Realms of Glass and Blood, Book 1

Bethany-Kris writing as

K. FOURNIER

For the things, and people, we wish were different.

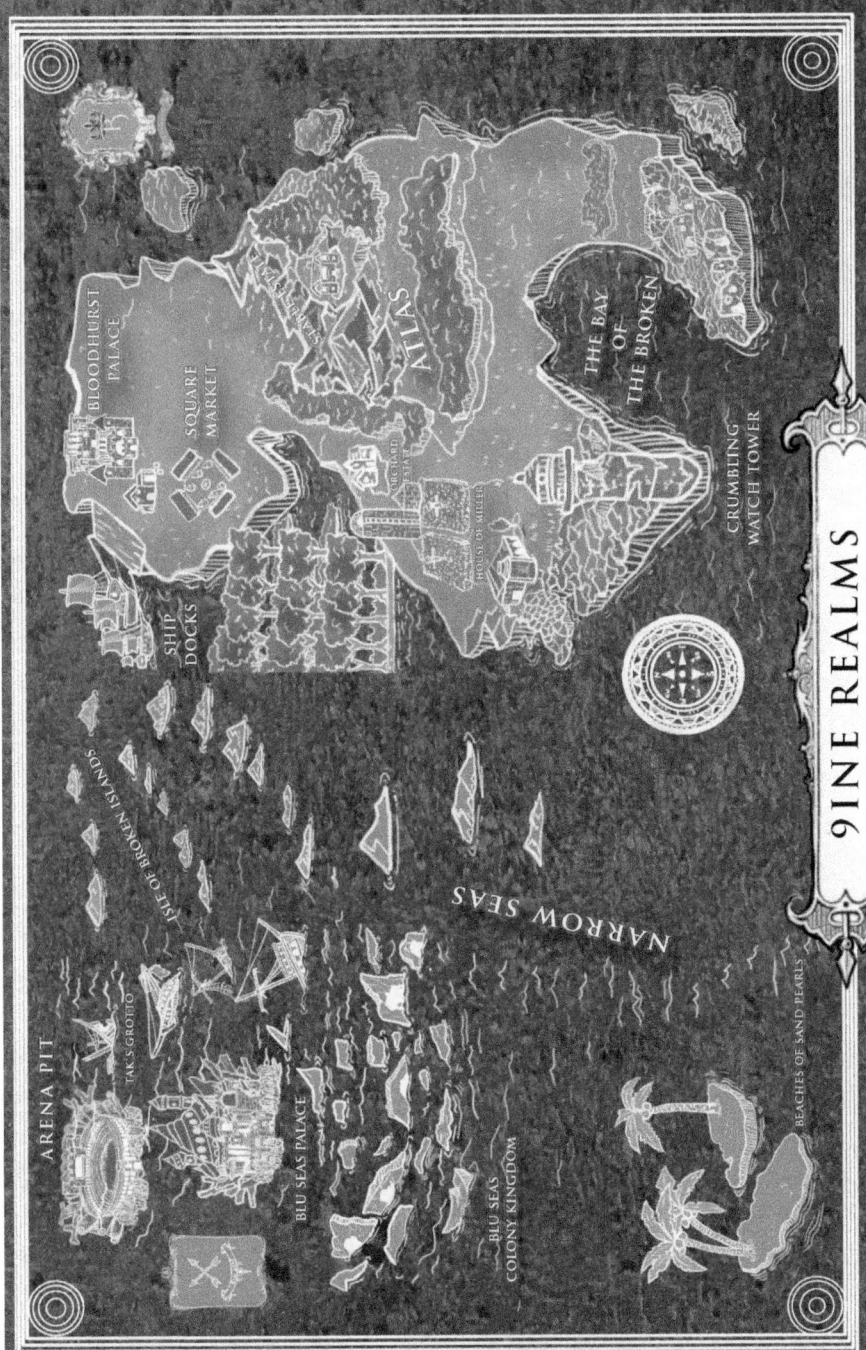

9INE REALMS

CONTENTS

A NOTE

Dearest readers,

I tried doing this note before I began writing, then during the writing of Songs of the Hunted, and now I am trying once more after it is finished. All 168000 plus words of it. So, let's hope this one is the one that works for me. My poor attempts to explain why I had to do this, expand and rewrite this piece of work, feels much the same way this book initially did to me when I had finished writing it the first time. Like it wasn't entirely right. As if I acutely knew, each time I was faced with the book or the idea of continuing the world on, no matter how hard I tried to ignore it, that it wasn't exactly how I wanted it to be. A need to fit the book into a fairytale theme for a collection that I ultimately didn't publish it with, and a word count limit in my mind, I shortened what I originally wanted The Hunted to be and lost some of the elements I loved the most about what it could have been.

That was my mistake.

I knew it the second I hit publish, which I did publish it, because I felt I owed readers the book on the release date I had given, and so once it was out there, I tried to let it go. Literally, I burned everything related to the 9ine Realms in my mountain of notes because I one hundred percent felt like I couldn't continue the story unless I went back and made the first book what I truly wanted it to be.

But I had never done that before and didn't really know if I wanted to for a long while. I'm going to blame a hard two years for that, honestly.

And maybe, a part of me believed I was not ready, or the storyteller, to write this.

Well, it's done now. I guess that answers that.

I'm sorry it may hurt and if you are a reader of which the distressing/disturbing warning in the blurb is not sufficient for you, then you will find a better detailed list of TWs at bethanykris.com/soth.

XO,
K. Fournier/BK

1. THE PRIZE OF THE BLU SEAS

Anthia, Queen of the Blu Seas

One season before capture …

"What they say, is it true?"

"What do they say, your grace?" Anthia asked.

"That they hunt you," came the reply that chilled her to the bone. Not because of the words the king used, but the way he said it. As if it were a challenge he might like to take up. "Your kind—the men—they hunt you down and take you in front of anyone who can see, and that is how they claim you as theirs. Is it true?"

How dare he?

The thought seared through Anthia's thoughts like the bright star overhead that streaked through the purple sky as it fell from its otherworldly throne. *How dare he ask me that?* As if the bond between mates was nothing more than a hunt between a merman and his chosen female, instead of the unbreakable, life-lasting tether to another soul that it truly was for her people. The song between two souls that connected kin across seas and lands. A choice to irrevocably, in most all cases, leash oneself to another even if it meant a fight to the death for it.

He had no right to ask about that.

Of her thirty trips around the sun, seventeen of them spent sitting on the throne of sea glass that once belonged to her father, for a short time, and his before him for much longer, no one spoke to her the way the Bloodhurst King just did. In all the realms of the 9ine that she had visited or seen, never had another being spoken to her so abrasively, either. No king, or ordinary man, no fire breather or even a man of the seas.

None.

Those customs and traditions, their secrets, were not for those who could not experience them. Only sea people could speak on such things freely. But not this man.

Not this landwalker.

He had no concept of how much he just offended her, and if anything, the tap of his leather, laced boot against the glossy ship deck told her that he expected an answer. And probably sooner rather than later.

It took a heavy breath of sea air expelling from her mouth and neck gills, and the squawk of gull birds overhead to give Anthia something else to affix her stare upon, anything except King Misael. Only a few years on his throne and barely beyond his twenty-fifth year, if her sources could be trusted, she heard rumors that he shared a similar affliction to his now-dead father before him.

A taste for sea women.

They just didn't like them *free*.

The way he appraised her every time he looked at her made Anthia think those rumors had a tad more than a touch of truth to them.

The king felt entirely too close to her in that moment for her to speak the way she wanted to when he had a broad sword hanging at his back. Not to mention, guards waiting beyond the gangway connecting their ship to the one at their left, another at their right, and her people were scattered between the seas and the jagged cliffs carved into the land surrounding them.

"You're asking after things that are not of your place or people," she tried to say kindly, even gently, adding that, "The ways of the people of the seas are coveted and protected from those who would try to use it against us."

"How would I use that against you?" he asked back, seemingly unconcerned with her reasoning for not answering his inquiry. "People on land, we wed and bed. Your kind, well, you hunt and fuck. Say it."

No, *that* was the most disrespectful and disgusting filth someone had ever had the indecency to say to her, and by all the seas and the stars, Anthia did not know how she lasted standing next to the king on the ship's deck for so long. She bet the longer she spent there with him, even if they could benefit from the ships, the more he would take her silence and indifference to his behavior as acceptance.

How far might he take it?

Men like him were predictable.

"How about a question for a question instead?" she returned. "If you answer mine, I'll reply in kind."

"Depends on your question, Queen."

Of course, it did.

The challenge didn't scare her a bit.

"Is it true that your father died at the hands of a mermaid in his bedchambers and you had her burned in the square while they coronated you, King Bloodhurst? That you covered it up and buried him with a funeral pyre so no one would know that he got what he deserved?"

The king's jaw tightened. "That was two questions."

And neither needed answered, honestly.

Nonetheless, their time here, this entire charade between them, was just about over. Appealing to a man with known questionable honor was a losing game, and Anthia wasn't the queen who could afford to fail her colony of people. Refusing to even let her brows knot with the frustration caused by the king and let him know he'd rattled her, she simply released a sigh.

"I'm bound by an oath I spoke to the Gods and seas on the day they crowned me to give my life for my people to live how they always have for thousands of centuries. Not even a king with fancy ships set all out like gifts for me will change that," she said, gesturing to the flags whipping above, each embroidered with a cursive B and the Bloodhurst crown. "I did not come here to speak with you about the ways of my people, your grace."

Icey, blade-colored eyes turned on the queen of seas where she stood in the middle of the large ship's upper deck to survey the peace offering made to her between two kings she couldn't trust. That, above everything else, Anthia believed without a doubt. Well, that and the fact that King Misael Bloodhurst's eyes on her felt like dirty hands reaching under the low-cut collar of her bodice to get a palmful of something that wasn't his. And the landwalker wasn't even touching her. His gaze remained affixed to the brand of her royal status on her throat for long enough that the intensity made her swallow. Every royal line to sit on the Blu Seas throne accepted the brand to denote and mark them. Her family's had been on their throat, but the king of a now-dead line that came before her grandfather had his family branded on their palms. She was concerned with the level of interest the king showed in her brand, really.

"That there," he said, gesturing to her throat. "Do you remember it—did it hurt?"

"Not particularly. And probably. We're also not talking about that, your grace."

"I wonder if that might make it easier to find you?"

Even knowing the Bloodhurst King watched her, bold and unashamed in the way he drank in what he could see the shape of her legs beneath her gown's slit skirt, and bare feet, she pretended he wasn't. Better not to give his blatant interest any time or mind, lest he think she want it. And she certainly would not be entertaining any talk of *finding* her. Whatever that meant.

Gods forbid it, she prayed silently to the beings above land and below the seas. Anyone who might be listening.

The last thing she needed was a landwalker king to think this meeting was anything but exactly what he and she agreed it would be. A small fleet of three ships from his Royal Naval Guard in exchange for the endless piles of sea glass he stole from their seas to sell to the King of the Red Seas two seasons before.

This meeting, and his offering to her along with the gold from the King of the Red Seas in the belly of each ship, was a long time coming.

But something about it also felt wrong.

Anthia couldn't put her finger, or a fin, on what it was.

Thankfully, they no longer had to fight to protect that precious resource from the bastard on land. *For now.* She bet his mind was as fickle as the winds that rolled through their realms during the season storms, though, and like the winds, his decision could change faster than she would be able to prepare.

She would have to worry about keeping the mostly unbreakable, meltable and moldable clear stone from getting into the landwalkers' hands another time. Besides, her High Master of the Army assured her they wouldn't get even a pebble once the safety of the upcoming storm season passed and the landwalkers put their ships back at the ports and moors. But for her, an even more pressing matter was at hand.

Instead of sea glass only found in the Blu Seas that she was sure the landwalkers would pull from the seafloor until nothing was left, she worried the king had once again taken a liking to pilfering something else from her kingdom just as his father had done before him. Something far more precious and important.

The sheer fabric of her skirt billowed wildly around her legs with the next gust of wind, giving the king an even better view of her body. She regretted the choice in attire in that very instant, wishing she had ordered her maidens to put any other gown into the watertight trunks for their trip to land but the one she now wore. Well, what was done couldn't be helped now. Anthia would deal with how the gown made her feel, and every other frustration, later. The very second she finished with this terrible idea of Zale's, once her father's truest and loyal friend, and now her most trusted advisor because of it, in fact. It was only his assurance that the gold, and even the ships, were paid for by the King of the Red Seas that dragged her from the seas on this day to face Misael. And with this nonsense with him out of the way, she could figure out another solution to her colony's latest problem. The missing caravan of her people, that was.

A large part of the cause of those missing mermaids—and the goods and young they had been traveling with—she was sure stared her straight in the face when she finally turned to grace the young king with what he seemed to desperately want and need from her: *her attention.*

Apparently, wasn't that exactly why they stood where they did on this day of all days? A king and queen with far better things to do, undoubtedly, but the landwalker went through a lot of trouble for this to happen.

Anthia wanted to know why.

"I could say the ships and gold are enough to make right your wrongs of seasons past," Anthia said quietly, "but I fear accepting either thing from you or the King of the Red Seas will simply lead one, or both, of you into believing that you can do it to me—to *us*—again. At that point, will you wait so kindly and gallantly for me when I bring my army to your shores, King?"

"Is that a threat?"

"How many of my kind, and *our* things, have you pulled from the seas?" she returned just as hotly as he. "I don't need to make threats, your grace, because that would mean I foolishly believed they could work on you and make you see reason."

Clearly, King Misael Bloodhurst saw no reason that was not one of his own making.

"No, this isn't a threat," Anthia added, her tone leveling coolly, "it's a promise."

"If you think to—"

"Whose turn is it to speak, your grace? At my tables, I let the person needing the loudest voice hold a dagger of sea glass and only when it exchanges hands does another voice join the chorus. Shall we also do that here?"

The fire that flashed in the king's eyes would have frightened a weaker woman, but Anthia simply tilted her chin up subtly to square her jaw the way he did with his. The two of them, as different as the land and seas around them, continued their silent battle of wills until he broke it first by glancing away with a boisterous laugh.

As if this was all in jest.

Just a big joke.

"Well," the king muttered heavily, "It wasn't as if you answered me in any other way that I've tried to get you to speak, mermaid queen."

Was that what he wanted? Had he done all this *just* to speak with her? After menacing and terrorizing her kingdom and their colony since before he even took his throne, all this just to speak? Something smelled terribly foul, and it definitely was not the gathering, rising seafoam starting to fill up the bay where the ships took port.

Anthia didn't give him a reaction to the pet name that his tone twisted to be something that made her stomach clench almost painfully.

No, she wouldn't entertain a messenger sent from him time and time again, season after season, but the King of the Red Seas, a man who bled a different color than her but swam and changed in the seas as she did ... Well, he was a separate matter altogether. Even if Nodan had made the purchase of their stolen resources, it was the respect of their kind to give another the opportunity to make things right.

When it could be done, of course.

The seas might run through their people's veins, but it did not look fondly upon their blood staining the waters, either. They were the water. When possible, war should always be avoided. How they treated the land and seas, well, the Gods would treat them in kind.

She chanced another look at the young king to find him watching her again, and thought, *All of us, or none of us.*

King Misael took his time dragging those cold, gray eyes of his back up her body to where they needed to be. The turn of her shoulders, and a flick of her wrists at the collar dropped the cloak at her back more around her front to give her exposed skin showing off a spattering of sparkling scales down the middle of her chest a bit more modesty. At least, he didn't continue to let his attention linger longer than he already had when she finally made a physical show of her displeasure with it, but it was still too much for her.

All of this was too much.

It took but a few words from this man who called himself a king for her to understand—and well—that he did not see the crown of twisted, sharp pointed sea glass on her head as something that made her anything close to his equal. She was now glad she'd accepted the cloak of heavy fur-lined velvet from her maiden after their trip through the Blu Seas brought them to the bay carved into the south end of the continent named Atlas for its centered position to the circle of other realms across the 9ine. She tried not to let her gaze stay too long on any one crumbling structure on the face of the jagged cliffs above them but some she could name from memory alone because of the stories passed down to her by her father and grandfather. The latter of whom once ruled both these lands and seas from his palace that used to be seen from Atlas as if floating on the water's surface.

But that time was long gone.

The kings before her were not ready to face the House of Bloodhurst, and their weakness had always been the land anyway. As it appeared, Anthia also wouldn't get a choice in whether the man made a mess out of her reign like his father did to the kings of the seas before he was even born.

"Are the ships and the King's gold not to your favor?" the king asked.

A lot of things were not particularly to her liking, but Anthia didn't think it would benefit either of them for her to go about naming her list. Besides, it was quite a long one.

"No," she settled on saying, "they are not, I'm afraid."

"Pardon me?" King Misael all but spat her way.

That was either not the answer he expected to hear, or worse, not the one he wanted if the sudden and severe pinch of his broad brow was any indication. As handsome as any other king still in his best years from a good bloodline with enough ambition to get themselves onto the throne, she was sure he didn't lack companionship. His seeming fascination with her made no sense to Anthia.

Hadn't her advisor even said he had a wife—the closet thing a landwalker could get to a mate?

Anthia had gone along with this meeting as much as she could, but there wasn't a single part of her that cared to stand there and do it for one second longer. All this day had done was prove to her that the King of Atlas would never bend or break, and certainly, not in a way that would change him for the better.

People were who they were.

She believed this man was a monster.

Her heart—owned by her people and the seas so much so that she had refused for all of her many turns around the sun to mate lest it break the bond she'd already made—told her so. Misael Bloodhurst, King of Atlas, wanted nothing good from her. Whatever it was he did want, she would make good and sure he didn't get it.

"Send the gold back to the Red Seas," she said then, turning away from the Atlas king without the proper respect of a goodbye, "and tell the king there that he can choke on the betrothal he offered me to protect the Blu Seas from you."

She wouldn't sacrifice herself to one man for another. Not her crown, her kingdom, and not even her body. None of these men would get anything from her.

"*Where are you going?*" the king thundered behind her. "We're not done talking, mermaid queen!"

"Oh, aren't we?" she asked back, scoffing.

She was certainly done.

"Queen Anthia?" came the call from a familiar voice somewhere down on the rocky shore of the portion of bay that remained ledgeless. She didn't bother to look Zale's way. The advisor would figure out soon enough that this meeting had not exactly gone according to plan, but he should have known that from the start. She'd not kept her feelings hidden before they'd even arrived.

"And what of my fleet?" Misael shouted at her back. "Do you know the trouble I went through to deliver these to you?"

"I'll take them if only to show the people of my kingdom what sails to look for when we burn them to the seafloor, King."

"You'll regret this, mermaid!"

Anthia didn't think so.

She also didn't take the gangplank down to the waiting rowboat that should have ferried her back to the shoreline where her maidens waited to help her change into something more suitable for underwater travel. It didn't seem like a bright idea considering the way Misael's armored guards turned on her with hands ready to unsheathe their swords when she first walked away from their king.

Instead, she took the rear steps of the ship's deck to the captain's port until her feet found the railing ledge and the bay waited down below to greet her.

"Find another realm to line your kingdom and house's pockets, Misael," Anthia told the fuming king, "because it will no longer be mine."

The murder in his eyes told her that the sea glass, ships, and all the rest was probably nothing compared to the vision of her walking away from him because he wasn't worth it.

"I'll get what I want," he returned through clenched teeth. "One way or another."

She would let him think as much.

So be it.

The water did greet her sweetly, like a nuzzle from a mother, when she dived from the ship's stern. The currents called her home; the very second the water filled her lungs and her legs and feet changed. From flesh and bone to a tail of blue-green scales, and an elongated, delicate tail fin of blue and black markings. Bone melded to bone; muscles expanded with the life of their seas; skin melted to sparkling scales. What the land exposed, the seas protected. The last thing Misael would have seen had he been looking before all of Anthia disappeared under the surface of the bay. She wouldn't break the surface until she was back in the safe waters of her Blu Seas, but those waiting under the surface found her before she had even made it out of the bay completely.

She could already hear the *tsk*s of her maidens for ruining a gown and cloak that could have been used again, but she made no apologies about ripping the garments away from her lithe form because they slowed her down as she cut through the water.

"Your majesty?" came the chirp of one guard. "Is everything all right?"

In the water, their mother tongue traveled like the calls of other underwater mammals. Noises from clicks, whistles, chirps, and hisses that made up words she didn't want to waste time hearing from the people calling for her. No, the more space she put between her and the Atlas king, the better she would feel.

Surely.

So, why didn't she believe it?

"My Queen?" the guard asked again.

"I don't trust him," was all she managed to say at first. It should be all that needed said, frankly. Tak, the youngest of all her personal guards but also her favorite because of his length of time serving her family from his youngest years, barely ten then, was still a young merman even if he had already reached adult age. His youth did not stop her from posting him at the end of her chamber of suites in the palace more often than anyone else. She liked his conversation, his ideas, and frankly, his company at times.

Not that the guard had ever stepped out of line with her.

"He wants something from me, I don't know what it is other than me." *But he can't have that,* she didn't say out loud. "I can't trust him not to be plotting against me while I stand there beside him and give him the opportunity to do it. No, I don't trust him at all, and we'll accept nothing from him. Not even one of his godforsaken ships."

She let that statement be her final one on the matter—whoever needed to carry it on to the rest of her gaggle of advisors and guards would do so.

It seemed to be enough for the guard. Tak slowed his swimming pace to fall in line behind her. She didn't wait for the rest of the royal caravan made up of her maidens, guards, and advisors to catch up before she slipped into the stream carrying water back out into the seas from the bay.

It was in moments like these that Anthia sometimes wondered what it would be like to forget the crown on her head and the duty in her heart, but alas, somethings were just not possible. The same way the Gods had doomed their kind to need both the land and sea to survive, she was also hopelessly devoted in her duty as queen—the very last of her bloodline, in fact, and her kingdom, no matter how much they loved and adored her, knew it.

Worse yet, what if the land king knew it, too?

Mattue Bloodhurst, Bastard Prince of Atlas and Advisor and Sword to the King

There was something to be said about the gleam in his older half-brother's eye as King Misael was brought from the ships to the bay's shore where their gathered group waited for him. Anyone with any sense would know that look in Misael's cold eyes and what it meant.

Unfortunately, none of them, but especially not Mattue, could get out of the way as they usually might when Misael seemed fit to murder the first person within his reach. The king stomped his way off the boat as soon as it hit the rocky bottom, likely ruining his leather boots as he trampled through water to reach Mattue who knew better than to speak first.

History taught him that wouldn't work out well.

"She's a beautiful bitch, but a bitch, nonetheless," the king muttered once he stood in front of his brother, still affixing his attention to the mouth of the bay where the mermaid queen had taken her leave. "And like every bitch before her, she'll learn, too."

"One might think you would need to keep her standing in one spot for more than a handful of minutes to get her to listen to anything you have to say, but she did not seem very willing, your grace."

Misael's anger turned on Mattue in a blink. "And what exactly is that supposed to mean, *brother?*"

Mattue tipped his head down, lowering his gaze from Misael to soothe his sudden outburst. Nothing new with his brother, of course.

"I only meant," he clarified quietly, "that you put forth all this effort today, and many days before it with the Red King, to get her here in front of you, and for what? You produced ships and gold before her as if it was a dowry and expected her to react pleasantly? I highly doubt that is how a woman of her kind is courted, my lord."

The king sighed heavily, clearly annoyed, but he brightened slightly as his favorite white stallion was led down the path from the rim of the bay by a stable boy in faded, drab blue. Their conversation stalled as the caravan of horses were delivered, and those who would lead the trip back to the Stable Estate began the journey while Misael and Mattue waited at the rear with four knights, members of the Bloodhurst King's personal Guard of Swords.

"The ships are a minor inconvenience," Mattue said in an effort to please his brother somehow. "They'll be returned to the ports, and we won't be out any ships. Tis not a bad thing that she didn't want them, King."

Misael scowled. "Fair enough. And the gold in the bow's bellies?"

Mattue laughed loudly, drawing in the attention of the guards waiting for them to heel into the horses they had mounted. "We take it, of course. Tell the King of the Red Seas that she accepted his apology—what difference does it make? He won't know any better."

"He might in a few seasons' time, should the two of them ... Oh, I don't know, meet?"

"Will she last that long, brother?"

He didn't call Misael king that time.

Not even *my Grace* or *my lord* as he often allowed Mattue in private. No, this time he treated Misael as an equal—even if the king wasn't—because he wanted to tell his older brother something important. The very fact that there were people surrounding Misael who knew him even better than he did himself.

Mattue included.

Misael stayed quiet atop his horse, but his stare once again followed the same path that the mermaid had taken to leave the king behind.

"How long will you be able to keep it in check, do you think?" Mattue pressed.

He was good at that, see.

Pressing in the right places.

Even sore ones.

His brother was no better than their father before him. Mattue was proof of their dead father's sins just like Misael's inability to control even his stare was proof of his own. Misael did not need to speak the truth into existence for it to be fact, but Mattue would let his brother believe as much if that's what it took to get him to just admit what he wanted.

What was *obvious.*

"Is it true what I heard about their mates?" the king asked suddenly, seemingly changing directions in their conversation altogether. Without warning, too. Except Mattue did not think the change was all that different from the initial topic between them.

"Was that what you were talking to her about on the ship's deck?"

Misael shrugged his wide shoulders, but he wouldn't look his brother in the eye. "Perhaps, but what I discussed with her is of no true importance to you. And now I am asking you the question, brother, and out of the two of us, you would know about the mermaids better than me, I suppose. No?"

At that, Mattue bowed his head to his brother. A silent offer of apology and respect that he didn't think Misael cared for but demanded all the same.

Before he could properly answer the king, a chirp from the bay, a shriek from the seas, and a hiss he knew his brother couldn't hear signaled the last of the mermaids to find the mouth of the sea. The shriek, he did hear, and Misael recognized it, too, if the way his gaze swung back to his brother and landed on the throat Mattue rarely kept covered.

The indents of his sealed gills were barely even visible. Closed shortly after his birth with needle and spun steel, and never spoken of again.

It had taken him many years of hearing the sea people's language to begin to understand it, and even speak it back in some cases, but he felt no attachment to the half of him that didn't really feel like his.

"Well, you tell me, brother," the king said, his hands tightening around the leather reins of his waiting horse. "How should I court that mermaid when she won't even grace me with her voice for more than a handful of moments? How do they find their mates?"

"They hunt them," Mattue replied. "They make them bleed."

Or, that was what he knew of it.

"Then, she would be mine?"

"I don't know, would she be? If she births you boys like my mother did for Father, will you name them a bastard like he did me?"

Misael didn't answer that.

Honestly, he didn't have to because the two children already birthed to him by mermaids, and not his wife, answered the question considering they were now in line to the throne. Pushing the bastard, Mattue, even further down the line of succession. Although, if this wife was anything like Misael's last, she wouldn't last longer than her former counterpart before she, too, was discovered drowned in a lake.

"I want that mermaid, Mattue."

"Clearly," he mumbled in reply.

As if Misael's constant, obsessive focus on the Queen of the Blu Seas wasn't a new thing, when in truth, his brother had been seeking the woman out for more than a handful of years. She had only recently become aware of it, mostly because Misael stopped playing coy with the cunt.

Her interest, however … Well, that was another thing.

Misael's sharp expression turned on him again. "She is, by far, the most beautiful thing I have ever seen crawl out of that sea. *I want her.*"

Did he expect Mattue to jump into the sea and chase the beautiful queen to bring him back to the king himself?

Not likely.

"And the harem of slaves you already keep to fuck when you please, my King?" Mattue asked back just as fast. Not to mention, the laws his brother put in place on the lands of Atlas so that he could carry on their father's legacy of catching and bleeding or breeding mermaids, and also hunting them to sell to the pleasure houses in the cities stretched across the realm. It made relations with other realms of the sea in the 9ine a bit difficult, but nothing they hadn't worked out thus far.

"Those were Father's. I only kept them because they have nothing. Perhaps, we could sell them all—I hear they fetch a good price."

Right.

Mattue rolled his eyes, but out of his brother's line of sight. Whatever lie Misael needed to tell himself to sleep through each long night. He might very well sell their father's old slaves, but that mattered little to him.

If only Mattue cared, but no. He gave no regard to his brother's morals, dealings, or the sanctity of Misael's soul. Those were not his problems. Unless the king decided to go ahead and make it so.

Like he had with this.

"Perhaps," his brother said then, like he was making a deal with Mattue, "she will be the one that starts my own collection. Doesn't she make the perfect piece? The greatest prize of the Blu Seas. I'm due a good hunt and sail, too."

This time, Mattue opted not to reply.

It would do no good.

It surely wouldn't save the mermaid queen from an inevitable fate because that had already been decided. He bet his brother made the choice long before this day ever came to pass, in fact.

"The next orchard season," the king stated then, making it final just like that. "After the storms—we hunt her, brother."

"And you're not at all concerned that taking their queen, who, as I understand it, they love dearly, won't cause Atlas or the crown any trouble?"

"Well, that's for you to figure out, isn't it?"

The king spoke, and so shall it be.

Mattue nodded once. "I will make it so."

At that, Misael spurred on his horse with a swift kick of his heels into the beast, leaving Mattue in the billowing dust kicked up by his brother climbing the steep hill to the ridge of the bay. Without as much as a goodbye.

Nothing unusual to see here.

Mattue had long become accustomed to being his brother's shadow, and in it, and he couldn't care less if Misael bothered to say goodbye. Besides, now he had planning to do.

And he rather liked doing that.

2. THE CROWN OF A QUEEN

175 days later; a sunset before capture …

Tak, High Guard of the Blu Seas

"Your majesty, the maidens are ready whenever you are," Tak spoke at the cracked doors of his queen's throne room. From her seat of twisted sea glass on a platform of bright pink coral she nodded in his direction to say she had heard him. It was the relieved roll of her eyes which her advisor speaking from down below didn't see that made Tak chuckle.

"Okay, the rest will have to wait, Zale," Anthia said then, interrupting whatever the older merman was about to say when she stood up from her chair. Plucking her crown from where it hung for safe keeping on one point of the large throne arms, she winked Tak's way when the advisor finally noticed that there had, in fact, been an interruption.

"Well, just a moment," Zale said quickly.

"The ladies have been waiting all day for us to get a start on this trip to the Isle of Broken Islands. What could possibly need to be said that we haven't already discussed all day, Zale?" Anthia sighed, giving the advisor a sharp arch of her brow as she placed her crown neatly on her head, around the large ball of her braided, black hair. "If this is about the landwalker king again, I've already told you—the Broken Islands off the coast of Atlas *is* ours, and furthermore, our women need what we forage there. Before the oncoming storm season rolling in, ends, the High Guard will be posted across the islands for all of north and west Atlas to see. Let Misael Bloodhurst come into the seas, then, Zale."

"I'm am very aware how you feel on that matter."

"Good, then there won't be another meeting with the landwalker king and my council to discuss said issues, will there?"

"No, my Queen."

From the moment Anthia started to speak as if she meant for her advisor to listen, the merman did. Wisely, too. A gentle woman, and loving enough to feel like anyone's mother if they got close enough to the queen, she also accepted nothing less than utmost respect from everyone. In return, she offered her subjects the same.

"Lift your head, Zale," Anthia muttered low.

He did, but only to watch her swim toward Tak still waiting at the entry to the throne room in the cracked open doors.

"That other thing, Queen," Zale called after her.

"What is it?"

She never turned around.

"Your named successor, actually."

14

That did freeze her trek, but she spun around too fast for Tak to decipher the look that crossed her face. He could tell by the movement of Anthia's arms that she crossed them over her chest as she asked Zale, "And what about *that?*"

He shuffled a bit on his tail fin and played with rolling his hands together, mumbling something about, "Perhaps it's better Tak is here—a witness to this and all."

The guard at the door cleared his throat, but no one paid him any mind. That was fine. Tak had become accustomed to being privy to conversations of merpeople—most usually women, but occasionally those closest to the queen, regardless of sex—and pretending as if he wasn't. Tak had heard and seen things since his tenth year when the royal palace adopted the orphaned children of the last war; a lot of things. Things that he would never repeat or speak again because he owed the souls that called this palace home his very life.

He owed them everything.

Anthia, and her long dead kin.

"If I may be frank?" the advisor finally asked.

"Go on about it, Zale. Just get it out."

"You've gone through your list of suitors, madame. You've made it clear from your fourteenth year that you would never settle into a mating pair or companionship, but you also have not had any children. I don't say that for us to discuss your reasoning for private choices. I say it because we are in treacherous years, and now is the time to make these things clear."

Anthia's head bobbed slowly. "And what isn't clear?"

"I beg your pardon ... my Queen?"

"I thought we were being frank," Anthia returned edgily.

"Well, we are, but—"

"I'll answer my own question, Zale. Laws of the Four Seas dictate that the crown be passed onto the oldest and highest advisor to the late monarch when there are no proven blood heirs. In my case, that would be you. Again, what isn't clear?"

Tak heard the queen's point just fine, but he couldn't say whether or not the advisor did. Or maybe the man did understand that he had started to walk a very fine line with Anthia. *Who* would be the next ruler of the Blu Seas kingdom after her leave from the throne had always been clear to anyone that knew their laws. And all of them did.

Bowing in her direction, Zale murmured, "As I said, Tak had come and now was a good time with a witness to these things. Formalities, Anthia."

"*Mmhmm*, well ... The time for being frank is over, Zale."

"Right, my Queen." The advisor bowed again. "Have a good night away with the ladies on the Isle of Broken Islands and safe trip both ways."

Tak understood exactly why the advisor decided to clear up the issue when the queen turned fast on her tail and cut through the water for the door after their exchange, but the fury in her eyes kept Tak from trailing the queen as she exited the throne room. He did turn, readying to follow and do his duty, but something stopped him.

A flash of movement from the side of his vision had Tak looking back as he moved away from the doors and back into the hallway. There, he found Zale turning to stare at the shadowy throne of molted and twisted sea glass that Anthia had left behind.

He could not imagine what it felt like to know you would become the next king, or how the weight of that duty would sit on a person. So, he gave the advisor privacy and headed after the queen. It didn't take Tak long to catch up with Anthia, but instead of the queen turning right at the end of high-walled corridor where her caravan of maidens waited to begin the trip to the islands, she went left. Straight into the side courtyard of a coral maze. By the time he slipped out behind her, she had already moved sideways, out of view of the doorway where she could press her back against the wall.

She gulped in three breaths, and each came out a little shakier than the last.

"I'm sorry," she whispered, "just t-tell the ladies I need a m-mom—"

"Anthia," Tak murmured softly, "tis okay to take a moment, your majesty. They would not even want to go if they were not going with you."

She nodded at his soft assurance, and her head dropped a bit to take those violet eyes of hers—the same color as his—out of his view completely.

"That shouldn't have upset me, he was right," she admitted quietly.

One couldn't see anything from tears when someone cried in the water except for the trickle of a shimmer. Without thinking, Tak reached out and brushed away the proof of the queen's sadness with the side of his knuckle. Just the way she had for him as an orphaned merboy who so desperately missed his own mother.

"Cry to be happy again, we have time," he told her.

He wasn't exactly sure what about the advisor's discussion of succession put Anthia into tears, but Tak wouldn't ask unless she offered the information, either. He still knew his place even after all these years.

Even now, as her friend.

Anthia cried it out.

Tak guarded the door silently all the while.

Eventually, he heard her sniffle and the scrub of her palms against her face before she told him, "You are more than welcome to take your leave of post to start your own hunting trip early, you know? I'm sure the caravan has more than enough guards for a single night. The trip isn't even as long as the one we took to the Beaches of Sand Pearls during the last storm."

"Exactly. *During* a storm, your majesty."

The random bursts of bad weather that came before the long-term, regular season of storms that stretched on and on was bad for the landwalkers, but a life-saver for the people of the sea that had never been scared of the violent weather changes.

Anthia nodded to his point as she came to stand beside him again. "I do think you could afford a bit of time away. You're always in the palace, Tak. Have you even started working on your own home?"

He grinned down at her. "I have, in fact."

"Have you slept in it?"

Tak laughed loudly. "I have not."

"Well, you should fix that."

"Sure, after this trip to the islands," he returned, shrugging one bare shoulder. "Because under no circumstances would I allow my queen to travel with anyone *but* me to hold the sword at her back."

"Allow me, huh?"

He chuckled. "Poor choice of words, perhaps."

She tipped her chin down, not meeting his gaze as she asked, "Did you know I had a sitting with a lovely merwoman last week—on your behalf?"

That news sent Tak's brows lifting high. "Oh?"

"Missa, my maiden."

Ah.

All at once, he figured out what the queen had been trying to tell him.

"She is lovely," he said.

"And would be a good mate for you which is what she asked for, should you find yourself at all curious. The two of you would make a good match and since you're both of adult-age, we don't have to discuss *why* she's coming to me to ask, but I assume you've spent some time together."

"She is lovely," Tak repeated, "but I needn't take a mate to be happy, my Queen."

Anthia nodded once. "Sure, but is that it?"

"Is what it?"

"Your reason—is it only that or something else? Not because you're holding out or waiting for someone else, say?"

Now it was Tak's turn to ask for clarity.

"Are we being frank?" he asked, wanting to drop the pretenses of policy and procedure in their conversation altogether.

Anthia smiled up at him, but it didn't quite reach her eyes like it usually did. "Please."

"If you're asking if I pine after you," Tak said, not wasting time or breath with anything that would ease them into this, "then the answer is no. If I had a mother after they killed mine, it was you. Like a lot of young men and women in this colony. We were never going to be like that, and neither of us needed to say it to know it was true, Anthia. The state of me needn't be a worry for you, especially in that regard. I assure you."

"Fair enough," she replied under her breath.

"However," he added.

That made her cock an eyebrow again. "What?"

"My duty to you is far more important to me than bonding myself to someone I may not be able to give myself to completely because my heart is split. Half with them, half here. I need all of it or none of it to be where it should be, your majesty."

His declaration made Anthia let out a heavy breath as she shook her head and glanced away from him.

"You may not be my lover, Tak, but you still know how to say all the right things, exactly as you should."

"My duty will remain with you, if it pleases you."

"I know," she said only a little sadly, "but I do wish for you to find someone. It doesn't have to be today."

"Perhaps. Someday. Shall we find the maidens?"

At that question, Anthia nodded. "Yes, please. Are you helping us pick sea lilies this year, Tak, or will you be staying in the seas again?"

"I think we both know the answer to that as one of us has to be watching things and not picking flowers, hmm?" he returned, smirking.

Sea lilies were a coveted resource made up of long fire-red stems and blue teardrop shaped petals. The plant was not necessarily easy to find in the 9ine, but it did grow wild and well in the wetlands beyond the beaches of the Isle of Broken Islands. Boiled petals in sea water and imbibed still warm would abort a merwoman's pregnancy within the month without ill effects, but chewed raw or packed along the gum, and then the petals soothed the achy mouths of their young as they teethed. Tak only knew these things because he had spent so much time with the palace maidens as a young boy, and now man, that they allowed him that privilege. However, not all mermen were lucky enough to know the secrets of the sea lily, or many other numerous things he did because of his place, and his deep respect for Anthia and the other palace maidens kept those ways of the merwomen safe with him.

As it always would.

"You're no fun at all, Tak," the queen scolded him halfheartedly as they exited the coral maze together. He didn't mind. Mostly, because she was smiling again. That was far better than when she cried.

"One of us can be fun," he returned, "and the other has to wield a sword."

"Well, let's hope not, anyway."

Gods, please, Tak prayed.

Let it be a safe trip for them all.

Anthia

The queen slipped her bare feet into the wet, grassy muck that came all the way up to her knees just so that she could reach the largest of the sea lilies in a pod of several. As was their way, she only took one from a bunch, leaving the rest on the stem to fall and produce even more the next year. Harvesting the lilies that way took longer but also left behind more than enough for someone else or the land. Not that anyone else came to the Broken Islands except for them.

And perhaps, the landwalkers.

She couldn't be sure.

The ways of those on land—even the women of their kind—was an enigma to Anthia, and most of the mermaids in her close circles. A complete unknown, and in a way, that bothered her because there was a part of her that knew even though the seas and land divided them, her people and theirs were more alike than any of them probably knew.

Under the skin, where it counted, how different could they really be?

"Are we going deeper into this pond, do you think?" the maiden to Anthia's left asked.

Missa, actually.

"I think we have just about enough between us and the others, actually."

"Oh, good. I love doing this, but the *smell*."

Anthia laughed. "Wetlands *always* smell."

Thankfully, the sweet merwoman didn't take the news of Tak's refusal to mate with her too harshly. It seemed it was an answer she already knew, because she asked the source herself before coming to the queen, but she had thought that perhaps Anthia's voice might help sway Tak's decision.

Clearly, the man knew what he was doing.

They ought to let him do it, then.

Anthia had just turned to leave the muck and smelly wetness behind when the first whistle cut through the chilly night air. The stillness of the winds helped the warning to travel from one side of the islands to the other, but they would have heard it regardless of how hard the wind blew. A second followed the first, and that one, she recognized.

Tak's confirmation of spotted ships sent every mermaid running for the seas whether their arms were full or not.

"Hurry, hurry, they're coming in from both sides of the Isle—they're painted black!"

Oh, Gods.

How would they have seen them?

How would her guards have even known?

"What?" Anthia heard Missa hiss at her left. "What did they just say?"

"The ships," Anthia replied as the satchel of lilies she had filled spilled to the ground, and she trampled every single one on her way into the sea.

"What of the ships, your majesty? What about them?"

"They're black."

Ghosts of the sea.

Ghosts *on* the sea.

Anthia's blood, warm in her body despite the shockingly cold water that filled her lungs when she got that first breath, ran entirely cold. The implication thudded painfully in her chest with every racing beat of her heart as she searched in the darkness of the water for the one thing she knew would protect her above all else.

He'd been holding her dagger from her pack, too.

"*Run! Run!*" shouted those from the sea to those still on land.

"*Under the islands, out of reach of the nets!*"

Someone else called for her, specifically. The merman she needed to find.

Tak.

"*Queen!*"

"I'm here! Tak, I'm here!"

He came up fast behind her before she even understood it was him, in fact. Her dagger of sea glass found its way from his palm to hers, and then his hand found her upper arm to yank her deeper into the waters. Like everyone else, they dived for the underside of the many wetland islands broken into scattered pieces that stretched in two separate jagged lines off the north-western coast of Atlas. Their noise in the water quieted the longer the gathered mermaids huddled together until no chirp, click, or hiss passed anyone's lips. She could barely breathe but for the fact their huddle kept her in the very middle with Tak holding the heel of his sword in both hands, the tip pointed down at the ledge of the broken island's underwater shelf where they currently hid.

"Shall we send the guards to scout?" she asked.

"And confirm the four ships we already spotted at each end of the isle?" he returned. "If we don't send them to their deaths, then it is for useless information because I already know what they're trying to do."

"Which is *what*?"

"Covering both ends. They think we're all going one way or another because underneath the islands, no one knows the caves between the Broken Islands well enough to get from one side to another. They change every fucking year."

He wasn't wrong.

Her muffled noise of horror didn't go unnoticed by her favorite guard. Tak glanced back at her, his brow pinching a bit in concern. "It'll be okay, Anthia."

"Will it? Will it, really?"

"Why do you ask me like that? As long as we stay here," he told her, "then we're all safe."

"I ask you like that because for the first time, the ships are black, and somehow, those black ships are at either end of the Broken Islands as if they somehow knew we would be here, too. Tak, I only planned this with the maidens recently."

Too recently. They did that on purpose because it kept their traveling caravans safer.

He seemed to understand her implication that someone would have needed to help the ghost ships along with the information about their trip. Worse yet, what neither of them said, was that they both knew exactly who had been to the land recently.

"I was trying to calm you," he murmured.

"Don't calm me, Tak. Help me save my people."

A nod answered her back. "Of course."

"How long can we stay here?"

"Days, but not many."

Right.

"Long enough for the palace to send someone else to look for us when we don't arrive back tomorrow evening, I suppose? What, then? The ships catch a fleet of my guards, and we still lose."

"No, *they* do," he replied. "You'd still be in the seas where you belong."

She heard what he didn't say.

With us.

The situation unfolding before Anthia left her numb and still as she closed her eyes and tried to find the composure she so badly needed in those moments. She wished she could still hear the voice of her father and grandfather—their words of love and wisdom kept her going as queen when she was all alone to do it. She couldn't remember her mother, a chosen companion of her father who had died during birth, but she fingered the pearl ring belonging to her on Anthia's middle finger, circling it around and around until finally, she just knew.

"Do you think they came for a whole catch of us or just one, Tak?" she whispered.

He didn't answer.

"I know you heard me."

"*Stop it.*"

"Do you think it's the land king?"

All at once, Tak turned on her. With the lack of room, how he managed to keep his blade tight to his own body and not cut anyone else around them, she wasn't sure. The fire in his gaze rooted her to the spot, but the silence from them all continued to echo. No one else would lift their heads or turn their gaze to look at the queen and her guard in those seconds.

"I said stop it—don't even *think* what you're thinking," he snapped at her.

"Do you think it is him or not?"

Tak's jaw worked with the struggle of the words he tried to keep inside, but the battle of his duty eventually won. "Who else would it be?"

"Right," she said quietly.

"Anthia …"

"Who else would he want but me? I can save us all from being captured—"

"It's not us if there's no you, Queen."

Fair enough.

But it changed nothing.

"I will swim to his nets alone," she told him, "and you are to let me."

His mouth opened to speak.

She beat him to it when she took her mother's ring from her finger and placed it into Tak's hand, closing his fingers around it so that her decision was clear.

And final.

"You will let me."

Tak

If the two moons overhead could be seen through the clouds, the landwalkers on the ship just a swim stroke away from Tak might have seen the way his eyes glowed at the surface of the water. Alas, the dark night that had worked to the land king's favor to hide his ships now slanted to Tak's benefit as his hand finally skimmed the rough edge of wet wood along the bow.

Overhead, he listened for what was important.

Down below, he did what he fucking had to.

I'm sorry, Anthia.

She could punish him for going against her wishes later. He'd accept whatever she dealt him with a smile.

Even if it hurt.

"Well, brother, are you satisfied? I told you the price for the hunter's ships and time would be worth it."

"You're very lucky that I am in a good mood at the moment, Mattue," came a familiar voice from overhead. "Otherwise, I'd wipe that smirk off your face."

Tak clenched his teeth so hard his jaw ached to keep from hissing at the very sound of the land king's voice. But it was what the man told the queen overhead next, still being hoisted higher in a net, that made him wish he already had the blade at his back against the king's throat. 9ine hells, even the dagger Anthia made him take would do.

"I've fucked them in that form, too, darling," the king said, the smug satisfaction coating his every word. "Hold onto that last bit of the sea. It'll never taste the same again."

"*What was that?*"

"Torches to the side!" came the order.

"*Down*," Tak hissed to the mermaids currently surrounding the ship. Would she punish them all for this? She had to know they'd try.

They loved her.

They *needed* her.

Under the surface of the rocking waves, Tak peered back up to see the distorted glow of fire that brightened the water for the sailors overhead. He waited what felt like an eternity, long after the torches disappeared, before he gave the order for everyone to rise.

Of course, he came up and heard the worst thing of all.

"Oh, there are her legs." Misael Bloodhurst laughed darkly, adding to someone that Tak couldn't see, "It always amuses me the way we keep catching them with so little clothes. If not for the fact she can still swim away, I wouldn't even wait until I got her back and safe to get a taste."

"Well, unless you're going to fuck her in the cage in front of everyone," came the voice of the man who called the king his *brother*, "you're going to have to wait until we get back to the shore, at least."

"Can we clip her there, Mattue, do you think?"

Clip her?

What did that mean?

The landwalker named Mattue, the brother, sighed noisily. Irritated. "I wouldn't—it's still early enough for there to be some activity in the port, you see. You have her, Misael, she's here. Look at her, brother. *You have her.* Let it go for a moment. Just a little."

This time, it was the king whose air rushed out in a breath of loud relief.

"Yes, tis true, I do," he replied. "She is finally mine. Property of the king."

"I'm not yours, and I'll never be," Anthia hissed viciously, not that her fight earned her a reply from the king.

"Get up and walk, bitch," someone else, a new voice, ordered. "In the cage with you."

And with those words, with her fight, Tak took that dagger given to him by his queen and stabbed it high into the bow. As high as he could reach. Another mermaid at his back handed him another as he used the one already stuck in to hang from before he jammed in another blade higher than the first. It took two more before he finally pulled himself up onto the railing of the ship, expelling the sea to find his legs, and the very first thing he laid eyes on was a landwalker standing up from where he had bent down to tie the sail ropes.

Today is the day I collect another skull that I'll send to the seafloor, Tak thought, *and unfortunately, it is to be yours.*

The man didn't even see Tak coming for his throat until it was too late. He barely had time to stand straight all the way before the merman's hands found the wet, warmth of the innards that tried to vibrate with a scream. Too late. He crushed the cords, muscles, and everything else from inside the man's throat and then yanked it all the way out. Hot, red spurts of the man's blood spattered Tak, the ship deck, and the landwalker trying to run away from the next mermaid to come over the railing.

He let the dead landwalker hit the railing of the ship before the corpse flipped over the side, and Tak then grabbed the sword at his back, the screech of the sea glass blade hitting the first broadsword to come upon him with the force of the man's swing. He hadn't expected Tak's block, and his face suffered the fate for it with the next swing of the long sea glass blade. Another three landwalkers found their fates at the end of his blade in quick succession.

Finally, with a stride of room to move on every side of him, Tak searched for the only thing on the ship that he really needed to find. The struggle and screams of the landwalkers from bow to stern was music to his ears. The song of the seas. But the next scream to cut across the deck of the ship stopped every mermaid, even him, in their tracks. Now, he didn't need to try to find his queen.

He'd never *unsee* her.

The next crack of the braided, black leather whip a little more than the length of him in the king's hand hit Anthia across her chest and face, splitting her skin savagely. Her purple blood misted the air and speckled the deck. The essence of her life in the air could be tasted on the next breath every one of her kind on that ship took after that moment. Their blood could change the very air around them, but in that moment, time just stood still.

Sea air wouldn't taste the same.

"Tell them, *tell them who you belong to!*" he snarled at her. He didn't relent, even as her hands came up and she turned her back to him, begging to be spared another strike, he didn't.

He hit her again and again.

And again.

The speed was dizzying.

He showed no mercy.

No care.

Even as Anthia stopped trying to protect herself, simply falling to her knees with her body bloodstained and full of broken welts, trembling and sobbing on a gag of pain, he didn't stop whipping her.

Not until she finally croaked out a painful, "*Leave me, I am ...*"

The whip raised again, but it didn't fly yet. 'Say. It."

"*I am property of the king.*"

"Queen," Tak tried to say.

Another strike of the whip came.

Anthia screamed again.

Tak just wanted to die. Every crack of the leather against her erased a part of him, ripping the human side of his nature, his happiness and joy, and even every fond memory out of his mind so that the only thing it would replay for the rest of his life was the sight of his queen on her knees.

Bloody, abused.

Unprotected.

"*Tell them again—tell them until they know it!*"

"S-stop, please," she pleaded softly.

The king finally did, but he loomed over her with his chest still heaving, and his fury burning brightly as he turned to the rest of the ship.

"Tell them," he ordered her.

"*L-leave,*" Anthia spoke in their language.

Even the landwalkers, or those left alive, around them had come to a standstill to watch the horror of the king's treatment of the broken queen.

Tak answered her back, clicking to her, "*Please, Anthia, please ...*"

"I will pull every mermaid from these seas and let you watch them burn one by one, my little queen. And when I am done, I will release you back to the nothingness that will be left for you to find in these seas. *If* you can still swim."

"Tak, it's okay," she told him, still in their tongues. But her head remained bent down so all he had to judge of her words was the shudder of her bloody spine.

It wasn't okay.

It *wasn't*.

"Give her that ring from me. When you find her."

The king couldn't know what words the shaking mermaid spoke, but it didn't matter. His cruelty continued with another brutal strike of the whip that sent Anthia flying up so that when she screamed, her eyes landed directly on Tak.

"*Please*," she whispered.

His blade still raised and bloody, his head shaking to deny what his heart screamed for him to do, he took that first step back. He couldn't see her get hit again.

"Worry not, brother," said the man named Mattue who wore a similar fur cloak to that of the king. "Her kind doesn't scar easily. That'll all heal up nicely. Mostly."

"I'm sorry," Tak told the queen, then.

For everything.

All of this.

He called those words to her for as far as he could swim and still see the ships.

At the surface of the seas, he watched the ghost ships disappear as the heads of his kind began bobbing back under the choppy water one by one, and he was finally alone.

Tak made a promise, then.

No matter what, this wasn't over.

No matter what, he would find his queen.

Or he would die trying.

"Back from the Broken Islands so soon?" Zale asked as a quiet Tak entered the darkened throne room.

He wasn't at all surprised to see the advisor had taken up residence of the space over the course of the evening and long day of travel back. He always did head the kingdom when Anthia took short and long leaves from the palace, but Tak didn't believe for a second that was the reason for the man's apparent comfort sitting there. Not now.

Zale didn't even look surprised at the item Tak held before him.

Anthia's crown.

"The queen has been captured," Tak said. "I'll be taking the army inland before day breaks. They already have a head start and—"

"You'll do no such thing," Zale interjected calmly.

"The queen—"

"Is not here," replied the advisor simply. As if it really *was* that simple.

"And in her absence, the word of law is mine. I say you won't take the guard to Atlas, and so you won't, my lord."

Tak's brow knotted. "Don't call me that, I'm not a man of status beyond my guardship."

"Tomorrow, you will be High Master of the Guard, in fact." Zale lifted his hands from his lap and opened his arms wide, adding, "You'll be a bit busy there in that position—guarding a kingdom, and all. There won't be time for taking the army to the land for a single merwoman, Tak."

"A single—do you hear yourself?" the guard asked sharply. "We are talking about the *queen!*"

"I have talked about the queen far more than I wanted to in these past handful of days. I need not hear you start on it, too."

He couldn't ignore it anymore. He'd thought … *maybe* he was wrong.

But no. Zale's betrayal stared Tak blatantly in the face.

"It *was* you," he accused. "You did this. You helped them."

"I did what I had to for this kingdom. He wouldn't have stopped. The land king—"

"You didn't see what he did to her!" Tak roared back so loudly that the stained sea glass windows of the throne room overlooking the coral maze courtyard shook.

Instantly, Zale lifted from the sea glass throne and cut down the stairs faster than Tak could blink. The advisor straightened to his full height just a foot away from the guard, and he snatched the crown from Tak's hands without grace or care to the way it cut the merman's fingers and palms.

That pain was nothing. After that ship, he could feel nothing.

Zale placed the crown atop his head, squared his shoulders and jaw against the taller form of the guard standing in front of him, and repeated, "I did what I had to. Now, you will do what you have to—protecting these people. Bowing to *me.*"

His insides ached. Standing there, he felt like he could rot away.

Tak just nodded, and he did fall to his tail, bending for the King of the Blu Seas because he had no other choice.

He didn't lie to the new king, though.

"On my life, I will never raise a blade to protect or defend you," Tak told him.

"So be it," Zale returned, looking down at the guard, unfettered, "but they still need you."

3. THE DAY TWO MERMAIDS DIED

20 days after capture ....

Anthia

It took fifteen days for the king's caravan to deliver Anthia to the palace built into the jagged coastal rocks on the north side of Atlas. By the fourteenth, she could have climbed out of her skin from how severe it itched. Only once had she been out of the seas long enough to leech its salt from her skin, a visit to the Emerald Lands in her youth after she'd been crowned, but that realm of sea and water had warm salt pools ready to use.

The King of Atlas did, too.

In his empty harem of gilded gold and marble pillars holding strong a vaulted ceiling made of stained sea glass roses, in fact. Anthia was more surprised to find the section of palace, a monster of stairwells, corridors like mazes, and more rooms than she ever cared to count, empty to begin with. Especially after the travel where she had heard more than one landwalker guard minding her remark about the harem, and the many women inside it.

But no.

She found it empty. Even the servants seemed to disappear when they weren't needed. Somehow, as if it were possible, Anthia felt alone. She couldn't decide whether or not that was a good thing. Five days in the palace, her life already forever altered and changed in a way that could never be undone, and only now would she allow herself to feel it.

Worse yet, it was the one moment, with her alone in the long pool of warm sea water healing and soothing her still-healing wounds, some newer than others, that she felt truly safe to weep. A great many things could earn her some form of physical violence meant to act as a punishment to teach her. Or, just for the amusement of a very cruel king. A fist to the face, a whip again, or the worst of all, during one encampment on their travel, she could be stripped, beat, and made to walk amongst landwalkers who said and did whatever they wanted to her until she was finally behind the flaps of the king's tent. Where he demanded she be, regularly.

But the things that happened in there?

That was no safe place, either.

So, she did.

Finally.

Anthia cried.

Rocking into her own palms, she allowed herself that time to let out what had been building from the moment the king pulled her from the sea. Every shudder of her shoulders rocked down her body, making her legs tremble under the pool of water and causing the freshest of all her injuries to flare with pain in the worst way.

Because of it, of *that*, she cried harder.

A small voice inside Anthia whispered for her to get it out, but get on with it, too. Tis okay to need time to be sad in order to be happy again, as a wise merman once told her, but there would be no happiness at the end of this road of agony and suffering.

Only survival.

This court of gold and blood was nothing like the one she left behind, and while the palace might not be busy with much life at the moment, it soon would be if she could trust the gossip that passed through the walls.

The end of the Orchard Season was upon the landwalkers. The final stretch of a half a year of good weather, crops to tend, and land to repair where it needed it after the Season of Storms. Apparently, the king had planned the hunt for her to end shortly before his court filled with noblemen and women of the land, and anyone else wishing to speak to the House of Bloodhurst, for what would be the last time of the season.

No one, however, mentioned the harem of slaves. Not where they were, when the group of females would be back, or even if they were coming back. She didn't even know how many mermaids, if that was the collective harem, there were to the Bloodhurst name.

Property of the crown.

Owned by the king.

She'd heard that far more than she wanted to.

Taking one last wet breath of broken air in to settle her heart and help dry the tears, Anthia let it all go. The soreness between her legs. The bruises of various coloring that had become like a necklace around her throat. Even the bloody stumps where her pinky toes had once been that now stung the most in the pool of warm sea water.

It was okay, though.

That pain meant it was healing.

She closed her eyes, sunk beneath the water, let it fill her lungs to find her tail again, and she let the rest of it go. Suspended under the water, seeing nothing and hearing only the trickle of the water canals bringing fresh seawater in, she could almost pretend like none of this was real and she was back where she should be.

Almost.

It wasn't clever or safe to be too distracted, even behind the walls of the harem, in this awful place, so Anthia didn't stay under the surface of the water for too long before the soft *pat-pat* of something up above had her surfacing. She stayed under the water enough that it was only the bridge of her nose upward visible to the person that now walked along the edge of the pool.

The sight of the landwalker careless and carefree in loose trousers and bare-chested, surveying her in the water like a prized catch enraged her. He had the nerve to smile at her as if she should be as pleased to see him as he was her.

But no.

Out of everyone here, even the man who raped her daily and had destroyed her fin so that she could never swim in the seas again, she hated the man before her the most.

For a *very* good reason, too.

Mattue

"You're looking ... sour tonight," Mattue noted to the merwoman in the pool. "That isn't a very nice look on you, I must say."

Her stare said one thing: *if only I cared what you had to say.*

"Is the itching better with the pool? I've heard your kind needs it."

Still, he got nothing from her.

Nothing but a stare that willed him to die.

It wasn't often he visited the harem that took up a large portion of the palace's center between two of the three floors. The rooms here didn't have doors, there were no sharp objects to use, and the windows couldn't be opened or used as a means of escape. It was the safest place to deal with the slaves his brother kept like pets, but he just didn't like it.

"If you wish for it to be such a way, this can be a one-way conversation, Anthia," Mattue told her.

He really didn't mind.

Finally, the merwoman lifted her mouth out of the water just enough to tell him, "Get away from me."

Mattue chuckled. "I cannot, unfortunately."

Anthia continued glaring at him as if she could will him to burn on the spot. If a stare had the ability to turn a man to ash, he would be.

"What do you want, then?" she demanded. "Say it, and leave."

At that, she went right back under the water, but this time, she swam away from him, turning her back to find the other edge of the pool where she lingered without looking at him. Mattue didn't mind her mood and wasn't all that offended by her lack of conversational skills, considering the circumstances.

She was due a bit of defiance. He was one of the few men in this palace who would not beat her for it, but he could order it to be done.

If that was how she wanted to play.

"Shall I call Durel for the whip?" Mattue asked quietly.

That did it.

The very mention of a sword to the king who *enjoyed* using the whip, and he got exactly what he wanted from her.

Slowly, Anthia spun in the water to face him again but her head still remained bobbing half in, half out of the water so that she could keep her sea breath and tail. If she felt safer that way, he couldn't say but frankly, the tail would do her no good for speed or strength any longer. Not after her smallest toes had been taken by the king's surgeon and left her tail shifting into some mangled semblance of what it used to be. A punishment used in other sea and land realms for mermaids that did their people, or royals, wrong. Misael had adopted it for other purposes.

"I heard you broke the jaw of the surgeon after the first toe," Mattue noted.

Her lips found the surface again for her to hiss at him, "And he could have got a lot worse."

"Mmm, had to chain you to the table and everything ... but again, that was only as I had been told."

"Are you wanting to hear it again from the source?"

No, he saw the jaw of the man. It wouldn't be the same, and he would be stuck eating only what he could pour into his mouth in some form of liquid, or ... liquid-like substance. Apparently, the surgeon was not as kind or careful about taking her second one, and every soul on that wing of the palace heard her screams.

"If you want him to quit roping you against bedposts or shackling you to the walls in his rooms as he fucks you—"

"He *rapes* me," Anthia snarled back. "How dare you? He rapes me!"

And he liked it, too.

Misael loved it, in fact.

He didn't care *how* he got the mermaid queen, or bedded her, for that matter, just that he did. So, if she wanted to fight and bleed her way through every interaction with his older half-brother, then that was the path she would have to walk. Which he thought, she did not understand in the slightest.

This didn't have to be so fucking difficult.

Mattue tipped his head sideways slightly, as if to almost concede her point. But not quite. "You are property of the crown, and the king will do with you as he sees fit. If fucking you is what he wants to do, then it will be done, regardless of your will and wishes which I think you understand by now. What you call it to yourself is no concern of his or mine, but you might consider—"

"*Fuck off.*"

Mattue blinked twice. "What?"

Never a lady at court, no one but a whore in the pleasure houses perhaps, had spoken to him in such a way. Men, all the time. His brother, every time they spoke. A *woman*? A slave, better yet?

Absolutely not.

"I will get that whip," he threatened.

"Get it, you bastard. He fucks me less when I'm broken, anyway."

Fair enough.

'Twas true.

Misael didn't mind beating the mermaid to teach her a lesson or make her listen, but he didn't want her limp and lifeless from being bled out after someone took it a little too far. Then, he couldn't indulge his obsession by forcing her to dine and talk with him at all hours of the day and night whether she wanted his company or time.

Her displeasure was not important to the king.

Yet.

"Tell me why you're so angry," Mattue requested.

Softly, even. Letting his tone drop a bit so that she might trust him enough to tell him the truth. Not that he honestly thought it would work. And it didn't.

"Jump from the nearest high cliff," Anthia replied blithely.

"Now—"

"Better yet," she interjected, pushing away from the edge of the pool to move closer to his side, "come a bit nearer to me and I'll make it fast and easy."

Mattue took one small step away from the pool, then. "Anthia, it need not be this way."

"Are you getting the whip?"

"Do you want to be raped or cared for tonight?"

The question stopped her swim in its tracks instantly. "Every time he puts himself inside me, he rapes me, Mattue."

She could call it what she liked, he told himself. That was not the point.

"But it needn't be that way," the advisor returned quietly. "He does not care how he has you so long as he does. If fighting you around a bedchamber or dining table is all the interaction you're going to give him, then so be it. He'll take it. You're getting just what you've been asking him for, mermaid."

Anthia's brow dipped as she sunk a little lower into the water until only her eyes were visible. It told him that she was waiting to hear what he would say next instead of taking her turn to speak. Smart, really.

Mattue rarely spoke unless it needed to be heard. Or, to get what he wanted. They could also be the same things but that wasn't for him to figure out.

"Tomorrow, what is left of the old harem will return from where they've been housed for the last while. He sold off the rest a season ago. There will not be many who join you, but you will no longer be alone. Will that help with your sadness, do you think?"

He hated the sound of a weeping woman because it grated on his nerves like a blacksmith's hammer against an anvil. That was why he waited so long before entering the harem.

She didn't come back out of the water to answer that question, instead, she popped up to ask him something else instead. "Why would you want to help me at all?"

"This isn't about you, believe me."

At her narrowed eyes, he shrugged.

"I'm tired of listening to him bitch about it, and *you*, truth be," he muttered. "Every daybreak when he takes a meal with me, it's exhausting."

Truly, it was. Another morning spent willing the skies to strike him dead as he listened to Misael bemoan his newest toy was out of the question which was precisely why he found himself in this godforsaken place talking to her at all.

Anthia sneered. "Poor little halfling, you. You're just as much his pet as me."

It hadn't taken her long to notice his sealed gills. He thought she hated him more because of it, too.

"Perhaps, I am," Mattue said, "but which one of us is free?"

She said nothing.

He didn't need her to.

"It shouldn't take you long to figure out the dynamics here will not be the same as what it was for you and your people in the seas. Here, the most loved gets her way. Here, it is whatever it takes to please the king."

Anthia lifted from the water again. "The *king* is a monster."

"Perhaps," Mattue agreed once more, "but is he the monster you know or one you don't?"

That was the better question.

And with that, he left her to it.

Turning on his heel, Mattue headed back for the guarded, gated exit of the harem where the waiting swords of the king's knights would allow him to leave. Over his shoulder, he told her, "Misael will be calling on you tonight and it can be easy or hard, Anthia."

"But it'll never be true."

No, *that*, Mattue knew.

All too well, really.

Nothing here was ever true. The king and his court had always been a game where winners kept their heads and everyone else suffered a far less pleasant fate. She would learn to play it as well as Mattue had over the years, or she, too, like so many before her, would die trying to fight the game Misael wanted to play with her.

There was no point in fighting.

The king always got what he wanted in the end, anyway.

Anthia

King Misael did call on her that night, as Mattue promised the bastard would. A guard in full armor, including the helmet with a red and gold feather that matched the colors of the Bloodhurst sigil, walked her through the maze of stairways and corridors attached to the harem that led them straight into the rear of the king's private bedchambers. A suite of rooms that, if he had no desire, Misael didn't need to leave as it had everything he could possibly want. A table to eat and entertain. Access to his private courtyards. More than enough rooms to have guests, for him to keep a library of books, and even one with a set of miniature ships and buildings that sat atop a landscape that looked a lot like Atlas.

And *her* seas, too.

He never let her touch those, though.

Frankly, she didn't want to touch anything that belonged to him, but she might burn his models if ever given the chance and could get away with it. It wasn't out of the realm of possibilities.

"Face down at the end of the bed," the king said as soon as the guard delivered her to his rear doors that had been locked until he produced a skeleton key for it. He preferred the position for ease of access to muffle her noise when needed. "You know where to find the ropes."

The man covered in steel grabbed Anthia tightly around her upper arm, yanking her nearer to the room connected to this one. The room with his bed. Her chest ached with the slamming of her pounding heart against her ribcage. For a split second, the war she had been fighting in her heart for twenty days came to an end at the prospect of being tied down, legs and arms spread wide, for the king to have his way with her once more.

"Please don't tie me down like that again," she quietly said to Misael.

He heard her, though.

The tensing of his shoulders said as much, but it took him a while before he finally turned around to face the knight tasked with delivering her and Anthia, but he only looked to the guard with his next orders.

"Leave her with me."

"Sire?"

Misael jerked his head toward the door. "Take your leave."

Anthia tried to catch her breath and swallow the invisible rocks in her throat while the guard left, the king leaned against his table of models, and she stood in the middle of the room, silent. Twisting her fingers together because her nerves wouldn't settle, and she was very aware of the edge she currently walked with the king.

"Are you hungry?" he asked after the rear door to the chamber shut. "Thirsty, perhaps?"

"I am not."

Misael nodded. "Would you like some entertainment—"

"No."

He didn't seem bothered by her interruption which was an action that had gotten her slapped and insulted by him before. The king's chin lifted subtly then, and his gaze narrowed in on her as if there was something in her eyes or face that he needed to find. He searched hard for it, but as she had nothing to hide, he didn't find it.

"I wasn't even going to entertain trying to converse or bother with you tonight which was why I would have had him tie you to the bed at the start—what's changed?"

"We're not exactly bothering *or* conversing, are we?"

"A little," the king returned.

She knew what he didn't say.

More than we ever have before now.

"It's very lonely here," she said softly.

A noise of consideration echoed from across the large room. "Is it?"

"Perhaps it doesn't seem that way to you."

"Even when you have companions to fill your days between me and my desires, they will not be ones with your best interests at heart. Nor will you find them kind ... at times."

Right.

So she had been told.

Without warning, Misael stood straight, pushing away from his table of models for him to pace back and forth in his loose fitting trousers and tan undershirt that remained unlaced at the collar. Her gown, what good it was practically sheer with a cut down the front to her navel and slits up both thighs, had been shoved at her from the guard when he came to retrieve her.

At least, she liked it more than the robes.

Those didn't even tie closed.

Nudity had never been a taboo or struggle for her growing up in the seas where most everyone didn't have the time or need for clothes between jewelry and other things to keep oneself modest when needed. Now, she wished more than anything for the ability to cover her body.

"I would like to ask you for something," she admitted.

Just like that, the king's pacing stopped. His gaze snapped to her so quickly that she almost startled in shock, but thought better of it. Showing this man that she understood his level of infatuation and fascination with her bordered on insanity would not be a clever thing to do. It was not just obsession when he had gone as far as to hunt her in her own seas, like a mate would have if he had been capable of being the one she chose to take her.

Instead, he'd done it how he *had* to.

Then, he proceeded to do everything and anything he could to her to make it clear that she could never go back. She knew it was more than being owned by the king. This was more to him than adding another slave to his growing harem she had yet to even meet.

And by the Gods, Anthia would use it.

Against him.

For herself.

Whatever it took.

She'd play his game—his war of hearts.

And she would win.

"I would like to go for a walk tomorrow, if possible," she murmured. "I'm locked away all day and I see nothing."

"I'll take you."

Instantly.

He said it *so* easily.

Anthia understood exactly what Mattue had been trying to get her to see earlier.

"With proper clothes for me, too?" she asked.

At that question, Misael turned on her and crossed the room in a few strides until he was upon her, and his knuckle found the underside of her chin. Lifting there so that her gaze met his, it took every ounce of willpower and self-control that she had not to cringe, shudder, or pull away from him.

She would play this game.

She would survive him.

"What color gown would you like?" the king asked. "I'll have an assortment brought in for you to pick your favorites."

Blue, like her seas.

That's what she wanted to say.

Instead, Anthia told him, "Something red, something gold."

His grin bloomed at her pick of his house's colors.

Would this be so hard?

He practically already loved her, anyway.

"It will be done," he vowed.

"And sea lilies?" she dared to ask, then.

"What of those—what *are* those?"

Hoping he didn't notice the tremor in her fingertips, she stroked his chest overtop his shirt where she could focus her gaze and settle her nerves without him noticing it. She needed just a moment to control her voice, to keep her tone steady.

He wouldn't know, after this moment, that she never wanted to touch him, or he her, again. That the very idea disgusted her more than he would ever understand. He wouldn't know that she bled the first time he raped her because she had never taken a lover in all her years and not from his brutality, although that hadn't helped, either. She had never been touched until him, and the choices she would have to make after this night left her believing she would never be touched by another again.

If she was lucky.

If she played the game right.

"My favorite flower," she lied, smiling up at him and feeling far too small. If this was what her life here would be until her end of days, then so be it.

But he wouldn't take it all from her.

She wouldn't give him that.

"I like for them to fill my rooms."

"Tell me where to find them," he replied, bending down close enough so that their noses touched, and she could taste his next breath when he added, "and I will fill every room."

Anthia did what she had to, then. She made her deal with a monster. The only one she knew.

She kissed him.

That choice changed a lot of things.

For one, the king's harem didn't arrive the next day. Not that Misael cared to tell Anthia why he waited another five days, after the entire court had flooded back in behind the high palace walls, before he allowed the return of his enslaved mermaids.

It wasn't exactly hard to figure out.

She didn't leave his bed except to visit his private latrines and attached bathing suite for even one of those days and nights. Oh, they walked *his* private gardens, of course. Nowhere else.

Anthia stood next to Misael just beyond the heavy gold and red drapery of an upstairs veranda overlooking the entry hall. Filled wall to wall down below with ladies and lords, traders and merchants, the queen and her sister, Gistell and Gillian, and their horde of ladies, all of whom she was forbidden to look at or speak to. Even beggars lingered when they weren't being shouted at near the muddy doors. The whole hall waited. No one looked Anthia's way when someone down below glanced up at the king. A step off to the side and back from him, where he liked her to be, she had a bit of privacy from the stares, anyway, thanks to the drapery.

She, on the other hand, could still see the gathered court.

"Not long now," Mattue said, coming up behind them.

"I thought I heard the horses," the king replied.

I thought I heard a snake, Anthia thought, taking care not to glare too hard at Mattue. She still didn't trust him. Not even if, in some way, he *had* helped her. If a man could watch his own kind be used and abused, if he also hid that part of himself so that he looked more like them than his own, then he was not someone with honor or morals.

He was not someone to trust.

Their exchange ended quickly because sure enough, the gallop of hooves against cobblestone and the roll of wheels had everyone down below whispering and turning for the door again.

"Do they not know which ones you've kept?" Mattue asked.

"No one does," Misael returned.

"I do."

Mattue's gaze turned on her at the declaration, wide but confused.

Misael only chuckled, not noticing his brother's attention on her. "Ah, that's right. She does. We spoke a little about each of them. Better she keeps them in mind and minding them, anyhow, if she's to be using the set of suites just off from the harem."

"The *private* suites?" Mattue asked suddenly.

Misael turned on him with a scowl, and the large collar of white fox fur cloak he wore shuddered with the swift movement. "What of it?"

"They're unlocked, my King."

"The guards are right there, brother. She's walked around this palace all day with one behind her. No one even said a thing."

"Could they, *brother*?" Mattue cocked an eyebrow challengingly. "Better yet, *would* they?"

The tension between the two made Anthia step in because now did not seem like the best time for a discussion of this matter. Nor did she like the way Mattue tried to undo a good deal of the hard work Anthia had put in over the last few days with the king.

"And the little princes, too," she added quietly, smiling a bit when Misael glanced over at her. "We talked a little of them, too."

Her mention of them, and that *they* made her happy to know they were alive and well, boys with blood of half her kind—had the king softening. It was the only thing that did soften him to the children that he told her about with his head between her thighs as she desperately tried to keep her mind somewhere else so that her body wouldn't feel the things he did to it.

Sometimes, it still did.

She felt guilty, so disgusting, for that, too.

"And them," he agreed, nodding.

Not that he spoke very fondly or lovingly of his two sons born to mermaids. Simply that they had been taken from their mothers and given to appropriate ladies and lords to raise until they were suitable to return to court. One had seen four years since his naming day a month after his birth. Another, barely a season.

A season.

Many were born.

Many died trying to come out of their mothers, too.

Apparently.

Noise and loud chatter down below greeted the two mermaids that entered the hall. Both women—one a redhead from the Red Seas sold to Misael's father by the king there for her misdeeds and the other, a heavily pregnant mermaid from the Blu Seas—wore the same robes Anthia still had to adorn when she entered the harem pool and suites.

Or whenever her king asked.

Sometimes, he did so sweetly.

Outside, at least, she now had trunks of beautiful gowns to make sure she was appropriately dressed whenever she felt the need. So, perhaps she did lie, then. He let her out of the room for the seamstress and tailor who came to deliver her clothing and do whatever alterations required on the spot.

No one in these lands refused the king.

Of anything.

"Ah, there they are, all is well," the king muttered as the two mermaids passed like a spectacle of entertainment for the people down below. The dark-haired mermaid with her hands cradling her protruding stomach made Anthia's heart ache for more reasons than she cared to explain. She felt for the redhead from the Red Seas who glared her way down the hall and dared someone to even speak to her, but Anthia knew her kind, too. Her heart called to the one from the Blu Seas.

She knew that one, pregnant by Misael, by name.

"Fun," Mattue muttered dryly. "Now that all that is over, shall we go on the ride? The horses are ready, and I think we need to talk."

"Not with that tone and attitude."

"You are the king—"

"Exactly," Misael interjected sharply.

He turned to Anthia like he might speak, but she was too fast for him, and frankly, she had other things to do at the moment.

"I'm starting to itch again."

He'd believe the lie because it had been a good spread of days.

The king's nose crinkled. "Not in my bed. To the pool with you."

"As it pleases you," she replied with a curtsey.

Like that, Anthia was dismissed, and she left Misael behind to deal with his meddling brother. There was something—someone—more important for her to find. She kept her head down and met the gaze of no one as a guard followed close behind her, his armor rattling with every step to keep up with her fast pace. Once she finally reached the harem—it took all day to learn these halls—the knights of the sword posted at the gate of gold to let her in, handed over what she had left behind five days before.

Her sheer robe.

Anthia said nothing as she unlaced the ties to the red gown with cap sleeves and modestly cut bodice trimmed with gold thread detailing to make every seam and hemline look like scales. She thought it was beautiful.

And appropriate.

Once it was off and in a pile on the floor, she slipped on the robe.

The guard behind her stepped forward, already reaching to pick up her gown left behind when she walked forward.

"Put it in the trunk," she told him.

He nodded back, not even questioning her.

See, tides *could* turn here.

Even if they didn't realize it yet.

Inside the harem, Anthia found the one of two mermaids that Misael had decided to keep from his father's old collection wading in the pool, naked, belly big, and with her tail and destroyed fin. She almost looked happy.

Peaceful.

"Merae," Anthia said softly.

Instantly, the dark-haired mermaid's lower half slipped into the pool so that she floated upright, and her gaze found the person who called her name. A face she should know because Anthia knew hers just as well. Of course, the mermaid stared for a long while at the brand on her throat, as well.

"Qu—"

Anthia shook her head. "I'm just Anthia here, if we could."

Merae nodded but the sadness in her eyes couldn't be overlooked. It didn't just stop at her gaze, though. The woman, a bit younger than herself, seemed coated in it.

"Missa has missed you so dearly."

The mergirl had barely been beyond her sixteenth year when she was captured, the older sister of one of Anthia's maidens. Finally old enough to walk on the land as the curse in their blood of the Blu Seas allowed the change as they came into adulthood.

"And I have missed her," Merae replied, barely managing a smile.

She had been so happy to know there was at least one mermaid returning that she could share some level of trust with, but seeing the way Merae couldn't even bear to hold her gaze to someone else's for more than a few moments broke her inside.

Another piece of her gone.

"The king told me that this is your second baby?"

"The first was his father's. I don't see him. I'd not even expelled his life sack and cord before they took him from me."

Anthia's hands shook, but she kept them clasped tightly together at her middle. "I'm sorry."

"She doesn't want you to be sorry for her," came a new voice from the side.

Anthia looked that way to find the redheaded mermaid from the Red Seas, exceptionally beautiful with her vivid green eyes and heart-shaped face, and a head full unruly, corkscrew curls. Her skin, a shade of light golden brown, remained bare head to toe—no robe—as she stared Anthia down from an open room in the hallway of suites full of open beds.

Beds she hoped she *never* used.

"She wants to die," Tora added just the same way she had delivered her words to greet Anthia. As if all of this bored her to death, and she was absolutely sick of it.

"What?" Anthia asked.

"Who are you?"

"I am Anthia. And you are Tora—no need for pleasantries as I'm aware that you don't like to share, will bite me, and have some boundaries about your person and space. Let's just get all that right out of the way, okay?"

Tora's stare narrowed in on Anthia. "Excuse—"

She went back to Merae, cutting the other mermaid off. She could take her mood and problems somewhere else to someone else. Anthia didn't care to hear it.

"They'll take this one from me, too," Merae whispered brokenly. "Boy or girl, it doesn't matter. Some of them, I've heard they don't even claim, or so I've been told. What *do* they do with them?"

That, Anthia didn't know.

"I'm sure Misael won't take your baby," Anthia tried to soothe, saying that, "and if the last was his father's, then—"

"They're not different men, they are the same exact breed," Tora murmured, now sounding tired.

"I wasn't going to say that."

"Good. Don't be stupid enough to think it, either."

That might be the only thing the redhead said that Anthia did care to heed.

"Fair enough," she conceded before turning on Merae once more. "She isn't right, is she?"

Merae's violet eyes dropped from view once more. "She isn't wrong, let's just say."

"Not even for your baby, at least?"

"That's not hers, either," Tora said before the other two could speak again. "Property of the crown and king."

Babies were *not* property. One's young was the most precious and important thing. Which was why having the choice to reproduce or not had always been only a merwoman's to make.

Anthia didn't correct her.

"Doesn't matter," Merae sniffled out, turning away from Anthia so her back faced her within the pool. "I'd do it myself, if I could, but we don't even get the freedom enough for me to do that."

"Can't even jump to the rocks," Tora agreed.

"Why would you say that?" Anthia asked her. "That's … *awful.*"

The redhead only arched one brow at the queen. Then, she turned on Merae.

"I'll do it for you," she said.

"What?" the other two women asked at the same time.

Tora only spoke to Merae. "Kill you. I can do it right now."

"You're lying."

Was this … happening?

Or some act?

A joke Misael had played on her?

"I am not lying," Tora replied to Merae. "Ask me."

"Do it, plea—"

"*No!*" Anthia rushed to say.

But it was too late.

Tora was far closer to Merae than Anthia when the redhead dived for the pregnant woman already in her tail form in the pool. Anthia would never have touched the water and still expected to live. Merae gave one shriek of terror before Tora pulled her beneath the depths of the pool. Anthia screamed for the guards to help as she raced to the water's edge to find both ladies in tail form at the deepest end of the pool where one held the other down.

She stuck her fingers from both hands into Merae's neck, deeply

42

plugging her gills, while her longer, *stronger* tail pinned the other mermaid under the depths of the pool.

"*Gods, help her—help us, please!*" Anthia screamed when the guards finally came in with a holler and clatter. It was too late. It took minutes to drown a mermaid. Not very long at all, really.

She watched two mermaids die that day—the other lost her head. King Misael Bloodhurst's harem went straight back to one.

Just Anthia.

For a little while …

The king made collars the law of the land for slaves after the incident of which no one was allowed to speak; with spikes that filled the gills on both sides of his slave's neck, they could no longer change or even stay under the water without drowning from being unable to breathe. Should they change, it was a death sentence. They could not expel the water or breathe in the water. They would drown just like a landwalker.

Made of iron and measured to spec, unbreakable, and permanent to the wearer. She wore the first one. Hers was custom unlike every other collar the mermaids wore—inscribed with Misael's sigil but designed to droop in a V-shape down the hollow of her throat.

Anthia's brand wasn't visible for anyone who entered the harem or court to see after that. Ever.

She truly felt like a queen of no one. Of nothing.

More importantly, the collars served another purpose, and that was the *only* reason she allowed that bastard to smile, so pleased, as he placed it around her neck for the blacksmith to seal it. No matter how strong or capable the slave, she couldn't change any longer in the pool without signing her own death order. Anthia made damned sure what happened that day in the harem between the mermaids *never* happened again.

Even if she was a queen of nothing and no one—maybe—that didn't change who and what she was inside. It didn't change the heart beating in her chest that screamed in agony every day for the safety and comfort of familiar seas that she would never see again. She would always protect her people.

Here, she just had to do it differently.

4. THE WAR OF HEARTS

9 years after capture …

Anthia

A single flower taunted Anthia.

Just one.

Pick the damn thing—do it.

She ignored that hissing voice in the back of her mind even though it was probably right. It usually was, anyway.

It's been sixty days!

Again, with that fucking voice. As if Anthia didn't know how long it had been since she last drank a properly boiled sea lily tea. Enough for the two moons of their world to change through their many phases twice, their way of measuring months passing into seasons. But as Misael had done in many years past, a trip to the Stable House—an estate deep in the dense, forested peninsula centering Atlas—kept them away from court where he made sure she always had her favorite flower somewhere within reach. Not that he ever learned the true reason why, and if she cared to keep his favor, she would never tell him.

They all made sacrifices to remain alive here.

This was her *constant.*

"*Ugh!*" Anthia angrily, and exhausted, snarled at the poor flower.

It took her hours to find it, and she only had a bit of sea water saved from their pools at the palace to use if she had found it. She was going to be in so much trouble when she finally took the black horse named Nightwind back to the stables after stealing him from his field when she noticed him tacked up and ready to go. She wasn't to leave the stable house or its very large property without a guard, or more, depending on the time of year and political circumstances in the king's court.

Misael allowed her many freedoms. Still.

Many.

While back at court before their recent trip to the stables, she had even been given a choice of newly bought slaves from the realms of green to make her pick of which to be her ladies. They would have been called her maidens in the waters, and Misael wouldn't let her pick from any of the dozen Blu mermaids he had meticulously selected from every ship's catch season after season … no, just the Emerald Land caravan that he took her all the way to the square to see. Nonetheless, those ladies were not for Misael's enjoyment, although things had happened, and they were given nearly as many freedoms as her simply to serve and keep her pleased.

She did pick two. It was all she had been allowed.

Misael added one to his harem—another mermaid disappeared from the count by the next morning as a sacrifice to keep Anthia's king's number at a nice, even sixteen, and he never told her what happened to the rest of that catch of a traveling caravan. He liked a little more than a dozen, though. His favorite number for the harem, including her in the bunch. And as he constantly reminded her, she was still his first.

His most important.

His *love*.

But there were rules he never bent.

Not even once.

So far, in the long nine years she warmed his bed and remained his ever-faithful companion and confidant, he had never let her go off alone. That would mean he trusted her to come back to him, and he didn't. She knew it without him telling her as much.

Between them, words were not always needed.

Misael never struck her again after those first twenty days unless she raised a hand, or weapon, to him first. There had been times, of course— they could fight as well as they fucked, honestly. Usually over the harem, and that he wouldn't *stop*. That it wasn't just the mermaids he collected to show off like a sideshow to the court and fuck when he pleased. No, it was the business Atlas had made out of the trafficking of her people—of people like her and her own. It was the creams upon creams meant for skin, hands and nails, faces and everywhere else mixed with the magic that could only be found inside of someone like her. It was the tea pills sold at the markets made from mermaid blood that he, himself, had started to use as the years passed them, and he began to show his age in ways that only added to his face made up of strong lines and prominent features. A line at his eye corners, like bird's feet. A single piece of gray in his hair or beard.

The lotions and teas, all of it smelled sickly sweet. Like their blood rotting in the waters. She made him wash before touching her when she could still smell it on him.

Meanwhile, Anthia did not age. She would be well into her nineteenth or so year before she started to look as if she was reaching her middle life— and even then, a sea siren's beauty never faded.

Anthia could not pick the lily she had risked so much to find on this day. There was only one left, and none had fallen to give back to the ground for another good growing season. Clearly, someone else had found the rare bushel in the small wetland deep in the forest—or perhaps they planted it themselves to come back to—and needed it more than she did.

By the time she returned to court, she would be too far along to, one, hide it from Misael because he knew her body as well as, if not better than, she did, and for two, drink the tea, anyway. There were time limits on such things unless a merwoman wished to suffer more. It was not easy to hold the very same baby in your arms that you chose to kill when you could trace their little features, see yourself in them, never hear their gurgles and whimpers or feel their suckle, and cry over them for hours because you almost always birthed them alone.

Anthia had never done that. *Yet.* She had never needed to do more than a painful night-long shedding of purple blood that was similar to a landwalker woman's monthly moons.

Over the years, however, she'd needed to help many that did make that choice.

These were not small sacrifices.

They left scars that often gaped.

Now, she faced her own horrifying choice. Anthia didn't know what to do or worse, where to begin.

Well, that was a lie.

Right now, she had to return to Misael.

At least, she thought while standing to move away from the flower that had been taunting her for far too long, *he'll know you'll come back to him now.*

Perhaps, that would soften him.

Soften … whatever came next.

She tried not to think of that, head still turned down, and she spun to come back the way she came. Up a small knoll of tall, wet grass where she left the horse, Nightwind, tied to a tree branch.

"Are you not taking the lily?" came a familiar voice from overhead.

In terror, Anthia's head snapped up and her eyes widened when they landed on the man waiting for her at the top of the hill.

Misael.

"I-I …" Anthia looked back to the lily to give her some time to find a lie. *Anything.* She turned back around, forcing on a smile that still shook at the edges. "I only noticed it and wanted to—"

"I know what it does for you—for them, my love."

The trembling that had started to work itself throughout her entire body, even her fingertips, came to a sudden standstill. She couldn't even feel the wind or hear the wildness of the nature living around her. No, all she could see were those blade-colored, sharp as ever, eyes of Misael driving her into place. Sticking her into the very ground under her feet, daring her to deny it.

"Sometimes, I want to ask you …" Momentarily, his gaze broke hers as if he needed to look away to say what he was about to. "Just, I want to ask you not to lie to me, but I don't because I'm not sure you could. Or would."

Was that another thing he allowed her?

All these lies between them?

"How did you figure it out?" she asked.

Misael shrugged, and the action made his barrel-like chest lift heavily. Covered in his favorite leather breastplate over a fancy shirt, red with gold thread as he preferred, that she had sewn his initials into the breast pocket, he loomed impossibly tall standing so far up there. The fact that she could not see his broadsword at his side or back, he would wear it either places, told her a lot.

He had been *very* distracted in his need to find her.

"The palace has a lot of eyes and ears."

She nodded, accepting that. After all, even Mattue could understand the language between the mermaids, as long as he was actively listening, and they didn't speak too low or quickly to make it hard for him. Which they did.

But then, Misael added quieter, needing to glance away from her yet again when he murmured, "And you, my love, you talk in your sleep. There are things that weigh heavy on your heart and perhaps your dreams are the only place in which you feel safest to speak."

"So, you let me."

"I let you do many things, Anthia."

The way he said it, almost accusatory, although she didn't know why unless it was anger over her running to seek out a sea lily, rattled Anthia. Not in a good way.

"And I've given and let you do many things, Misael," she returned hotly. "Far more, far worse things, than not giving you a baby."

Even under the thick, dark beard that he had let grow for the last year, she could see how he clenched his jaw at the truth she threw at his feet. But, as if fighting with her was not what he wanted to do, he scrubbed his hand over his jaw and jerked his head back toward the way he must have come. A silent order for her to follow him.

"Are you not going to do it, then?" he asked her after she climbed the hill and stared at his retreating back.

Her brow dipped. "Do what?"

In a wildflower field a far stone's throw away, Misael's horse grazed next to hers. Alone. It seemed he did not bring the gaggle of guards or even his younger half-brother, to find her. He came by himself. Perhaps, someone had seen the direction she went. Mattue knew the land better than any of them having lived in the Stable Estate, amongst other properties, like they were his own, compliments of the king.

As for the horses, Misael still liked the beasts white, and a little irritable like her, so when he whistled to his horse to call it, Queenie, as he affectionately shortened from her longer name, Queenthia, the animal barely flicked her ear in his direction.

Well, she did blow her lips and spit toward him.

Anthia grinned.

"Little bitch," Misael muttered half-heartedly, but his tone quickly changed. "She's with her lover now, anyway. She's got no time for me. She was as mad at you as I was for taking Wind."

"He needed a good ride, anyway."

"That is not the point!"

His sudden shout seemed to still the very air around them. Other than the birds in trees that his noise sent flying into the sky.

"I was coming back to you," she tried to say.

He didn't reply to that.

"Misael—"

"Are you not going to do it?"

Again with that question.

"I asked you what you meant—you didn't answer me!"

This conversation would be a lot easier for her to manage if he would just stop walking away from her, and it seemed like her own yell back at him finally did it. Misael swung back around on her, every towering inch of him that was a good head and shoulders above her, came upon her like a storm cloud, dark and heavy, that she could never get out from under.

Somedays, that was okay and she didn't want to.

Moments like these, though?

He terrified her.

She still knew what he could do.

Even if he no longer did it to her.

His hand grabbed her jaw, but Anthia pulled away from him and took a step back from his reach entirely.

"Don't you touch me—we're not fighting and fucking this one out, my King."

"I don't want to fuck you. I want to strangle you."

Anthia snapped even further back from him, gasping. "Because I was here doing the same thing I've done every month for years? It apparently didn't make you want to kill me then."

"*Why*," he roared at her, hands flying out in front of him as he needed her to see the way they trembled with his fury, "couldn't you just ask *me*?"

"I—"

"No," he interjected just a tone lower but still too loud for a man of his standing. Emotional, Misael was *not*. "No, you lie to me. *Lied* to me, in fact. Many times. We could have spent this day looking for what you so clearly wanted and needed, if you had just told me, but instead you did *this*!"

"How do you expect me to tell you?"

"The same way—"

"'Tis *my* only choice, Misael, my sin to bear."

At her declaration, the fire in his gaze dimmed slightly. Not entirely, but enough that she knew he was listening.

"You're not hearing me, Anthia," he returned, shaking his head. "You broke rules—you are special, but you are not when you force my hand! And there is an entire estate of guards, of servants, who expect me to drag you back there bleeding and bloody. You should have seen the smirk on Mattue. That *bastard*."

That made her take another step back.

"Stop walking away from me," Misael snarled.

"Will you? Will you do that to me again?"

"*Why do you do this to me?*" he yelled back at her, louder again.

Only this time, his tears fell.

She had never seen him cry.

Ever.

"If you beat me like that again, I swear to the Gods I will—"

"What?" he threatened, daring to take a step toward her. "Cut me in my sleep? Jump from a cliff the next chance you have? Kill another of my babies?"

Ah, so that was what the problem was for him.

How he could let her do it, but also be angry about it and say nothing for so long, told Anthia that this man was more than what she even knew and understood of him. There were places, spots inside Misael, that she had yet to reach.

How many were there?

Would she ever know them all?

This was still a very dangerous game between them. The finest line sat between love and hate. It was this moment, now, when Anthia finally admitted to herself that, like him, she too straddled that line with him more often than she didn't.

"Are you not doing it?" he asked again, quietly.

Now, Anthia thought she understood what he had been asking.

"I didn't pick it. I have nothing. Doesn't that tell you something?"

"You could take it when we get back to the palace in a month's time. We both know the number of times someone has found what they have found in the sewers and—"

"Stop it," Anthia whispered brokenly.

He was right.

But he also wasn't.

Anthia used two fingers to rub at the spot between her eyes to stop the prickle of tears threatening to clog her throat. "I have done what I had to, Misael."

"I know you have, darling."

But he wasn't sorry.

Neither was she, mostly.

And that made them both monsters now.

"I hate what you've done to me," she said through chattering teeth.

Now, she cried.

He just watched her, silently.

Even the horses, not far away at all now, lifted their heads from the flowers they chomped on to survey the riders. Their attention gave her something to focus on as Misael started talking again.

"Truth be, the only reason I didn't call you on this years ago was because I knew you were right to do it—and frankly, to let the others do it."

"W-what?" she asked, rather speechless.

"Do you want to know the real reason my father started pilfering your precious sea glass, and I kept up the tradition when I took the throne?"

"Not particularly. I think I can make a safe bet."

It was a valuable resource.

"We needed windows. His slaves would jump from the highest ones if they weren't shackled or chained up every damned day."

Oh, Gods.

Anthia felt sick.

"I know when things have crossed the line," Misael added.

"But to be fair, you are not a very good judge of it."

He didn't concede her point, asking instead, "How happy is my court when there are mermaids and infants dying every other month or season? When they're all fighting and weeping every time they have another baby taken away. It's …"

"It's cruel."

Misael's gaze tracked her face as he asked, "Is that all you would call it? I thought you might tell me, once again, that I'm disgusting."

"It very much is. You are. All of it is, and you still in this very moment think that you have every right to do that to us, as if we don't breathe and cry and bleed the same. Like my pain isn't sometimes also yours."

He let out a hard but shaky gust of breath.

"I know that something, in here," he said, pointing to his chest, "is wrong with me. I needn't have you say it, too."

"But I also stopped telling you that because I know it hurts you to hear me say those things to you. Because you love me and you have this image of yourself that you want me to see, that you need me to see, so I don't tell you anything anymore. And we're all just happy to play make believe."

Another sacrifice for her to wear like the collar around her throat. She just didn't know what it would mean to, yet. Some sins, she would take to her grave.

"Because you love me," Misael said as if he knew her thoughts.

Out of all the things she could whisper in this man's ear, that was the thing he wanted to hear from her the very most. And sure, a part of her did love Misael. She loved the part of him that was just hers, when it was only them, and in the moments where time suspended and they could just pretend.

Pretend he had not kidnapped her from her seas.

Stripped her of her crown, of her culture, home, and people. Those very rare times when that night he whipped her bloody on a ship didn't matter, and the weeks that followed weren't that painful to revisit in her memories. It didn't happen often, but loving him also wasn't an impossibility.

A part of her did, simply put.

And a part of her didn't.

She could never undo what he had done, and neither could he, nor would he, so there would always be that piece of her where he could not reach. Anthia wouldn't apologize for it. She couldn't reach it, either.

"I cannot birth a dead baby," Anthia whispered painfully.

Misael's shoulders fell a bit. "Is it even still early enough? We could head back before planned, or—"

"It would not matter if he could fit in my palm, I would *die*, Misael."

Her tears still hadn't stopped even if his finally had. Jaw trembling, he chewed over words he didn't speak while glaring at the sky overhead filled with fluffy white clouds to give them some respite from the sun.

"Gods," he muttered under his breath, "I just wanted a good hunt today."

"It would be too late by the time we go back. It already is, if I'm being honest."

He nodded once.

"Right," Misael said heavily, "and how do you know that? Women, they miss their sheddings, and you—"

"The waters of my womb are my seas—I know, Misael. My kind, we know."

He didn't question her. Something he never offered anyone else almost all of the time. Not a few moments before, he had called her a liar, yet every time Anthia opened her mouth and spoke, Misael let her have her words.

Sometimes, she hated and loved him for it, too.

"I won't be able to let you name them."

Anthia nodded, already knowing that. It was the least of her concerns.

"If half the neck has gills—"

"They'll be closed, I know."

But she had time to work on that.

"The lord, the baby's ward, could be Matt—"

"Please don't take my baby away from me," Anthia whispered, willing to plead if that's what it would take.

"Is that why—all these years?"

He'd never asked her outright, but she knew he wanted a baby from her.

51

No, that was not *only* why.

Not at first.

Time changed a lot of things, though.

"Please don't take them away from me, Misael."

The request was not a simple one. Not in the slightest. There had never been another that was allowed to keep their young, the child immediately being confiscated to the crown after birth. If he allowed her this, it would take some work and forethought. Care not to make the rest of the harem jealous or even allow the palace gossip to spread like a disease the way it sometimes did. All of it, poison.

If he granted her this, it would change more than he ever had for her before.

"You'll stay here," Misael said, breaking the silence between them first.

"What?"

"To birth the child, whatever it is. Mattue will be between here and the House of Miller when he isn't at the palace. There are more than enough servants to accommodate you, and you're already past the leeching so you shouldn't be in any distress. Comfortable, I mean."

"You ... Are you saying you want me to stay here until I have the child?"

"Did I stutter?"

"You cannot give to me what you won't give them."

"I can do whatever I please, Anthia. I am the king."

"That isn't fair."

And she knew it.

"If it is a boy, he *will* be put into the line of succession. He will be given the same treatment, educated and raised the same, as the previous two I accepted."

"And if it is a girl?"

"Would you live your days out here?" he asked, gesturing around them at the beautiful serenity that was such a bright contrast to the pain between them. "Somewhere else, perhaps?"

Misael turned back around on her.

"Anywhere. One of the many estates and castles I have all over Atlas. You've seen them all. Not even the last wife made her way through all of them before she found her way into a grave like the one before her, so would you?"

Ah, yes, Gistell.

Once *she* noticed Anthia, and not in a good way, the queen didn't last long. Misael swore he would not marry again, and there wasn't a soul willing to stand against him in protest of the decision. No one thought anything of the finger mark bruises around the queen's throat, or her broken neck when Misael passed the incident off as a wagon accident.

"Pick a house," he told her, "raise our daughter, and live out your days. Would you be happy?"

"And what, wait for you to visit me whenever you please?"

"Would you miss me?"

"I might like you more if I see you less," she offered back truthfully.

It made him smile, all handsome and as smug as could be.

"Allowing you this child, some semblance of raising it, will leave you a target in the harem—you will not return into the gilded rooms, and you are not to be alone with any merwomen."

"*Misael* You can't do that to me, they need—"

"There will always be sea lilies available."

"That is but *one* thing they need from me!"

His gaze nailed into hers, and the murder she found there stopped the very breath in her chest. "If even one of those mermaids killed you and took you from me because she was jealous or angry, or anything, Anthia. Anything at all, if they took you from me, I would spend every last day of my life pulling what I could find of them from the seas just to make them bleed so I might feel some semblance of better. I've dreamt of it. I know right where I'd *start*."

"Mis—"

"You are *mine*. No one takes you from me *but* me."

"What of my ladies?"

"I'll move them here, for now."

"And do you think Mattue—"

"He can go to whatever hell awaits us. He's lucky I still give him access to the crown with two heirs ahead of him. His time is just about up." He glanced her way, his gaze tracking down to her stomach when he added, "If this one is a boy, that will be three, and he will be taken from the line of succession entirely. Unless all of my sons died."

"You said the lord to oversee his education and raising would *be* Mattue, though."

"He still has his place. We all have our duties. Even you, darling."

He crushed far too many wildflowers in his short trek to close the distance between them, and this time when his hand found her jaw, she didn't pull away. He tipped her face up, nuzzling his nose with hers. Soft and sweet compared to the sting of his fingers holding her tight enough to hurt.

"You still think I'm going to run away, don't you?" she asked just before he kissed her. "That you've not done enough things, or taken enough from me, to make me stay here forever with you?"

Against her lips, he nodded. But then he pulled away, yanked her along with him in the field, and gave her a soft pat to the stomach when they reached the horses where he helped her saddle up.

"Less now, though," he admitted from the ground, his hand still firm against her middle.

"I hope you know that also makes you a monster."

Misael let her go then, and climbed his own horse as he gave her a sidelong look. "And which one of us doesn't want to admit to ourselves that we like that, my love? A meal to feast on your thoughts."

He didn't let her reply before heeling into the horse and taking off. Frankly, she was grateful. As it appeared, Misael was still willing to allow her a few lies.

Anthia soon followed behind.

Mattue

A season later …

"Where is he? *Where is she?*" the voice thundered through the house when Misael finally arrived.

Eight days after the birth of his newest son.

Mattue remained in the entry of the Stable Estate until his brother and guards finally spotted him once they entered under the doorway.

"Your grace," Mattue greeted, bowing to the king.

Misael, too busy for pleasantries, policies, or politics, passed Mattue by without as much as a glance. "I said, where is she?"

"Upstairs in her chambers with the baby. The same place she's been since he was born. They're fine. Both are perfectly fine."

"You said another two weeks!" Misael shouted over his shoulder at his brother.

Mattue tried not to roll his eyes.

And failed.

"Yes, well," he muttered back, climbing the winding stairwell up, "birth is a tricky thing like that. When the child might come is—"

"I've had *many* children, Mattue, and you have had none. One of us is far better versed on pregnancy and childbirth than the other, let me say."

"And which number did you birth of those many, exactly?"

The question shut his brother up.

Mattue took that as a win.

The guards, and whatever other people his brother had brought along in his traveling caravan didn't follow the king and advisor to the second level of the large Stable House. Meant to hold the king's personal collection of horses, his very favorites, it also needed to be large enough to entertain, to have a good hunting party, and to house everyone who could please a king.

Thankfully, Misael used the property less frequently than he had in his youth, but Mattue adored it. This, and a few others, were his only respites. Giving it up to his brother's favorite whore for a little more than a season for her to privately carry and birth the king's next child was but a small price to pay even if it had left him feeling like a babysitter, of sorts. He almost liked her, really.

Anthia, that was.

Not like his brother did.

Not like the court did.

Not like anyone did.

No, Mattue respected Anthia for the game she played, and the battle he had only now realized she'd won. It was all the more apparent to Mattue that she had been successful in her war of hearts with Misael when the king finally found her in the west hall of the home, tucked beneath blankets with a bundled baby nestled between her crossed legs.

Misael's whole face lit up.

Even his eyes—and those were always cold.

"There he is," Anthia said, glancing up from the baby to lay eyes on the king. "You're only a little late."

"He's eight days old."

"And eats like a horse," she returned. "I told you I wasn't lying in for months and months just to be weak for him when he needed me strong. Birth is war, too, Misael, you do what you have to."

A smile twitched at his brother's lips, but then Misael turned to Mattue, scowling. "Leave us, would you?"

"Did you bring the surgeon?" Mattue asked first.

The boy would need his gills closed, but Mattue could not imagine how that was going to go over with Anthia. She had gotten a lot out of the king so far, sure, but saving her child that pain? Not possible.

Who would tell her that?

Misael's gaze shot back to Anthia. "Later."

"He'll need a proper naming day at the palace, so should we prepare a convoy for that in the next moon?"

"*Later*, brother," Misael repeated. "Leave, now."

"As it pleases you," he replied.

He was slow to go, though, wanting to watch the scene play out before him because he, too, still played a courtly game with the Bloodhurst King. As it were, Mattue found himself staring at his latest competition. The most danger to his place behind Misael.

Anthia, that was.

Gods, Mattue had been stupid.

What a hell of a game to win.

He smiled Anthia's way, then. "Well done," he told her.

She nodded back, smiling tiredly.

His praise of her had nothing to do with the baby boy she was now unwrapping to show her king, telling him, "Look at him, Misael, all chubby and pink. He's absolutely *precious*."

"He is, here ... let me see," the king replied, stepping deeper into the room with arms ready to take the baby. "Who is nursing him?"

"*Who?*" she shrieked back, cackling maniacally. "Me, Misael. He's my baby."

The king chuckled. "Yes, but we can have a nursemaid—"

"I'll cut her tits off. I *will*."

"And close the door, brother," Misael added, over his shoulder, at that threat from Anthia.

Likely a promise, really.

Well, the next decade or so should be fairly interesting.

Mattue nodded in the doorway, turning back to grab the handle that he had pretended to forget to pull shut on his way out. He saw one last thing before he did.

Misael holding a diapered, but otherwise naked, prince.

Never had he held a son. None of his babies. Most, Mattue knew for certain his brother had never even seen them, unless he claimed the child, before they were sold to rich lords and ladies incapable of reproducing—or just those with enough gold.

Not until the baby he would name Eryx.

The baby Mattue hated and loved the most.

The halfling he had once wished he could be.

The loved child he never was.

Not until Eryx did Mattue hate the king and his little sea queen. *Truly* hate them. That baby changed everything.

Anthia

"*He could rule the land and the seas, then, couldn't he?*"

"You're being ridiculous, my lord."

"Am I, or am I about to make your face bleed?"

"My apologies, I just—"

"*Shut up.*"

No, it was too late.

Their loud conversation in the hallway dragged Anthia from a very peaceful sleep. There was something to be said about the Bloodhurst brothers and the unstable, sometimes loving bond the two seemed to share. They plotted against and tortured one another as much as they defended and protected the other.

It was vicious.

And a treacherous thing.

They were also all the two had. A part of her recognized that for what it was, and why Misael kept his remaining bastard brother around despite the irritation it sometimes was. He cared for him—not always in a good way, but he did.

Anthia rarely stepped between the two, even still. After all these years.

That night, she did.

"If it had to happen to me, and the other halflings born, then it has to happen to him, too, Misael," Mattue said at the appearance of a sleepy, confused Anthia in the bedchamber doorway. "So, let it be done. It'll be within the hour now."

"*What?*"

At his declaration that *it* would be done so soon, Anthia found herself quite awake. She spun as Misael yelled her name and ran back into the bedchamber. Sure enough, the cradle where her newborn slept was gone. The ache in her breasts said she had been sleeping longer than she should have, but if no baby cried to be fed, how would she have heard him?

"I told you to let me sleep with him on the bed!" she screamed at Misael. "You did this, didn't you? You let them take him from me?"

"'Tis not done, yet, Anthia."

"It likely is," returned Mattue dryly.

"You said you wouldn't take him from me!"

She slung every word at him the same way she threw items from all over the room. A pillow. A goblet. The gold clock that told time by never stopping its constant swish-swish movement. Anything she could get her hands on, it crashed across the room between the walls, the opened door, and Misael.

"Get me my baby!"

"My lords?" came an unknown voice, muffled further down the hall.

It sounded like one of her ladies.

"Everything is fine, return to your chambers," Mattue snapped hurriedly.

"Okay, that is enough," Misael said, stepping into the room and closing the heavy door part of the way behind him. "Are you going to throw another thing at me?"

No, she wouldn't, actually.

Anthia grabbed the carving knife from the table that he'd used to cut her apples for her while she fed their son earlier in the evening. For a second, Misael looked as if he expected her to turn it on himself. Instead, she stuck that knife up under her own jaw. In under the bone, deep. Until it hurt. Until it bled. Until he understood that if he didn't do something right that very instant, his life would never be the same.

"Get me my baby," she hissed.

"*Dammit*," he swore, glaring at her. "Don't you dare try this shit with me after everything."

He dared to take a step forward.

She pulled the blade.

Two inches right.

"*Anthia, stop!*"

"Get my son or I'll bleed myself out on this fucking floor, Misael."

"Mattue's getting the baby," he assured, but he never moved again.

"You let them close his gills?"

"The laws are the laws," he tried to explain.

"Because you made them," she replied frankly, "and you could unmake them."

But he wouldn't.

When a monster shows you who they are, believe them.

So, he could stand there, and he could look at what he'd done. What he did to her. While she bled all over her silk nightgown and the floor.

By the time her baby was delivered back to the bedchambers and in her arms, she had left quite a puddle of deep violet staining her feet and the floors. It didn't matter. She let Misael staunch the wound, kissing her head as he mumbled about her being *fucking, bloody mad* while she climbed back into their bed to nurse their baby. His continued hiccups as he tried to eat against her breast told her that he had been crying.

Hard.

For a long while.

"What did they do to my baby?"

"Well, he screamed every second of the way to the stables where the surgeon did it," Mattue said where he leaned in the doorway. "But he often does that ... screams away from you, I mean."

She glared his way, but he only raised an eyebrow back.

Bastard.

"You don't take young from their mothers," she snapped at both of them.

Not her young, anyway.

The rest of the reason for her baby's distress was easy enough to see, and it broke her heart. Thin steel, spun like thread, created little crisscrosses around the line of each gill on the only side of his neck where he had them. All of them, sealed shut. As explained to her, after a year, they would remove the steel knots, another painful process.

He would never breathe in the seas.

"You don't know what you've taken from him," she whispered as she traced his little features with her fingertips.

"It is just—"

"I'll never forgive you for this," she told Misael, silencing his apology or whatever else he might try to say to justify this away.

Swearing her life on it even as he pressed his mouth firmer against her head with his next kiss, and his hand tightened around her arm almost painfully.

"Anthia …"

He made his choices.

As would she.

"Ever."

5. THE NEXT KING

Almost 5 years later …

Anthia

"Another," demanded a very greedy king.

Anthia shifted her naked form along Misael to give him the kiss he so badly wanted if the hunger in his eyes was any indication. But as swiftly as she gave him that taste of her tongue sliding along his and the barest sweep of their lips, she pulled back.

Miseal tried to grab for her, but the state that she had left him on the bed was quite a weakness for the king. Too limp, and dry now, to do much of anything except listen to the only woman in the realms who could hold his ear.

"Too late," she teased him, already stepping off the bed.

"Get back here, we're not done."

"I'm taking a piss."

An unhappy grunt answered her from the bed as she slipped away to do her business. By the time she was back, she had slipped on a robe of soft pink silk, a match to the beautiful nightgown Misael had just ruined in his haste to get off her. She tried not to pay it any mind where it now remained forgotten and tattered, thrown haphazardly over the black mountain bear fur blanket at the foot of the bed, if only because it was her favorite.

She just didn't care when it had happened.

If prompted right, Misael was a fantastic lover. Fucking him wasn't entirely a waste of her time, but coupling with him less often over the years left the king rightfully suspicious every time the two of them found themselves in bed together again. Whether it was because she wanted fucked, or had motives to get him more affectionate and compliant, he never assumed that consenting sex between them was anything but a bargain or deal.

"What do you want, then?" he asked, still breathing hard on the bed.

"At least tell me when it's a good lay."

"*It always is.*"

It sure was.

From the very first moment he put himself inside her, instantly lost his seed, and then proceeded to rape her to his second release as he told her almost the very same thing, in fact—*let's hope it's always like that, my little queen.*

Unsettled in her heart a bit, and not trusting herself to return to the bed when her mind had just opened an old and hidden wound without Misael knowing, she tried to buy herself some time. Leaning in the doorway connecting the private privy to the king's west room chambers in the Stable Estate, she toyed with the rope of silk meant to tie her robe, even picking endlessly at the fragile ends.

She knew when Misael's eyes finally turned on her again. The feeling of them on her had never changed in all these years—even from that first meeting on his falsely gifted ships. Sure, the way it felt changed over the years, but the effect of sensing it almost intimately never did. If there was any bond they now shared beyond their son that was true, it was that one.

Anthia remained property of the king.

"Is it about Eryx?" Misael asked quietly.

"'Tis," she simply said.

That felt easier.

Get it right out there, then.

Anthia nodded once to herself, silently relieved.

Misael's swallow sounded from the other side of the room. "What of it, then?"

"He's approaching his fifth year and—"

"Will return permanently to court under Mattue's ward."

So many things between them could have been different if only the Gods had opted to gift them anything else but the blade-eyed, black-haired baby with a chubby little prick between his legs. Not that she regretted a single thing about her baby, but the comparison was a contrast in her mind that she couldn't pretend didn't exist.

Misael could choose whichever of his sons that he wanted to be his heir, but girls were next to useless to these kings of land, it seemed. And for that matter, he played a game of favored roulette with the sons he did acknowledge. His oldest son, one he cared so little for that he married off to a continent a season away just to see him less than the effort he already didn't make, was a good example.

"You could have kept the oldest on Atlas," she finally said. "Why marry him away? Eryx didn't even *need* to be the spare, Misael."

"And now he is, so court it will be." Misael elbowed his large form higher in the bed until he found himself leaning back, satisfied, against the purple crushed velvet headboard. He arched an eyebrow at her, studying Anthia like all of this was still a game between them, and not like her child's life was about to again be irreparably changed. "He's not just a boy when he's mine, you see."

"I've always known that, but doesn't it mean something to you that you wouldn't have him without me? That I chose to give him to you?"

"Anthia, that is but one of two reasons why you still live and breathe."

She sucked in a shaky, broken breath. "This is why I fuck you before I talk to you now, my King."

Everything else between them went straight to *hell*, and swiftly.

"I know, darling."

"I'd like to return as well, then—to court," she clarified, bringing their conversation back to where it needed to be.

The king did not look pleased.

Her stays at court were always short and sweet. Anthia never re-entered the gilded rooms of the palace harem after birthing her child, and other than her old maidens who had been gone since the end of Eryx's first year, she never spent time with mermaids alone. Not without a guard, or several. But the infrequent, and short, trips to court gave Anthia an awareness of something she hadn't really planned for. Especially as she watched Misael from afar as their boy toddled along the courtyards and corridors beside him, and the court came to life with the king's exploits and personal dealings on display. Her son felt like a spectacle. A loved one, sure, but he was still just a baby.

Practically.

Having the king in a good mood and willing to entertain his court could make a whole week better—but seeing him with the princes, beginning their courtly life and education?

The court found it's happiest days.

The fact that Eryx was reaching his years where court life would take center stage as his proper education and training began put Anthia in a bad position. She neither wanted to return to that life full time, nor did she want to leave her son in the sole care of his father and uncle. But how could she possibly get Misael to understand that?

To him, he loved his son, yes, but the boy was just another thing. Something else of Misael's—something precious and adored, sure, but still just his to do with as he pleased.

"Misael, please—"

"Hush a moment, if you would. Although, truth be, it's easier to tell you no when you're not still dripping with my seed."

"I won't have another child to replace, or trade, for Eryx."

She was getting a little further along in her years to be carrying healthy pregnancies, anyway. Not that this was the right time for the discussion.

That quieted Misael and darkened his features in the already shadowy bedchamber.

"Is that who you think I am?" he asked, barely above a breath.

"I—"

"You think I would ask that of you, truly?"

"I think if you consider all things, it would not entirely be beneath you, my King."

"*Anthia*, I let it be your choice," he snapped, irritated instantly. "As it will always be!"

"Lower your voice—the second prince's wards are sleeping below us and you know Mattue listens through the walls for *everything*."

At that, Misael screwed his lips shut.

Not very happily.

"I don't know why I bothered bringing Sett and his whole house along—he doesn't even like hunting," the king grumbled irritably

"Someone," she returned, not playing coy at all as she eyed him, "thought the two boys would make good playmates—with what, nearly ten years between them?"

"Kings do not always make smart choices."

Obviously, she thought.

"No," Anthia muttered out loud, "but they never make the wrong ones, either, I'm told."

"Correct, my love."

A roll of her eyes answered his pet name.

Misael didn't seem to mind. "Are you coming back to bed?"

"Am I returning to court?"

"If you're sleeping in my chambers only."

Gods.

He played an impossible game.

"Misael—"

"Tis not fair if only you use what we still share against me, and not for I to—occasionally—turn the cards, is it?" he asked.

Bastard.

"Counter," Anthia returned.

Misael sighed, annoyed, from the bed. "What of it?"

At least, he let her make one.

"I keep him during the storms. You keep him in the good season."

Anthia expected an instant no.

That would still be half of a year without her son, but she didn't think Misael would enjoy being locked down in his palace with a boy who only cared when he ate, played, and made a sport out of hitting high leaves with his piss. And she truly hated time away at the palace when it was empty of any life.

"How does that counter benefit *me*?"

Of course, because all he wanted from her was sex and time shared between them.

"I am property of the king," Anthia said frankly, "and I'm quite aware, my lord, that you know precisely where to find me."

Misael eyed her in that way again—ravenous and hungry. "Every end of season, or ball or tourney for our son, you are to return for at least a fortnight."

Fourteen days?

Manageable.

"Easily done, my King."

"Is it decided, then?"

"I get him for the storms?"

"Until ten, Anthia," Misael replied, shrugging. "Then, his education will take him on travels. Tis important for a would-be king."

"*Would be*," she muttered, "you say that like it's a bad thing."

Misael's gaze stabbed into hers, murderous and unforgiving. "Look inside your heart, that part of it that I made mine and neither of us can change. Tis there, we know it is, even if it's dead. Even if it takes you to a place where you don't want to go, ask yourself, Anthia. What would you rather Eryx be, my love—the spare, or the next king?"

She did look there, *go* there, in her mind but she didn't answer him.

"Mattue will remain his ward, however, whatever the season, so start getting used to the idea of spending more time with him while you can, I suppose," Misael added, reminding Anthia that even with closeness and time to raise her son, someone else had all the say. They would make all the rules, too.

A goddamned *snake.*

Mattue

Clack. Snap. Thwack. Crack. Clack.

Slap.

"*Ow*," howled almost five-year-old Eryx from across the field.

"Don't poke me like that, then, you little bastard."

"*Sett!*" Mattue snarled, never once looking up from his book. "Not appropriate."

"Don't call my mother a *whore*," the younger Eyrx returned.

Had he missed something between the boys?

Oh, well.

Mattue tried to keep his gaze on the text in his hands, but the noise continued and the boy's crying became louder.

"Someone's going to get themselves a switch," Mattue warned dryly.

"Uncle Mattue, Sett—"

"*Shut up!*" came the snarl that finally lifted Mattue's head.

"Quite enough, Sett, thank you," Mattue called out.

Nothing and no one answered him back. All he really wanted to do was read his damned book, and he couldn't even see the children now.

Shit.

He truly disliked children. In a way that came from deep within his own heart and told him that he was not meant to be a father. The one thing he cared for about Eryx was the fact that the boy doted on him and adored him almost incessantly. The closest thing to his father, Eryx saw his uncle as something very near or similar to the same thing. As if he couldn't really tell that his uncle barely cared to have him within arm's reach, or that his patience constantly ran a little thin, and much to his mother's displeasure, the halfling couldn't seem to get enough of him. Anything he wanted to do, the boy found himself making a way to come along and do it, too. Mattue had not known it was possible to both adore something and will for it to die almost constantly until the third Bloodhurst princeling that became his ward.

Had he not liked his cock as much as he did, he would've had it taken off to prevent children of his own entirely, but alas, that didn't seem the way to go. A bit much, someone told him once, considering how spilling the seed down a woman's throat was always a good option. So, he kept his physical relations limited to what served him, and found himself acting the fool as the ward for his brother's child, anyway.

What wrongs had he done to their Gods to treat him this way? Honestly. He sacrificed every good first hunt of the year like he should and paid his tithes seasonally. Why did they deem fit to punish him so?

"Eryx?" Mattue asked, then, his gaze scanning the rolling field of wheat where the two halfling princes had been playing a game of knights.

He wasn't a very good minder.

Not of children, anyhow.

Sett, significantly older than his counterpart, could be a bully and a brat, when he wanted. Which was almost all of the time—baring the moments in his father's presence. Then, the little shit turned on his handsomest smile.

Out of all the boys, Sett looked *most* like Misael. Eryx, however, held the most affection, and that counted for a lot more. Mattue had a feeling this time around when brought to visit with his younger brother, Sett knew as much, too.

But one was still quite little even if he wielded a wooden sword like a boy twice his age, and the other could almost fit in his father's shoes. That was a big difference.

"Eryx!" Mattue called one more time, a bit louder and firmer. If his nephew heard him use that tone, the boy knew to return to the front of his uncle's boots *immediately*.

Yet, little Eryx did not come running.

Mattue finally discarded the godforsaken book to the ground and stood. The bit of extra height gave him visibility to what was happening just beyond the rolling knoll of tall grass. Well, what he could see of it, anyway.

Little boots, Eyrx's, kicking high in the air, his only fight against the much larger boy now sitting on his chest. The kid didn't make any sound, he couldn't call his uncle for help, and Mattue learned why as soon as he got close enough to find the reason. Sett had taken the blade end of his wooden sword and used it to pin against Eryx's throat.

His ward's face was *blue*.

"Little bastard, you're only the spare anyway," Sett hissed down at a struggling Eryx.

"Sett, stop it this instant, that's enough!" Mattue roared.

"Doesn't even know his *place*," the older boy spat.

Those words.

They were the ones that did it.

Something inside Mattue left at that moment. Whatever human part of him remained, tying him to the older child, disappeared in an instant.

Mattue just … *snapped*.

Later, when his brother called him on his lies, Mattue would use many excuses for his actions that day. From his irritation over minding the children when there were more than enough ladies in waiting to do it, to even crying and calling it an accident.

The truth?

Sett Bloodhurst got what he deserved.

Mattue deemed himself fit to serve it.

It took one good swing of Eryx's wooden sword, the pointy tip clenched tightly in Mattue's hand, and Sett fell to the side with his eyes blank and open. The force of the impact sent the second prince of Atlas' head smashing off a chunk of rock sticking out of the ground, adding another louder sickening crunch after the smack of the first. Blood poured from both sides of a broken prince's face.

"MOTHER!" Eryx screamed the very second he finally found his air.

Only two things saved Mattue's head that day.

The fact they were so far from the estate so no one could call him on the many lies he formed with his nephew on the long way back. And Eryx.

Eryx saved him, too.

The kid only had to say *one* thing in the end.

"He fell from the horse—do you hear me? He fell from his horse, Eryx."

"W-which horse, Uncle Mattue?"

Eryx asked a damned good question.

Nonetheless, he did as he was told. In return, not that little Eryx properly understood the implications of Mattue's actions that day, his uncle had made him the next king.

He hadn't even turned five.

Mattue made Eryx promise another thing.

Not to tell.

Perhaps that was the one and only mistake Mattue made that fateful day because trusting a child, even one that adored him, was simply a losing game. He didn't realize the error until much later, long after the sun had set, and Sett's ward along with the king's caravan began the journey home. With the dead prince's body in tow.

They would soon follow.

Apparently, there was to be a burial.

The thoughts of the prince's funeral were not what greeted Mattue awake in the darkened space of his bedchambers, however. No, that disturbance belonged to someone else entirely, and currently, she sat straddling his chest and placed the tip of a sharp blade under his chin. She dragged the blade down his throat slowly, inch by inch, letting him feel every one until she came to a stop against his hard swallow.

"Oh, good," Anthia murmured in the darkness, her violet eyes glowing silver in the two moons' light, "you're *awake*."

"Anthia, now—"

That blade of hers cut him, then. He felt the blood run warm down the cold, sharp edge.

"I'll gut your throat if you say even one more word," the mermaid hissed.

Once upon a time, he watched through a crack in the door as this woman stuck a knife in her own neck and threatened the only thing in the world that probably truly loved and needed her like no one else in all of the 9ine ever would. If she could do that to Misael, a man he believed she had cared for and possibly even loved despite his monstrosities for the sake of her child, then he did not doubt her willingness to hurt him.

Mattue meant little to nothing to Anthia.

Dirt under her shoes, really.

Until Eryx.

The one thing she was forced to share with him despite all the many things Mattue gave up for the comfort and peace of his brother's favorite whore.

Gods.

"Misael should have sent you back to the seas," Mattue snarled on the bed.

"I agree."

"I didn't hurt Eryx."

"You hurt his mind today, actually."

That reply had Mattue's brow dipping.

Anthia didn't give him long to think on it, though, before she drove that blade even harder against him. "Until the rest of my days, Mattue, if you ever lay a single hand or hurt a hair on my son, I will find you like this ... when you are weak and unprepared, and I will make sure you understand the pain that comes from a mother's fury. Do you understand me?"

What choice did he have?

Mattue nodded.

Anthia still didn't move.

Neither did her blade.

"Not one fucking hair, Mattue."

"I care for him, too."

"Not like I do."

No, that was true.

And his affections, unlike hers, were far more fickle.

"Did he tell you, then? About today?"

Finally, he felt the tremor rocking the blade and her hand. "What do you think?"

Yes, the boy did.

Just like when he screamed, Eryx called out for only one. No one else. That boy knew his safest seas.

"I am his mother," Anthia whispered from above him.

As if he could somehow forget it.

"Get off me," Mattue demanded.

Anthia nicked him once more, and good, with the blade again, but then she was gone. He felt her weight leave the bed, but even her figure was a shadowy blip across the room before the bedchamber door creaked.

Her knife?

She'd left that behind, tossing it at his cock as she took her leave. A final warning.

6. THE NEXT QUEEN

Many, many years later …

Poe, 2nd Princess and Heir to the Blu Seas

"Well done! Well done!" the king to Poe's left shouted, lifting from his throne of glass to clap for the sea snakes and their riders that clashed in the middle of the pit below. A dangerous sport when the beasts of the seas were thrice the length of the mermen riding them—the snakes winding and knotting to fight in the middle of the tourney ring while their masters wielded swords—and easily doubled the width. But it was also her father's favorite sport even if he was no longer allowed to participate as king.

Any excuse to throw a good tourney under the seas.

This one just happened to be hers.

An entire week of celebrations to mark her adult life, actually.

"You could be more excited for this," her father noted over his shoulder at her.

Could she?

"Of men attempting to kill one another for the sake of my favor?"

Zale didn't bother to hide his smirk. "Yes, Poe. Precisely that. For *you*. Someday, when you're queen, this colony will expect you to be up on your feet shouting and excited as I am."

Gods.

Did she really have to?

Snake fighting wasn't a favorite of hers. Poe lifted her chin a bit higher to better spy the happenings lower in the pit. Purple blood staining the water told her the knight from the Emerald Lands was likely losing to his Red Seas counterpart but how bad his injuries were in comparison to the snake blood in the water was a little hard to tell. Although, if Poe knew her father well enough, the loss to the Prince of the Red Seas always was the plan.

The roaring cheer of the crowd in their own balconies to watch the event made the royal's larger section vibrate with the noise and tail fins hitting the carved reef. If anything, the seven days of celebrations to mark her seventeenth year, and coming of age, had done something good for their small colony.

Any joy here was welcomed.

Happiness, even more so.

Her father, King Zale, learned to keep his people of the Blu Seas compliant with entertainment and small privileges that felt like freedom to a colony under his very strict control. Everything from their mating season to how far one could swim became laws spoken from the mouth of their king, and bereft to do much else but agree or be exiled from the colony, their people did what they had to, she supposed. Eventually, the king's proclamations of the laws and protections being for the better good even started to ring true.

Well, if one feared the landwalkers, anyhow.

Poe couldn't say she did.

In fact, she had never even seen one.

"*Yes!*" Zale cheered, pumping one fist high when the bloody battle below finally came to an end. The white snake brought along with the knight from the Emerald Lands lay dead on top of the rider doing his best to get out from under the beast. Deep in its neck, straight through to the other side, glistened the silver blade of the young—almost thirty-five—year-old son of the King of the Red Seas.

Not an heir to a throne of his own, he was his father's third child—the deal as she knew it was that he would take her home, as his father did with her oldest sister, Sarha, a year before. Then, she was expected to practically share a throne with him upon return to the Blu Seas when her birthright finally came to pass.

Besides, she wasn't even sure she would like the Red Seas.

Dismounting his snake and handing off the reins to a merman who came to retrieve the beast, Tordan, named very similarly to his father, like his brothers and sister, decided to take his blade back from the gravely wounded sea beast. The cruel and unforgiving sound the sword made coming out of the snake made Poe cringe, but her father only smiled impossibly wider when the prince held the bloody blade high.

"*Now*, you rise," Zale told her.

Demanded, really.

"Whether I like it or not," Poe mumbled, forcing on a smile as she still did what her father wanted. She wasn't the only one. The rest of the members of their royal family stood with the king and heir to his throne to celebrate the official winner of the tournament.

Rosel smiled in her daughter's direction. "He'll make a good match," she said of the prince.

Poe didn't return the sentiment, but that was only because she still had a part to play today, especially as the tourney was *for* her. The triumphant champion, a charming man she had spent a little bit of time with over the fortnight since his arrival—as she did with many of her possible suitors to arrive in the Blu Seas—swam his way to just beneath their balcony.

The blade of his sword did the rest.

In their tourneys, favors *were* the clothing and picked by the winners. The tip of his sword found the loose, twirling piece of sheer fabric woven into the strings of pearls hanging from around her waist. Much like the matching, and separate, unattached bodice which allowed her a bit more modesty for the day, the pieces of the lower gown were his to take.

Now.

His tail, a bright red like the stems of sea lilies from his waist to the jagged, flowy fins beneath him, made the bright green of his eyes even deeper, and the golden color of his skin glint in the sun rays that made their way this far down through the water. She only needed to look at him for a short while to understand why her older sister so easily fell for his father when that match had been made, but he, and his seas, were not at all what she wanted.

Now, she had to tell her father.

Tordan took three of her favors, leaving her with practically none left. Good thing the tourney had almost come to an end. *"Princess."*

She answered his nod back with her own. "A worthy win," she told him.

"Yes, well done," Zale spoke up.

The blowing horns of the sea trumpets in the pits called the prince away for the interim to begin before the final show of the tourney. And then, this awful week of a revolving door of suitors would come to an end for Poe.

Finally.

Behind her, she listened to the chatter of her sisters, Arelle, a year younger than her, and Coral, two years her junior, be quieted by one of their mother's maidens.

"Hush," said the merwoman. "'Tis not the time, girls."

"Well," Arelle said a little louder, "I just wanted to know if she even liked him."

No better time like the present, Poe thought at Arelle's dejected proclamation.

"I do not," she admitted loudly enough for their entire balcony to hear.

Next to her, Zale sighed loudly. "Daughter of mine—"

"If you might let me speak," Poe interjected sweetly.

Zale eyed her sullenly. "You won't mate with the prince from the Red Seas, will you?"

"Do you at least care to hear why?"

His gaze said he didn't.

But, his mouth did not speak.

Being his favorite child of the four he shared with her mother, Rosel, Poe knew exactly how far she could push her father's patience with her before it snapped entirely. Sitting amongst their closest kin and trusted people, he would not mind her speaking freely about such things if only because it kept the two of them from screaming at one another.

Usually.

"The knight they sent from the Emerald Lands—you know that king is more interested in his son being a match for someone else," Poe stated, choosing every word carefully. Some things, even if they involved her sisters, like who their father intended to mate Arelle off to, was not yet something they were old enough to discuss. And as the king of those lands hadn't even cared enough to send his son and heir, she would never have picked him based on the man they did send to represent him for the time being. As for the sister closest to her own age, until her own intended mate and companion found his way into their lands, many things about the mating, the bond, and other secrets of the merwomen would remain just that to Arelle—a secret.

Or it should.

Poe, too, had learned of some things early.

"So, let's take him off the table, shall we?" Poe asked her father.

"He's gone," Zale returned. "Pick another."

"The guardsmen were all worthy fighters, but there is no true benefit in mating with any one of them for me," Poe said about the various mermen who had taken up the challenge of winning her eye. "Although, it isn't hard to wonder why I'm a prize to them, let's be honest."

She quickly dispensed any notion that one of the other suitors who had traveled in the hopes of catching her interest were appropriate, either.

Her father was not impressed.

"Why discuss all the others before the prince?" Zale asked.

Down below, mermaids danced with silk ribbons of various colors twirling around them as the blood and carcass of the sea snake was carted away. The dancing maidens gave her something to focus on instead of the brutality lower down, or her father with his crown of twisted, glinting sea glass. A bigger version of the smaller crowns that she, her sisters, and their mother all wore during events like these or for other important things.

Zale, however, rarely removed his crown.

Even the throne he sat in, as gaudy and big as it was, traveled with the king. Even if he only went as far as to the arena pit carved into the great Blu reef to watch his favorite sport, the throne of glass came, too.

The way Rosel leaned back in her seat to whisper something to her younger daughters, remaining that way to talk a bit, told Poe that her mother was attempting to give them some privacy. And keep her little sisters out of the conversation while they were at it.

As complacent as ever.

Regal, always.

Rosel seemed fit in her place as queen consort to Zale, but their union, decided upon by her father and his advisors a few short years after he became king, was also every single reason why she did not wish to mate into the Red Seas. Would she be that queen, just a smiling arm piece for the man sitting beside her, after it was all said and done?

Would he take her seas?

"It wouldn't be madness to consider that he'll also want to rule," Poe said quietly.

Zale tipped his head her way. "Tis fair, he might want equality to you, but I'm sure the two of you could work those things out. You will have many moons to do so. There is lots of time."

Right, and it might be an easier decision for her to make if the two were mated and a bond inside her very blood and soul made it so.

It was nice that her father could talk his way out of the problem, as if his solution should also work for her. Poe disagreed. She didn't want the bond to make the choice for her. Looking over at her father, Poe could see herself reflected in him despite the obvious differences between the two like their sizes and his slightly browner of skin. But she also found what made the two the very same.

Their small grins.

Their violet eyes.

The crossed arrows, their royal family brand, burnt onto the back of their hand, given to her on her naming day shortly after her birth. Her red hair of unruly curls, a trait shared by all her sisters, that her father kept tied back in locks.

"He also cannot give me children," Poe pointed out, the one thing she hoped her father couldn't argue with.

"Sarha has—"

"A newborn by a companion who is not her king," Poe interrupted before Zale could even start. She didn't even mention how her sister was already pregnant with another child—again, not by her king, but that was Sarha's choice to make. It did not have to be Poe's. "Tis fine and well if she wishes to have children outside of her chosen one, and if they have that sort of understanding, but that is not *my* wish, Father."

Again, Zale sighed noisily.

He didn't demand she call him king like most everyone else, and perhaps that was why Poe always appealed to the father in Zale instead of the head of their colony. It took a long time—sixteen trips around their sun—for Poe to truly see Zale as a confidant alongside her father, and it probably had something to do with her sister leaving the year before. Had their mother given him any sons, Zale would have instantly designated that child to the throne after him. Sarha couldn't wait to leave the Blu Seas and didn't want his damned throne, so Zale was left with the one daughter who could stand to be in his presence because his younger two only cared for their mother.

That left Poe.

Zale's heir to the Blu Seas.

The next queen.

"A political match *is* to your benefit," Zale reminded her.

"Or is it more to yours?" she returned swiftly.

"They can be the same things."

She didn't think so.

"All those mermen, even that prince, they all have their own ambitions and motives for wanting me," she explained to her father.

"Isn't that usually how a good match is made?"

"And what if I have no ambition or motive for wanting them?"

The king settled back into his chair as the dancing mermaids in the pit began their long swim up, signaling the end of their intermission.

"You were already in talks with another kingdom to mate off Arelle," Poe stated.

"*Hush*, if you would," Zale threw at her, glancing back over his shoulder.

No, they mustn't let the girl who just began to walk on land know how their father planned to mate her off to another realm as soon as he was able for his own benefit. Not yet.

"Coral is far too young to consider anything yet," Poe added.

Not even old enough for her change to come on so that she, too, could travel the land.

"Why are we discussing this?" the king asked. "And now, for that matter?"

"That just left me—what are you trying to get from the King of the Red Seas that Sarha wasn't able to get for you, Father?"

"Must you think this is some ploy or plot of mine?" he asked her.

"What is the benefit?"

"Alliance. Allegiance. A bigger army. *Many* things, Poe. And all you have to do is share the blood, and let him catch you. After that, I am sure the two of you will figure out the rest. Sarha didn't even need to share the blood to get that done."

They all had their own choices to make.

Sarha made hers.

"You said I could choose my mate."

Zale's jaw clenched as the trumpeting started anew, wailing in a swirl around the arena pit. "Yes, and I even threw you a very expensive tournament that lasted the entire week of your naming day, provided you a whole list of possible suitors, and—"

"Only meant for me to truly pick the one. Is it really a choice when you've already decided the winner for me, Father?"

"Poe—"

"'Tis my right—*my* choice."

Part of her birthright, really, and she dared her father to argue it. Coming of age didn't just mean being seen as a proper adult woman in her colony, but it also marked the beginning of a new phase in her life, marked with learning about their women, ways, and customs. Being educated on the many secrets of merwomen that would someday be her responsibility to carry or pass on. Picking her companion—the one to teach her about her body and pleasure—who would also very likely turn into her mate by the end of the year was not a little thing.

It couldn't be overlooked.

Or the choice simply *made*.

No.

The next queen, or king, was allowed to decide their fate—mating was meant to be a permanent bond that could carry over land and seas, and she *had* to be willing. Zale couldn't force Poe's hand here, and she did not mind reminding him as much.

As someone did for her earlier that very same day, actually.

The Master of the Tournament entered the pit below to crown the Prince of the Red Seas the winner, presenting him with a sword made of sea glass. Then, atop his head, the tourney master placed a crown of carved sea driftwood.

"Your champion!" he called to the crowd.

Again, the reef around them vibrated from the noise and hammer of fins.

The prince turned to find Poe in the balcony once more, bowing to her.

She only nodded back.

Poe would kneel for no man except her mate.

And her mate would not be him.

Zale pointed after the prince who had now taken his leave from the pit for the time being until the ending of the tourney would call him and the other suitors back. The very same merman her father meant for her to take as a companion for the next year before they would officially mate during the landwalker's annual season of storms. Their safest time to hold their matings and have the bonded couple publicly witnessed by their colony. Something she had been allowed to do since the year before, once she reached her sixteenth year. And hers especially would be a season unlike any other for their colony in a long time as Sarha had not officially mated with her king in their traditional way.

Shouldn't it matter more that she picked her own mate, then?

Especially because Zale expected it to be such a spectacle?

"He, and his people, have traveled a very long way for this, for *you*," her father said.

Yes, his entire convoy, actually.

"And his trip back will find him just as well, I'm sure," Poe replied, unbothered.

Zale could not say the same.

"You kill me, daughter. You *wound* me, truly."

No, not at all.

Poe didn't think her father had the right perspective when it came to choosing the proper mate for her. All she needed to do was take a glance around at the many merpeople of their colony that filled the spacious arena, packing in every balcony until there wasn't any room left. Her season of mating would bring the same for them, allowing those who wanted to pair off to do so and make it official, but unlike her, they had to wait for their king's permission in that regard. She didn't doubt that some of the people of their colony—people that she would someday rule over—also probably held some bitterness toward her. That she was so freely allowed to choose from a line of prospective mermen, *knowing* she would mate with him, while they all had to get permission from her father to do almost anything, including bonding themselves to another or even having children.

It was all sad to her, really.

Even if the laws were made for their safety because the landwalkers of Atlas hunted them seasonally as if they were just another fish in the seas to catch and sell, this wasn't how they were supposed to live. It wasn't how their kind should live, frankly. But the youngest of their people were also the weakest, and needed a village of mermaids to help look after them in the seas, and the constant touch of their mother for the first year of life, on top of that, to keep them healthy and strong.

What else did one expect?

The landwalkers made it more dangerous for the people of their colony to mate off into pairs, and have large families. When those bonds between mates and kin were threatened, a mermaid would do unspeakable things to get back to the people they loved the most.

"Even though he is a third son," Zale said, being the first between them to speak again, "what he brings with him will improve the colony greatly, and his father promises much more that our people direly need. You should at least consider it."

As if she hadn't.

As if she slept at all this whole week.

"His father also keeps a harem of whores that his first wife heads and my sister joined," Poe muttered under her breath.

"What?"

"I dislike their ways, Father."

"You would learn to get used to it. We're losing more and more of our islands to the land king," Zale muttered after a moment. "How much longer can we do this?"

Poe still remained quiet in her seat. Perhaps, the answer to his question lay with the man who asked it in the first place.

"It is not just our people anymore that we need to protect. It is our livelihood and our kingdom. Our Blu Seas. We need a bigger army," he told her, barely glancing her way. "And you, Poe, you have a duty."

Again, as if she was unaware of these things.

"And when I can't produce a child with him because I bleed violet and he runs blue?" she asked. "Because this, *that*, it matters to me, too. And it should matter to *you*. It is our throne. Our line."

Zale's jaw worked with his irritation.

Her father was right that that third prince from another land was by far the most appropriate and suitable prospect lined up for her. A great warrior, he saw two battles and won with his older brothers taking over the smaller colonies of mermaids just beyond the borders of his father's Red Seas. Tordan was only two decades older than her, so they would still be close enough in age to enjoy their youth together, but all that mattered very little to Poe.

"He cannot make me a mother," she told her father for the last time, "and therefore, he cannot give me an heir."

Another choice of hers to make.

Her *right* as the next queen for the good of their people.

"A match with him would take many things away from me, Father."

"Forgive me for hoping they would be manageable things."

"Apparently not."

"Nothing I can say will change your mind?"

"Nothing," she confirmed.

"So, no match was made at the completion of your tourney today?" Zale asked, drumming his jeweled fingers to the arm of his throne. "The fortnight of suitors who bent over backward to please you—all that for nothing? Is that what you're telling me?"

Weren't these questions already answered?

She didn't mind clarifying.

"No match was made, Father."

Zale gave her a look, but said nothing. It was that moment when her mother decided to join the conversation as if Poe had asked her to. "There are other ways to be a mother," Rosel pointed out gently.

Fair enough.

"But being a mother is only half of my reason to refuse that merman," Poe replied.

The other half remained with her crown. The crown that would stay on *her* head to the kingdom that would remain with the people of the Blu Seas. And frankly, even one reason not to mate with a merman was enough for Poe—why bother with a prospect of which she already had two strikes against him?

Not worthy.

"Just because a merwoman *can* break the bond," Poe muttered lowly, making sure her sisters did not learn of things which they were not ready for, "doesn't mean I think she should. That doesn't mean I think she should pick the mate who she already can find reasons about him to refuse.

77

I don't want to have to break my bond. Or is that wrong of me? Because I am to be queen, should I not care what I want it to mean to me?"

Neither of her parents answered.

Thankfully, her sisters hadn't heard, either.

"This is not the time to speak of these things," Zale muttered unhappily.

"I just thought you wanted my decision, the reasons, to be clear, your majesty."

Might as well add policy and pretense into the conversation as well, as if her father wasn't already unhappy enough.

"As if it wasn't?"

Poe smiled her father's way. "You tell me."

"Tis your turn, isn't it?" the queen asked, reminding them all of where they were and what still needed to be done. She turned as quiet and sweet as always after asking her question, resting back into her seat the same way she faded into the background of her mate's rule over their people, and even her own family.

Rosel was not called their Humble Queen for nothing.

Some part of Poe knew her mother must like her position and life the way it was. Sometimes it irritated her like nothing else, and other times, Poe simply didn't care. If Rosel wished for different circumstances, then vocalizing as much to her mate would go a long way to forcing his hand. One needed to keep their mate happy.

Knowing as much told Poe that her mother must be—or things would not be the way they were. Simply put.

"Tis, best I handle it, then," her father replied.

Zale's hand reached over to touch the gleaming blue tail of scales of his wife and queen before he stood when the trumpeting came to an end. Finding the balcony, the king waited for the master of the tourney in his blue and green garb to announce Zale to the people before he would speak.

"His Royal Highness, Zale of the Blu Seas," came the loud call.

"For a satchel of sea gold, anyone brave enough to fight the High Master of the king's guard can attempt to claim their prize," the king announced to the murmuring crowd. "Any man of the seas willing, step forward. And may your braveness catch my daughter's eye."

Poe shot her father a grin as he sat back down. "You're getting warmer, Father."

"Am I?"

"I would pick from the Blu Seas."

In fact, she already had.

The way Zale watched her from his throne as the trumpets began anew, and the tourney master began calling for anyone of the seas who wished to challenge a much more skilled opponent for a worthy prize, the finale of the whole event, made Poe think he knew her thoughts, too.

"So tell me, who do you think should be your companion-turned-mate?" Zale asked. "Because I can't begin to hazard a guess of who you might pick if you've already so carefully found every flaw and possible reason as to why you can't, or won't, maintain the bond with any of the suitors that have been presented to you thus far."

Poe laughed lightly. "Now you're asking me?"

"Would it have been wise of me to ask before two other realms invested in this coming of age of yours?" her father returned, a little sardonically. "We all have our duties, little thing."

Poe's brow shot high, but she wisely chose to stay quiet. She would be remiss to admit that there were times in her life that it seemed like her father knew her better than she knew herself—even if he liked to wait to let her figure as much out.

"I think it's safe to bet you gave more thought to whom you think would fit than I did," Zale said, shrugging in his throne as the tourney master continued to try to find a worthy opponent of the High Master who hadn't even entered the pit yet. "So, who is it? Which merman of our colony do you want all for yourself?" His elbows found the arms of his throne while his fingers interlaced, and he leaned closer to Poe, saying almost conspiratorially, "Just tell me."

She grinned, and Zale offered her the same back. In some ways, perhaps sometimes in a lot of ways, they were more different than alike as individual people. But in their best moments as a king and his future heir, they were exactly the same. Exactly when they should be.

And the way she knew him, he also knew her.

Father and daughter, like kin should.

Their conversation was once again interrupted by the chants spreading throughout the arena as the High Master of the Royal Guard finally made an appearance at the entry of the far side of the deep pit. Even as the tourney master continued to call for an opponent who might take on Tak for the prize of sea gold, and the chance to catch the princess's attention, the rest of the people called to their favorite merman.

"*Tak of Zale! Tak of Zale!*"

Poe couldn't remember a time in her life when the High Master of her father's guard wasn't beloved by their people. He shared a tenuous, at best, relationship with the king despite all his duties revolving around the crown and the guard, but Tak of Zale, as their people called him because he had no kin left, orphaned decades before Poe was even born, was ever loyal. She thought Zale put up with the man's moods and attitude simply because the people loved him, but he was also the best fit for his position, too.

A constant backdrop in her life, usually on the very fringes making him all the more interesting and mysterious to her, and she found herself asking after Tak far more than she should. To anyone who would lend an ear to listen and had something to say back, actually. Almost everyone who knew the merman did have something to say about him—*interesting* things.

It had started to become a problem. Ask too much, and people tend to start asking things back. Questions that Poe was not ready to answer.

The tourney master, her father's cousin, who minded a smaller colony of their people further out from their palace, threw his arms wide to the crowd, making his robe of blue and green billow wide as his voice carried through the pit one more time.

"Is there anyone—anyone at all—who will challenge the king's High Guard? *Anyone?*"

It was partly the show put on by her kin that helped the crowd of merpeople stand and beat the reef again. Their true excitement, though?

Tak.

He was what everyone, including her, had been waiting for. What made the small entrance fee less unpleasant. To sit in the uncomfortable balconies and be fed for the day. To enjoy Water Orchard fruit slices soaked in liquor. All of it, the good and bad parts, were worth it for him.

A large part of what was left of their decimated colony was made up of the guards within their army and the families tied to them. She didn't exactly think that it was fair and right for the crown to pay a large portion of these people to protect the princesses, their family as a whole, and the kingdom, and then also proceed to take that same gold back from them in a form of a tourney meant to celebrate Poe.

Even if there was a prize at the end.

It all felt a little wrong. But the matter of her father's treasury was not of Poe's concern. Something he made very clear to her the first time she ever called him on his misappropriation of their kingdom's funds. Not until she got the crown and took the throne herself which wouldn't be for more than a century, at least. Unless her father abdicated or found his death very early.

Tak, in only a sea leather breastplate made of woven swatches and emblazoned with the crossed arrows of the Blu Seas, lifted his sword of sea glass with a strip of tar steel down the middle high for the crowd to see, setting them on fire all over again. Muscled and with shoulders wider than she thought her arms could reach, he was every bit a man. Her body felt it. Nearing his fiftieth year of life, he had been her father's highest royal guard, directing and overseeing the Blu Seas army just a step below her father, the king. At the call of the crowd, he swam deeper into the pit for everyone to get a chance to see him, waving his blade and doing a little trick that made her heart skip when she thought he might cut his deep golden skin. His head of black braids were tied into a rope down his back. Something she noticed he did whenever he was expected to sword fight. Only on very few occasions, the rarest of moments, but her luckiest ones, also, did Poe have the luxury of standing next to Tak in such a way that she understood just how tall he was compared to her.

The depth of the pit made it hard to appreciate his towering size from so far up. Her head would have to tilt all the way back for her to properly meet his gaze. But as she wasn't standing beside him or in front of him currently, and her father still eyed her beside him, she made some attempt to keep her thoughts and expression neutral as Tak surveyed the challenger who finally swam their way into the pit.

Already, even as the commoner merman proceeded to declare his love for Poe down below her balcony, she knew Tak would win in his one-on-one sword fight. Quickly, too.

The guard always did.

"Good luck to you," she told the merman waiting for her reply.

He nodded, and bowed.

Beyond him, another pair of eyes watched her.

Those, she *felt*.

A sword was handed over for the merman to use, and as the tourney master announced the challenger properly, Poe turned to her father.

"I want Tak," she said simply.

She figured he probably knew as much, already.

Zale's gaze had shifted away from hers, but she couldn't miss the clench of his hand around the arm of his throne. At the prick of one of the glass points, he loosened up a bit. "The guard, hmm?"

Down below, the fight began.

Poe only looked at her father. "He has seen battle twice in his life. Once when he was barely of age, and their realm joined to fight with another for a season—and another time just before you were crowned King," Poe said, "or so I heard. Is he not capable of protecting me as good or better than anyone else put before me?"

"His capability in that regard is not a concern of mine," her father murmured. "And the fact that he and his chosen guards accompanied you and your sisters on a handful of your trips away from the colony should say as much."

Good.

That was one point in her favor.

Zale's stare slid her way again. "However, I wouldn't say the second one you mentioned was a battle, per say."

"He guarded her, didn't he?" Poe asked softly, too quiet for their nearby companions to hear. "The queen we cannot name?"

Her father leaned in a little closer. "He was her favorite guard, yes."

As she knew it, and as the stories went, the queen before her father became king was captured by the landwalkers of Atlas, a continent controlled by a bloodthirsty land king, and presumably killed shortly thereafter. Zale had been her oldest advisor, and when her death left the realm without a blood heir, he took the throne.

Those details, however, were less interesting to Poe than the story of how Tak tried to save his queen on the night of her capture. Their people might not be permitted to whisper the old queen's name lest it cause discontent and unruliness in Zale's realm, but Tak's devotion and protection of her had certainly cemented his place in their kingdom and people.

His respect, that love, was truly earned.

Tak, stoic as always, barely graced the challenger with his attention until the two of them found themselves facing off in the middle of the pit. Even as the sea glass blades began to clash, with one man putting up a good fight but still being no match for the better trained and more experienced guard a head taller than him, Tak barely blinked.

He didn't frown.

Or grin.

Nothing.

That focus in his face as he easily tucked a swinging blade and spun close to the ground to return another swing with a far more powerful one of his own never changed. Despite the merman Tak fought being one of their own, it was a valiant and honorable death on his part up against the merman he faced, and when it finally happened, even his own kin cheered when the guard ended it all with one smooth blade strike.

A head fell to the seafloor.

It wasn't Tak's.

The energy that shot through the crowd sent every mermaid in the arena up from their seats, including Poe, to clap and cheer for the bloodstained merman below. Tak turned to the royal balcony to bow just as Poe glanced at her father.

Zale didn't look nearly as happy.

"I did hope you would pick the prince, though. A little," he admitted.

He passed a nod to Tak, who at that action, decided his duty had finished, and he could take his leave from the pit. Behind him, the tourney master called for him to take his prize, but Tak only turned back long enough to ask that it be given to the kin of the merman he had killed on that day.

"I want to be a *loved* queen," Poe stated, then.

Zale's head swung her way. "And you will be."

Would she?

After all her father had done to their people—after the things he let happen to them year after year? Would she, *really*?

Poe could plainly see the future she faced. She simply knew better than to say as much to her father. So, she told him in a different way. "You told me yourself—I could pick whoever I wanted, and I picked *him*. I want someone who comes from *our* people. A man of theirs, one that they love and would be overjoyed to see standing beside me; a man from the Blu Seas."

Zale's lips pursed a bit. "I suppose you'll say that his age is to your liking because he has some lived experience, and can teach you all sorts of things, too."

"It certainly isn't a strike against him."

There was something about Tak that spoke to her. Intimately. In a way she couldn't explain. She found it in the way he carried himself. How he watched people. Even when he engaged with those around him, young and old. All of it called to her like a song in the seas, a melody that could be her own.

"Might he challenge me a bit? *Handle* me?" she asked, smiling.

Zale said nothing.

"He won't want to take my crown. Or my kingdom. He's home to them, and he's home here. He's everything they love and all that I need."

At that, her father hummed a quiet sound.

"All that you need, you say," Zale noted under his breath.

Was that too much?

Or just enough?

She thanked the Gods that the thunderous noise from the mermaids in the pit was still too loud for their very private conversation to travel.

"The Red Seas might not be very kind to us when we send their prince home far earlier than he should have arrived, and without a mate, as well," her father said.

A feast for her thoughts.

"So promise me to those seas—upon the break of my bond with a man of my own seas," she argued, even though it ached. Even though she had *no* intention of ever ending what she believed could not be undone.

Zale didn't acknowledge the offer.

She chose then to tell her father the thing he needed to hear so that he could stand up and tell the waiting suitors their journey to find her heart had come to an unfortunate end.

"I heard he fought for her until the end," Poe said of Tak and the stories of the queen they could not speak. "I heard it was bloody and beautiful and *brave* … and that up until he couldn't, and only to save her pain, he fought for her until he had no choice but to stop. I heard that he even climbed the ship—is that true?"

Zale wouldn't look at her then.

Poe didn't care.

"What if that was me on that ship? She wasn't even his mate—what might he do for me?"

"Have you two even spoken more than a handful of words to one another?"

Instantly, Poe's mind was ravaged with the handful of memories that she did have of when Tak graced her with the irritated, almost annoyed, growl of his voice. Was it sickening that she could remember every single word of any sentence that he ever spoke to her?

Yeah, all of it.

"It's more scared of you than you are of it, Princess," Tak had once told a young, stumbling Poe as she tried to scuttle away from a crab with sharp claws.

And once, when she stumbled into the pit of riding snakes?

"You're in the wrong place, Princess," he'd joked at the sight of her horrified face inches away from a chained snake.

She supposed the more inappropriate side of her fascination with Tak started the year before just after the mating season to celebrate her sister's match had ended, Sarha left, and their people settled back into their grottos and palace life. Her guard, always posted at her chambers and waiting to follow her anywhere just a few paces behind, had been called away unexpectedly and Tak took his place.

Rather unexpectedly.

Without explanation, which she did not like.

When she, in the hurry and flurry of trying to figure out what was going on, demanded that he move away from her door, Tak essentially threatened to tie her to her bed should she give him any trouble that night. Perhaps it was her reaction to him, that she stayed in her doorway staring him down and daring him to do it, that made him speak to her again.

Women like you haunt me.

What obsession?

Poe wasn't obsessed with Tak.

No, because she practically loved him *already*. He had her nailed like a fish on a spear and didn't even know it. And ever since that moment, the merman who had been on the fringes of her life and the peripherals of her vision day in and day out, just on the outskirts, became Poe's instant focus for her almost all the time.

Whenever he was near, anyway.

Constantly. Perhaps it wasn't healthy, and maybe she could have saved her father a lot of time, effort, and riches for this fortnight of celebrations, but she already knew that nothing would change inside her heart. That thing growing in there?

It belonged to one.

He just didn't know it yet.

"We have spoken a few times," she settled on telling Zale of her moments with Tak. Her father still hadn't stood for the master of the tourney repeatedly calling his name.

"Not about *this*, I bet."

"Well, no, but—"

"Have you thought of what Tak might want? Did you consider that he's spent many a moon as he is, alone, happily living that way? No children, and rarely a companion that he keeps for more than—"

"An evening, or so I've heard," Poe said, uncaring for her rudeness. In fact, she did consider Tak's long period of loneliness and thought it was quite sad. But that was something she would ask Tak himself about, and not a discussion she would have with her father. Choices like those were not ones she thought a man like Tak would make easily. He probably had good reasons, and so, what if she gave him a reason to change his opinions?

"A queen should really not listen to rumors and gossip," her mother put in, reminding Poe that their conversation wasn't entirely private, after all.

Her father seemed to need the check into reality as well.

Zale finally stood from his throne but before he went to the balcony, he looked back at her. "I can't change your mind, then?"

"'Tis *my* choice, even if I let you believe for a little while that you could make it, Father."

This was her right.

The king regarded his waiting crowd. Every suitor below quieted to hear his fate.

"This has been a week of great hunts," Zale said to the quiet people and the gathered suitors now waiting down below. "Of greater feasts. The second princess of our seas, and myself, thank you all for making her coming of age truly an event we shall remember for decades. All for you, my people, you are the delight of our days, and we promise more happiness is to come, however, I regret to inform you …"

His crown of sea glass casted rainbows of color when he tipped his head to the side and caught another ray of sunlight under the seas.

"My daughter has not chosen one of you."

7. THE PRINCESS AND THE GUARD

Tak of Zale, High Master of the Royal Guard

"The King's requested your presence later on this evening in the throne room, if it pleases you, m-my lord," said the young palace merboy who often acted as a messenger of sorts for Zale.

"If it pleases me?"

"I—*sorry, sir*," the boy squeaked.

Using the cloth of woven barnacle to finish cleaning the only thing left sticky with violet blood—his sword—Tak examined the young that barely reached his waist in height, and who certainly didn't have the confidence to lift his gaze and meet the older merman's eyes. Despite the scarf of green and blue tied around his arm to designate him important to the palace and king, the merboy didn't look anywhere near ready to bring a message to Tak. 'Twas the way with some of the little ones whenever they were put in his presence—especially before they came of age and walked in the storms like the rest of them.

"Coda, is it?" Tak asked.

Nodding quickly, the merboy kept his gaze forced on something deeper in the stable pit where the guard kept their snakes.

"And when did the king tell you this?"

Coda's nose—a tiny, button thing he had taken from his mother who had been ripped from her seas like many before and after her—crinkled at the question. Tak had once been an orphan himself with this boy's mother. His father had been one of the mermen to train him, actually, and he found himself into a watery grave shortly after his mate's unfortunate fate. He knew this boy's face very well.

Honestly, he knew a lot of their colony well.

"Um," the merboy hummed.

Tak chuckled, and the lighthearted sound finally gave the young in front of them enough courage to swallow hard and lift his gaze. "Tis fine, you shouldn't speak of private conversations with the king. Even to me."

At those words, Coda focused on Tak's slightly bloody sword. It was an unfortunate part of being them—blood free and magical above the seas changed to a sticky, unpleasant mess in the salt water. As if it was trying to tell them it was the one place where their blood should never spill.

"Needn't be scared of me, little one," he told Coda quietly.

All he got was another nod.

Although, the day had probably seen the boy watch a man be killed at Tak's hands before he was then sent to bring that same murderer a message from the king, so who was he to talk of fear? It did bother him with the little ones being frightened of him, though. Especially because he meant them no harm, and one day, he would probably even train the boy in front of him.

"But nothing about the king is as it pleases me if the merman finds himself needing something from me. Should you find yourself needing to seek me out for another message from His Majesty, keep it in mind, and skip all the pleasantries. I only need to know the most important thing—what will irritate me."

"Shall be done," the merboy replied rather quickly.

Tak smiled a little, then. "Did he say what he wanted to speak with me for?"

This time, the boy didn't hesitate.

"He did not, my lord."

So, whether the king did or not, the boy had learned something between them that day. Tak would take it as a win. They would work on his fear of the older, larger merman on another day. They had plenty of time.

"Off with you," he ordered.

And off the merboy went.

Tak followed behind just to stop in the stable hole to see the merboy head across the causeway between the arena and stables to head for the trek through the coral forest leading back toward the palace made from sea glass and carved into coral reef and stone. From here, Tak could only see the pointed peaks. But he wasn't interested in Coda's journey, or the palace in the distance.

No, his eye was drawn to something else entirely. Wiping his blade down a final time before the rag was too soaked to be of any use, Tak tried not to let his gaze linger on the gaggle of princesses and their maidens backed by the line of four guards chosen by him to protect the horde of merwomen. He'd be a liar if he said he looked anywhere but the one leading the pack. The one redhead, the tallest of the golden three left, that stood out to him the most.

Poe.

With only two favors left around her waist at the end of her fortnight of celebrations, he found her a sight for sore eyes as she was—smiling and laughing to her sisters and the maidens following. Those who thought they knew her whispered that she would be a cold queen because she presented things frankly, even if it was cruel or hurtful, and without emotion, but he thought that was simply her way of handling difficult things.

Why soften the blow?

She was her father's daughter through and through. But her own person, just the same. As calculating as the king, ambitious enough to want the crown, and stunningly beautiful in a way that stopped every merman in her godforsaken path.

Tak was the exception.

Usually.

Apparently, just not today.

Well, perhaps not lately.

That young woman, just coming of age, was the greatest test of Tak's loyalty to the crown, and a threat to his personal self-control. Like he did with every other female to call the palace home, he swore to the king—as much as he despised Zale—to protect Poe at all costs, and act befitting of his position at the same time.

He doubted other guards stood toe to toe with her in her bedchamber doorway as she stared him down, and asked if he thought she might like being tied down by him. As if his threat to keep her in control when he'd been unexpectedly put on her post had been nothing more than an invitation for an evening.

That evening never happened.

Gods, sometimes, he wished that it did.

He tried not to notice the princess, and Zale's chosen heir, as much as possible considering the way she seemed to ask after him every chance she got. Yes, those in their colony who thought he would care to know about her interest had made him aware that a woman who spoke very little of anyone suddenly wanted to talk about him. Tak still wasn't sure if that was a good thing.

"Perhaps, the bastard just wants to thank you for keeping the guard on task and duty during these very important days," Tak muttered to himself, turning away from the sight still crossing the causeway. Not even he believed his own lies to himself. Just like everyone else in their colony, even those from faraway lands just there visiting, he, too, heard the king.

No companion was chosen.

Perhaps, then was when he should have known.

Tak chanced one more glance over his shoulder, finding the princess searching the busy movement of many merpeople on the causeway. The more time passed Tak by in life, he longed for the same things that those around him shared. Kin. Home. Memories. *Love.* He'd not found that sweet spot where his heart would be entirely in the right place, but the way it thudded hard in his chest the longer he stared at Princess Poe, the more he dared to wonder.

Has it been long enough?

The soft question, asked of him by the seas, sounded like the voices of his mothers. One believed that their kind were fated to find their mates from the moment they were born, as if the Gods and stars decided who it should be. The other had never even taken a king, but she would've asked those same things of him, too.

It wasn't other voices asking him things, then.

It became his own.

Is she why—all this time for her?

Poe

"Well, did she tell him?" croaked the oldest maiden of their colony.

Fragile in her favorite seat, in the deepest belly of the palace rooms where the water ran warmer from heated vents under the crust of the sea, Rayel asked the question to any one of the ladies, including Rosel, that filed into maiden chambers behind Poe. She only looked to the princess of the Blu Seas for her answer, though.

"Well ..."

"She did," Rosel said before her daughter could tease.

"Oh, good," the old maiden muttered, relieved.

Poe rolled her eyes the merwoman's way while two maidens worked on unclasping the remaining favors from her waist and removing the bodice of sheer, woven silk and pearls. "Did you really think I wouldn't tell my father that I had already chosen a mate?"

"I thought you would do what the king thinks is best because one of us is to be a queen, Poe, and the other knows the rights of merwomen. If it is one queen's right to choose not to mate, it is another's to decide who their mate shall be. The king knows it, too."

"Well, I did tell him. I won't mate into the Red Seas."

Rayel smiled, making her eyes crinkle at the edges. Those lines in her face and her grayed hair, tied neatly into a plait, were the only tells of her true age. That her three-hundredth year had started approaching.

The oldest left in their seas.

A precious holder of their secrets.

Poe had only now started to learn some of those things locked inside Rayel—she knew, unfortunately, it likely wouldn't be the old merwoman who also shared the rest of those secrets with her. When the time came, Poe hoped the seas took their maiden quickly. *Kindly*.

"Come here, child," Rayel murmured to Poe, reaching with her weathered hands.

Free of the busy maidens who had moved on to help her little sisters and mother remove their clothing and jewels to safely store away, Poe swam to the merwoman tucked into the farthest corner of the room. Bent down on her tail, it allowed Rayel to hold both sides of Poe's face in her hands as the two locked eyes.

"You're to be queen—it *must* be willing."

Poe nodded. "I know. It will."

"The king, he didn't argue?"

"Only a little."

Rayel grinned, making her faded violet eyes twinkle a bit. "But?"

"'Tis *my* right."

"There you are, Princess. And they will *all* know it."

Yes, they would.

"All right, out, out we go," Rosel ushered her younger daughters once they were free of expensive jewels.

Arelle danced around her mother's arms every step in the way in an attempt to turn back to Poe and the maiden. "But wait, I have questions, too!"

"And you will get to ask yours another season," their mother assured as a younger maiden followed the mergirls to take the princesses out. Rosel remained behind, and closed the chamber door.

She thought she heard the maiden add to Arelle, "'Tis not your season, child."

"I've seen my sixteenth year!" Arelle shouted back, loud enough to be heard outside in the corridor.

Her back pressed to the door, Rosel laughed at the antics of her third oldest daughter.

"That one will be more than willing come her time," she muttered. "Which should please her father immensely."

"Oh, perhaps," Rayel replied, "or who knows, she may even surprise you."

"Don't curse her—Arelle does that all on her own, far more than enough."

The old maiden simply smiled indulgently, but then her gaze turned on Poe again. Sharper in a blink, she asked, "Now, have you told him, yet?"

"I said I told the king."

"I think she means someone else, my daughter," Rosel said softly.

Oh.

"I have not yet spoken of these things with the High Master of the Guard," Poe informed, trying to keep her cheeks from turning pink. She wouldn't even be able to blame it on the warmer water.

"Tak, you mean."

"Yes. The lord of the—"

"Tak," Rayel interjected, making Poe grin wide.

"Stop teasing me."

"It must be who you want, Poe," the old merwoman said, the same warning she had told the princess since she came of age. Whenever she got the chance, and the king wasn't listening.

"And he is," she promised.

"Well, she needn't concern herself with bringing the topic to Tak, anyway," Rosel said as she left her spot at the door to collect the remaining favors from Poe's outfit that day. She waved them at her daughter. "I'll be keeping these for a baby."

"Would you?" Poe asked, only a little heartsick over the idea. Was it also sickening that she bet she could close her eyes and imagine what a baby of hers and Tak's would look like—a head full of dark curls and skin the color of sunkissed gold?

"Who knows, if you have a girl, perhaps she could wear them on the day of her mating."

Poe pouted a little. "My choice didn't take *my* favor, though."

Not that Tak could have done so, really.

"Perhaps," said the oldest in the room, "he didn't have to."

All over again, Poe nearly blushed. "I don't believe he even knows I exist," she muttered, only partly joking.

Tak did see her; he simply didn't look as often as she would like him to.

"I'm sure the merman knows more than he wants to about you, Princess," Rayel assured softly. "And as many years and pairs as he's seen, you can bet he craves a bond, too. Tis what we do—instinctual."

"Speaking of which," Rosel said to the two as Poe straightened to her full height once more. "Seems to me that someone in this room has a misunderstanding of the mating bond … if her words to her father are to be trusted."

Knowing her mother had to be talking about her, Poe narrowed her stare in on Rosel. "I'm right here, Mother."

She could speak like it, too.

"As I can see. Rayel?"

"What misunderstanding?" the eldest palace maiden asked.

"Someone—"

"*Tis me.*"

"Yes, Poe," her mother stated, tipping her head in Poe's direction, "seems to think after bonding, she could simply end it for this or that reason. Reasons she might have decided upon before even mating, in fact. What of that, Rayel?"

A chuckle echoed from the chair.

"I said, if a bond was to end, I could see why that might happen."

"The bond is permanent, even when gone. Tis simply a ghost inside you, then, a memory of what will never be. It cannot be undone, Poe. It can only be killed."

That statement had Poe's head swinging back around to meet the gaze that felt a lifetime away. Rayel shrugged her delicate shoulders, and went back to work on the pillow of beading she had left untouched in her lap after the group arrived back.

"And he will never be able to kill it," the mermaid added.

"But I could?"

"With love, we all can."

Poe's brow furrowed. "I don't—"

"That doesn't even make sense," came the annoyed voice of her younger sister.

All eyes in the room turned on the unruly, ever-defiant Arelle sneaking a listen in on their conversation at a crack in the chamber door. How she had managed to get away from her maiden, and open the door without them hearing, was anyone's guess.

Her sister, however annoying, should not be underestimated.

"Arelle!" their mother yelled desperately. "Go find your sister and maidens!"

"No," said the young mergirl, pushing the door further open. "That doesn't make sense. You can't kill things you love, Mother, so you can't kill the bond."

Arelle looked Rayel's way, daring the older merwoman to deny it.

Rayel only smiled softly.

A little sadly.

"Pray you never find out, child. *Pray* you never have to learn."

"'Tis permanent," Arelle said as if she had already made up her mind. "The bond cannot be undone. And because of that, Poe should pick who she likes."

"Should you?" their mother questioned.

Arelle's violet eyes gleamed with mischief. "'Tis not my season, I'm told, but I doubt I'll pull as much favor as Poe with the king."

The mention of their father made Poe think of something else. She swung around on her mother fast in the water.

"What did you mean—I needn't worry about discussing mating with Tak?"

Rosel's mouth opened and closed, but no words formed, confirming Poe's silent belief that her mother's offhanded comment had been accidental.

"Well, he—"

"*Mother*," Poe warned, her voice chilling.

There was another reason they whispered about her being the cold one amongst her sisters. The coldest jewel in the seas. Poe played games with no one. Not even her family.

"As far as I know it, the king asked to speak with him this evening privately," Rosel finally said, still not looking at her daughter.

"Without me?" she shrieked.

Arelle made a skittish noise behind her sister, always the first to bolt at the first sign of trouble. Smart, really. "Perhaps, I'll find Coral and my maidens now. I'll just take my leave …"

"When?" Poe demanded of her mother, paying her sister no mind.

The door clicked as Arelle left.

"Consider that if your father wished for you to be a part of the conversation, then you would be, Poe."

"He wouldn't even know that's who I wanted if not for me!"

Yes, she should be a part of the damned conversation. Besides, she didn't want this to be a one-way thing. How well received would her request of mating with Tak be when it was delivered to him by her *father*.

The fucking king.

"I needn't this be another duty for him," she snapped, angrily.

Gods forbid she wanted the merman to want her, too.

Rosel appeared unbothered at the show of emotion. "As I said, the king would have called on you, also, child."

Well, then.

Poe let her mother, subservient and pleasing to her king, think whatever she wanted. But the truth? Arelle wasn't the only princess in the palace able to sneak away and disappear down corridors.

Zale would learn as much, too.

The first moment Poe had to sneak off, she did just that, leaving their private chambers bustling with activity and laughter behind as soon as she was sure no one would see her leave.

"Princess?" called a guard at the doors when she slipped out.

His sea glass armor rattled a bit as he raced to follow her. Only the one of the two posted at the door, thankfully. By the third corridor, and the second spiral staircase up, she had lost the guard who might very well foil her plan to interrupt whatever trick her father thought to play. There was a chance he had already spoken to Tak, and probably sent the Prince of the Red Seas off on his unhappy way with his merry caravan, but she didn't allow herself to think much about it.

Poe never failed.

Not a possibility.

It wasn't long before Poe swam her way down the long corridor leading to the throne room where the king held all of his conversations when it wasn't insufferably late or early. The guards posted at the far end, on either side of the black A-frame doors that opened wide whenever Zale held an open court for any and everyone to see their king on his throne, passed a look between themselves at the princess's fast but silent approach.

She did not make eye contact with either merman; mostly, because she dared either of them to try and stop her as she got close enough for them to understand she intended to enter the throne room while the king was in a private meeting. Each held their post with a sword at their hip and a spear in hand, and the one on the right glanced her way as she took the three stairs up.

Already, she could hear her father through the crack in the tall doors.

"Princess—"

"Do *not*," she hissed at him near soundlessly.

The guard snapped back into place.

The thing that bothered her more was that if she could hear her father having a discussion with Tak from her position just outside the cracked doors, then so could his guards. It would not be long before news of Poe's true choice traveled within the colony.

Would the prince and the rest of her suitors even take their leave from the realm before it happened? She tried not to wallow on how that would be received. What good would it do her now?

"I'm telling you it exactly as she told me," Poe heard her father say. "She wants you as her companion, as she has a right to take one for the next year now that she's come of age and decided to mate, and I feel she intends to ask you to share the blood. She would let you take her as a mate."

Yes, she did, in fact plan to tell Tak exactly that.

Poe reached to push open the door to say just that, but the next voice to ring out stopped her.

"I'm not sure what would give her the impression that I was open to being her companion. That I am suitable to *be* her companion, your majesty."

Tak's words froze her on the other side of the doorway. Suddenly, the two men she had tried to avoid eye contact with entirely made great effort to turn their gazes anywhere but at the princess between them. She was only a little bit grateful for their pretenses and thoughtfulness, but it didn't make the situation any less horrifying.

"Apparently the tales of your protection and fight for the queen who shall not be named still travels amongst the people in our colony. My daughter has romanticized it, and you, in her head, the way most women do about those sorts of things," Zale muttered heavily. "How does it go—have you heard them tell it?"

"Can't say that I have, actually."

"Shame," the king returned.

Was it?

The mocking tone behind Zale's words said he felt differently. It wasn't just the High Guard with a strained, odd relationship between himself and the king. Poe noticed that her father lost his patience and will to be pleasant with Tak quite often, as well.

Nobody seemed to know why.

"But," Zale said then, the word cutting through a quiet throne room and into the hallway beyond, "Poe is also very strategic. Not like my other daughters. She's a bit more calculating. There's venom in her smile. I guess what I'm dancing around here is that picking you is probably not negotiable to her. She's thought this through."

"That queen we will not name," Tak said, not at all entertaining the king's comments about Poe and her motives, "ultimately did not need saving from the landwalkers that night, your majesty."

"I know that better than anyone," Zale replied hotly, "but I can't think of a reason why now would be the time to discuss it."

"Me either, but you said yourself that your daughter is using her idea of that night as a basis for the reason why I should be her mate ... well, I'm not sure she has the right impression of me."

"Are the tales they tell of it wrong?"

Tak didn't reply.

"Did you fight bravely?"

Zale got nothing.

"Was it bloody?"

Silence echoed.

"Did you climb the ship, my lord?"

"If you would kindly move on, your majesty," Tak muttered through what sounded like clenched teeth.

"What you tell my daughter of that night should only ever be in warning, and we can argue over the matter of how she sees it, but again, I couldn't care less. I'm sure you'll settle that between the two of you."

"At least give me the decency and respect of *asking* me, Zale."

"Pardon you?"

"Your majesty," Tak practically spat.

"Better. You've been alone all these years, she's better than anything you could have imagined, and there isn't a single reason for you to say no, Tak. I needn't really ask you, my lord."

Why did he have to make it sound like a *duty*?

"I think what matters more are the questions my daughter would ask of you. Would you do the same for Poe that you did for your precious queen—protect her until the very bitter end, up against it all? Would you fight everything, the Gods, the seas, the *world*? Could you do it for her? Would you?"

"My sword weighs half of what she does soaking wet—would she even be a worthy hunt for me or would I catch her before she could get beyond the palace gates?"

Even the guards chuckled at Tak's comment.

Enraged and in disbelief, Poe opted for that moment to barge into her father's throne room. She didn't even give the guards time to announce her properly, which should be a lesson for them as well.

Two pairs of eyes turned on her as she came to stand in the middle of the room, just a swim stroke away from the High Master of the Royal Guard. Between her father, and Tak, the merman in front of her was the only one who looked surprised at her presence.

Zale just glared behind her. "Well done, you're useless," he told the guards who stuck their heads in the room to apologize.

She didn't care about the king, or the guards.

No, she glared Tak down.

"Is that why you would say no—because you think I wouldn't be a good chase?" she demanded, putting a hand to her hip and holding his gaze, daring him to say that same thing to her face.

Out of all the reasons he could pick, he said *that* one?

Tak looked her up and down, and the slow trek of his gaze left an imprint on her body from her long tail fin to the very top of her head.

The king cleared his throat from the throne.

Poe didn't look his way.

Tak didn't move, either.

"Well?" she asked him. "At least have the nerve to look at me and say it."

This close, the merman's face was even more haunting. Made up of strong lines that chiseled out his jaw and chin, of eyes that spoke of dreams and horrors, and she swore the straight line of his plush lips twitched.

As if he might smile.

She wasn't ready to face *that*.

Tak already made her weak.

"Tell me," she told Tak, "that I am not a worthy chase. You just did— you said it easily. Do it again."

"Princess—"

Her stare narrowed in on him, and he instantly quieted. "How far?"

Tak's eyebrows lifted at the question. "I beg your pardon, Princess?"

"How far would I have to swim for the hunt to be worth it for you?"

Tak did grin, then.

It *was* devastating.

"To the Beaches of Sand Pearls—at least."

Poe's mouth dropped open. "That's twice as far as the Isle of Broken Islands."

As far as she had ever gone.

It was also in the opposite direction entirely.

"You asked, Princess," Tak returned calmly.

Poe's jaw snapped shut audibly, and she spoke through her teeth. "Are you saying that you think I couldn't do it?"

"I think—"

"Could I have just a moment to speak, please?" came the voice of the king.

Zale, King of the Blu Seas

"Polan, Dreel," Zale called to the guards beyond the doors. Two heads came into view almost instantly, and the guards looked just as sheepish as they had the first time they peeked into the throne room. "Close the doors and take your leave from the hall for a bit, would you?"

Zale was terribly careful about the merpeople he put on his posts—especially those who might overhear things he would rather they didn't. Those two were good guards, and while they wouldn't normally discuss private happenings with the king, he doubted this situation would be the same. After an entire fortnight of revolving suitors, all of which his daughter refused, he bet the colony would cheer and celebrate to hear Poe was determined to pick a mate within their home seas.

Never mind, the merman she did want.

That would make their people go absolutely mad—in a very good way. Zale might not be entirely on board with Poe's decision, but he couldn't deny that her choice wasn't necessarily a bad one, either. He sympathized with her reasoning for wanting Tak as a mate, and frankly, the choice would please their kingdom like no other. A happy realm meant complacent people, and less work for Zale to do to keep them all in mind, and minding, so to speak.

He could use this.

So, he started by saying nothing.

"As you wish, your majesty," said the taller of the two guards to the king's request. The other only nodded and followed his counterpart who closed the large doors to the throne room.

The door barely even clicked shut before Zale's daughter spoke again.

"If I made it to the beaches, you'd be willing?" she asked Tak.

"Tis more than how fast you are or how far you can go, Princess."

Poe nodded, but a little viciously. "Right, but that isn't what you just said, my lord."

"Tak, if you would. Just Tak, please."

"That isn't what you said, Tak."

"Did you consider that wasn't something I meant for you to hear?"

"I think you shouldn't say things in this palace if you don't want a royal to hear," she returned swiftly.

Zale held up a finger, drawing in their gazes as he murmured, "Ah, she does have a good point made there."

The two went right back to staring one another down as if he didn't even speak.

"I think you shouldn't say things about me," Poe added pointedly, "unless you're also willing to say those same things to me."

Tak's chin tipped down momentarily. "I will keep it in mind, Princess."

"Please, do."

The guard squared his shoulders, folded his hands in front of him, and looked Poe straight in her face when he told her, "I don't, however, think you could make it to those beaches without me catching you first. I don't think any woman in this colony could out swim me in these seas, including you."

Poe's hand found her hip again. "Is that so?"

Tak nodded once. "Yes, it is."

Poe's eyes widened a bit, but Zale knew that look in his daughter. The guard had challenged her and not even realized it. She couldn't—wouldn't—back down from that now. As the two seemed fit and fine to stand there glaring at one another and talking as if their king wasn't in the room, Zale leaned back in his throne, happy for a bit more privacy, and watched the show.

"Tis not necessarily meant to be an insult," Tak added quieter.

Poe cocked an eyebrow. "It is when you say it like you did."

"Well—"

"If I made it to the beaches, would you be willing?"

Tak sighed loudly, and finally broke the staring contest with the princess to glance back at the king who did nothing but smile back from his throne.

"Is this your doing?" Tak asked him.

"I offered her a prince and—"

"But I want *you*," Poe interjected, sending Tak's head swinging back in her direction. "And there isn't one single reason in these seas for you not to want me, too."

The way Tak's shoulders tensed told Zale that his daughter had hit a nerve.

"I should not have called you unworthy. Those were hurtful words, and

98

I'm sorry."

"I asked you a question," Poe replied, her expression made of stone and ice. "And I expect an answer. If I made it to the goddamned beaches, would you be willing?"

Once again, Zale put in his two cents, only when needed. "Ah, the princess has spoken. Tis not a request anymore."

"Shut up, King."

Zale guffawed from the throne. "I'll banish you, my lord."

Tak only stared at Poe.

He didn't care about the king, clearly.

"Tis *more* than making it to the beaches, Princess," Tak told her.

"We have a year to work those things out. I can end a companionship whenever I please. Nothing is permanent until we share the blood."

"Tis true," Zale put in, "she can."

Tak growled a noise of warning to the king low in the back of his throat. The sound sent a pink color flooding Poe's cheeks that she tried to hide by looking away from her father. Zale still saw it, and he thought Tak probably did, too.

Gods. She did have it bad.

At least, Poe was relentless when she wanted something.

In those quiet moments, as Tak looked the princess up and down one more time, Zale thought the other merman in the room was starting to understand that exact thing, as well. But he found himself bored with their verbal foreplay and made the decision for them.

The guard, and his daughter, could thank him later.

"Tis settled, then," Zale said from his seat. "A companionship will be announced to the colony between the two of you, and the rest shall work itself out, it seems."

Neither listened.

"Would you be willing?" Poe asked Tak one more time. "Or am I just some sliver under your skin that you can't get out?"

"It can be both for me, actually."

"Really? Are you mad to tell me that?"

"Just honest—you, of all people, should appreciate it, Princess."

"Did either of you hear me?" Zale questioned loudly.

Purposely.

The two across the room, who had obviously found something better between them, paid him absolutely no mind. That should be a good thing.

Tak took one step closer to Poe. "You misunderstand me. I know very well that you will make this worth it for me. I know all the reasons why you are more than worthy and why I am not worthy enough."

"And yet, you still wouldn't want to mate with me?"

"Perhaps," Tak returned, "it is you who would not want me in the end,

Princess."

"Not possible. You are of everything that I *dream*."

Tak didn't say another word after that soft, but sure, declaration. At least, he said nothing that suggested he would not take Poe on as a companion.

In the end, the king didn't settle it. The princess and her guard did.

Shortly after, they took their leave.

Zale's mate found him still sitting on his throne, mulling over the day and evening, and staring at nothing in particular. "Tis done," he told her.

Rosel's brow lifted in surprise. "Already? That was quick."

"Your second daughter—"

"*Our* second daughter, my King."

"Our second daughter has a way about her," Zale settled on saying. "And a mind all her own."

Rosel nodded as if she understood. "Poe does. She left the maiden chambers when no one was looking. Did she find you with her guard?"

"She did, of course."

His wife grinned up at him where she sat at his fin, waiting and sweet.

"Tis not a bad thing that she prefers a man of her seas, and Tak was the guard you considered sending as her … companion, should she have agreed to mate into the Red Seas. Didn't you fret for the last season about broaching the topic with the lord about it? Now you won't even have to. Little blessings."

Perhaps. He had put the guard in Poe's path a time or two knowing Tak was truly the one and only man of their seas that would be capable of catching the eye of his most fearless daughter. It wasn't hard for her to catch the attention of others, she was *the* prize, but it was not as easy to find a match worthy of her, as she pointed out herself. Better her father had sent her to another realm with a merman she knew she could trust to protect her wholly, and lean on if needed, than hope the prince of those seas would do it for her.

Besides, his other daughter did the same thing. He just hadn't picked the companion for her—Sarha let him do nothing except make the match with her King of the Red Seas.

"See, things do work out," Rosel told him, drumming her fingers to the scales on his tail.

Zale hummed under his breath. "You think?"

"I do."

"Then, it should be a very interesting year, my Queen, for us all."

"The colony will be quite happy."

Yes. And a happy colony also made for a happy—and safe—king. The only thing that truly mattered here.

8. THE COMPANION

152 days later ...

Poe

Choosing a companion and spending an entire year, barring any reasons to end it, in the companionship with said merman before sharing the blood was the rite of passage of any merwoman after coming of age. Should her family agree to her choice, or in the case of matches arranged under the agreement of all parties, the supervised companionship could begin. A courting, of sorts; a spread of time meant for the two to spend time together in settings that would allow them to get to know one another deeply, but without intimacy, so they could determine whether they were suitable to continue on together as a pair, a couple, in what would come. And with watchers.

Always with the spies until permission was finally given for the two to continue their companionship without all the extra pairs of eyes.

Not that Poe's maidens liked being called any sort of thing, and they were rather good about *losing* her at times.

Arelle, on the other hand ...

"This way now, hurry and hush," Poe whispered to Tak, yanking him by their hooked elbows into a hidden path on the coral maze that Arelle swam past every single time they were in the courtyard. Her maidens, who did know about the secret way to the middle, had been just around the bend behind them and probably wouldn't have seen the two enter at first. It gave them long enough for Arelle to realize her sister wasn't coming around the other corner, and for the maidens to figure out exactly the trick Poe had played on them all.

By then, the two would be in the very middle of the maze.

No one would say anything, truly.

Her father's private chambers, where he'd been spending his most recent days as their colony continued to thrive in storms that would come to an end and keep them deep beneath the seas, overlooked the maze and courtyard. *Someone* was watching them, surely.

She simply didn't want anyone to hear.

Tak laughed darkly under his breath, but followed her into the smaller slit in the coral to pop out on the other side. "Pulling another of your tricks again, Princess?"

She smirked back at him. "And what about it?"

This probably wouldn't be the last time she snuck the pair of them off in safe waters, and she was well aware that Tak only let her do as much because she always had a reason. Usually, because she intended for the two to have a conversation that would not be overheard. It wasn't long before they found themselves in the middle of the coral maze of various colors, and only then did she unhook her arm from his so the two could take a step back from one another.

There were *some* rules.

They tried to respect them.

Tak's violet eyes studiously watched the way Poe toyed with the belt of jewels hanging in various lengths to cover the swell of her hips and the cleft in her tail that she barely paid any mind to unless this merman was in her presence. Then, that spot that turned into her womanhood and entry to her womb when she exhaled the seas, ached more often than it didn't, and she had more than a little clue why.

"What is it?" Tak asked, already knowing.

"My mother told me that my father intends to ask me this evening if I am willing to continue with the companionship," Poe said quietly, looking down at her hands fiddling with precious stones again. "I wanted to ask you myself first. Tis on me to end it to him, I know, but—"

Her words died on her tongue when Tak stepped forward. Close enough that he could reach out to fiddle with the small dagger of sea glass, curled at the end like a hook, that she kept in a sheath at her waist made of braided leather. Something else *he* had made and given her during their many swims around the colonies and meals around the court's biggest table for feasts.

One of which was from the spoils of a hunting trip Tak took her on. He admitted later that he didn't think Poe would be the type of merwoman to get herself bloody in the seas for the sake of food and the thrill, but that he wouldn't hold it against her all the same. Whether she was the type or not, Poe went.

They killed a Great Black Shark, a beast five times the length of one of their men, and brought it home to the court and king. Tak later requested the beast's rib cage and bones, which was granted by the king, but he promised to tell her what it was all for later.

Later had yet to come, apparently.

"I will," Tak murmured finally, breaking the long stretch of silence between them. His gaze flicked up to meet hers, then, and Poe couldn't help but grin just a bit. Her companion, the best choice she had made in her short life yet, flashed his teeth right back. "Tell the king that we will be going ahead, Princess."

"Do you think we'll be free to do whatever, then?"

"In private?"

Poe wouldn't meet his gaze, then. "I think about that a lot."

"Good. You should."

And that was about as much of that topic as Tak would touch, but it was just enough to get that soft, warm cleft of hers almost throbbing again. The sensation quickly faded at Arelle's shout.

"You're lying, there is no secret way to the middle—she's not there!" her sister called loudly to someone just beyond the wall. Probably, to the maidens.

Sure enough, Arelle almost tripped over her tail fin at the sight of her sister and the merman waiting for her in the middle of the coral maze. Tak had thought to put a little bit more distance between them at the sound of Arelle, but there was no hiding the flush in her cheeks that Poe willed away with the helpful rub of her fingertips.

"*Whew*," she muttered, fanning her face in the water for the bubbles to help cool it off and turning away from Arelle who had looked back for the maidens. "Too close, that."

"She is here, I guess."

"Sorry, Princess," Tak murmured low, so only Poe could hear.

No, he wasn't.

Tak knew good and well what he did to her.

"Go off and swim in the maze, then," Poe told her sister. "We're talking."

"You promised to race with us today, Poe."

"I will," she tried to assure Arelle.

The way the mergirl's angry, and perhaps jealous, gaze turned on Tak in that moment told her older sister a lot. This year of her sister's companionship leading into her mating would teach Arelle a lot, but with that education into her womanhood would also lay bare how unfair her own lack of choices would eventually be when it came her time.

Poe worried a lot about that.

Arelle sighed loudly, her sharp gaze darting between Tak and her sister once more before she turned and swam out of view. Not long after, the maidens took their positions at the one entry to the middle, giving Poe a knowing look that said they had caught onto her little trick, but turned their back to allow the two privacy all the same.

"Murder in her eyes, that one," Poe said of her sister.

Tak chuckled. "I think that's you, actually. But I like it. Let's everyone know exactly where you stand and that you damn well mean it."

Poe's head snapped his way, and he arched an eyebrow at her.

"That one," he said of Arelle, "well, isn't she also losing her sister little by little, in these days that have become ours?"

He wasn't wrong.

"Murder in my eyes, hmm?" she asked.

Tak grinned. "*Woman*, I said I liked it."

He had been very careful to do that ever since that night in the throne room where his offhand remark about a worthy chase in her regard. They never talked about that, specifically, again, but anytime he complimented her in a way that was unusual, but Poe still liked, he always made sure to clarify.

Just so she understood, and she did with him, *very* well.

"It's always been the same look, too," Tak added, making Poe laugh about herself in a way that she usually didn't. "Whenever you put your mind to something—that time you were twelve and your father wouldn't let you and your sisters take the maidens beyond the colony for a picnic. It took us two days to find you."

"We weren't even that lost!" she half shouted, still laughing. It drew the gaze of one of her four maidens to check on the two, but the woman only smiled at the conversation she could probably only partly follow.

"The look," Tak replied, "never changed. That was the point. Outswimming every guard put on your halls. Learning all the tricks of how to beat everyone foolish enough to ask you to race. The look doesn't change."

The more he talked, Poe usually became enraptured, happy to lose herself in every single word. This time, she only heard one thing.

"Your refusal of my companionship at first had nothing to do with my speed or the worth of my chase, did it?" she whispered.

"One of us could probably outswim the other in these seas, given the right circumstances, Princess. Certainly."

And it was her.

Absolutely.

However, he might be the only man in their realm and seas able to catch her, too.

"So, what was the reason?" she asked, remembering to keep their conversation quiet.

"Must we—"

"Are we doing this right?"

Her soft question silenced him instantly.

Then, Tak nodded.

"So, we start with truth," Poe said.

"The truth?" he laughed sadly, but he eyed her in a way that felt almost predatory. His stare settled so heavily on her that Poe found herself gulping in more water to breathe easier or help the feeling.

Nothing worked.

Nothing would until she had time away with Tak from everything and every*one*. Soon. That should happen soon. Her father had no reason to make them wait when both of them were of adult age and agreed to a bond at the beginning of the next storm season.

"Is there more than one reason?" she asked. "Is that why you struggle to tell me?"

Tak snorted. "What, do you think I have an entire list?"

"Perhaps. Who am I to know, you've spent all this time alone already, so I am sure you've come to that decision through a great deal of thinking. It couldn't have been an easy thing."

"The easiest—because it was the right thing."

Oh.

"You're not entirely what I expected," she admitted. He ended up being much, *much* more. A conversation with him could be both challenging and entertaining. He had a mind of his own about most things, like her. He let her talk—*loved* to hear her excited about something. But as much as he seemed to adore her, the part of Poe that clung to the love she felt for her father was something Tak pulled back from. Often. Enough that she had noticed. "Not that it is a bad thing."

"Saying yes to you also wasn't that hard, even if I was willing to tell the king anything to get him out of my face," Tak muttered, then.

"That was why you said it?"

"I couldn't tell him the true reason."

"Would you tell me?"

Tak's gaze darted to the line of four maidens with their backs still turned. None of them gave any indication that their conversation could be overheard, but he still lowered his clicking to her in the water all the same.

It didn't make his words any less painful.

"Telling you is just as bad, worse even, to me—how do you tell a woman that her father is setting her up to be the queen that fails? How do you tell her that awful thing when she loves him?"

"Why would you say that to me?" Poe asked. "Why would you say that of your king?"

To talk of the king like that was treason and reason for death. In fact, she'd seen merman be killed for less in her father's kingdom. Tak looked entirely unconcerned with her attempt at a warning.

"He's got, what, another hundred years on his throne? Perhaps a little less, or a bit more depending on if he sees the end of his natural life, and then when he finally hands this kingdom, the colony, over to you … have you thought at all what will be left of it, Princess? What, *who*, will be left for you to rule over?" he asked her quietly, softer than before. "Seasonally, the landwalkers are taking a dozen of us. Tis two a year for their best hunts. We're getting to numbers that we can accurately count within the colony. What a sad legacy that is for him to willingly, knowingly, leave for you. He sold your oldest sister off, would have done the same for you, and who knows what he's got planned for the other two. They're too young yet, I suppose. Our people, they're birthing a third of what is being captured a year. Consider what that also means. *Consider* that there will not be a kingdom for you to come into," Tak finished, looking away from her the entire time he delivered blow after blow to her rose-tinted world.

He did it one more time, repeating, "The queen who fa—"

She didn't let him get the words out again, and no doubt, Tak would appreciate the irony of the sea glass dagger he gifted to her being the very same thing that she put against his throat in that moment. He hadn't blinked, didn't even get the chance to turn his head back toward her before she had closed the distance between them, and his next swallow found the edge of her blade.

"*Don't you call me that,*" she hissed, the fierceness and fire in her matching the blaze that she found lit in him when he finally looked down at her. Every breath between them ached, and her hand trembled because she didn't want to put her blade to his throat, but he couldn't say *that.*

"I will do many things, but not that," she told him.

"Princess?" came the concerned call of one of her maidens.

Poe didn't look away from Tak, who also never broke their connected stare despite the interruption. They really should—it wouldn't be good for word to get back to her father that for any reason she pulled a blade on Tak.

"'Twas the only reason I would have refused you," he said as a sticky dribble of his blood made its way down the edge of the blade slowly.

"You could have just asked me if I thought my father was a fool."

"Should I ask that of his next chosen queen?"

She didn't really have the answer.

Tak shrugged, still unbothered by her blade that had left him with the tiniest of cuts. "Otherwise, there is nothing about you that does not call to my seas. I swear, I already hear your heartbeat."

Gods.

Challenge her, he did.

And he did it so well.

Poe dragged in a hard, shaky breath. "I will *not* be the queen who fails."

"Not anymore, Princess."

At that, she dropped the hooked dagger.

Still bloody from him, she sheathed it.

"'Tis fine," she assured her maidens. Or tried. "Just a game between us."

Tak shot her a look that said he could turn that blade into a game if she truly wanted. She pretended as if she hadn't seen.

Arelle had made her way back to the middle of the maze by the time the maidens allowed them a false sense of privacy again. From the edge where she held onto the coral wall of the maze, Arelle watched her sister and Tak.

"You said you would race!"

"And I will," Poe muttered, more than a little annoyed.

"But if your father has underestimated you once, he'll do it again—make sure every time is worth it," Tak murmured as he passed her by to leave her behind.

Poe's pinky finger caught his on the way, stopping him to wait for her, but his finger only wrapped tighter around hers as he did. "But you don't, right?"

"Underestimate you, Princess?"

Yes, that.

That terrible, awful thing.

She nodded.

Tak grinned, and the sight made her heart skip a whole beat. "Never, not once, and perhaps with me at your back, you *can't* fail. In the end, the one reason to say no was truly more of a reason why I should agree."

And so, here they were.

"I picked the right man of my seas, didn't I?" she asked.

He reached for her then, without warning or permission. His hand found the side of her neck and face, holding warm and tight in the cold water. It wasn't an inappropriate way to touch her before their private companionship had properly begun, but the way she felt her head tip back for him as he inched closer, like he might kiss her, that toed the line.

Just a bit.

He didn't close the gap.

Tak didn't kiss her, either.

Even if she would have begged him to. And on the Gods, on her life, on her crown and her seas, she would have. Had he only asked her to.

No, he told her something instead. He gave her something far more important. Everything, really.

"Tis only fair if you're the heart of mine, Poe."

92 days later ...

The little incident with the dagger in the maze did get back to the king. Unfortunately. To make matters worse, when Poe and Tak wouldn't give a proper reason for what caused it, the king made the pairing wait for another half of a season before he broached the topic of allowing their private companionship again.

Zale did that on purpose. For no other reason than to piss her off, surely.

Just like when he finally granted it.

He gave Poe no forewarning that it would happen, did so at the dining table for the whole court to hear, and proceeded to announce the other couples in the room that would be allowed to mate in the upcoming season. Poe was stuck between her own private joy at finally being allowed to close a door on prying eyes whenever she wanted with Tak, for any reason she pleased, but her excitement was dampened by the manipulation she could plainly see.

It was obvious why her father did it now. That he had allowed other companionships, and now matings to coincide with hers meant the king saw Poe's relationship and soon-to-be bond as nothing more than something he could use.

"And a draw—there will be one of those this year, too," the king stated from the head of his table, loudly.

It silenced everyone.

No one even breathed.

Poe finally found the stare of her own companion at the far end of the room. Tak no longer watched the king if Poe was in his line of vision. He only looked for the heart of his seas.

"A draw for who will go on to have young this year in the colony," the king clarified.

What they all had been waiting for.

Except Poe.

It was just another ploy of Zale's.

A way to manipulate his court and kingdom further. The way the massive space lit up with a catacomb of noise in the water as hands hit the tables and mermaids lifted from their seats to cheer about the news of a lottery for allowed pregnancies between mated pairs, it all just served to tie Poe's heart into a knot that she wouldn't be able to undo.

She should be happy, too.

Instead, all she could do was see it for what it was.

Well, until Tak caught her eye again.

Back where he stood near the doors leading out of the dining hall, he tipped his head in the same way he always did to silently tell her to come to him. With most everyone in the court filling the halls for the feast demanded by the king—his intentions for doing so being more obvious to Poe, now—the rest of the palace would be quite empty.

"*Now*," Tak mouthed at her before he slipped between the crack in the doors.

As he wished.

It wasn't a hard choice for her, and she didn't hesitate to hold her maidens back when two tried to follow. The two guards that kept a respectable distance were a necessity wherever she went, even with Tak usually, but only when she wanted them to be.

And she didn't want them near her.

Not right now.

But, the king told them to follow. Thankfully, Poe had exited the dining hall as well before the mermen got that okay from the king.

It gave her a head start.

She followed the scent of Tak in the water—a skill of hers that he had helped her hone with every hunting trip the two took deep in the seas. She headed down the first corridor, turned right to find another, and found him around the corner at the far end at the left. Well, more like he found her.

His hand did.

It found her neck, anyway.

Tak yanked her into the darkened corridor with strong hands that made her body comply for him the second he touched her. It didn't matter if it was his pinky finding the side of her hand to stroke or his gaze making silent demands. It all felt so intimate to her. And after so long of being forced to stand side by side, respectably, with Tak to please the king and colony, those first few seconds of his hands exploring the shape of her body, from the swell of her hips to the soft mounds of her breasts, were pure bliss to her.

Exquisite.

Her back to the wall, she sighed when his hand found her neck again. Instinctually, her head fell back for him, and he found her mouth there, full lips pink and his to take. He did, kissing her hard and backing her tighter against the wall until her chest flattened against his leather breastplate and their tails tangled.

The way his fingertips had grazed over the contours of her flesh so softly, his mouth, at first, did the same. Exploring and testing, teasing her with soft flicks and gentle pulls of his teeth to get her to open up. Against him, she found a breathless sort of peace, and when he started to try to pull away, Poe refused to let him. Kissing him deeper, harder, holding his wrists and pulling him back into her.

No, they were not *done*.

Not even when he murmured along the seam of her trembling lips, "I promised the king no defiling in the palace, Princess."

His admission finally had her pulling back.

Their burning gazes met.

"You knew he would allow us our private companionship tonight?" she asked.

"He said as much to me when he came to ask about my plans for the royal guards when we move into the season of mating. You realize the entire colony is coming to watch, don't you?"

Watch *them*, he meant.

Poe swallowed hard, and nodded. "They might not see it all, but—"

"Some will. Some will see—and hear—everything. Even the way you look and sound for me."

The only part of this whole thing that made her nervous, really. That didn't mean she wasn't entirely confident and sure in her decision to move forward. "

"And then we shall never be disputed—our bond is *true*."

He kissed her again, harder than before. Teeth scraping her top and bottom lip and his fingers found the best place to squeeze at her sides.

The *clink-clink* of armor approaching had Tak stepping back from Poe to make things appear more appropriate between them. Entirely too far, in her opinion, considering the way she ached for him to imprint himself against her once more.

"The good news," he told her not a moment before the guards finally caught up to the princess and her companion, "is that I told you father I would be taking you away for most of the evening the very first chance I could—I'm following through on that."

"Tonight?"

Tak's smile bloomed. "Aren't we getting a little close to the mating? You've barely even practiced, and even if you are fast, ask yourself—*do I know these seas as well as he?* I'll give you a head start tonight. I'll count to one hundred, even, if it pleases you, Princess."

Didn't he know already?

"Everything about you pleases me, Tak. That is precisely my joy."

And perhaps, the only problem.

"Ah, there you two are."

She didn't acknowledge the guards who rounded the corner, nor did she look away from Tak.

"Where am I swimming to?"

"Try to reach the edge of the colony."

"What, now?" asked a guard.

Tak paid him no mind, either. "Win, and I'll show you my grotto."

Oh, Poe very much liked that prize. Of course, he just had to give her even more ambition to win.

"Deal," she said.

9. FEAR AND PAIN

Tak

The guards in the darkened, empty corridor of the palace's east end, now bereft of a princess who wisely chose not to waste her valuable head start, continued their rambling worries and questions. Tak answered none of them and spoke only what was of utmost importance for the mermen in armor to know.

"Should we not tell the king of your plans?"

"Are you mad, my lord? Where did the princess go?"

"Needn't bother the king with anything," Tak said, still counting down from one hundred inside his head. He wouldn't give Poe a second more because he couldn't afford to. She was terribly fast in the water, and a smart competitor against others because she thought tactfully and carefully. Besides that, her only weakness was the outskirts of their colony, where he told her to *attempt* to make it, because he knew her father kept the princesses under a tight leash of just where exactly they could go.

She could make it further, to the Isle of Broken Islands, because he had accompanied the maidens there to forage with Poe and her sisters. But they were only allowed to go in the depths of the worst storms when there would be no chance of a landwalker's ships on the seas. Not unless the man wished for death, of course. It made finding what the merpeople needed a bit harder, of course, leaving them using the scraps of what was left and rationing it amongst those who needed it more than others.

It was all a little sickening, really.

Nonetheless, he couldn't let Poe get too far beyond the boundary of the colony—even if they were approaching safer times because they were leading into the storm season. Violent waves and sea storms that hit randomly and didn't stay for very long often kept the landwalkers from venturing too far beyond their very safe coasts. The thunderous pace of his heart inside his constricting chest just wouldn't allow Tak to give Poe the opportunity to make it beyond where he considered it safe without him.

Storms or not.

Nearly down his count, he told the guards who stared at him as if he had lost his head or fin, and said, "Tis a waste of your precious time—because you'll need to attempt to keep pace with me—to return to the king for clarification on something he needn't concern himself with at the moment. His Majesty already knows of my plans this evening, and if you were not informed, well, now you are."

"Keep pace—"

"Now, yes."

Tak finally hit zero in his head, and with that, he offered the guards no other explanation as he followed the route Poe had taken through the palace by following her scent lingering in the water passing in the halls.

"My lord!" he heard called out behind him.

The guards truly were a nuisance, but needed, and so he couldn't complain that the king made the demand of him, for now, to keep their post on Poe. Tak found the scent of his soon-to-be mate dissipated like a cloud in front of his face the moment he found himself beyond the palace walls at the rear end of the coral. His head swung one way fast, and then the other. She could have went straight, but the taste of her in the water wouldn't have weakened like it did when—

"My lord," said a guard where he stood off to the side, in the corner of the large square.

The merman looked up. Nothing else, but it was enough for Tak to understand exactly the reason for the lack of scent. Poe's tail fin, every glorious inch, would have dispersed the trail as she jutted straight up. Clever. She found the first place to exit the palace and with no ceiling to stop her, and headed high where the slipstreams were the strongest. His momentary confusion allowed her a few more seconds ahead of him. Not enough, he hoped, to get her into the narrow sea separating their colony and the islands that became denser and more forested the closer they came to the shores of Atlas.

Many, those closest, were the landwalkers'. Atlas Islands.

Ah, yes. Up she went.

"Good girl, my Princess," Tak murmured under his breath as he headed upward, soon finding that unique mix of flora and seas above in the water.

As much as her little trick did work his heart into overdrive with worry, he was still pleased that she had found a way to outsmart him. After everything—even with this, she made him eat any regretful words he had dared to speak about her for no other reason than his pride.

He couldn't have very well told the king that he wanted Poe. Her, of course, but not her father. He would have used that, somehow, against Tak. Surely. Zale, well, the only thing Tak had left for that bastard was the pointy end of the sea glass blade. Alas, as he wasn't quite ready to lose his head with his life just beginning, in a way, so he kept those violent urges in check. He still owed the colony, and his people, his life, after all.

And not at the hand of their king. A false one wasn't worth the sacrifice to sate his own satisfaction, anyway.

Tak paid no mind to whether the guards had been able to keep pace with him, but he safely doubted it based on his past experiences with the mermen. They wouldn't be too far behind, no matter, so he picked up his pace to hit the upper slipstream that would carry him toward the band of narrow sea where he would find Poe.

Or catch her first, hopefully.

He hadn't told her to take the race farther.

She still might—wouldn't that be just like her?

Chirps and whistles followed Tak as those of the court and colony outside must have caught into the princess's game with her guard, and people stopped to watch them go. The darkness in the water, of the skies beyond the surface of crashing waves, made it hard for him to see very far ahead of him but as long as he had her scent, the rest didn't matter. He'd follow that until he couldn't and let instinct do the rest as it usually did. Most of his life had been spent hunting for sustenance in these seas from a very young age. He was not weak in these waters.

Yet, neither was Poe.

So, when her scent took him to the very edge of the slipstream, beyond the scattering of the remaining sunken ships and broken islands made of rocks that was their colony, where many landwalkers lost their life, lending them grottos and homes, it disappeared again. Tak knew Poe had done it.

She'd won their race.

And she continued, heading straight into the narrow sea.

Tak came out the slipstream shouting for her in the nothingness of the raging waters. "*Poe!*"

Not princess, like he knew he should.

No, just her name ripping out of him desperately. Clawing its way out of his chest to explode through the water like the taste of his own fear spreading around him. Tak was there in an instant—on a *ship* again. He couldn't breathe and every slam of his heart in his chest sounded like the lashing of whips against already-broken skin.

Her pleas had stayed with him the longest.

He'd finally stopped dreaming of that night.

It took *decades*.

"*Poe!*"

Her twinkling laugh, sly and pleased, was all he heard before she rushed him from below. She had no concept of the absolute terror that waged a war inside Tak as her arms snaked around him, and their bodies crashed together before he could properly comprehend what had happened. The force propelled them both higher. Her laughter echoed all around them, and she was still blissfully unaware of the trauma that had cracked open the invisible wound left inside his chest.

Gods, he wanted her to remain that way.

"I *won*," he heard her whisper.

She did.

One could not afford Poe extra seconds in a race. She would use every single one. Tak considered this a lesson well learned on his part.

They broke the surface of the water just long enough for Tak to gasp in a lungful of wet sea air before he dragged them both back down. He needed to get as far away from the taste of his own fear in the water as he could, but it was far easier to do with Poe's lithe, trembling body molded against his. Their tails tangled as he turned them into a downward spiral, sending them both headfirst toward the seafloor.

A very long swim down.

He kissed her on the way, hard, long and *deep*. Until he knew she couldn't breathe because his own lungs ached for the seas. He poured every bit of fear and numbness that had taken over him, before and tonight, into the way he found paradise against this woman's lips. It was easier to lose himself in her simple pleasures as her body woke up grinding against his than it was to go back to a memory he would rather not relive.

And then Poe bit him.

The sharp tug of her teeth against his bottom lip was the last thing he felt before his back slammed into the sandy seafloor. It was too dark to see the cloud of silt that must have bloomed around their bodies making impact with the ground, but he felt the way it covered them both when it once again settled. Tak would have liked to put his attention on Poe's hands, capturing his own, dragging one to her chest and another to her the apex of her tail but something scratched at his back.

Something very bad.

"Move," he snapped.

He wanted to kiss away the hurt that pinched her face, but Tak could explain later. His arms locked around her as he shoved her further away from the bottom of the sea.

"What is—"

"Wait," Tak said quietly, his gaze scouring the darkness in a circle around them for anything out of place. Even a hint would send him swimming with Poe in his arms whether she wanted to go or not, that was not of his concern.

"Don't move," he told her, finally letting Poe go.

Remaining still for a period allowed their eyes to adjust to the shape of one another and whatever was closest to them in the darkness, including what he swam back down to the seafloor to show her. Running his fingers through the silt, he found the scratchy, woven netting that had greeted his back not moments before. Pulling it up a bit, they could then see how flat the dark netting rested against the bottom, and as Tak swam along still pulling it up from the sandy bottom where it laid hidden, he could feel the water change.

Poe's change.

"Oh, Gods," she breathed. "I've ... I've never seen one."

"A net, or a landwalker?"

"Both," Poe admitted.

"How far have you swam—how close did you get to those lands?"

Her gaze wouldn't meet his, then. All he could see of it before she took it away entirely was the crescent, silver sliver in the darkness, anyway. He had considered like many of them, even himself, that Poe would dare to go to Atlas should she have the chance and think it was safe. She was clever enough to know she had to hide doing so from everyone—probably even him.

But no.

Tak *needed* to know.

"Just tell me," he said, tone soft.

"If I can sneak away—I only do it in the storms."

"How far?"

"The edge of the orchard."

Gods.

Those were his favorite fruit, too.

Tak's jaw clenched, but his own reasons for keeping quiet stopped him from telling her not to go to the forbidden lands of Atlas. Instead, he let the netting go from his fingers and it fell back to the seafloor, disappearing under the silt almost entirely.

"Tis getting a bit close to storms for them to be out placing nets, isn't it?"

What would that matter?

The land king planned ahead.

Often.

"That wasn't here a fortnight ago—and the way it's sitting … Well, is something weighing it down? Think like them, Princess. If you knew where you placed the netting, could you come back to retrieve it, and if you know it's in a place where your prey travels, your likelihood of coming up with something is a bit greater, in those cases."

"How would they get it up from the sea? This far down?"

"Rope and hooks," Tak said, not even sure if he was right. That's how he would do it, though. A ship on either end of the net, a few lines and hooks to drag along the bottom, and lift. Simple, really.

"They find new ways every season that they get back onto these seas," he muttered, irritated. "New ways to rip us from them. They're not even releasing the men anymore."

"*What?*"

The horror that lit up Poe's voice had Tak spinning back around in the water to face her. Her gaze, wide and distraught, lingered on the seafloor and the netting no longer visible to anyone who needed to see it.

"He's not told you that, has he?" Tak asked.

He couldn't quite see the way Poe fidgeted but the twitch of her tail said she did, nonetheless. "Have you considered he might not want us to worry?"

115

"Before it was just women—now, they take men and children, too. A princess's worry should be the least of your father's concerns when he doesn't even know what they're doing with the people of his seas!" Tak shouted.

He instantly wished he hadn't.

Not because Poe's head dropped to hide her own guilt or from his emotions that got the better of him as he faced yet another harsh truth about the extinction of their people.

No, not for those reasons.

"I'm sorry, I know it isn't your fault," he murmured, heading for her.

Poe let him capture her to apologize with more than just his words. She sniffed away tears he couldn't see in the dark water while he dotted soft kisses along the lines of her beautiful face. Across her cheeks that lifted in a soft smile for him. Over her eyelids that closed for each kiss. Down the bridge of her pleasant nose and across the silken seam of her tempting lips.

Only then did she finally kiss him back.

"Forgive me?" he requested as her face tilted sideways in the cradle of his palms.

"Do you trust me when I say that I know it isn't right?"

Tak nodded. "Of course."

But at that very moment, what could she do?

Tak understood that, too.

"Then, I forgive you," Poe murmured.

He sealed her words with another searing kiss, finding her lips parting for him almost instantly for a taste of her mouth and the lash of her tongue against his own. What distance remained between them left when their hands tangled and their fingers interlaced as tails coiled, and her body found its home tight along the contours of his.

"Easy, Princess," he warned quietly as the soft pulse of her cleft pressed into his rigid stomach. The valley between her bare breasts, otherwise covered by her long hair and innumerable, delicate chains hanging from her throat at varying lengths, made a soft cushion to rest his chin as he told her, "Our night is still young."

"We're in the middle of the seas, *who* will know—"

"My lord!"

"My lord?"

"Princess!"

"Them," Tak said, chuckling as he felt her suddenly pull away.

Poe, too distracted with him, squeaked embarrassedly under her breath. "You could have told me!"

"Down here—we've got a problem," he called to the guards somewhere overhead. To Poe, Tak only said, "And not feel the way you want me? Not hardly."

"Oh … *You!*"

Her indignant, but breathless, exclamation only made Tak grin, but he put on a more serious face when the guards found them. He made quick work of showing the two the nets, and how easy it could be for their sea glass blades to cut through it.

"Find the ends, cut off whatever is anchoring it down, and take this back to the palace to show the king," Tak said, one finger hooked around a square in the netting.

"And you, my lord?" the taller of the two guards asked.

Over his shoulder, he found Poe waiting. At least, her gaze no longer fixated on the netting he showed the guards. Mostly, because she was too busy staring at him.

'Twas a good night.

Before all … *this.*

He still wanted to end it that way for her.

"After, find us at my grotto. I'll be ready to return the princess to her palace chambers."

Tak's grotto, a home he had worked on for most of his adult life, existed from the remnants of a sunken ship's bow and the underwater cave where it had come to rest. The cave had a hole carved in the rocky ceiling, a feature he had added to allow sunlight from the one piece of the cave that jutted out of the sea surface. Only swirling bubbles that burst at the surface spoke of what waited for the pair down below. Poe dived under the water and followed Tak without him needing to tell her as much, and she didn't speak again until the two had entered the wide crack in the bow that allowed them entrance to his one sanctuary.

A net bulging with skulls awaited them.

Poe peered up at it, curious. "How many are in there?"

"I stopped counting around sixty or so. Seemed redundant, really."

Her brows lifted higher. "And the purpose?"

"Does it bother you?"

"Not at all."

Good, because the grotto only got darker from that point, not that he told her as much. Everything about the space he chose to live and exist, to hold what was precious and important when he wasn't there to do it, came with a warning. The skulls were just the start. Any kill of which he saved the bones hung in the corridor beyond the broken ship where the grotto opened to a larger, partially underwater cave.

"I let the crabs eat the flesh off them and return to where I left them," he explained about the skulls as he headed deeper into the grotto. "Less mess here, I suppose."

Poe followed, but she still glanced back at the skulls. "Which was your favorite?"

What a strange question.

He reveled in it.

"Hmm," Tak muttered, finding Poe's hand to pull her along with him past the bones hanging in the corridor.

She stopped at a particular set.

Large ribs.

Sharp teeth.

It all hung from jagged rocks, tied to cords of sea leather.

"Is that our shark?"

"The Great Black bitch," Tak confirmed, laughing. Tak had baited the beast and let Poe do the honor of killing it. Never had she looked more like his wildest dreams than she did surrounded in a haze of bloody water, a kill to her name. "'Tis almost clean and ready."

"For what?"

Tak only shrugged.

It wasn't time for that.

Besides, Poe liked surprises. He planned to keep this one.

"Come along, now."

"You didn't tell me which skull you liked most—or why."

Which was what he suspected she cared more to learn.

"My favorite of the skulls were the ones I collected from the ship that sank to make my home. It felt appropriate. Both that I used their deaths as a warning, and that their souls know their bones were simply added to a larger collection of misdeeds. The herring for all others who might think to make a similar choice."

"Your misdeeds, or theirs?"

Tak smirked. "What do you think?"

Poe winked back. "Only asking, my lord."

That title—one he'd always hated and never wanted—had a growl rumbling low in the back of his throat when it slipped from her pretty, pink lips. The sound was the only warning Tak allowed Poe before he crowded her against the wall just before the cave opened up much wider. Nose to nose, eye to eye, she curled her tail like a coil around his. Now, she wasn't the only one locked in place as she cocked her head to the side as if to ask him, *Now what?*

"Ask me," he murmured, every word brushing over her lips.

Poe's eyes searched his. "For what?"

"Ask me to show you why it feels so good to press yourself against me until there's no space left. Ask me to touch you the way you did on the seafloor—but use words, Princess. *Ask me.*"

"If I can't call you my lord—"

"*Poe*, heart of my seas, ask me."

Her breath hitched when his hand slid lower on her stomach where he felt her muscles clench and twitch with every slow inch.

"You'll show me?" she asked, then, oh, so softly.

Yes, he would.

That was why they were here; why she picked him. A man of her choosing, proven and worthy, to guide her into the depths of her intimate womanhood. He understood that once a woman of their kind came of age, she was given some education on coupling, the prevention of unwanted births, and even self-pleasure. It wasn't, however, acceptable for her to curiously explore those things unless she had taken a companion, or if she was not well into her adult years and settled into her life.

In her case, the companion was him.

"Poe," he murmured against the seam of her lips in a tender kiss, "I'll show you everything. *Anything.*"

If only she asked.

Instead, she told him.

That worked, too.

"*Then, show me.*"

He let her find his hand and take it lower, until his fingertips found the silken ridge of the cleft at the apex of Poe's tail. A shuddering breath pulled its way out of her at his first stroke of two fingers along the sides of the tender spot. He found her tail cleft warm and soft, glove-like around the fingers that he used to edge her. Even her tail fin quivered like her chin when the next stroke of his fingers went a little deeper. Her body moved with the motions, daring to rise higher as another gasp tumbled from her parted lips.

"You ache for me," Tak said against the hollow of Poe's throat as she pressed her head back into the wall as if that would relieve the tension she probably felt. Not likely. "'Tis why you always feel it, why your stare lingers, and you can't hide the heat." Poe's moans reverberated under the water and the heat of her cleft hugged his fingers impossibly tighter. He nuzzled her throat, feeling her head turn to seek the affection even as he kept the same pace sliding his fingers in and out of her. Massaging the top ridge of her cleft with every stroke; ignoring his own discomfort as her tail tightened painfully around his own to the point of cracking bones. "'Tis almost there, Princess, let me feel it."

"P-*Poe*," she breathed back.

It was only fair.

Like this, what did it even matter?

He pulled her chin down, making them lock gazes again as the bliss threatened to shut her eyes on him altogether.

"Mine, then," he said. "*My* Poe."

Her reply came in a broken cry that he only partially caught with a kiss as all at once, her tail unfurled from him, and her bliss gave way. She couldn't form words beyond the deep groan of satisfaction as her trembling body fell into his, and he all too happily caught her, letting her head tuck along the crook in his check.

"That," he told her, "is always mine to give, and yours to *sweetly* receive, my love."

Poe laughed weakly. "And just how do I do so sweetly?"

Tak grinned, pulling her away from the wall and cradling Poe to swim into the widening cave. "You have lots of time to learn."

And when it benefitted her, he doubted it would take Poe long to catch on to some of his more baser preferences. He could make soft love all night long, but there was a time and place for that sort of thing. 'Twas better when it wasn't overdone. He much preferred finding paradise at the very edge of control where no one cared to live. Where pain mixed with pleasure and every breath shared between two became one.

They craved it, their kind.

To let go wholly.

Completely.

Only in their weakest moments, their most private, could they.

"Is that—"

Poe didn't get to finish her question before Tak broke the surface of the underwater wave. The only piece where, beyond the rock, it reached above the seas, sticking out dangerously and jaggedly. Half the cave remained a pool of water while the other sat on a shelf carved into the shiny rock with a hole in the top above. Shelves of weapons, knickknacks, stacks of his books and other land things that he watched Poe eye curiously, surrounded the nest of pillows and blankets in the very middle that made up his bed.

Well, theirs, now.

He had never shared it with anyone.

Until now.

"Tis yours," he told Poe, placing her to sit on the ledge. Her hands found his shoulders to hold while he stayed in the water, holding his sea breath as she peered around the enclave. She, too, kept her tail for a moment. "All of it."

"Smells like the seas."

Tak smiled. "Oh?"

"And *you*."

With her words came the last of the water from her lungs, rushing out of her gills and down her shoulders. He had seen Poe take to land with her legs, but it was quite another thing for him to feel her scales and muscle melt away to the clenching thighs that he suddenly looked down to find his own hands now shaking against. Every part of her that would be only his was mere inches from his face, and shamefully, he had to remind himself that everything from here had to be on her terms.

Everything.

If he did it the right way, and he would for Poe because she deserved a companion who treated her preciously and with the respect that she should have, then his needs and desires came second. Last, even, to the pace she set between them and the requests she might make in between. He deserved to do it right for both of them, frankly.

Tak glanced right back up at a smirking Poe. "You planned that."

She flashed her teeth. "I did, too."

Little pest.

He adored her for it, though.

Tak drummed his fingers against the jump of her thighs before suddenly pushing away from her to float back in the water, dipping down to take another breath of the water to keep his tail. "Go explore and settle your mind of all its questions about what you can find snooping through my things. I'll float."

Still kicking her bare legs back and forth in the water, her knees pressed firmly together, Poe peered up at the cavernous rock that dripped with the occasional water drop. She was a treat for his mind sitting with her palms propped against her knees, the flames of her red hair sticking in wet ringlets down her back, nipples hard in the chilled air, and her skin prickled from his last touch.

"Is it really mine, though?"

Tak righted himself and popped back out of the water instantly. "What do you mean?"

"How often will I actually get to be here? I've never spent more than three nights away from the palace."

"As often as you like."

Poe glanced down at him, cocking an eyebrow. "You think?"

Well ...

"As often as you like, with me," he added as a caveat. And whatever guard, or two, that the king would have posted at Tak's grotto to see the princess back and forth safely. "We needn't be stuck under water in that palace together constantly. You're not on the throne yet, Princess."

Poe smiled at the title that time. "No, I'm not, I suppose."

As if their chat was all the encouragement she needed, Poe finally stood from the ledge. Tak did not turn away in the water fast enough to avert his gaze from somewhere else other than the peek he got of her round backside, and the sliver of her sex when she bent over before getting up.

"Well, aren't you coming, too?" she asked him.

Tak made a wave from how fast he spun around. "Pardon?"

She stood next to the shelves of weapons and various items that Tak kept close in case he had a need. Corked jars of salves for wounds and dried flowers from all over the lands of their seas to cure, aid, or kill, depending on one's need. Poe's fingers settled on the spine of something else entirely on the shelf.

A book, actually.

"How do you get these here?"

"Watertight sacks," he admitted.

"Can you read?"

A slightly harder question, if only because it could lead her to ask more. Still, he answered her truthfully.

"Yes and write the landwalkers' language. Some."

"How?"

Of course.

Of course, she asked that.

Tak sighed loudly, making Poe glance his way with furrowed brows. "The queen before your father … she had all the palace orphans, and any young in the colony who were sent by their parents, educated in the language. I was one of those. We learned to speak it and read. Some texts, if treated properly in the vinegar made from water orchard fruit, retains its form and ink even after being made wet. She used to have a library. 'Twas her grandfather's. We spent an hour a day reading tales of all kinds with her in the coral maze. Well … tis a favorite memory of mine."

"A dear one, I imagine," Poe replied. "Will you ever tell me about her?"

The question froze him in place. "An—"

He stopped, flinching as he almost said her name.

"The old queen?"

Poe wouldn't meet his gaze as her cheeks and neck heated with a flush. "I have been told that you were close, and I wondered—"

Ah.

"Not that sort of close," he interjected softly before Poe could continue. "But if you're asking, then yes, I loved, and still do, her dearly."

Poe nodded, then. "And you *won't* tell me about her?"

How could he?

How could he possibly speak any words to Poe about a women he had loved so very much that his love and loyalty caused her unimaginable pain? That night and ship? It was his greatest shame.

"I cannot," Tak said simply.

"Okay."

Tak nodded and dipped under the water to take another pull of water. By the time he came back up, Poe had opened the book, and he watched the way her gaze skimmed down whatever she found on the pages between her hands.

"What are these?"

"Letters," he said. "Words. I could teach you. You're quick and clever, so it wouldn't take long at all for you to catch on."

She showed him the book. "So, what does it say?"

"The Lies of Halflings."

No author.

No publishing date.

Nothing to give away who had written down such crucial information, in story form, about mermaids of the Blu Seas and the people who walked on their lands. However, Tak had read the text at least a dozen times, could recite it probably by heart, and it still took him no closer to knowing what happened to the queen all those many years ago. After the risk he took to even get a book like that, well, he damn well better read it.

Until it was imprinted in the back of his damn skull.

Poe's puckered brow turned on him again. "The *Lies* of Halflings?"

"'Tis—"

"Where did you get this?"

He could have lied.

Maybe he should have.

"You are not the only one who sometimes travels to the forbidden lands when it is safe to do so."

Poe straightened a little bit, tipping her chin up as she regarded him silently.

"Why?" she eventually asked.

"I lost something."

Everyone did, really.

Tak shrugged. "For a while, I dared to think I could get it back."

Poe's gaze softened.

The sight of her there cemented something else for Tak. Another important decision.

"'Tis okay," he told her quietly, smiling sadly. "I am looking at the reason I needn't risk looking anymore."

It could be both right and heartbreaking, but she didn't have to know as much. He did not need her to make his pain her own for him to love her.

He already did.

Poe placed the book back on the rough, wooden shelf he'd balanced there by using sharp rocks jutting out from the wall. "Are you getting out of the water with me?"

"I can stay here for as long as you would like or want me to, actually."

"I know what you can do—what you *will* do," she pressed, "as long as it's what I tell you to do."

"Or not," he returned.

Poe nodded. "Or not, Tak. I know and I trust you. Join me?"

Well, she asked.

So, he did.

Tak swam back to the ledge, pulled himself up, and let go of his sea breath to find his legs when he fully emerged from the water. The curse of their kind to only walk the land after they reached their sixteenth year was truly just the beginning. Men would not copulate for their own pleasure or even take a respectful piss, unless they walked on land and found their legs. Their women had the gift, and pain, of bringing children into the world. Men were made to suffer with a smaller cleft than that of the female while in tail form, which brought them *no* pleasure at all, to eliminate.

Poe's gaze darted away from Tak after he stood on the ledge. Specifically, she looked away from the part of him that swung heavy and thick, even soft, between his muscular legs. The loose pack he typically wore strung around his waist would cover his manhood when he walked on land, but he just didn't have a need for it under most other circumstances. Nakedness wasn't exactly taboo to their people, but with the loss of ignorance came a certain appreciation and respect for the parts of themselves that their tail kept otherwise hidden and protected.

Nevermind, what that part of him would do to *her*.

Poe surely knew it.

Her focus went back to whatever she could find on various makeshift shelves and in piles on the damp floor. He chuckled as he headed for the bed where a crumpled blanket, a quilt of many colors, laid along the sloped edge. Plucking it up, he fanned it wide to wrap around Poe as he came up behind her.

"Here," he told her as she turned to face him.

"I'm not cold," she replied, eyeing the quilt.

"No, nervous, I think."

Her gaze snapped up to his.

The quilt created a barrier between them, a curtain of privacy, of sorts, which was not his intention, but it did make it easier for Poe to hold his stare. Not that it helped at all with the pink coloring her cheeks and flushing her chest.

Her hand flew up to snatch the quilt and pull it lower between them when she said, without flinching, "I'm not nervous, either."

Yes, she was.

The difference?

Poe knew, in her heart, that she had nothing to fear from the man standing across from her. Tak could be a lot of things, but a monster was not one of them. Not when it came to her.

So be it.

Tak flung the quilt wide, then, billowing it out behind Poe so that when he pulled it tight, it hugged her back and yanked her straight into his naked body. Skin to skin, still wet from the seas, and hidden in the cocoon of his making, Poe stared up at him through her dark lashes. His greatest temptation personified.

Just waiting for him to take.

"So, you will teach me to read, then?" she asked.

"I'm going to teach you a great many things, heart of my seas."

Her lips curved upwards, pleased. Those arms of hers that she had tucked against his chest unfolded and moved down without a word from her to explain what she planned to do. Tak soon learned when her smooth palms found his soft cock, one tight above the other, to stroke and tug him awake.

"Tonight?" Poe asked.

"I honestly hadn't even planned on even getting out of the damn water but—" Tak's words died on his tongue when he groaned thickly, a long echo of her name, as the tip of her thumb found the head of his cock to circle. "Who taught you that?"

Poe grinned. "Finish your sentence first."

Indignant, but broken, air passed his lips instead.

"*Poe*, Gods—do that again. Harder."

She did, looking very pleased.

Air cut through his lips in a hiss when she tightened her grip a bit on the next stroke, making his knees weak. She earned herself another of his moans for that one. Well deserved, truly.

"Like that?"

"'Tis perfect, my love."

She was perfect.

"No one taught me," she admitted, leaning forward for her lips to find the patch of scales that followed the contours of his chest down, even in this form. She kissed a burning path down his skin, leaving Tak holding the quilt high and staring at the sight beneath him as she knelt, too. Down she went, lower until her knees pressed into cold stone, and she was eye level with her hands, and his hard cock, thick enough that her fingers couldn't close around the shaft now. "But I'm allowed to touch you, too."

"Yes, you are," he assured through a hard swallow.

"And women whisper," Poe added quieter, her breath ghosting along his shaft. He chanced another glance down to find her enraptured by her hands wrapped around his cock, her pupils blown wide with lust. Would he find her wet? Slick and hot and *so wet* for him if he reached down to check that spot between her thighs? Tak didn't.

Not yet.

He couldn't.

That still had to be on her.

"You didn't finish what you were saying," Poe pointed out ever so sweetly, her lashes fluttering up.

Oh, Gods.

"What was it?" Tak tried to remember, even closing his eyes to try to rid the vision of her pouting lips terribly close to his cock.

She took that moment to swallow him, actually.

He didn't get his answer, although he was sure it had something to do with the water, but what did it honestly matter now? Not for one second had he considered tonight would be the one when Poe allowed him these sorts of privileges with her, but he was helpless to do anything but mercifully hand himself over to her.

However she wanted him.

The wet, silken seam of her lips engulfed his shaft, and the sound that vibrated from her throat, a muffled moan at the taste of him, sent violent shivers racing down his spine. She kept one hand on his cock to pump him as she used her lips and tongue to learn the things that coaxed the noises from her companion, and Tak was happy to let her explore. Her other found his thigh clenched tight, flattening to the ridges of his muscles before her fingernails dug in when she took him impossibly deeper into her throat and swallowed.

Nope, that did it.

That and her eyes staring up at him as her nose nuzzled his skin. *That* made Tak lose it all.

"Swallow it," he told Poe who could no doubt feel the pulsing on the underside of his shaft.

She did.

Every drop of him, she drank it down.

Spill the first seed, forsake the pregnancy.

A lesson of their kind as old as time.

He had not considered that was Poe's intention when she had dropped to her knees in front of him until he thought about her admission—*women whisper*—and she finally released his cock with a grin, showing her teeth and tongue to him. Next time, he'd paint her lips and neck. After that, a new part. Her ass, perhaps.

He made many plans.

"All gone, my lord."

He did not mind the bastardly title nearly as much when she said it like that.

Tak's throat bobbed from another hard swallow, and he remembered what it was that his mind had lost in the process of this woman making him weak in the knees. He hadn't planned to get out of the water. This night was never meant to go this far.

It still didn't have to continue.

"Poe, are we ending our night here or—"

The shake of her head, making red ringlets stick to her shoulders, answered him as she stood. His arms found her shoulders, cloaking her with the quilt again in a cocoon, while soft grazes of her fingers continued to explore the part of him that ached again. Painfully. She sought his mouth for a tender kiss, and then a harder, deeper one that made Tak sigh shakily against her pillowy pout that still tasted of him.

Of his *seed*.

"Tis what I want," she told him, her tone reassuring to him and sure to herself, although soft. "*You*. All of you. I want what is mine."

And so, she would have it.

The part of him he had been keeping just below the surface, lest he push them too far, came out to play with Poe when he cupped her face between the ends of the quilt in his hands, stared into her eyes brimming with her own lust. His thumbs pressed against her lips, rapping once and then twice as he closed his eyes, rocked them both, and tried to make a choice. He felt her smile against his skin.

"Please," he heard her breathe against his thumb pads.

Their noses nuzzled between pecks of their lips, another nod from her to tell him that it was okay, and Tak let it go.

He'd done it as she wanted.

She wanted *him* now.

"I'll eat the taste of me out of you when we're done," he promised her. "Yours, *mine*—the blood. All of it. And you'll know what the heavens taste like, then, Poe. Straight from the mouth of *me*."

Poe's eyes flew wide at his words; at the implication. But when her gaze dropped to his lips again, the yearning flared in her eyes like never before. He started with that—kissing her with a force that could bruise, the force propelling Poe in the direction that Tak took them both. She needn't worry about tripping on his nest-turned-bed because he'd swept her into his arms at the ridge, stepping into the middle without even breaking their kiss.

She inched backward in the slope of the bed, on her elbows, curling her fingers for him to follow. And he did, on his knees, crawling to her like a man ready to worship.

Because he was.

"Open and show me all of you, Poe," he demanded when his hands found her trembling knees.

He no longer thought that was her nerves.

Excitement.

Desire.

Need.

Not fear, though.

Everything *but.*

He started at her pubic bone when she finally widened her thighs for him, sucking, kissing and biting on the spot until his mark was left behind. *Everyone* would know, then. Each one he left behind, the path trailing up over her navel, between her breasts, and then her neck until he stopped at the spot behind her ear, every mark would tell them all.

She *was* a woman now.

His.

She mewled and gasped, her body arching against him the longer and harder he sucked on the spot behind her ear. Then, his teeth found the tender spot just to leave it *blue.*

"*Tak,*" Poe managed to get out.

The whole time, he'd felt her hands between them, exploring her sex and relieving the ache that had to be deep there. The wet sounds of her fingers finding paradise had him sucking in air through his clenched teeth. The smell of her, tart and hot and untouched coated the cavernous space until it was every breath that he dragged in.

"Remember how that bit of sting just helped your ache, Princess," he murmured in Poe's ear as she finally found her first orgasm under her own hands, melting into the softness beneath her.

Lips parted, eyes heavy, she watched him slowly loom high over her, shoulders rolling side to side as he looked down.

"It will always be good," he promised. "I will always make you feel as you do just now—limbless and sated."

"Will you?"

"Even when it hurts, my love."

And it would.

This time.

Sometimes.

"And I promise you'll like it even then, too," Tak added lower, dropping down to kiss her quivering lips. "Now, turn over. I have an idea."

He helped her, spinning Poe in the bed so that her knees rested against the sloped wall of the bed, and her arms could lean over the side. Over her shoulder, she watched him fit in behind her, kissing along the line of her shoulders until her mouth was against his own again. He let her lose herself in the lashing of their tongues as he tucked one of her hands in his and directed it between her thighs. The first touch of her cum, slick against his fingertips, coated both their fingers. Using one of hers, and one of his own, he rubbed hard circles into her clit as he swallowed every desperate moan and plead that she tried to release with kiss after kiss.

And then he took her.

Fitting his cock against her from behind, guiding himself with the hand she hadn't concerned herself with until she felt him pressing there. 'Twas better done fast, lost in pleasure, but the flare of her eyes told him that she knew it was coming.

Good.

He wanted her to.

The tight heat that engulfed Tak's cock was like no other. He'd taken lovers—his loneliness didn't need to extend quite that far, at least, not all the time. None of them had ripped the breath out of his lungs the way the first flex of his hips did sending his cock home. That's what she was.

Home.

Instinctually, instantly, Poe tried to pull away. Too full, no doubt, and stretched with him as he settled in deep, a cry like no other fled her. Hitching at the end, and piercing to his heart, it bounced off the walls and reverberated back to them.

"Easy," he shushed against her shaking shoulder, holding her tight to the stop with an arm locked around her waist. "Moving won't make it better."

Her fingers had stilled between her legs, but his did not. He slowed the intensity to something he hoped would be more pleasurable, and the drop of her head over the edge of the bed told him that it was. Tak could not understand how his balls already felt like they were back in his throat with another orgasm threatening to humiliate him before he had even made his good again for her, but goddamn, he hoped it was always like that for them.

"Gods, your cunt is squeezing me so hard I can't breathe," Tak grunted against Poe's shoulder.

She couldn't talk.

That beat of his fingers, circling tight circles against wet, swollen flesh had served its purpose. As the release barreled toward her, he felt it in the squeeze of him inside her and the trembling in her thighs. Even had she fell into bliss suddenly, her noises gave it away. By the time she chased the wave of pleasure again, she had started to rock against him.

"Tak! *Gods* ..."

Her moan faded into something longer, more primal, when he answered her orgasm, and the movement of her body, with the snap of his own hips. Back and forth, slow but deep. Until that noise of her was muffled against the edge of the bed, and her arms hung limply over the edge.

What he could hear?

A guttural, pleased, "*Yes.*"

Pain changed pleasure.

One simply had to appreciate it.

All it took was Tak lifting higher from Poe, using one hand to hold her back and lower half against the sloped wall, and he could see himself coming out glistening and tinged violet with the maidenhead of the woman who would be his mate. All sense was lost to him, then.

Entirely.

Her last hiss of pleasure laced pain milked him into release like the walls of her pussy hugging around him impossibly tight. One last thrust found him deep, he held her there for every last drop of seed that came from him. Tak still couldn't talk, breathe, or think when he, sadly, pulled himself from Poe and turned her over. He didn't think her hands fell crossed over her breasts to hide them from him, but because she could do nothing else with them for the moment.

He panted heavily.

Legs still open for him, so did she.

"I wanted a man who knew how to be a lover," Poe whispered.

"You got him."

Her next breath came out wet and heavy.

Tak made good on his other promise, then, starting that path of kisses back down where he could eat. Poe, unashamed and starting to grin again, pushed up to her elbows to watch him.

Later, with her nestled and napping under Tak's arm, he forced himself to leave the princess at the sound of a familiar clicking. Coming from under the water and outside the grotto, he heard Poe call for him just before he dived under the sea. At his door, so to speak, he found the guards waiting.

"Did you show the king the net?" he asked.

The look shared between the guards told him exactly what the king had thought of that.

"He told us to get it out of his sight, my lord."

Gods.

Zale would kill them all, surely.

"The princess and I will be out shortly," Tak told the two before returning inside the grotto. A lie that he had no intention of following through.

He found Poe awake and peering over the nest edge at him when he surfaced, pulled himself up, and exhaled his last sea breath.

"Are you taking me back?" she asked.

"Perhaps, they think I am. Let them go beyond the net," he returned frankly. "I'll take you back to the palace when you're ready. Did you want me to read?"

"Oh, yes, please." Poe preened, but then scowled at him playfully. "You are taking me back, yes?"

"Of course."

Still bruised and loved by him, it would *be* a swim for her. One he would gladly, and proudly, follow her on. Many had done it before her, and many would after her. Like their mating, these things had been done and seen between their kind for many, *many* centuries. He'd heard rumors that women on land could be ruined by the whisper of men who even suggested about the things she did in private with a lover.

A shame, really.

Their people?

The journey into adulthood, including sex and its discovery, was celebrated. Usually. When done appropriately.

Tak went for one of the shelves on the wall and grabbed two things. Although they both looked the same except for the color of the covers. Books. One gold with the embossed outline of a landwalker on the front, or … a halfling, considering the apt title.

The other had no words, just a leather top that he flipped open after setting the other book aside. Poe leaned up to see what was so important inside the other book that he brought from the shelf, but the pucker of her brow had him laughing at her surprise.

He'd hollowed out the middle.

Inside sat a band of gold, topped by a crown pearl.

"Oh," Poe whispered softly. "'Tis very pretty."

"'Tis yours," Tak said, pulling the ring from the hiding spot where it had waited for many, many years. Once upon a time, he'd thought this day would never come. That he wouldn't want it to, actually.

Then, came Poe.

The heart of his broken seas.

"'Tis yours," Tak repeated as he found the band fit perfectly on the middle finger of her right hand. The first one he tried. "A gift from my mother. For you."

She had to have questions, knowing that he truly had no mother for quite a long time, long since considered an orphan. He appreciated that she didn't ask.

Somethings … Tak may never be ready.

Poe's gaze dropped to the ring, and Tak leaned down to kiss and nuzzle the side of her cheek, adding, "I will be honored to be your mate, Poe. To share the blood."

When he stood straight again, tears had stained her cheeks. He used his thumbs to wipe them away before bending down to kiss what remained smeared to her lips.

"You are mine," she whispered.

Tak nodded back. "I am yours."

10. THE MATES

34 days later …

Zale, King of the Blu Seas

"The very delight of the court," Zale's mate said from her seat to his right, beside his ornate throne.

Zale looked up from the raw fish he'd been sawing into to find where Rosel's attention had traveled. It wasn't hard to figure out. The entire room couldn't look away from the pair dancing to the music provided by the king's court. The princess only had eyes for the guard. Tak, well, he smiled.

Actually smiled.

"Tis a sight," Zale agreed, but then his eyes narrowed at something else on his daughter the closer she spun toward the king.

He tried not to fixate on the teeth marks peeking out on Poe's nape every time she twirled and her red hair flew wide, but alas …

"Am I going to need to speak to the guard about minding the look of the princess?" he asked Rosel quietly, careful not to bring the other two people at their table into the conversation. Arelle, nearing her seventeenth year, and Coral, who would only soon take to the land, were not ready for the ways between men and women.

"Perhaps," his mate returned softly, "you should mind your own thoughts, my King."

Zale's head snapped her way. "What did you just say to me?"

Even as kindly, and respectfully, as she had offered the statement to him, it was so unlike Rosel to speak against something Zale said that he just couldn't wrap his mind around that it had even just happened. Even though it did.

Even though he heard it himself.

He just could not.

Rosel's gaze flitted away to find the delight of their colony still dancing much to the pleasure of the packed dining hall that acted as a ballroom, when required. A clap spread throughout the merpeople, hands and fins slapping to the beat as Poe and Tak circled one another closer and closer, stares locked as Poe grinned and showed him her tongue … almost, *playfully*. The teasing sneer Tak offered her back before he captured her in his arms to take them another round around the court at the loud cheer of the watching crowd made it appear as if the guard saw no other but the one before him.

Never, *ever*, would Poe have behaved the way she just did—silly and carefree—until the merman opposite her. Something about the guard softened Zale's daughter in a way that didn't go unnoticed. By anyone, really. Instantly, it was as if her choice to pick the mate of her desires and make the bond aged her a decade in maturity, frighteningly.

Zale almost didn't recognize her.

Or Tak, even.

Playful, he was not.

Serious, severe, and insufferable to the bitter end, yes. Tak didn't, however, dance, not since he was a boy, and he certainly didn't take long swims with a merwoman at his side around the colony regularly. He didn't do a lot of the things he did now … after Poe.

One had not just changed the other.

It went both ways.

"Are you going to explain what you just said to me?" Zale asked Rosel, still tempering his tone to mind the children not too far away.

As if the one wasn't already asking to see the matings that year. *Gods.* Girls were the punishment for all his wrongs, Zale was sure of it.

"Need I?" Rosel returned.

"*Ros*—"

"Are you trying to make everyone look at us?" his mate asked, smiling and waving when the group closest to their table heard the king's voice raise and turned their way. Eventually, the lords and their ladies went back to the better entertainment.

"You accepted Poe's right to pick a mate of her choosing, made them wait far longer than any other for their witnessed courtship, and then you granted the lord permission to take his privacy with the princess. She is of age, Zale," Rose murmured, finally looking back to him, but now with a fire in her eyes that warned him to mind it. "She is a woman—in less than thirty days, she will be *his* mate."

"I know what that means."

"Do you?"

"Yes, I—"

"My King, if you think to control the princess and her guard after the blood is shared, and the bond is done the way you do the rest of the people in this colony, I warn you, consequences could be dire. There are some things, things that cannot even be made laws because the Gods have touched them, that you should not breach."

Zale's teeth clenched hard as he swallowed against snapping at Rosel for her audacity to interrupt him. Even if her warning had been due.

"She is as good as his, now, Zale," his mate reminded him, as if he needed it. Well, perhaps, he had. "If it were any other woman in this colony, she would not even remain with her parents until the mating happened. Perhaps, *that* is his way of accepting there is still a pretense for the three of you to maintain. She is still here."

"You think?"

Rosel's delicate shoulders, bare but for the jewels she wore around her neck and in her hair to cover her breasts. "I do. And of what's bothered you," she added, her gaze traveling to Poe and taking his own with it.

The two had stopped dancing to share a kiss, a mostly appropriate one, now that the music had stopped. However, the bite mark was visible again from the way the lord's hand swept back Poe's hair to cradle her head in his large hand. As if he wanted the room to see.

Any man *would.*

"What of it?" Zale asked, although he had a feeling about what she might say.

"'Tis not of your concern what a grown woman consents to, privately, with her chosen one."

"Even if that woman is my daughter?"

Rosel arched one brow in challenge. "Even then. The guard needn't mind his desires, only what Poe likes, for that matter, but you certainly could do some minding of your own in that regard, my King. She is already as good as his," Rosel repeated, glancing over at him once more with softness in her eyes now. "To the court, she is. To her, she is. To him—"

"I get it."

Well, then …

Never had Zale ever been put in his place, by his mate no less, quite so simply. Of course, Rosel did make good points, and she wasn't wrong about any of it. Not that he particularly liked the entire situation, but he stuffed down the urge to call the guard for a discussion later, or even, take away his privileges with the princess. As it was, Zale probably pushed that line a lot making the merman wait until this very evening to even allow him a full night away from the palace with Poe, but Zale had to do *something.*

What he could, anyway.

As his mate said, bond or not, perhaps Zale should not test that beast too much lest it bite him right in the ass.

The two were … *close.*

Bonded without the shared blood.

He just didn't know why.

Perhaps, that was the problem.

Zale had started to lose his friend.

"Does it feel the same, Father?" Arelle asked to his right.

Zale leaned that way to converse with one of two of his daughters who usually didn't care to be in his presence most of the time. Kingly duties, a lack of want to be a parent to young, and the need for an heir put him in the position he found himself with his children. Some, he fared better. Others, not so much.

"What, Princess?"

"Poe. And Sarha. Does it feel the same to watch another go?"

Zale had not expected that.

He wasn't at all ready.

Arelle knew it if the way she arched a red eyebrow at him was any indication.

"It does not," he admitted truthfully after clearing his throat.

"Poe is happy."

"Sarha was, too," the king reminded the princess.

Arelle nodded. "For different reasons. One couldn't stand to stay, the other couldn't consider leaving."

"Tis more than that, child," Zale told her, almost warningly.

Arelle didn't behave as if she'd heard it. "Is it?"

"These are not discussions for you, anyway."

"No, nothing is, I suppose," the princess muttered. "Is it true you've already picked my mate? Do I not even get to *dream*?"

Ah, now the king understood.

All too well, really.

"Princess—"

Arelle's blazing violet gaze turned violently on her father. "Tis not fair. I wouldn't even have asked for the things you did for Poe. I didn't need tourneys, or great hunts, not feasts, or even the line of suitors, just—"

"What?" the king interrupted sharply. "What would *you* need, Arelle? Do you know what a kingdom needs? What our people need?"

"A choice," his daughter said quietly.

A little sadly, too.

"Just a choice, *maybe*."

Zale let out a heavy breath, eyeing the princess in the middle of the room who had started another dance at the encouragement of the court. "You will have what counts—the year to do as you please and settle things. He is a prince. A someday king. Of land *and* seas. A match that is far more than you could have hoped for, and you will not be one of many."

At that admission, Arelle glanced his way with furrowed brows.

"What do you mean?"

Damn him.

"Tis not important, what is, is that he is more than suitable, and out of his pick—which I'm sure would have made your possible choices look pitiful in comparison, mind—I was told that you were it."

Not once did his daughter ask him *who* had wanted her for a mate. Instead of what he expected from her, gratefulness for a good match, Arelle's brow puckered again. She still didn't look particularly happy.

Zale could fix that.

Sometimes.

"And I discussed it with your mother," he told her, noting the way Arelle perked up immensely at the comment.

"Did you, about what?"

Oh, she knew.

The girl had *not* stopped asking.

"We agreed you're at a respectable age to witness the matings this season," he told her.

The third princess squealed.

The other one, further down, scowled now.

"Not me?" Coral asked.

Zale sighed, loudly.

Girls.

They truly were his burden for every sin.

"'Tis not your season, child," someone nearby said for the king.

Thank the Gods.

Poe

29 days later ...

"Are you nervous, Princess?" one maiden asked.

"No."

"Are you excited?" her mother questioned, winking as she brushed through the tangles of Poe's hair one last time.

Poe hesitated. "Yes?"

Laughter filtered through the chambers at the way she posed the question. The many maidens who had gathered to link one interlocking piece of sea glass after another around her waist, a tradition as old as their time for the willingly hunted, by the women around her who had cared and helped her grow into her adulthood. Even her sister, Arelle, had been given her own piece of the sea glass chain to link onto the one that Poe's mate would attempt to break. Before long, Poe had a chain that went all the way around her waist, with extra length that hung down her tail.

"Giving him extra feet to catch me," she joked, rattling the chain of glass.

A different kind of laugh passed around the room, then. Huskier, maybe. More *knowing*.

All over again, Poe was reminded of why she answered the question with another one. She had long accepted that her hunt, sharing of the blood, and mating would be witnessed by anyone able to keep up with the princess and her guard—or those already waiting at the Beaches of Sand Pearls. Accepting that made nerves useless because she couldn't change how important this event truly was, and as it *was* her bond, let them see.

Let them all know.

"I'm just ready, I think," Poe said then, quietly.

Silencing the room entirely.

Her mother smiled softly. "'Tis your season, Poe. Your *time*."

It was.

It felt a little surreal now that the day—or stormy night, rather—had arrived. After this, her life would never be the same.

Poe welcomed it.

She craved it.

It wasn't long before the knock at the chamber doors took the princess, her kin, and the maidens on the long journey up from the belly of the palace. Guards headed the group that swam, cloaked or jeweled modestly in some way, behind a naked Poe. Other than the pearl ring on her index finger, that Tak would remove shortly before his hunt began, she wore nothing.

She would come into the bond with her chain and blood. He would come into it with a blade, and the same. The only thing between them left to share.

After it all, two became one.

The overall act of splitting skin and sharing blood could be done easily enough, and once done, the heat and instinct would do the rest. Then, the song between the pair would be heard forever. However, those of the Blu Seas had long observed the rite of hunting one's chosen and earned mate to make them share the blood. The same way one of their men might hunt down a beast to bring back to feed his family for a fortnight, they hunted their mate to create the bond that would continue until the end of their days.

After being kept from Tak for seven passes of the moons, his eyes were nailed to Poe before the palace doors had even opened to show her waiting and all he had to see through were the sea glass panels. Tradition demanded the pairing be separated for at least a half of a fortnight, during which they could not speak or see one another, and she felt the effect that had on Tak standing just a dozen swim strokes away from her. He couldn't take his eyes off Poe, and she bet he was looking for every mark, love bite, and bruise that he had left scattered over her body the last time he had fucked her before they forced the two into the customary separation, but they had all faded.

One by one, day after day.

He'd make up for it tonight, no doubt.

Poe had to keep her head down.

Until the hunt began, anyway.

It didn't matter, she still felt him watching her. Under her lashes, she found him restlessly pacing in the water as Tak toyed with the hooked sea glass dagger that he had asked her to give back to him for now. She had not understood why, but seeing him hold it, knowing *that* was the blade he had chosen for them, made Poe realize something else.

That day in the maze?

That was not when Tak had decided he wanted to continue their companionship, or when he agreed to share the blood with Poe. Nor was it that evening in the grotto. In the throne room, when she challenged his words of her unworthiness? Even he had said that was all a lie.

Tak gifted Poe that dagger the very same night that her father told him of her desire to have him as a companion, and mate. His first gift to her. He came to her chambers later, with permission, or so she was told, to thank her for honoring him with the choice to still refuse her later—an agreement between only them—and give her the dagger.

She bet … *knew*, really … that was when Tak decided.

Long before he ever told her.

He had truly believed that she would not want him at the end of it all. That they would not be standing where they were as if she hadn't dreamt of this from the first moment she realized she *could* choose.

As if he had not been the only, the very one, thing she wanted from the beginning.

Poe would gladly—again—prove Tak wrong.

The Master of the Hunt announced the princess as the king approached her from the front, blocking her vision of Tak the closer her father came, but she wasn't supposed to be looking, anyway. She didn't hear the crowd that called for their princess and hollered joyfully for the night ahead—'twas not just their mating, after all. Many others would find themselves bonded come morning, but it was only once Tak had successfully captured Poe that the others could also begin.

The king spared *no* expense.

Zale did the most to make everyone happy.

With the lottery added to the mix for those who wished to breed could enter to win permission from the king, it would be a greater year than their colony had seen in a long while. Poe made herself go back into the present moment instead of lingering on the thoughts that constantly chased her now about her father's decisions as the head of their kingdom.

Didn't she deserve this night?

Couldn't she go back to being the queen-in-waiting later?

"I am told this is as far as I am going this evening," the king said to Poe as he came to a stop in front of her.

"You needn't watch—"

"I need not, no," Zale agreed, chuckling. "I will hear more than enough about it to last me decades, I'm sure. Good luck, Daughter. I hear you'll need it."

At those words, Poe chanced a quick glance up as her father headed beyond her to where Rosel waited, maidens and her other daughters at the ready. They would be the first to set off the trail of those who would follow the princess and the guard.

Well, except Zale.

And of course, she still found Tak watching her.

Just now, more intently.

Was it almost time?

She couldn't remember—

"You have but a moment, my lord. I am counting," warned the Master of the Hunt.

If the merman's words irritated Tak, she couldn't tell. Already seemingly restless and on edge, he stalked toward her after handing his dagger off to a guard who swam forward to take it. He couldn't bring it forward with him yet.

He'd have to go back for it.

Poe continued to keep her head down—as she needed to—even as Tak came to stand in front of her, his breathing deep, but steady.

"Your ring, Princess?" he asked her, his tone dark and lovely.

It wrapped around her, promising wicked things.

Poe held out her hand, and Tak took his time pulling the pearl band from her middle finger, telling her as he did, "I've missed you."

"Terribly," she agreed softly.

Through her lashes, she caught his hint of a smile.

"The storms are heavy—it will be a hard swim," he warned.

She nodded once. "Still to the Beaches of Sand Pearls?"

"You better make it there. I think you'll look beautiful spread out against the sand, bleeding beneath me. Tis why I chose it. But I'm not opposed to dragging you out of the water, either, my mate."

They weren't that, yet.

Yet, they were.

In a way, she bet Tak did want her to be a worthy hunt, as many mermen before him did for the woman of their choosing. Yet, with his words, she also understood that how far she made it wouldn't matter to Tak in the end.

Perhaps, it never did.

He wanted her, regardless.

He'd take her from the seas, should he need to.

He loved her already.

There was no going back now.

A palace boy, one she recognized as a favorite of her father's, rushed forward to take the ring from Tak who didn't even look the young's way as he handed it off.

"Thank you, Coda," Tak murmured to the merboy who scurried off.

"When do I get it back?"

"The very moment you ask."

"Tis—"

Poe never got to ask her question.

The clash of sea glass cymbals had Tak spinning around in an instant, heading for his dagger. The roar of the colony filled the water at the same time Poe heard a familiar voice shout out behind her.

"*Go, Poe!*"

Her sister.

The only one who would be allowed to watch, should she so choose.

Those few seconds it would take Tak to reach his blade where he had been made to leave it in the hand of the guard was the only head start Poe had to use. Nothing else, and nothing less. She tried not to waste very many of them.

Tak would afford her none later.

If she won, it'd be fair.

He'd make her earn it, too.

Poe headed straight up, sending the people gathered down below whistling and calling out even more excitedly than before.

She heard Tak yell for her, as well. Louder to her than everyone else, somehow. Above the noise of all others, his echoed all around her.

"Tis always the slipstreams with you, Princess," he taunted her, laughing all the while. He wasn't wrong.

She didn't even look back.

Poe couldn't afford those lost seconds, either.

Tak had not lied about the strength of the storm as she found the slipstreams weaker with the crashing surface more violent than usual. The darkness saturated the waters around and in front of Poe, making it hard to see and even more difficult to navigate a route she had never raced. Oh, she had plenty of practice play-racing Tak over the period of their companionship, but never the intended trek of their final hunt.

He'd done that on purpose, surely.

By chance, if Tak meant for the confusion to thunder in Poe's heart and thrum through her veins as she sped up and headed for the bands of islands where their bond could begin, then he had succeeded. If anything, the thrill made it better for Poe. The spiking adrenaline pushed her harder in the water as chirps, whistles, and clicks echoed in the distance.

Well, all around, really.

She couldn't pay attention to whom she passed—or even where. The princess didn't have the time to answer any calls or wishes for good luck.

No, just the hunter at her back.

Tak.

"Aha, got you, Princess," she heard Tak say, very close behind her.

No, he didn't.

Almost, though.

She dropped, then. Diving low to come out of the slipstream without warning, and glancing up to see Tak's grasp miss the chain of sea glass trailing behind her by the barest graze of his fingertips, and he flipped and tumbled overhead. *He* felt the loss.

She heard it.

Poe reveled in her win, cackling at her trick.

"*Fuck*," he snarled. "Get back here!"

Her laughter answered him back, as breathless as it was.

"To the beaches, my lord," Poe called back to him, teasing him this time.

It was only fair.

His growl chased behind her as he righted himself to head in her direction again. She used the darkness of the water to her advantage while she still had it—who knew when, or if, the storms would clear, and the moonlight gave Tak a better chance of catching her—and headed deep in the sea, cutting downward in a spiral that moved her faster through the water than even the slipstreams.

Poe decided to remain as close to the seafloor as she could until the rocky bottom began to slope upward and turn *sandy*. If Tak had expected her to use the slipstream the entire time, than her ability to navigate her way from home to sands of pearls just by the silt she skimmed with her fingertips should keep her at least one step ahead of him.

So to speak.

What she knew took her forever to swim only felt like minutes, somehow. It was only then, as she felt the seafloor slope to say the belly was approaching land, that she chanced a look over her shoulder to discover nothing.

Darkness.

In the far distance, she could hear chirps.

Happy water shrieks.

But not—

Poe dared to slow down.

For only a *breath*.

"Eyes on the prize, Princess," Tak hissed in her ear as he barreled into the side of her, sending them both rolling up the slope of sandy silt.

She had made the mistake of looking for him—she should have known

141

he was always there whether she saw or heard him, it didn't matter. Tak, who would never take his eyes off his prized prey, likely saw her momentary loss of speed and attention in the water and struck.

A good hunter never hesitated.

"*No!*" Poe shrieked in disbelief.

Tak's husky, dark, and *pleased* laughter echoed all around them in the rolling, raging waters. His arms locked around her like bars as they continued tumbling along and through silt, creating a cloud that made it hard to breathe in the darkness.

"I can't believe I got you before you hit that fucking beach," she heard him mutter through satisfied, arrogant chuckles. The blaze of his gaze locked on hers to glow silver in the darkness.

It wasn't over yet.

Poe had not bled, or lost, *yet.*

'Twas her right, what she did next. To fight for it, to make him *earn* it. Tak wouldn't have wanted Poe to do it any other way—he'd tell her that himself later, when it wouldn't really matter at all. So, she felt no guilt about it.

None when she bit his lip so hard she tasted his blood and the shock of her sudden fight and threat caused Tak to make his only mistake. His arms let her go, and he'd never wrapped his tail around hers to begin with. Poe flipped backward out of the water, and her tail fin kicked him hard, sending more violet blood from Tak blooming in the water as he groaned in pain. In all the years she knew him, never had another made the merman bleed. She didn't wait around to see whether it was his nose, mouth, or both, bleeding.

She headed for the beaches.

With white sand as soft as pearls.

Tak's laughter, sinister in the best way, reverberated louder in the water than the clicks and hisses starting to get closer.

Poe realized how close she was to the surface, to the shores, because of the wave that caught her unexpectedly and threw her into the air when it rolled. She came back down into the water too fast to lose her sea breath, not that she wanted to, and dived as deeply as she could to get out of the strongest currents from the raging storm.

Doing so put her back in Tak's path, though.

Instantly.

This time when he rushed her against the seafloor, Poe had nowhere to go but wherever the two ended up after they finally stopped rolling. Hooked dagger in hand that he already started twisting into the chains of her belt of sea glass, he did not make the same mistake as last time. One hand held her throat, squeezing out her breath just the way she liked best, and the next rolling wave pulled them both out of the water, and gone was her sea breath. She only realized Tak was also walking, dragging her into shallower, sandier, water when the kicking of her legs embedded her heels into soft sand.

Her fight stopped all at once when, dagger in hand still woven into her chains, Tak lifted and dropped Poe hard to the beach where the water barely kissed. Her gills flared wide with a gasping, shuddering breath when his hand found her throat again, his triumphant smirk clouded her vision, and the chains bit painfully into her skin as he twisted the dagger again.

Bleeding from both his mouth and nose, he made rivulets of violet down her trembling flesh, from the valleys of her breasts down to where it pooled against sea glass and inside her navel.

He didn't look mad.

Not even hurt.

Just *hers*.

"*We did it*," she breathed, only now understanding how close they had both come to winning. But didn't they? After all, they were the prize.

"Well done," her lover murmured back.

It was the only softness that he allowed her that night, beyond his kisses, words, and the pleasure. Everything else about it mixed with pain. From the way Tak broke the chain of sea glass, turning unbreakable links fragile with braided pressure, the shards scattering wide and cutting them both to his knees that forced her legs so far apart that she whined. Still, he did not ease up.

Their blood changed the air, then. As droplets from above fell warm, wet, and purple into the wounds of hers below—everything blackened. The edges of her vision. The wet air in her lungs. There was no beach, or storm, or sky. No clicks and whistles or words. Even the sound of her own pleasure, when his hand found her throat and the other flattened to the smeared mess on her stomach, Tak drove himself home inside her for the first time in a week, and Poe heard nothing.

Air crackling, blood spattering. Wind screaming, seas spitting.

She heard nothing but him.

The bond began.

Her axis abruptly tilted.

All she saw were violet eyes.

"Well done, my Princess," he panted above her heavily.

His next thrust sent her jerking back, but also had her telling him, "*I'm yours.*"

"I know."

Time stood still for Poe, then. In an instant, irrevocably, Tak became the very song of her seas.

Arelle, Third Princess of the Blu Seas

"Well?" came the click of a worried merwoman beneath the seas. "Is it done?"

Arelle's head broke the surface of the choppy waters to find the storm had eased only enough for her to find the answer to her mother's question. Many, *many* yards away, on the beach, cradled in the arms of her mate who rocked and nuzzled her in shallow water, she found the answer.

"Tis done," Arelle whispered back from above.

Rosel would hear.

The queen always did.

"Is she okay?" Arelle asked the maiden who bobbed along the surface nearby. "Poe, I mean?"

She knew this had been what her sister wanted, the greatest of all her desires, probably more than anything else, but her soft crying carried over the stormy waters. Arelle could hear it, and likely, so could everyone else.

"Tis a lot," the maiden replied gently to the younger mergirl, apparently not yet ready to do the very same things that Poe had just done. "All of it, and at the end, you're not the same. Nothing will ever be the way it was again."

Arelle nodded. "That would be a lot, I suppose."

"Hmm, yes."

"Shall we get a start on rounding back for the others?" asked another maiden.

Arelle wouldn't get a say on whether she watched the other matings that evening, but honestly, she didn't care as she knew very well when it *was* her season, her time, it would not look like Poe's. It would not look like anyone's.

She took one glance back at her sister and the merman now holding her face, their stares connected as his lips moved with words Arelle could not hear. It was the way Poe looked back at her mate, though, that made Arelle's young heart ache.

She'd told her father she wanted a choice.

Really, she wanted to look at her mate like *that*. As her sister did just then, life forever different, but hopelessly happy and in love all the same.

She wanted to feel that.

Arelle knew she wouldn't.

11. SONG OF HER SEAS

Poe

A season later ...

The smack of bare feet and the splatter of water droplets against sandstone woke Poe in the grotto. One eye cracked open, and from the nested bed, she found the source of her broken slumber dropping three sea leather sacks, each sealed with braided cords wrapped many times around the neck to keep it shut. One bag, heavier than the others, knocked over a pile of books Poe had left sitting there to go back to.

Tak always let her choose which they read.

"Dammit," she heard him grunt under his breath.

"Hey," she muttered, unhappily.

Tak's head swung her way, and it was only then that she realized the amount of light illuminating the grotto cave from the hole up above. A bright, blue sky peeked out from beyond what she could see overhead, and her brows furrowed.

"Poe ..."

She instantly looked back at Tak.

At the watertight sacks.

At the sky, *again*.

"Did you go to the forbidden lands?" she asked.

She didn't actually need her mate to answer her question when the sight of him still wet from emerging out of the water and the sacks told her more than enough. And even if those didn't, something else hit her, then. The smell lingered on him despite the seas that had probably washed him the whole way home. It didn't matter. Poe knew her mate, and that strange something she smelled lingering in the air could come from nowhere else. Not even water could wash that scent away when it embedded itself into one's hair, the lines of their skin, and even in the very air they breathed.

She knew that smell well.

Fire.

Smoke.

"Did you burn something?" she asked, then.

Tak hid the sudden tremor rocking his left hand by scrubbing it down his jaw, but he never looked away from her. He wouldn't lie. "Two ships— a dock, too."

She had not expected him to deliver news like that so frankly. Unbothered, as if it wasn't at all a problem. When it was, in fact, a huge one because he left her sleeping, hearing the hum of his song even in her dreams where he lulled her nightly. The fact she hadn't heard him leave, felt him while he was gone all night, and only now woke up to his return said her mate had called to her all night, singing the song of her seas.

He wouldn't need to be next to her, then.

It would be like he already was.

"Tak!"

"Are we to behave as if you didn't take your sister to the bay before the storms ended to show her the—"

"During storms!" she shouted back at him, instantly enraged. Which was not at all the same thing that he just did—the risk was not even close.

Tak's gaze darted back over his shoulder, at the surface of settled water. "Lower your voice. The king's guards are still posted there from last night."

"Do they not question you when you come back?" she snapped at him.

Tak swung back around on her. "Not if they know what's fucking good for them."

Of course.

Tak went about unpacking the bags when Poe huffed, and turned herself away from him. She even went as far as to snag the quilt she had kicked off in the night to cover her nakedness from her mate—not allowing him the pleasure of seeing that, either, while she was mad at him.

"Needn't hide from me, tis pointless, my precious. I can picture your cunt with my eyes closed, Poe. I can fuck it and make it squeeze the life out of me with them shut, too, remember."

Ugh.

"Prick," she hissed beneath the blanket. "How could you do that?"

Something not nearly as heavy smacked against the cave floor, loudly.

"What?" he asked.

"How could you do that to me—convince me to sleep in your arms, use our tether to keep me feeling safe in sleep, just to leave the first moment you could?"

"Is that what it is?" he asked softly.

Poe pulled the blanket down to glare at nothing in particular. Definitely not the merman on the other side of the cave staring at her as if she had just offered him a lifeline. Tak despised it when the two fought, and let her know as much the first time they so much as argued about what to eat. The bond did not mean a pair wouldn't fight, or would suddenly find themselves in a constantly pleasant companionship for the rest of their long lives.

No, they were still people.

Each their own.

Sometimes, annoyingly so.

"And to go to the forbidden lands, too," she added after a moment, just to drive the point home. "Tis dangerous, but I know I do it, too."

Tak exhaled heavily. "I'm sorry. I—"

"At least tell me before."

Or should he?

Would she want to know why, instantly, that he wasn't there for her to wake up to some random morning?

"Will you tell me, then?" he returned, viciously.

The only source of true contention between the two was the fact that neither of them spoke, to promise or otherwise, to each other about the forbidden lands of Atlas. Not what either did while there, when they went, or anything else, really. Well, mostly.

But he did it far more than her. He went there more often than he should, and they both knew it.

"I thought you said you stopped looking," she whispered, then, sad again.

"Poe, good *Gods*," Tak uttered through clenched teeth.

She didn't even hear his footsteps across the cave before the pads of his fingertips found her hair to sink in deep. His lips found hers, and then the tip of her nose before he kissed a line across her forehead. Helpless to do anything but let her mate adore her and apologize the way he wanted to, she listened to his murmured words against her skin.

"I would not be looking in this season—for *anything*," he said, kissing her again.

Poe said nothing.

His thumb swept along her cheekbone, and then he kissed the same spot. "I cut nets in the narrow seas, burnt two ships near the bay, and a newer dock at the Isle of Broken Islands."

Her gaze tipped up to meet his. "Were there landwalkers on the ship?"

His hands tightened a bit on her face. "Yes."

"Oh, my—"

"Most sleeping," he interjected quickly, pressing another hard kiss to her mouth that quieted her. There, he whispered, "Whatever hunt they just planned ended last night, and you can't be mad at me for doing that, Poe. You *can't*."

He was right.

It still terrified her.

"Stop it," she muttered, pushing him away, then.

Tak let her go, but he watched her intently, his face darkened and shadowed, as he headed back for the sacks. Or, whatever he took out of them. "I did get some things."

"From the ships?"

He shrugged. "What I could, anyway."

She knew he wouldn't have had much time—from what she had managed to get him to tell her about his unspoken protection of their colony, there were always lookouts awake on the ships at night. However, if he could kill them first, and silently, that gave him a few moments before making the choice, and doing the deed, to sink the ship.

"You'll like this," he murmured, bending down and picking up a folded swath of soft looking silver fabric.

"Is that …?"

"A bolt of land silk. There were different flags on one of the ships. I think they'd done something with that recently. 'Tis the color you want for the cradle, isn't it?"

He held it out to her like a treat she could take, if she pleased. Poe eyed the bolt of precious fabric where it hovered, midair, between them. Briefly, her gaze darted to the corner of the cave, not far away from their bed, where the bones of their shark had finally taken form. He didn't hide it from her as he prepped and smoothed the bones, and then shaped the many ribs into a cradle that rocked by using braided leather to knot and wrap the joints where needed for support. She never hid her desire from him to be a mother, although they had been made to wait for permission from the king like everyone else in the colony, but Tak began their journey long before a baby could grow in the seas of her womb.

It took him months to make it, piece by careful piece. Lovingly constructed by hands and eyes that took his work seriously so that every inch was perfect—just as their child would be. Like her, and without him telling Poe as much, she knew that he loved their child that didn't even exist yet just as much as she.

Tak just showed it differently.

The teeth from the beast, however, remained untouched. Still hanging in the grotto corridor, in fact.

"Another surprise," Tak said.

But he didn't tell her what.

"Are you going to take it?" Tak asked her.

Poe didn't. "You didn't go scouting for ships and nets just to find something like this for me, did you?"

"It was happenstance, Poe. I swear it. Perhaps, the Gods are telling me with finding this that I am doing the right thing."

"Until they catch you."

"*If* they catch me," he replied.

She snatched the bolt from him, then, angrily, but she quickly tossed it aside. "If should not be an option, either."

She would not live on if he did not come back to her.

Poe could swear on it.

"Your father won't do it," Tak told her, returning to the sacks. "The guards, either. He orders them not to. What if the next is one of your sisters, a maiden, or—"

"This is why we cannot speak of it to each other, isn't it?" Poe asked, the tears starting to form and roll heavily down her cheeks. "Because we both know it's wrong for the other to go, but it's only selfishness that drives us to say it, and then we bicker endlessly."

"And still, we do. We go."

Yes, they did.

"I found you something else, too," Tak murmured, his tone lighting up with bemusement like she had never heard.

Poe dared to roll a bit in the bed to watch him pick up the sack he had not yet untied. The one out of the three left to unpack. It also moved rather suddenly when Tak held it up higher for her to see which made Poe sit up straighter in their bed.

"What is in that?"

"Something amazing," he replied, grinning. "I'm only giving it to you if you're no longer mad at me, though."

He still played a hard game.

Poe sighed, glancing away. "I guess."

"You *guess*?"

He stomped right back over to her to snatch her chin in his hand and pull her face toward his where he took the kiss from her lips. His right to, honestly. She pecked him back before he finally let go.

"I'm *mostly* not mad," Poe told him.

Tak crinkled his nose. "Good enough, I suppose. Here."

He dropped the sack in the nest with her, right between her crossed legs. The wiggling inside the leather, drawstring bag continued, making her stare warily at it without putting her hands anywhere near it.

"What is it?"

"Something else to love for a time," Tak replied. "Let her get your scent good before you open it up—they don't like men."

"They—*what*?"

What did he bring home to her?

"Silk and nets weren't the only thing on those godforsaken ships," Tak muttered, returning to the various items he'll pulled from the bags. Some oil, corked in a bottle, that would make lighting a fire easy. Flint, for sparks. His favorite hunting knife. Apparently, he hadn't found very much stuff to fill his sacks if he came back with mostly the same things he took when he left. "She must have been caught up in their nets. Tis a shame—she only needs a cave, really. She's the only kind in these seas that can walk great distances on the land. They're quite smart, and if you have time, you can even train them."

"She?"

"Males have pink underneath. The females are entirely black. Tis a deep violet, really, but you can't see that if she's not directly in the light."

"Underneath *what*?"

Tak grinned her way. "Their tentacles. Open the sack, my love."

Poe finally did.

An octopus, with a middle as round as Poe's head and as black as night, flew out of the sack. And promptly stuck all eight tentacles across Poe's chest and neck. She gasped at the gentle kiss of the creature's suckers pulling against her skin but it got no harder, certainly not painful, and the tentacles curling around her arms and neck didn't tighten much at all.

"See, she likes you already," Tak murmured, then.

Poe, still as a rock, laughed weakly. "And she doesn't like you?"

"She tried to stick her tentacle down my throat when I pulled her from the cage they had her in," he replied frankly. "She can rip out a man's tongue. They will bond to *women*. Only."

Blinking, Poe glanced down as the black octopus crawled down to the nest where it then proceeded to go straight up and over the edge. The last thing they saw of her was a curled tentacle before it disappeared under the surface of the water.

"Oh, no," Poe muttered.

"Tis okay, she'll know she's safe. She needs the cave, really."

Poe squinted his way. "For what?"

"Just a safe place. Are you going to give her a name?"

She smiled his way. "Perhaps."

"I'll have to watch her when I'm traveling in and out, now. She might get a tad mean. Your kind are territorial."

Poe laughed at the picture forming in her head of her mate, scared of a little octopus. "Our kind?"

"Females."

Well, he wasn't wrong.

"Sofian," she said, deciding on the name just like that.

"Goddess of Fertility—mother of young."

"Protector of mates," Poe added of the sea deity, one of the first of their kind to have swam their seas, or so the stories went, anyhow. "Queen of the Seas."

"Tis a good name, my mate," Tak told her, stepping close enough to bend down and capture another kiss. He groaned into it, making her moan. "Another," he demanded.

She gave it, too.

This one lingered, it *lasted*, and he let her pull him into the nest as their tongues and limbs tangled. Back where burnt ships and cut nets and cold beds didn't have to matter. Not when nothing separated them. Nothing but skin.

12. SISTERS OF THE SEA

Arelle

A season later ...

In the vast expanse of the Blu Seas, the water always matched the sky. It never failed, and it was what Arelle enjoyed the most as she skimmed along the surface of the water and followed her two sisters.

Poe led the pack—a year older than Arelle's eighteen, now—with Coral close behind and all too willing to hang off every word that left their older sister's lips.

What was it like to change, Arelle? Did you just know how to walk? Will I feel different?

Then, Coral had turned sixteen and the curse swimming through their blood took hold. She no longer needed to ask her sister those kinds of questions when she was able to experience them for herself. Instead, her questions turned on Poe. The only older sister who remained in their kingdom, and mated, that had experienced something she hadn't.

Arelle didn't take it to heart.

Mostly.

A storm was rolling in to batter the realm of Atlas, the Blu Seas surrounding it, and the small bands of islands throughout the seas where the three women currently called home, with their grottos safe from any hunters. Not that the storms would bother the sisters—it was the safest time for a mermaid to ... well, live. The air became wet. Travel for the landwalkers on Atlas turned dangerous. The sea, too rough for their ships and weapons and *nets*.

Not that Arelle, or the rest of her sisters, were supposed to know anything about the people who could only walk on land. Their ways and motives were only whispered about when they learned something new from someone else. Although, Poe would fill in blanks, when her younger sisters asked ... sometimes.

"Down we go," Poe said when bubbles burst in a small swirling pool. The only sign that beneath the dark waters of the churning sea there was a small enclave that led into her sister's grotto. An underwater haven, private to Poe and her mate, made up from the remnants of a sunken ship, and the cave carved from one of the rocky islands above. Another entrance to the grotto waited behind the curtain of a waterfall but the sisters couldn't use it to swim through like this one. In fact, they'd have to climb very sharp rocks, so truly, it wasn't really an entrance at all. "And then, Coral, I will tell you all about the mating."

Coral let out a happy chirp—one that even underwater, her sisters would understand to be a pleased *yes*. Poe dove under the water first, the shimmer of the green-blue scales with similar markings to Arelle's on her tail and fins, slapping the surface before she disappeared into the rolling, black sea.

"You're coming, yes?" Coral asked Arelle, her excitement vibrating in the water. "You can't go back to the palace yet, Arelle."

It wasn't very long ago that Arelle, herself, had asked these same never-ending questions, pestering any and everyone who cared to listen. Or rather, whoever would listen and indulge her. 'Twas only fair to let it be Coral's turn. *Tis not your season.* Coral would likely hear those words far more than enough in the coming year just as Arelle had, and so, because she didn't think it would hurt …

Well, she simply couldn't tell her sister no.

"Yes?" Coral asked again.

She smiled, struck by despite how young Coral was, even if she was only a year younger than Arelle, they still seemed like mirrors of each other. The same vibrant, fire-colored hair plastered to dainty features and cherry-red lips. People in their colony called the sisters of the Blu Seas the most beautiful. The golden sisters.

Sirens of the water with wide violet eyes framed by long, dark lashes. Full lips shaped like bows that sang tempting songs capable of sinking ships, drawing in men, and even the sea creatures if they needed. Faces round like the sun when it dared to peek through the clouds, temples spattered with speckles of sparkling scales and olive-toned skin that glimmered like gold in the water.

As if that wasn't enough to say the three were sisters—their fourth sister, the oldest, Sarha, as good as mated and gone from the realm, shared their same, distinct features—the burned scar on the back of their left hand certainly did. Two arrows, one atop the other, crossed. The sign of royalty.

Royals of the Blu Seas.

"Arelle, yes or no?"

"I'm coming," she assured her sister.

Another happy chirp came from Coral before the girl darted closer to the spot where Poe had disappeared moments before.

Arelle peeked over her shoulder to look for the guards the king constantly sent to watch them. The three mermen, imposing in their stature with spears at the ready, all lined up shoulder to shoulder with a watchful eye on her, waited for when she would head under the water to the grotto. At least they stayed far enough back that the sisters' conversation remained private. That probably had a lot to do with Poe's mate overseeing the entirety of the guard. It allowed the young merwomen a bit of privilege.

Or as her father might say, just enough rope to hang oneself with.

Coral slipped under the water, then. Arelle didn't hesitate to follow, spiraling down twenty feet deep into dark water in mere seconds until the broken bow of a sunken ship came into view and she slipped within the hole, careful not to touch the jagged edges of the broken wood. The ship had sunk decades ago, much like the others surrounding the dangerous Atlas Islands. The nearby regions provided safe shelter to many mermaids in their colony.

Homes where the landwalkers couldn't touch. Not without endangering themselves, too.

A few feet ahead of her, Coral was quick to hang her twisted crown of sea glass on a piece of wood that stuck out from the wall of the ship, and Arelle did the same with her own. They ducked low to avoid the hanging netting their older sister's mate used as a warning to anyone who entered his grotto. Skulls bunched like lumpy balls in a low-hanging net; a morbid decoration Arelle had never quite gained the courage to ask about.

At least, not entirely.

Who did the skulls belong to?

Their kind?

The landwalkers?

Both?

They looked so much alike—when they weren't in the water, of course—that Arelle thought it would probably be difficult to tell the difference between their skulls.

"Wish he'd take that down," Coral muttered, quickly looking away from the netting full of skulls. "It's unsettling."

Yes, much like the rest of the grotto. A dark black from the walls of stone the home had been carved into just beyond the sunken ship, with bones as decoration and glowing fish trapped in overturned glass bowls to provide a little bit of light. The water in the grotto tasted of her sister and Poe's mate as it passed Arelle's lips and she exhaled through the gills in her throat.

She didn't have one of those yet—a mate, that was. Although with her eighteenth year passed, it was only a matter of time. Her suitor had already been chosen a long time ago, his travel to her finally underway, and once he arrived, she too would find herself in a situation similar to her older sister. Only unlike Poe, Arelle would not be staying in this kingdom—she would leave with her mate to return to his homelands.

It wasn't that which bothered her. It was everything that had to come before. All the things that wouldn't be.

Coral shrieked as the black-purple octopus Poe seemed to like so much flicked a sticky tentacle a little too close to her face when they passed by its small den before entering the largest portion of their sister's grotto. "It feels dark and ... where is the color or the pretty things, Arelle? Where is *Poe?*"

Arelle laughed softly, saying quietly so the sister in question wouldn't hear, "Can't you taste her in the water? *Everywhere*, Coral. She's everywhere."

These things. This place.

All of it.

"It's just as much hers," Arelle said, refusing to fill in other blanks for Coral. On those subjects, like the bond between mates and the complexities of a relationship involving private, individual people, her sister would have to help herself. "Besides, consider, Tak leads Father's guard but also spends his time hunting creatures in the sea, and you think he wouldn't have a penchant for all things malevolent? The man doesn't go anywhere without something sharp in his hand."

Or very near to his back. She noticed he didn't carry his sword as much as he used to, though, instead opting for sharp knives and daggers. Often, belts of them.

Her sister chuffed but didn't reply.

In the water, they only used their mother tongue. A language made up of noises produced from their throats that traveled even in the choppiest of seas; one the humans hadn't learned, despite how easily the mermaids absorbed their language and ways.

"Could always go back to the palace if you don't like my grotto," Poe said as the two entered the largest section of the underwater cave.

The cave reached so high under the island that, at the very top, a hole big enough for two allowed them a view of dribbling water and a rocky ledge.

Arelle didn't want to go back to the palace but she wouldn't tell her sisters that fact. There was nothing waiting for her there. Except, perhaps, the suffocating control of her father, and a court that couldn't seem to look away whenever she was in view. Her season had finally arrived, after all.

Poe didn't give the two a chance to respond before she lifted herself to sit on the ledge. What seawater remained in her lungs exasperated in her next exhale, sliding down from the gills at her throat and over her breasts, which were covered by the long length of her hair and a draping necklace made of jewels and shells. Just like that, with her first breath of air instead of water, her sister's shimmering scales disappeared by the churning water where she rested her tail.

Gone was her fin and the blue-green scales. All the black markings.

In its place were her sister's very human legs and bare feet. Poe stood from the edge, walking to sit where she kept all her favorite things in her grotto. Arelle followed suit, pulling herself out of the water at the rocky ledge and letting the curse—although some of their kind believed it to be magic—take hold and change her, too. Despite how it looked to see her scales melt away into legs and feet, it never felt like anything more than a tickle racing over her skin and through her blood. The first few times were painful, but after? Nothing.

Coral, on the other hand, stayed skimming the surface. Arelle passed her a look, shaking her head at the same time and asking, "How are you ever going to be comfortable on your legs if you don't use them?"

"I use them," Coral replied.

A bit too defensively, really.

"Not nearly enough," Poe muttered when she picked up an old, leather-bound book from the floor. She flipped through the pages, clearly knowing where she had left off. Arelle often wondered how her sister managed to get books, not to mention, keep them from getting ruined in the very damp, earth-smelling grotto. Besides that, how had she even learned to read? But the fact that her sisters didn't tell their father that Poe had items from the forbidden lands was the only reason why she allowed them into her grotto at all. "Yet, you want to take to land every other day."

"I just—"

"Need to learn to use your legs. What if you need to run?"

Coral quieted.

Arelle dropped next to her sister's seat, enjoying the smooth, cold rock against her skin. As naked as the day she slipped from her mother's womb, she stared up into the hole of black overhead, considering the storms again.

"How long do you think the storm season will last this year?" she asked.

Poe grinned slyly.

Out of all of her sisters, Poe could be the most dangerous, Arelle thought. Calculating, always able to say the right thing, and capable of great violence when she knew she could get away with it. Beautiful, too, and the only one of Arelle's sisters who had been able to pick her own mate—a merman who was just as prone to enjoying the darker things as she was.

"Long enough, I hope," Poe replied.

"For what?" Coral asked.

"I'd like a child this season."

That silenced the grotto but for the constant *drip drip drip* of water.

"Will Father—"

Poe's stare cut to Coral, stopping her from asking more. "I've been mated for a year—why wouldn't he allow me to have a child this season? Tis my right to continue my line when I choose, and I think he wouldn't argue it if need be."

She had a point.

Not that it would make a difference to their father. As king, Zale made all the choices for the people in his underwater kingdom. Because when even getting pregnant required them to change and leave the sea where they were most vulnerable, although birth could happen in either form … Nonetheless, it was a risk. Not to mention, having young meant his people would protect them more than even him or themselves.

"I just don't understand," Coral muttered, her cheeks pinking when her sisters' attention turned on her. "I'm not allowed to ask."

Ah, yes.

Not even the king's children, or his mate for that matter, were exempt from his control. The girls spent less time with their mother as they got older, maidens stepping in where Zale demanded Rosel stay away. As for them, their father believed the less they knew about the ways of their people and their traditions the less they'd want to be included, or so Arelle thought.

That was never the case. He'd not yet learned.

Coral, ever curious, had no understanding of mating although she would gain a companion in the coming years to teach her everything. Except she wanted to know now.

"How does it ... work?" Coral asked.

"Which?" Poe replied.

"Sex."

Coral promptly turned as red as the hair on their heads. She wouldn't even meet their stare, was far more interested in making circles in the water with her fingertip, and even bobbed beneath the surface as if she were taking another sea breath.

"Anyone can fuck," Poe said, sighing. "Fucking is just that—fucking. A bit different with your tail than in your walking form, but you should know about that, don't you? Your cleft, Coral ..."

Their stares turned on their youngest sister, who still didn't seem to want to look back at them. Coral might be the most curious, but she was also the one who wasn't at all ready to be grown.

Arelle decided to give the girl an easy out for this side of the conversation. Only because she didn't think Coral understood anything about sex as a merwoman because her younger sister hadn't yet had sex or a true desire to have it. "You'll learn soon. A companion will be picked to teach you everything. It'll come easy."

Poe sighed. "But if you want a child ..."

"We can only conceive when we're like this," Arelle added when her older sister didn't elaborate, waving at her naked legs. "And when we give birth, too. The curse, again."

Beside her, Poe laughed a tinkling sound. "A curse—doesn't feel like that when the thrall comes, the heat begins, and the bond starts. The magic that gives us the bond also gives us the pain"

"And how does that work?" Coral asked, at least managing not to squeak with her embarrassment that time.

Arelle allowed Poe to answer, knowing good and well she didn't have the firsthand experience to give Coral.

"It's ..." Poe's gaze darted to Coral, and then to Arelle before going back to the book in her hands. "It's instinctual, a need in your blood, Coral, and when it is your time, you will know what to do. That's all I can tell you now."

Coral's fingers danced along the rocky ledge of the grotto. "So, when the storms come, we take to land."

"Right, Coral." Poe nodded. "We have to take to land."

"Where the landwalkers are."

"Not always. The storms scare them. They're not like us—they die in the water."

"We die in the water sometimes," Coral pointed out. "Right?"

"But the water doesn't kill us when we can breathe in it. They can't."

"*Oh.*"

"Anyway," Poe said, flipping another page in her book, "I want a child this season. I'll have to ask if Father will allow me that. It'll make others want the same, which means, for one, that people will need to go to the land, but more importantly, that he'll have to do another lottery for those who desire young in the colony, and he might not like the idea so soon after the last. We had almost a dozen infants born since my mating."

"Tis a lot," Arelle whispered, knowing how that would fare for her sister's odds with Zale.

Not well at all.

Poe's mating had brought with it many other mated pairs during her season, and like her, those couples would undoubtedly want children. But their numbers were not great anymore. With each season, it seemed as though the landwalkers found more cunning ways to capture them. With children to protect, it made everything even more dangerous.

Their father wouldn't like that. Disobeying him—for anything—meant punishments sometimes worse than death. It was, after all, how he kept his people firmly in line. She learned that very early on in her life.

Arelle looked to Coral who had grown quiet, staring down at her nails, which she picked nervously.

"The landwalkers—they believe we're like this because we're magical. They're wrong. This has always been a curse," Arelle said, knowing her sister would understand she meant their shifting forms. "We're doomed to need the sea as desperately as we need the land to survive. And now that they've taken the safety of one from us, they're determined to take the other, too."

"Tis only a matter of time," Poe agreed softly, "before every single one of us in these seas are gone."

Because they were the hunted, and thought to be magical, their blood became a coveted resource. Arelle just thought they were doomed. Doomed to be the prey of those who walked on land.

Forever.

"Where is your mate?" Arelle asked Poe of Tak, the High Guard of their father's army.

"Hunting. I made him go—get away from the palace and do something he enjoys. I want to give him a surprise when he gets back. His favorite fruit, I think. He'll like that."

Arelle's brow lifted high. "Do you mean the fruit from—"

"The west side of Atlas, yes. The water orchard. Tis the only place it grows, now."

"You can't go there," Coral whispered. "It's forbidden."

Poe rolled her eyes. "Everything is forbidden, but only if others know you did it."

Arelle did smile at that. Poe wasn't wrong. Plus, if not for her sister, she would have never had the courage to go to those lands herself, even if she did stay in the water when she visited.

"I'll go with you to get the fruit," she told her older sister. "Tomorrow, when the court is distracted with Father?"

"It'll be the perfect time. The guards fall back with the others and tend to stay away. Easier to slip out, of course. And the storms are coming in and out so quickly as we approach the season that I doubt there are any ships left on the waters at all."

"I want to go, too," Coral spoke up.

She was back to that whine again.

The older sisters shared a look.

"She stays with you," Poe warned. "She doesn't understand anything. And I have other things to worry about than looking after her."

"Hey!"

They ignored Coral.

"She stays with me," Arelle agreed, and then she gave Coral another look. "That is, if she doesn't decide to stay."

What was the worst that could happen?

13. THE KING'S CLEVER WHORE

Anthia

"Ah, there you are."

Anthia dropped into a proper curtsey for the king at her arrival to his private chambers in the farthest wing of the lord and lady's orchard estate. His favorite place to visit at this time in the year when the season of harvesting the water fruit from the tall, knotty trees had practically come to an end, and as he would proclaim, the fruit tasted sweetest.

She just liked the peace.

Thankfully, she was also a welcomed guest, if not altogether ignored during parties and events, because her personal servitude to Misael allowed her such privileges. She tried not to take it for granted, but she also wished that he would let her settle somewhere without him for a while now that their son had grown into a man.

So far, no such luck.

"Here I am," Anthia returned sweetly. "You know I'm never too far away."

"Still a bit out of reach, though, no?"

She didn't return that question from the king with a proper answer, mostly because she didn't entirely understand what he meant. It could mean a lot of things. Many years with this man, however, had taught her that assuming things about Misael Bloodhurst could be a dangerous game with rarely any winners, so she probed at him first.

"Did you need something?" she asked.

Misael's careful expression crackled momentarily when she took a couple of steps into the room, watching the way she folded her hands against her middle. For a moment, the stoicism in his face faded for her to see the pining behind his eyes. He couldn't control it with her. He *tried*.

In all these years, that had never changed. He still wanted her, and now, he just wanted her in a different way. But alas, those days between them were long gone.

"I always need things from you, my love."

"Which things are we needing, specifically?" Anthia asked, letting her tone do the talking for her. She was not here to play a guessing game of words with him; they both had far better things to do, surely, given the guest who would be turning up anytime to begin the evening festivities.

"A woman that cares to converse with me, for one."

The sharpness in his voice couldn't be missed.

Anthia put on a smile for Misael. "Never have I ever not listened to every word that came out of your mouth, my King."

It was the truth.

Mostly.

Across the room in an ornate chair at the end of the bed where an estate boy helped the king to pull on and lace up his boots, Misael watched her in the same way he always did. Sharp eyes, an expression that told her just how well he knew she was lying, and then there was the sadness between them. Filling their constant and great divide. Nothing he had tried to do or say over the years—and her king had done a lot, even agreeing to send their son off the continent to another realm for two entire years at her request—closed that gap and filled the space with something, anything, different.

No, he hurt her.

Irreparably.

Misael proved that there was no limit to how far he would go. Not to hurt her. Not to make her stay. And she wasn't special in that regard, for certain. It did not matter if it was his child, a whore he loved, or the kingdom beneath his feet, if it served his own purpose, even taking his child's ability to breathe in water away, then so be it. He would do it, and the king didn't apologize for it, either.

Anthia never forgot those facts of her life, and because she couldn't, neither did the king. That was his burden to carry. Until the end of his days.

"Go," the king ordered the boy after his second boot was on.

"You don't want me to lace—"

"Get out *now!*" Misael snapped.

Anthia watched the boy scurry past her with a frown before she turned back on the king. "That wasn't at all nice. He was only trying to serve you, my lord."

"Off with his head, then, and yours," the king returned in jest.

Anthia arched a single eyebrow. "You wouldn't cut off my head, King."

"No," he admitted rather quickly, although not surprising, "it is still far too precious to me. I called for you before the night's events began to let you know that I made the head of the stable keep aware if you come out looking for my horse, that is his signal you are fine to head off alone to the orchard. If it pleases you."

Any other words died on her tongue. On the rarest of occasions, when they were in certain places where they had shared special moments and memories together, Misael sometimes allowed her time away. Atop a horse galloping along the edge of cliffs or through the forest somewhere, even with the collar around her throat, she could almost close her eyes and pretend to be free.

Almost.

And yet, not entirely.

Something—someone, really—else always called her back to where she needed to be. That thing calling her home was the only reason Misael trusted to let her go, too, knowing she wouldn't leave the remaining piece of her heart left behind with him: their son.

He didn't once try not to be a bastard. 9ine hells, he would say he was one himself. He was not beneath using their child as the tether to her, but because doing so meant having a hand in raising her son, even from afar for a good portion of his life and without any real say most times, that was priceless to her. No one else, no other mermaid to birth Misael a halfling of his blood and name, had been granted permission to exist alongside their child. Only Anthia.

In fact, he had even started taking the ones who got pregnant from the harem entirely. Where they went to carry their pregnancies and birth their children was anyone's guess, and not one she particularly wanted to hazard. Nor did she care to ask Misael.

A monster never minded being one, after all.

Nonetheless, for her son, she made the sacrifice willingly. Misael did allow her those privileges with Eryx.

Partly.

So, Misael still had her, or as much as she had left to give him, anyway.

"Oh, well, I thank you," she eventually said. "I hadn't considered a proper ride this evening when the crowd settles and isn't looking, but I might. Now."

"Would you ride with me?"

"*Well* ..."

The way she twisted the word said it all, surely.

"We used to do that here—remember the hammock between the orchard trees ... Oh, what was it we learned that night, my little queen?"

That quieted Anthia completely.

The king didn't miss it.

"I asked a question."

"I know you did," she replied softly, "but that was almost a year before you gave me my baby, and we both know what happened then. I couldn't care less about a water orchard full of floating blossoms where we had sex and dreamt of our child. Not when less than a year later you took my son from my arms, put him in his cradle beside me, and then convinced me to sleep in yours like he would be safe. But we both know he wasn't. All those nights of his life that I slept with him in my arms, and on the only one that he didn't because you were there, you let them take him from me, and they changed him forever, my King."

She made sure to add that title on, just in case.

Misael's anger could still be a tricky thing.

"I hate it sometimes, how you don't even try anymore," he murmured, every word aching.

"Try what?"

"To pretend to care at all about me, I suppose. There was a time, days, when I remember you looking forward to seeing me again. You'd even smile at the sight of me."

A long time ago, maybe.

Anthia picked at her nails, something she rarely did unless unsettled. "I do care about you in some ways, and I have never treated you like I did not, even when you gave me every reason to do just that, Misael. Even still, now, today. Here I am standing with you having a conversation that I would rather not—one I don't even think you truly deserve. But I do it because a part of me does care, can't you see that?"

"I do, but—"

"'Tis not the care you want. Just say it. You can't make me love you again, my King."

"Have I not given you everything? Gods, he even *loves* you, Anthia. Not that he ever has me."

"Why did you have to take everything from me first to do it? Why do you still take from me even today?"

She refused to acknowledge the *he* in Misael's remark. She never spoke a bad word about the king in front of their son, but Misael's very actions, life, and kingdom said far more than he ever could about how their son should feel and treat the other half of his blood.

Anthia's pointed question had Misael dropping his gaze from her sight altogether. "Fair enough, perhaps, but you've not loved me in a long time, either, my little queen," Misael returned. "And that was what I meant."

That was true.

Not like she used to.

Not how he wanted.

"But let's be frank," he added, shrugging, "I know why we've found ourselves here, too. And it helps to know you did love me once, I suppose."

He liked to remind her of that often.

Another burden of hers to wear.

"I do love one thing about you. Still."

Misael almost smiled. "What is that?"

"The part of our son that comes from you. The one thing about him that couldn't possibly come from anyone, or anywhere, else. I love that the most."

Misael nodded at the admission, but nothing more. Their child could have been a lot of things with a father like Misael. The king himself was proof of that, and so she had no qualms or complaints about the young man they were still forced to share, even if he was a bit hard to manage and had an attitude all his own, at times. As Eryx had grown older, and spent more time being educated and raised how the king deemed fit away from the court, the less attached he seemed to their son. Mostly, because every return that brought Eryx back to the king, he was less and less like Misael with a mind that could think for itself and a heart that knew his seas.

Oh, she knew Misael loved Eryx, so much so that their child had been given a life of freedom none of the other princes of the realm had ever truly known, but that meant little when in the end, he barely had the love of their son returned.

Not like she did.

Misael knew as much, too.

Then, the king jerked his chin at the open door behind him. "Close that, would you? Gods only know who's out there listening."

He did have a point.

The years had also taught them that.

She closed the door, and he spoke as soon as she did.

"I am considering arranging another potential marriage for Eryx, and I would greatly appreciate it if you could convince him of how this is in his best political interests as the current heir to my throne," Misael told her. "Tonight seems like a perfect opportunity because the two of you will surely have a moment at some point."

Really?

That again?

This man did not learn.

Anthia tried hard not to roll her eyes. "How old was Eryx when you purchased his first whore?"

"Fifteen."

"And what happened?"

"He sent her back to me with a two-word letter sealed with his family ring."

That letter?

It read *fuck* and *you*.

Eryx did *not* return to court after the season ended that year, either. In fact, he packed his horse in the middle of the night, and headed to the other side of Atlas on his first solo journey without a caravan, guide, guards, or otherwise. Misael sent a party after him. Three months later, they found him settled, pleased with himself, and no longer a boy who had yet to taste a woman, where he ended up at the House of Miller.

His most *favorite* place in all of the realm.

Anthia could have saved Misael a lot of time and heartache about where to find Eryx. Instead, she gladly suffered those months by his side, alone when he was at his very worst, so that Eryx didn't always have to be his father's son. Sometimes, he came out better when he learned to be his own man first.

"And his first betrothal, also chosen and arranged by you?" she asked.

"Four years ago," Misael grunted unhappily.

"Which ended …?"

"Badly."

"Yes, it did, thank you. You've sent that boy—"

"He is a man now. You can't keep seeing him as a baby, Anthia. He is a man meant to be *king*."

"Push him from your loins, hold him bloody and wet from your insides, and tell me that very same thing, my King, please."

Still, despite that space and hatred between them, he gave her all of her words. And he didn't argue them with her.

"He has been all over the lands," Misael finally said, a little angrily. He stood up from his chair having laced his boot, and paced the floor back and forth at the end of the bed until his mind seemed to find the words he needed. "He's been from one side of this continent to the other looking for a wife and couldn't find one. I even sent him to the Red Seas. I let you convince me to send him somewhere else to see another way, and even then ... even then, he came back alone to spite me. Where else is he going to go to find a suitable match? I need the boy married, Anthia. I need him *married*."

Oh, now he was a boy?

When it suited Misael to say it?

"No, you sent him to look for a wife. He did many other—" *more interesting*, she thought "—things while there, that's all."

And did not apologize for it.

Eryx had run his father's patience oh, so thin.

Anthia respected their son a little for it.

Misael should, too.

"Convince him for me, please," Misael said. "We both know he'll care more if he hears it from you."

Anthia shrugged, but nodded nonetheless. Whatever got her out of this godforsaken conversation. Another lie between them. There were many of those piled up over the years. Some that hurt less than others.

She would say nothing to Eryx about his prospects for marriage, and if a betrothal did happen, she would happily find her son a way straight out of it if he so pleased. Which he would tell her if that was what he wanted; he told her everything.

But that is not what a clever whore tells her king.

"Will you find me tonight?" Misael asked as he crossed the room, readying to leave. He stopped next to her, finding her skin with his knuckle to lift her gaze as he had so many times in the past. "Even to have tea and a conversation with me?"

"Must I? Don't they have someone for you here, my King?"

No, she didn't even try to pretend.

Not anymore.

Misael sighed, dropping his hand and leaving her without his touch as he muttered, "At least the lady of the house is a halfling."

"Good, then your dick will still get hard. I heard she had eyes for our son, too—don't offer him that one, he knows the shit you try to pull under his feet, and he hates it."

At that warning, Misael laughed darkly and the sound followed him out of the room even over the loud creak of the opening door. She didn't know which thing about the king was worse. That even his favored son, the only left living and remaining on the continent, was barely tolerable to him on most days. Or that he made a game out of finding every fuck his sons had ever had, and it then became his personal conquest to try to lay them all himself while at it.

Well, as long as the woman was at least a halfling.

Honestly, the answer to which would be worse was probably both things. Misael Bloodhurst was still a monster; a monster who knew himself, even. The monster who couldn't change, and because of that, here she would be, by his side although he couldn't even make her fuck him anymore, until the very last of her days.

How tragically ironic for him, really.

Their Gods had funny ways.

14. THE DAY A QUEEN DIED

Eryx, Prince of Atlas

It would be a difficult season of storms. The extended, quarter-round window to the left of Eryx's chair gave him an ample view of the darkening sky beyond the stained sea glass. Although, if he were being fair, the sun hadn't peeked through the clouds that day at all and the distance looked even bleaker, which meant the season had already begun to roll through.

Soon, he and the rest of the realm would find themselves shuttered away from the safety of the wind, torrential rains, and the rest of the dangers that came with this time of the year.

He didn't look forward to that. It meant needing to stick closer to the court and his father. Not even his son could deny the king.

Usually.

A throat clearing drew Eryx's attention back to the party, and his father sitting a few paces away in his gaudy throne. The monument of a chair dominated the room with the back sitting high at six feet tall, and wide enough that he'd not seen a man's shoulders be able to fill the width. Not that he'd seen anyone but his father sit in that chair. Ornamental carvings curved the arms and legs, coils of gold spun around the edges of the throne as if it weren't ostentatious enough.

In the morning light, with its placement in front of the windows, the chair glinted brightly in the room. The first thing one noticed when coming into the main room of any house his father used during his travels, since the throne came with the king.

And the man sitting in the chair?

Not much better.

"Yes?" Eryx asked from his smaller chair.

His father raised an eyebrow. A good sign, if there ever was one, of the man's displeasure at Eryx's lack of interest in a day and party that were meant to be for him. Or rather, his twentieth birthday celebration.

He wished he cared.

Except he didn't.

The king tilted his head to the side, bringing Eryx's attention to the man who waited just beyond the stairs leading up to the platform where their thrones rested. With the sky dark outside, and only candles in the ballroom of the estate house, it almost seemed like the dinner party had gone long into the evening.

It hadn't.

It was only a little past midday.

The season, again.

Gods, get it over with, he prayed silently.

Eryx stared at the man and woman, both well-dressed with jewels on their fingers and gold hanging from their throats, waiting for them to greet him properly as was custom. One of the servants of the house stepped forward with her head tipped down as to keep herself from meeting the prince's gaze.

In a simple gray dress that didn't showcase much of her figure or expose too much skin, one might think the woman was just a servant. Even he'd thought so at first glance. If not for the silver shackle around her throat that practically covered the entire delicate column and designated her a slave. Had her hair been pulled back, the spattering of shimmering scales at her temples would have given away her true breed as well. Sometimes, the mermaids blended in far too well with the rest of them when they walked on land.

The slave stepped up to speak. "Prince Eryx Bloodhurst of Atlas, the Lord and Lady of the house would like to—"

Eryx's father was quick to quiet the slave with a slice of his hand through the air. "Return to your position, quietly and quickly."

The slave did as she was told, but not before daring to defy the laws of the land by raising her head. Violet eyes—another sign of her heritage—flashed with indignation and anger. She spun sharply on her heel and returned to the spot behind the waiting man and woman.

"King Misael, your highness, I apologize for my slave," the man spoke up, doing his best to look apologetic. "She sometimes forgets her place. Rather new, that one. Bought her from the last hunts."

"That so?" his father asked, seemingly having found something to focus his attention on instead of Eryx for the moment.

"Yes, Sire."

Misael nodded, his sharp gaze slicing through the crowd to find the slave woman while he tipped his head back. The candlelight caught the jewels encrusted around the rim and pointed tips of his gold crown. "Bring her to my rooms later, then. I enjoy teaching them how to behave around the royal family."

It wasn't even a request. The king didn't have to make those in these lands. Here, he made every law. All Misael ever had to do was point a finger, and he was given what he wanted. It was their way.

Eryx wasn't much different in that regard, but he didn't share a lot of the same interests. He didn't find quite the same enjoyment in fucking and keeping slaves for sport like his father, and too many others, did. A bit too much work, honestly.

Mattue, the advisor appointed by his father to Eryx when he had been just a young boy—and also his uncle, through his father's bloodline—stepped forward. Always waiting in the shadows for his moments.

"Prince," Mattue said, hands clasped at the front of his closed fur cloak before he bent over subtly at the middle in some semblance of a bow, "the Lord and Lady simply wanted to give their greetings, congratulate you on your twentieth year, and thank you for allowing them to host you at their estate for this evening."

Was that all?

All this conversation for that?

9ine hells.

"Could have sent up a message through Mattue," Eryx replied dryly. "No need for a scene."

Out of the corner of his eye, he could see the clear frown that pulled his father's mouth down at the corners. He had a record of how many times he could displease his father in a day—twenty-two. Sometimes, he made a sport out of breaking said record. Misael made it easy.

It wasn't as though his father would punish him. Eryx was the only living son Misael had left on Atlas. The oldest had been sent to their closest neighboring realm the moment he'd turned seventeen, married off to a princess of an unworthy royal family to keep the peace and continue their trade of slaves.

His other brothers—the one before him and the only boy that came after in the line of succession?

Dead, now.

Eryx was his father's last hope.

Misael let out a sigh and waved at a servant who dared to move in the corner of the room and draw in his attention. "You—*boy*! I want another drink. Hurry with it."

The estate boy—who looked no older than thirteen—bowed with a quick nod. "Yes, Sire, right away."

Soft chatter returned to the room, and soon the music started playing. With no clear effort from Eryx to converse with the man and woman of the house, they were also led away, and he was left to his seat too close to his father, and his own thoughts.

Mostly.

Mattue joined him, stepping behind his nephew where he liked to place himself. That way, he could whisper all sorts of things into Eryx's ear the same way he'd done from the time he was a boy. No one ever thought anything of it, being that Mattue was his advisor. He was also one of his father's most trusted members of the court, considering they shared blood. And yet, Eryx did not think people realized how manipulative his uncle could be when he wanted. As a young boy, he'd often fallen into Mattue's trap.

Not so much as a man, however.

"Your father thought you might like the Lady," Mattue noted. "Her husband was even willing to share her for the evening, had she caught your eye."

Eryx's lip curled up at the edge before he plucked the goblet from the arm of his chair and downed what remained of the red wine in one gulp. Setting the gold cup down harder than he should, he let out a dark laugh. "I don't, and won't, fuck women he picks for me. I wouldn't care if she were the queen of the skies—which is a possibility, if the rumors I've heard of his next attempt at a betrothal for me are to be trusted. If he picks her, then I won't touch her, Mattue. Not that Lady, and not a bitch with a dragon, either."

"Eryx, that is only a—"

"It only means he wants to fuck her himself."

Mattue didn't even bother to deny it.

There was no lie, so he couldn't.

Deciding to switch to his advisor tone, Mattue said, "The storms are rolling in. You'll return to the north-west court with your father when the rest of the royal caravan begins the trip back. He's decided. Over the season, you'll have ample opportunity to consider each and every woman in the land who he believes is appropriate for your position, and should none of them please you, yes, he may be considering another realm for your match. However, he hopes, and wants, you to have picked one to marry in your own lands once the season has passed and a wedding can be had. You've already been to the Red Seas, so he isn't willing to send you away again."

Was Eryx supposed to be listening?

He really wasn't.

Despite having to listen to Mattue because he'd been appointed by his father, Eryx didn't actually care to do anything the man wanted or told him to do. Not unless it benefitted him in some way.

Tit for tat.

"Get him to lay off that for another year at least, would you?" he muttered.

His gaze swept the crowd, searching for someone who should have been milling near the rear of the room like she usually did. His mother, that was. The only person in this entire realm that he gave any care or concern to at all.

"What—a marriage?"

"Yes, that."

"Eryx, your twenty years have passed. It's time to marry."

Horseshit.

Total *horseshit*.

"I can marry anytime. You posed it like I was meant to pick a woman. Which woman has he already picked for me? I'm sure she'll be just as respectable and fertile in another year as she is right now, no? I'll marry no one when this season passes, and if he wants me to marry whichever cunt he's picked for me, then he'll wait another year, anyway. Whoever she is."

Hell, his father had probably already had a taste of the woman. Eryx wouldn't rush to have his.

Mattue sighed. "You seem frustrated. Perhaps you should take the Lady of the house to bed tonight. Drink a bit, then fuck away your mood. The rest of the court would appreciate it, Prince."

Right, right.

"Undoubtedly not," Eryx murmured.

He was still searching for that familiar face in the crowd—her clothes would, of course, be a bit finer than those around her, considering she was favored by his father within the court and had been for longer than Eryx was alive. Something else his mother never did was try to hide what made her so unique amongst the people with whom she was allowed to mingle.

And he couldn't find her.

Eryx had a feeling he knew exactly where his mother had gone when she'd had the chance to slip away from the room and people. Events like these often allowed her less attention from his father, and she used it to her advantage.

"You have that look—the quietness in you—again," Mattue noted.

"Do I?"

"Mmhmm."

Eryx stood from his throne, saying, "If they ask, tell them I went to take a piss."

"Are you? Taking a piss, I mean."

He gave Mattue a smirk, feeling the weight of his crown tilt with his head as he met the man's dark eyes with his own stormy, blade-colored orbs when he replied, "Well, as long as that's what you tell them, then it really doesn't matter what I actually do, now does it?"

His uncle didn't respond.

Eryx didn't really need him to.

If there was such a thing as love—if it was true and real like fairy tales and myths suggested—then that's what Eryx felt for his mother. Not the romantic love that women in the realm cooed about when they thought men weren't close enough to hear, but something else entirely.

A love worth more, maybe.

More loyal.

Far more coveted.

Real.

A true love.

His father spent years fucking his way through slaves before discarding them. A lot like he did to any wife he took, almost all of whom died under circumstances no one really understood when the truth had never been told. All his brothers had come from women kept in his father's harem of slaves, and yet none of them had ever seemed to care for their mothers the way Eryx did.

He wasn't sure why that was except for a few theories. Perhaps it was because their mothers hated the children they'd been forced to birth, and his mother never had, as some suggested. He thought it had more to do with the way the infants, and their mothers, were treated but to speak of those things meant treason.

Eryx rather liked his head, currently.

He also didn't understand why it felt like he could hear his mother wherever he went. Even when she wasn't with him, she was there. As much a part of him as the blood running through his veins, she was just there. He didn't tell anyone—they wouldn't understand, and he couldn't trust anyone enough to disclose the bond—but he knew his mother was aware. She simply wouldn't tell him why.

"I knew you would be here," he said, smiling when Anthia turned her hooded head in his direction when the horse approached the water orchard. Rows of water fruit trees stretched through long channels with deep sea water on either side. He listened to the wind whispering through waving branches with low-hanging fruit. The water fruit was best at the start of the storm season, in his opinion, but everyone liked it at different times in the year. The final harvest would happen soon, and the fruit would be good to store for the coming season. "Always your favorite spot, Mama."

He had her dark hair, twisted with curls down past his ears, while hers was long enough to touch the small of her back when she let it down. He also had her small lips that seemed perpetually turned into a smirk, even when he didn't realize it. And the sharp lines that made up her delicate features, although from his boyhood to adulthood, his had become harder and more masculine.

"You're going to ruin your cloak," he added, dismounting from the horse that he'd taken from the estate's stables earlier. He saw hers on the way in. A white beast usually used by the king. "It's not meant to be worn in the rain."

At least, not the one she was currently wearing. The satin fabric would be ruined by the time he got her back to the house.

"It's not raining."

"Yet."

Anthia shrugged, her hand raising to touch the silver shackle at her throat. Unlike most, his mother's was always kept shined and gleaming, and fell down the hollow of her throat in the shape of a V. The crown resting upon a cursive B carved into the metal designated her a royal whore.

He hated that.

More than even she knew.

"I like the wetness, Eryx," his mother returned, "because it smells like home."

"The sea," he returned. "That's what you mean."

She merely smiled.

Once he was close enough for his mother to reach out and touch him, she did just that. Her warm palm came up to rest against his cheek, soft against the roughness of his few days' worth of facial hair. A heady gust of wind pushed back the hood of her cloak, causing it to fall around her shoulders and open a bit to showcase the velvety green gown that had been chosen for her to wear that day. The low neckline did nothing to hide the collar at her throat.

She preferred her hair up, when the style of the time was to wear it down, and she refused to let them paint her face to hide the spattering of scales at her temples. Because if she was going to be kept as a prize, then she demanded to be shown like one. She liked sandals on her feet instead of the tightly laced shoes with clunky platforms on the heels, or wedges, that gave women a bit of height. The sandals showcased the empty spots where her pinky toes had once been, before the surgeons clipped them to devastate her. They would have become the tips of her fin tail should she shift in water. The loss made it harder for her to escape.

His mother was a slave. A mermaid. Everyone in the land would balk at the title, and yet Anthia seemed to find a way to carry it all with pride. She shoved it right back in their faces, and her favor from the king allowed it.

"You never tell me about it," he said.

"What, the sea?" Anthia asked.

"That, and them … You before this. Any of it."

"I did when you were younger. Sang the stories, when they allowed me to have you. Someone told them that's what I was doing, and they made me stop when you were quite young."

Eryx's brow dipped. "Why?"

"You already know the answer to that."

He really didn't think he did.

Anthia shrugged almost helplessly when he didn't reply, and her hand slid down from his cheek to allow her fingertips to glide over the side of his throat. His clothing for the day didn't require the usual scarf he would wear to hide what he always allowed his mother to openly touch there. The pulse of his heart beat beneath the spot, overtop scars that had faded with time. Just because they were faded, however, didn't mean that the gills the surgeons had sewn shut after his birth hadn't once allowed him to breathe. They existed, even if he now was incapable of using them. Then, they took them away.

After all, he couldn't be a slave.

He had to be human.

Or he had to look like it.

"Because then you'd empathize, Eryx. And you can't be what your father wants you to be when you care more for a slave than you do the people that slave is meant to serve." Just as quickly as his mother's mood seemed to turn dark, she smiled brightly and dropped her hand back to her side. "Walk with me?"

"You know, if they catch you leaving the estate without a guard ..."

"They'll whip me until I bleed purple, lock me in a chamber, and ... well, what else could they do? What would the king do now, hmm? He's already done and taken it all. If only the punishment scared me now."

He wished it did scare her. Wished so much he could protect her more.

He stayed close to his mother's side as they headed down one row of the trees. Plucking one of the low-hanging, white and red fruits from the tree, he offered it to his mother, knowing it was her favorite. She didn't get it nearly enough.

"How did the hunt go over the past season?" she asked, her fingernail dragging through the soft skin of the fruit to peel it back like a knife might. "I've only heard whispers about it."

"Not well," he replied, "and it looks like most of the catches will be used for trading or harvest, because they can't afford to keep any of them. Not with what the hunters promised the king, and what he promised the neighboring realm for the coming year's trades."

His mother hummed under her breath, nodding but otherwise saying nothing about the hunt. She never did—or maybe it was that she learned not to over time. He couldn't be sure. Sometimes, he found it interesting how she could stand to listen to people talk about the hunting, capture, and subsequent sale of her own people without as much as a frown on her face. He supposed she didn't have much of a choice.

And neither did Atlas.

Their realm was only guaranteed safety from war with other kingdoms if they could continue to produce worthy goods in their trades, especially as their ability to mine sea glass from the seas had lessened significantly in the last decade. Creatures from the sea, with blood that bled purple and could produce results in medicines that cured ailments and slowed aging were definitely a commodity most other realms in the world weren't currently offering. It was also why the mermaids remained young-looking once reaching adulthood, their aging taking a decade or longer to show what a human's year would for them. And while mermaids elsewhere had the capability and power to defend their people, the ones in the Blu Seas did not.

The people of Atlas took advantage.

Often.

While his mother chewed on a piece of the fruit she'd broken off from the five prongs at the bottom, he listened to the wind dancing through the orchard. Others wouldn't dare to stand out in this weather, knowing a storm was on the way while the sky swirled black, violent, and loud overhead. He'd never been as afraid of it as the rest of them were.

Neither had his mother.

"You never tried to run."

So many did.

And were killed for it, too.

"No," his mother said quietly.

"Why?"

Anthia's walk came to a stop, and so did Eryx's beside her. Her violet eyes—the one thing he hadn't taken from her because he wasn't full-blooded like she was—met his stare that matched his father's. Perhaps, the only thing he had taken from Misael that he wished he hadn't. Eyes that turned stormy like the seas or blade-colored in his anger and passion. He mirrored his mother's soft smile. "Now, that, you really should know the answer to."

"I think I do."

"But maybe you want me to say it?"

"Maybe," he agreed.

"For you. I never ran because of you. I let the king believe whatever he needs to, of course, but from the moment I knew you existed, Eryx, I could never be anywhere else. In a way, you were the last thing that tied me to my own seas."

So yes, he had known. He was just selfish enough to admit he liked that answer. Even if he shouldn't. After all, it meant he had a mother. For all this time, too. His selfishness? That also came from his father, for sure.

"Do you know why else I sang to you?" his mother asked. "When you were little, I mean."

"I don't even remember it."

"Not here," his mother said, pointing at her right ear and winking. Then, she pointed at her heart before also gesturing at her mind. "But in these places, you can't forget them. Where they *can't* hear them. The sea songs—the siren's calls, Eryx. It's the thrall, the magic in our blood, the bond of the mermaids. Families hear them singing for miles. Mates, even farther. Through waters and storms and wars … we hear them inside. You hear them, too. Why did you think you came to find me here?"

"I thought the songs were a way of warning …"

Anthia grinned. "Or a way to call someone home."

The wind blew again, and this time, his mother sang with it, the melody twisting and curling with the breeze and through the trees. He stood right beside her, heard the song as clear as day, but it almost seemed to echo within him, too.

Except when she stopped …

Well, the song didn't.

But it wasn't his mother singing anymore.

Anthia's head tipped up, and the paleness of her face became far more prominent when her eyes widened like the two moons beginning to peek through the heavy, dark clouds overhead. The song continued on, coming closer and … higher?

Eryx looked upward into the fruit trees. "Who is sing—"

His mother made an inhuman noise. "*Run.*"

His stare snapped back to his mother. "What?"

"You're more like them than us, and that's all the mermaids will see. Run, Eryx."

She didn't give him the chance to argue about it. The singing in what seemed like the trees above them came louder with every passing second. Her hand locked around his wrist, and she darted back up the channel of high water fruit trees. She ran like the wind, but he was still faster. It didn't matter because he stayed behind her as they weaved through the narrow trail beside the trees, avoiding low hanging branches that swung in the suddenly heavy winds.

The storm had arrived. He should have listened to the rustling of the leaves. The creak of branches.

He might have heard the mermaid when she dropped down on top of them. Except he didn't. Not until it was too late.

Red hair and violet eyes. Fingernails sharpened like claws that dug into his throat and teeth bared with a vicious hiss slipping past snarling lips. She was naked, shifted from her water form to walk on land although she attacked from the trees.

Eryx's mother's screams pierced through the howling winds, but from which direction he couldn't be sure. All he could see was violet eyes and fire-red hair intent on ripping the throat right out of his fucking neck.

Arelle

"And then what happens?"

Arelle sighed, willing her younger sister to focus on the last leg of their trip to the west side of Atlas, and less on things that didn't concern her yet. "Has anyone told you that sometimes, you ask too many questions?"

Coral skipped ahead of her in the water, her tail smacking the rough surface of the water to splash her sister before slipping over on her back with a grin. She skimmed along the choppy surface, all the while looking like she was quite proud of herself. "Actually, they do."

"Do you think that may be a hint, then?"

"Never."

Arelle laughed because, really, what else could she do? "You're asking me about things I can't give you the answers to, Coral."

"But you've been there. You saw it."

"I saw some of the matings, yes."

Since witnesses to matings proved paired couples' bonds beyond any doubt, it was quite common for the colony—but especially the royals—to go along and be a part of the traditions. Even if it was from afar. And, she had learned quite a bit doing so.

"And?"

Arelle could see just how close to the west side of Atlas they were. Already past the safe band of the Atlas Islands that separated their territory and the narrow seas, now was the time she knew they needed to be quiet and pay attention. To everything. She'd heard the tales of ships coming out of the fog—like ghosts appearing where they hadn't been just a moment before. She remembered hearing stories from merpeople who had managed to escape about how the landwalkers would lay nets along openings in the bays or on the seafloor before drawing them up fast when they weren't expecting it.

Of course, Coral had never experienced those things, and being sheltered meant she hadn't been around enough of their kind to hear those same stories that made Arelle wary and cautious.

"Well," Arelle told her sister, "if we manage to make it back to the colony alive tonight, then you should get all the answers to your questions soon enough. But if you keep talking so I can't pay attention until we get to the water orchard, then we might not make it back at all."

The widening of Coral's violet eyes and the way her pretty face fell almost made Arelle feel bad for her sharp tone and snarky words. She really couldn't afford to sympathize when nothing she'd said was a lie.

Yes, the sky was a swirling black mass. Yes, the winds were high, and the rain pouring down had turned rather cold and harsh. A storm had come in faster than it'd taken them to get from the band of islands to the shore of the mainland. The water was already choppy, a dark reflection of the clouds overhead, while lightning streaked through the tunneling clouds starting to reach down toward the sea below. The season of storms had finally arrived, which meant they were safe.

Arelle didn't trust that. It meant they should be safe. She would take no risks.

"Come on, we're almost there and I'm sure Poe is waiting," Arelle told Coral. "And then I promise, when we get back, I will tell you all about what I saw and what you can expect this season. Okay?"

Coral chirped happily in response, but it didn't quite skip over the waves like it usually would. Maybe Arelle had been a little harsh, and besides, Coral was still forever curious. She couldn't expect the girl to change just because she was now of age. She didn't understand what was expected of her yet, and like the rest of them, would learn in time what she had to do.

For herself.

For their people.

For their life.

It all came with time.

"Let's hurry," Arelle said, swimming ahead of Coral who had now flipped back to her belly on the surface of the waves. "Poe might have managed to leave court ahead of us, but she won't start picking any fruit unless we're there to help her carry it all home."

"Her mate must really like it for her to come here."

Ah, there it was.

Arelle heard Coral's wariness.

Maybe it was because they were now so close to the orchard that they could see the waterways between each row of the fruit trees perfectly fine. There was no going back now; they were in landwalker territory. A well-aimed arrow could end it all.

"It's dark, the storm is here, and it's the safest time for us to be out," Arelle assured, heading for one of the waterways. She'd sing for her sister, and no doubt, Poe would call back, so they could easily find each other in the large orchard. "The landwalkers are scared of this time of year. Don't worry, okay? We just have to be fast and careful, that's all."

Glancing back at her little sister, Arelle saw Coral's nod and figured that was good enough. They were here. What would be the point in turning back now? It wouldn't be worth very much, especially if their father found out that they disobeyed him, tricked their guards, and came to the forbidden lands.

Slipping into the mouth of one waterway canal, Arelle listened in the wind, ready to call for her sister. Before she could even open her mouth, a noise whipping through the trees had her perking her head higher. The water in the canals was maybe six feet or a little deeper—certainly not enough for her to stand straight with her fin to the canal floor and still have her head above water.

"Coral, wait," Arelle snapped, still trying to come higher out of the water to hear that sound better. "Listen."

"What?"

Coral spun a fast circle in the water, making more noise than she needed to. Because of course. Arelle said nothing. She simply waited. It would come again, that noise, if it was what she thought it was.

And then there it came, with the next rush of wind, as clear as day. It sounded familiar, and then it didn't. Angry, scared, and violent. That's what her sister's call felt like. It had Arelle's anxiety picking up with the fast beats of her heart and made her want to turn right around and leave.

Was that—

"Is someone here?" Coral asked.

"Someone is here with Poe."

Because that's what she could hear. Her sister, but something—someone—else, too. That was the only reason why Arelle decided to chase the sound. Poe was out there in the orchard, and she didn't know what was happening to her. But something was. It would have to be for her sister to let out high-pitched shrieks like that.

"Arelle!"

Coral's terrified shout echoed behind her, but Arelle kept moving forward through the waterway. She didn't think she had time to stop and explain but she shouldn't need to. Coral was just as capable of hearing the same thing she was. She could have told her sister to stay back, but instinct kept her swimming as fast as she could to get to the source of Poe's screeching.

The noise became louder to Arelle's right, and when she had the chance, she slipped between an opening in the waterways for another canal. She hadn't expected to be so close to the source of the noise, but when she broke the surface of the water … it was there that she found it.

A mess.

Chaos.

It all happened so fast, and she didn't have the time to react, even if she had been able to take in the sight before her. Of her sister's hands wrapped tightly around the throat of a landwalker—a man—where she had him pinned to the ground. Maybe it was the shock of his position, but her sister was substantially smaller than the man, yet she didn't give him an inch. The woman a few feet away edged closer, hands out to grab … something. The man, or her sister, Arelle didn't know.

It was the shriek the woman let loose, the violent familiar call of their people that had Arelle snapping back in the water. The violet eyes of the woman flashed before she sprang forward, barreling into the side of Poe and sending her older sister toppling off the man.

Arelle's heart jumped into her throat. "Poe!"

"Help her!" Coral screeched.

She would have.

Except Arelle didn't have time.

The slapping, flailing arms and legs of her naked sister and the other woman—who had eyes like them and sounded like they did—tangled together before they slipped off the embankment and into the canal. Under the water they went, and Arelle followed just as fast.

But not before looking up.

Straight at the landwalker.

She took a second; a single deep breath.

He had hair like the darkest skies.

Eyes the color of the seas and steel.

A sea of blue.

Even in his terror, scrambling to the side of the embankment with red blood dribbling from his busted mouth, the strong lines of his face seared into her mind's eye. He was, by far, one of the most handsome men she had ever seen in her life.

"Help!" he shouted back over his shoulder at nothing and no one in particular before his gaze snapped back to the bubbles bursting at the surface of the water.

She didn't stop to appreciate it, but even under the water, she could still see his face. Even as she rushed through the murky water to find her sister and help Poe, she still saw the landwalker in her mind.

The fight between the woman and Poe continued under the water with no sign of stopping when Arelle finally got the two in her sights. It was Coral rushing in beside her that stopped her from going any closer. She pushed her sister back, the warning hissing from her lips under the water, "Stay back."

Arelle looked over her shoulder in just enough time to see Poe push away from the woman whose cloak and green gown had tangled around her legs and arms. And then everything changed.

Just as fast as before.

Just as shocking.

The woman dragged in water, her mouth opening to suck in like she was going to breathe, and her body changed. Those legs swirled with water, her eyes widening in fear as the familiar tail and fin of their kind took its place. The straps that had held sandals to her feet drifted to the floor of the canal, but Arelle was stuck staring at something else.

Her tail.

It was wrong.

Ruined.

The tips gone—jagged where it should have been sharp. A good chunk on either side of the woman's tail was entirely missing.

How?

Who did that to her?

The landwalkers?

The sound that escaped Arelle matched the confusion that spilled from Coral.

"What's wrong with her? Why is she dressed like that? Help her!"

In the water, Coral's fearful questions came out as a high pitch in her fear. Her words slammed into Arelle one after another in their mother tongue. Poe floated backward, her own tail back in place of the legs she had been fighting with on the land. Her face was the same mask of shock that her sisters wore.

Of course, they'd heard the stories. Yes, they knew what their people said.

None of them had ever seen it firsthand, though. None of the sisters knew for sure that the warnings were true. That when the landwalkers were successful in their hunts of the merpeople, they kept them like slaves. Mutilated them to keep them from running, amongst many other horror stories that she didn't even like to think about.

"Help her!" Coral cried again. "Look at her neck! She can't breathe like that, Arelle!"

What?

Arelle did, horrified by the way the woman clawed at the heavy, thick band of metal encasing her throat. With her hair spilling out of the style it had been before she'd fallen into the water, it was hard to tell if that collar-like device went all the way around her throat, but given how white her face turned as she opened her mouth and tried to breathe ...

It did go all around and somehow, it must also keep her gills filled. So tight, in fact, she couldn't breathe. She could take in water to cause the change, but she could not expel it in the way she needed to in order to return back. Shifting in the water like that would be a death sentence.

And like the landwalkers, without her gills able to expel the water from her lungs, she would drown.

Die.

"Help her!"

"We have to get out of here," Poe snapped, turning fast away from the woman who couldn't swim well with her tail mutilated like it was, and still couldn't breathe.

Arelle couldn't move.

"Poe—"

"We have to leave!"

"But …" Coral swam around Arelle's side, edging closer to the still-struggling woman whose violet eyes—eyes so much like theirs that it hurt—looked between her sisters. The woman couldn't swim or get herself to the surface, not that it would do any good now. "We should help her, Poe."

"Let her die. Look at what they did to her."

"Poe!"

Arelle reached for Coral, ready to drag their younger sister back and away from the … well, she couldn't quite call the helpless mermaid woman dangerous, could she? Not like she was. "Poe is right, we have to leave, Coral."

They had already risked too much.

This had gone too far.

"No."

Poe had already turned to go down the canal. Arelle looked that way, peering through the dark murkiness of the water to call for her sister to wait.

"Help me … to the sea … take me into the seas."

The words slithered through the water like an eel slipping along the seafloor. The merwoman's voice so faint and painful that it made her flinch. And yet, she used their language, her pleas enough to make Arelle hesitate.

A second too long.

Long enough for Coral to grab the sea glass blade sharpened from the strongest of sea stones that Arelle kept strapped to her hip with a piece of leather wrapped in seaweed to keep it safe. Her little sister slipped out of her reach, heading for the merwoman just ten feet away in the water.

"Coral!"

It happened so fast.

Too fast.

Coral reached for the woman, only wanting to help because that's who she was … sweet and curious and so foolish. Not at all scared, though she should be. Except when she extended that blade, ready to cut the contraption from the woman's throat, purple exploded in the water.

Blood.

Their blood.

Because the woman struck back, whether from fear that she was about to be killed or for some other reason that Arelle didn't yet understand … she attacked. Grabbing the blade from Coral, she first slashed it across the younger girl's face, and then plunged it deep into her chest.

Violet all around.

It swirled and danced.

She could taste it in the water.

Arelle screamed, darting forward in the water to help her sister when Poe finally came back. She cut past Arelle so fast that she was only a blur of shimmering scales and red hair. Terrified Poe might be the next to find herself on the wrong end of the blade the other woman now had, Arelle swam into the fray as well.

Poe had her own knife, though. And hands that were fast with every strike. Their fight sent them farther down the canal, even as Arelle swam circles around the two women, trying to find that safe opening to help.

"Poe, we have to help Coral—Poe!"

Poe heard nothing.

Every swing of her arm caused another slice.

More purple in the water.

It was all Arelle could see.

"I want to die in my seas," the dying woman whispered, begging. "*Please.*"

Arelle couldn't see Coral anymore.

They were too far down the canal.

"Please, let me die in the seas ..."

"*Poe,*" Arelle pleaded, "*Poe, stop!*"

Even above the shrieks of her sister, her own cries, and the woman's pleas, Arelle realized she could hear something else through the water.

Something outside of the water.

"Anthia!"

Footsteps pounding against earth accompanied the painful calls.

"*Mother!*"

Eryx

"Mother!"

The water bubbled and swirled in the canal, bursting with rising purple streaks that almost seemed to glow with electricity when it reached the surface.

Blood, he knew.

But did it belong to his mother, or one of the mermaids?

He couldn't be sure.

And that fucking killed Eryx.

But then the bubbles began to swirl, and through the murky water of the canals, he could see shimmering scales moving. Twisting and circling, making water kick up near the surface, although that was about as much as he could discern.

His heart thumped hard in his throat, his fingernails digging deep into the soft earth of the side of the embankment. More than anything, he wanted to get in that water, but the skies raged overhead, water dumping harder than ever, and he wasn't nearly as strong as a mermaid was in the water.

That much, he knew.

It would be like throwing himself to the fucking wolves. Had they been on land … if only he had a sword in his hands … But he had none of that. He was the weak one here.

The water shifted again, changing and spreading with more purple. The shimmering a few feet below moved, and it was only his desire to find or see his mother that sent Eryx rushing to his feet. It probably wasn't the smart thing to do, and the sea was most dangerous when the storms raged overhead, but he pushed to his feet and followed the bubbling, swirling water.

Where was she?

Why had she attacked the merwoman when he had been seconds away from turning the situation around?

Oh, he knew …

Of course, she'd want to protect him. His entire life had been about her protecting him. Like an instinct his mother couldn't ignore, and one he shouldn't expect her to.

Eryx shouted for his mother over and over, chasing the moving water in the canal all the way down the orchard. He ducked the swinging branches, cold wind and icy water slapping against his bare chest even as he tried to keep from stumbling over muddy earth and the roots of the trees that stuck up everywhere.

He was failing again.

He would never be able to help her.

"Mother!"

He couldn't keep up with the movement in the water, and by the time he reached the end, the purple streaks of blood began to spread farther out into the sea. Overhead, the clouds screamed with their rage, tunneling dangerously with what he knew would soon touch the ground closest to the shores and devastate everything.

Him included.

And yet, he still slid down the end of the embankment, his ripped pants and ruined shoes doing nothing to protect him from the cold water. Except he barely felt it at all. His own blood tasted tangy on his lips, the scratches against his chest from where his shirt had been torn off stinging against the saltwater and heavy rain. Even as the waves came higher, the water turning choppier than ever, he moved farther into it all.

Closer to danger.

To his mother.

He called for her again.

The skies answered back with its own cry.

A warning, maybe.

It could take him under. If the current hit him just right, or a wave ... he'd be entirely fucked, drawn out to sea and unable to swim back. Not when he couldn't breathe under the water.

The realization was painful.

She wouldn't be able to breathe, either. Despite being born and raised in the sea, in her current circumstance, she wouldn't even be able to save herself.

Her collar ... impossible to take off. An item that made it impossible for her to breathe once shifted in the seas.

Eryx couldn't move.

He just called for her—begged for his mother again. Cried for her until his chest ached and the sheet of tears felt like they had become his very own face. His words disappeared into treacherous water and blackened skies. His soul went with it. What remained of him that had any good left was lost with every call for his mother that went unanswered.

Vanished like his pleas.

As did his sanity.

All of it.

Gone.

15. NEVER GO BACK

Arelle

"We have to go back!"

Poe kept swimming ahead of Arelle. She acted as though she hadn't heard her sister's shout under the raging water, but Arelle knew better.

"Poe, we have to go back for Coral!"

Poe's tail beat hard in the water, her fin slicing back and forth so fast that she made a slipstream for Arelle to follow. That didn't change the fact that her sister still wasn't answering her.

"Poe—"

Faster than Arelle could blink, her sister spun around. She nearly ran right into Poe, both of them straightening up as the dark water around them moved so harshly that it rocked them both on the spot. She barely noticed it at all, however, because she was more focused on the way her sister was looking at her.

So mad.

Teeth grinding.

Violet eyes narrowed.

Streaked with the purple of their kind, the blood an electric shade under the dark water. Like this, it practically glowed. She could reach out and try to wipe the blood off her sister's face, but it wouldn't do her any good. In water, their blood became sticky and hard to clean. It would take more than a swipe of a hand to wash it away.

Another sign of their wrongs.

A reminder that wouldn't leave.

They would pay for this.

"What?" Poe snapped.

Her sister's red hair, the same shade as her own, haloed around her shoulders in the water. It made Poe look more like the warrior her mate was than the princess she was supposed to be still covered in another's blood. After seeing what her sister had done back at the water orchard, Arelle had a right to be hesitant now.

How easily Poe struck out with violence.

It was shocking.

"We have to go back for Coral," Arelle whispered.

Poe's stare cut to somewhere over Arelle's shoulder. Into the depth of the now-black sea and the water that churned dangerously even beneath the surface. It was no wonder why this time of the year scared the humans into hunkering down within buildings where the strong winds and cutting rains couldn't touch them. If she had not grown up in these seasons, the storms might very well terrify her into seclusion as well.

"For what? Why would we go back there?" Poe demanded.

"Because she's our—"

"She's dead. And nothing, absolutely *nothing* we do from this moment on, will make that better. Not for you, I, or her. Nothing, Arelle."

Arelle's chest ached. The water she breathed in stuttered on the inhale and hurt when it came back out. "You can't be sure she's dead. She might not be. We should—"

"Arelle, *enough*."

Crying underwater could be an interesting, if not strange, experience. The tears couldn't be seen, sure, but the whimpers and sounds could travel for miles under the water. Her chest became tighter the longer she tried to hold back the urge to let out her pain. She'd tried her very best to pretend what Poe said wasn't the case, but she knew it was true.

Saw it herself.

She was right there.

"Arelle, she is gone," Poe said firmly. "And we cannot make it better for anyone else. Only ourselves."

She couldn't accept that.

"But … shouldn't we go back?" Arelle asked, her voice fainter than she wanted it to be. Against her older sisters, she'd always been the quieter one when they were all in a group together. Their personalities were so much bigger and more present than hers. Not that it mattered, because as the third sister, so far from the throne, she'd never needed to make herself known against her siblings unless it served her to do so. Sometimes, it was better to be able to fade into the background. It was a hard role to step out from, but this couldn't be the same. It was their little sister. "We need to go back—she's our kin. We can take her home, Poe."

"Go back and get her?" Poe's laughter came out as a sharp chirp that made Arelle flinch from the viciousness of it all. "Why? She's dead, you foolish girl. And if we go back there, what do you think the chances are that the human didn't call for help? If we go back there, we're only asking to die, too."

"So what, we just leave her there to rot?"

"What else would you do?"

"Go get her!"

Even Arelle was shocked at the level of her shout. At how strong she sounded, and the way it made Poe straighten up a little more in the water. For a long while, the two sisters simply stared at one another.

Things were changing.

Arelle could feel it all around them.

More things were about to change, too.

How could it not now?

"If you want to go back, then fine. Be stupid, get yourself killed. I don't care."

Poe's words might have hurt, if only Arelle found them shocking. Except she didn't because she had learned over her years that Poe really only cared for herself when the line was drawn between her and someone else, barring her mate, of course. If it benefitted her, then she made an effort to show concern for those around her. Otherwise, she just didn't give a damn. Arelle had hoped that becoming a queen, responsible for an entire kingdom, would change that side of Poe.

Alas, that time for her sister had not yet come.

"I will be going back to the colony—to our father. The *king*, Arelle. In case you forgot. You do realize what's going to happen once he finds out we disobeyed him and went to the forbidden lands, don't you? Only to come back without one of his children, yes? So yes, you want to be foolish and go back, then do it. But I am going home."

Right.

Poe had always been the favored one, though. The daughter who could do no wrong. Even their oldest sister, Sarha, who should have taken their father's throne, had been married off to a colony from another realm while Poe had been left here as the new heir with the benefit of picking her very own mate from a line of suitors.

The rest of them, however?

Well, the other sisters knew where they stood.

"Go home," Arelle said, finally finding the strength in her voice again, "but I am going back for Coral. Even if it is just for her body."

"Do what you must."

"And you, sister."

Poe nodded once, her gaze flicking behind Arelle into the darkness of the sea from which they'd swum. She didn't even look at her sister before turning in the water and darting away. Arelle waited until she could no longer see her sister's shimmering scales, or the glowing purple streaks of blood that would remain stained on her for days.

Only then did Arelle turn back for Coral.

She already knew, though, that the chances of retrieving her sister's body was unlikely. The water had risen too much, and with the currents becoming stronger from the waves on the surface, chances were Coral's remains had been pulled out to the narrow seas where slipstreams could leave the body anywhere.

Not that it mattered.

She had to try.

This was her fault. She'd brought Coral along, even though she'd known the girl was too young. The very least she could do was go back for her.

Wasn't it?

Poe

Every thundering beat of Poe's heart came with a scream in her mind. A horrifying scream that she knew for sure would cut through the seas and straight through the heart of the man who answered her back. She swam harder and faster than she had ever before, until every breath ached and each collapse of her lungs made it feel like her ribs hollowed into her cramping chest.

She had misjudged …

Her mistake could never be undone.

All too aware of how badly this could end for her, how it would reflect upon her mate, Poe never once considered what her father would do to her on that long swim back. Her regret and fear washed over her in crashing waves for her mate, and perhaps a little for herself.

Tak and she collided at the outskirts of the colony. Not far from their grotto. Still sticky with violet blood that she hadn't been able to clean or swim off, smeared from her face to her fin, and unable to properly breathe, she just sobbed as he held her.

Cried as he tried to shush her; trembled as his own panic grew the more Poe managed to gasp out. Did any of it make sense?

Could he put the story together?

Her mind had fractured a lot of it.

Did not r-realize …

S-someone already there …

Couldn't hear …

Tried … stay quiet …

In t-trees …

She misjudged what she saw, made the wrong choice out of pride and anger, and it only got worse from there. Her mate did not understand the full scope of her wrongs yet, oh, but he would.

"Poe, tis okay, my heart," Tak murmured in her ear, his nose nuzzling against the skin behind her ear. All the while, he held her locked in bar-tight arms as if she were a scared child that had run away from a monster. Except it was her.

She was the monster.

"He had a crown and a sword, I-I-I thought—"

"*Hush*," he told her, the demand clear, "and let me take you home."

She pulled back from him with another sob. "Your hunt—"

"The grotto, *come*."

As if he gave her a choice.

In fact, her mate had never handled her as roughly or harshly as he did that day dragging her through choppy waters until they were back in the safety and privacy of their grotto. Where he pulled her from the water to sit her on the ledge, but she smacked his hands away that tried to wash the proof of her sins from her body even after she had changed back to her legs.

"Stop, it will come off like this," he hissed at her, cupping another palmful to bring to her blood-soaked hair. "Try to tell me it all from the beginning again—we can fix this, Poe."

"*You stop.*"

Tak did.

Instantly.

With the choice came a bit of distance between the two, but Poe could only hiccup and swallow the uncontrollable sobs that just wouldn't leave her. She tipped her head back to stare up at the hole and take a fresher breath of air only to see Sofian drop from above as soon as her gaze found her pet.

The second the octopus landed in Poe's lap, an unforgiving tentacle snapped out with a loud crack at the merman in the water, sending him jerking back fast enough to create a wave.

"Tis okay," she tried to soothe Sofian whose tentacles squeezed impossibly tight around Poe's wrists and fingers, little suckers kissing against another's blood.

"Send her off," Tak muttered.

"She's confused," Poe returned shakily.

"Yes, and me, too."

Fair enough.

It took a little while to get the octopus back onto the stone, and she dared another warning at Tak before diving into the water. He quickly pulled himself out onto the ledge when he realized the depths hiding his lower half were no longer safe.

"My only regret," he said under his breath, still glaring at the surface of the water, standing on bare feet now.

"She is not a regret, don't say that. She loves me."

Her only baby, so far.

Sometimes, Sofian left the cave for days. The first time, Poe had panicked. But then, her pet came back with all eight tentacles wrapped around various items she brought back from the land. Most were unusable or confusing to Poe, but some, like a knife with a jagged teeth, were incredibly valuable.

"He's going to know I go to the forbidden lands," Poe whispered.

She felt her mate's gaze shift back to her, but she couldn't look away from the edge of the stone ledge. Her shame made it so.

"He might … he might punish me, or—"

"He won't do that to you, Poe. Zale favors you, and you know it."

"My sister is *dead*!"

Tak flinched, but otherwise, said nothing.

So, apparently he had managed to understand some of her mess in the seas.

"What if he tells me that because of this, he won't grant us a child?"

Her mate moved toward her. "Poe—"

She couldn't let that happen.

Pushing off the ledge to slip back into the water before Tak could even say another word, he shouted after her. She kept going. Tak would do what he had to—for her, she knew it. And so, as would she.

For him, *them*, she would lie, and she would make her father believe that she would never go back.

Arelle didn't make it far enough to enter the same canal of the water orchard where the attack happened because she knew that she wasn't alone. Even if she couldn't hear the noise coming from somewhere above the surface of the water, she would have still felt that something wasn't quite right.

Before she could think better of the decision, Arelle skimmed the surface of the choppy water. Overhead, a blackened sky shifted and circled with clouds that were already creating tunnels that would be most dangerous if they reached down to the ground. Add that into the violence of the water, ready to drag its next victim under the waves, and she could practically smell the season's arrival with every breath she took.

But none of that really mattered.

Not when the form near the shore of the water orchard caught her attention, and suddenly, she was unable to look away. He stood nearly chest-deep in the dangerous water. Without a shirt or cloak, even in the darkness, the landwalker's skin gleamed with a golden tint as the bands of muscles that made up his chest clenched with his next shout.

"Anthia!"

Arelle dragged in a lungful of sea-salt-infused air.

"Mother!"

She had wanted to cry earlier for her sister.

He was crying.

And that just made her so mad for reasons even she couldn't understand. That sudden swell of rage, as risky as the sea she waded within, had her wishing she could take the landwalker's life away from him.

From all of them.

If not for everything they had done to her people, this wouldn't have happened at all.

He shouted again.

Arelle almost sank under the water.

Before she could do that and get as far away from the hauntingly beautiful man on the shore who made her want to kill, and this terrible place ... his gaze skimmed the surface of the sea again. His stare landed right on her. They locked eyes; there was no denying the fact he could see her just fine from her safe position where she doubted he would go.

For a second, nothing happened.

The wind seemed to quiet.

She didn't notice the water.

And even from a good distance away, she could still hear the way he dragged in a breath that sputtered with the water crashing against his chest. If he didn't get out of the sea soon, it would pull him under.

Good, one part of her thought.

And what a shame, another bit whispered.

"I'll kill you," she heard him promise into the wind, "if it's the last thing I ever do, little mermaid."

Her heart skipped a beat.

And then two.

She didn't need to wonder ...

She could feel his threat was true.

Arelle sank under the water.

Let their Gods handle him.

She couldn't.

Arelle wished she could say that she hurried back to the colony, but in fact, she didn't do that at all. She warred with herself, knowing there wouldn't be any way to hide what happened or how, in the end ... she would be the one blamed for her sister's death. She considered hiding but knew that wouldn't do any good when her father would simply send someone to search for her.

And they would find her.

She certainly couldn't go back to the land. She didn't have her own grotto to hide within, not that it would make a difference if she did, when her father's guards could simply come inside and drag her out.

There was no choice, really.

She had to go back.

Before she had even reached the long wall of twisted coral that protected her father's palace from the rest of the colony, the merpeople had already begun to gather. They lined either side of her, separating to let her through without pause and never meeting her gaze. A few hundred or so— probably the entire colony of her people.

Just a few decades ago, their numbers had been much larger. Their colony, although that was at least a century or more before she had been born—according to those who were willing to talk about that time—had been one of the biggest in the 9ine Realms, in fact. Now, they were dwindling. Well, almost already extinct.

Year by year ...

Season after season ...

They were hunted.

And now, they had so few left.

Today, another had died. Except it wasn't just any mermaid, but a princess. The youngest of the royal sisters. She bet the people were asking that if they couldn't even keep the royals safe from the landwalkers, then how would they keep the rest of them safe?

Look at their numbers.

Their whispers and chirps reached her ears, a few of their statements discernable enough for her to hear even though she tried to ignore them. That was impossible, honestly, and while some of what she heard felt like accusations ... they were not unwarranted.

Arelle knew that better than anyone.

It also told her a lot about what would be waiting behind the wall of coral when she met with her father. If only because the merpeople seemed to already know that something bad had happened. Some outright said Coral's name.

How quickly word could spread ...

Her father's reign as King of the Blu Seas had long been tainted with questions and more unknowns than were favorable. He'd taken the throne after the previous queen had been captured and killed ... or so everyone assumed. With no heirs and no family left from her bloodline, it was left to her advisor to fill the role.

Arelle's father.

Many didn't like that the people hadn't been given a choice. Others were angry their queen hadn't been avenged, or even … searched for, really. The landwalker's hunting became far more common after that, leaving very little time for the colony to revolt against their new king when what they really needed was his protection.

Or so she had always been told.

Arelle had the distinct feeling their people regretted that now more often than they ever had before. She couldn't say that she blamed them.

She didn't try to meet their stares, either. Didn't force any of the people in the colony to risk being seen stepping out of place on account of her. Undoubtedly, that would only earn them a punishment for their empathy or even their anger.

At the gates leading into her father's palace, the guards waited in their usual positions. With spears at the ready. Instead of looking directly at her as she passed by to enter, they kept their stares turned on the seafloor beneath them. She wished she could be surprised to see her personal guards waiting just beyond the gates, but she wasn't.

And they didn't speak, either.

In fact, the two men who accompanied her almost everywhere—except when she'd escaped them earlier while the court was full—didn't even move to follow her until she had passed them by entirely. They trailed behind at an acceptable distance, and it was only then that she considered what they might also face for her decisions today.

Arelle had never felt worse.

The entire guard had come out to witness her shameful return, it seemed. The mermen with their weapons in hand lined the pathway leading to the palace on either side, much like the rest of the colony's people had outside the coral wall. Until that moment, she had kept her head high … fearing what would happen next, but willing to accept it.

As she neared the palace entrance, she finally lowered her head. The weight of her errors resting heavily on her shoulders had never been more present.

Her father's palace—carved from sandstone, sea glass, and the largest part of the coral reef—was usually busy no matter the time of day. There was always someone coming or going. Servants moving from here to there to do their duties. And yet on that evening, Arelle swam through silent, dark halls. She didn't need to be told where to go.

She already knew.

The first thing Arelle noticed when she entered the somber throne room where her father liked to waste away his days wasn't any one person in particular, but rather the entire group. Not to mention, the scene they made.

Her father, Zale, standing in front of his throne. Crown placed behind him on the seat as though the weight of it was currently too heavy for him to carry.

His advisors spread around the room, gazes turned away from her or down to the floor.

Her sister, Poe, standing half behind her mate who seemed to have finally returned safely from his hunting trip.

Her mother wasn't there.

That wasn't unusual.

"Why?" her father asked.

His voice boomed, carrying heavily through the water to stop Arelle in her tracks. His tense stance, fin flattened to the floor of the room and head tipped back, was a good indication to her that she was not welcomed to come any closer than she already had.

Arelle's gaze darted to Poe, who quickly looked away. "Why, what?"

"Why disobey me? Why, when I have given you and your sisters everything, would you so blatantly disrespect the rules put forth for you, Arelle? And now look what it has caused."

Again, she looked to Poe.

Her sister still wouldn't look at her.

What had she told their father? She didn't have to wonder for very long just how her sister had spun the tale of their travels to the water orchard, and the forbidden lands.

"Was the fruit worth your sister's life?"

She swallowed hard and let the words slide down her throat instead of slipping past her lips. Nothing she could or would say here would make any difference, not if Poe had taken the chance to spin her lies about what had happened before Arelle had even returned to the colony.

Would it matter even if she had come back straight away?

Probably not.

She wasn't the favored one.

"Everyone knows," Zale said, his tone staying just the same. "Now that not even my princesses can be trusted to obey me, and what do you have to show for it, Arelle?"

Poe was still streaked with purple blood.

Whom had she said it belonged to?

"Arelle."

Her father's shout snapped her attention back to him.

There was a look in her father's eye—a gleam she had only seen on a few occasions before this moment. One that said he was beyond care. It was a shame that was focused on her, but it told her a great many things in that moment.

The story had already been told.

A lie spun.

He believed whatever he'd been told by Poe, and whoever else, and Arelle would be the sacrifice for his rage because of it.

"Nothing," she whispered. "I have nothing to show for it."

The bitterness she felt for Poe couldn't be contained, but with her sister's mate standing in front of her as a wall of protection, she couldn't even see the contempt Arelle shot her way. Maybe that was for the better.

"You put us all in danger by dragging not only yourself but your sisters to the forbidden lands," her father said, turning to pick up his crown from the seat of the throne. "You never considered what it would mean to the colony or to my reign. And it shows."

Arelle dragged in a lungful of water, ready to apologize even if this hadn't been entirely her fault. Her father stopped her with a rising palm, saying only, "A lesson will be made out of you—you'll spend the season of storms isolated from the colony. If you cannot think about them, you will not be with them."

What?

Arelle moved an inch or two forward. "But—"

"Word came in from a traveling messenger, as well. Your intended mate will not arrive as planned. Something is holding him that he will need to handle. You're not needed this season, and it'll do us all well to not have to see your face while we try to move on from the loss you've caused us."

"I didn't—"

"Not a single word, Arelle."

A flick of his wrist was all it took for her guards to close the distance they'd been keeping since her arrival. Their grips tightened around her arms, pulling her backward and farther away from her father and the rest of the merpeople in the throne room.

She knew better than to speak.

Her father's warning had been clear.

And still, she dared to ask, "Will I be with Mother?"

Zale's laughter taunted her.

She'd hear it for days.

"Absolutely not."

16. TO RUIN A KING

Eryx

Every breath Eryx dragged into his lungs ached deep inside his chest. Made harder by the blinding winds that cut off his air when he did try to breathe and sucked in water from the rain that pounded down from the stormy skies overhead. He was surprised that he was capable of breathing at all, really.

Not to mention, the effort it took.

The pain he felt.

He didn't guide his horse back to the estate where his father and the rest of the court were staying the night. Frankly, he didn't have the wherewithal to do anything at all when he was barely able to stay atop his goddamn horse.

No, the animal took them back on its own. Eryx simply focused on staying atop the beast because even that was a challenge.

Not because of the raging storm, although it didn't really help, but rather, everything else. The agony still ripping through his heart over the woman he'd been forced to leave behind and hadn't even seen rise out of the waters after watching her fall into its depths.

If that weren't bad enough, the water had nearly taken him, too. As he'd tried to climb out of the crashing waves on the canal, still looking over his shoulder to watch the spot where the red-headed mermaid with the violet eyes had been only seconds before—he would never forget her face, now—the water had come rushing in higher. He'd lost his step and was dragged out to where he couldn't even touch down in the sea. With the water churning so forcefully, he'd been sure he was about to drown much the same way he'd just witnessed his mother do.

It'd taken every ounce of his effort to get back to the shore; never once had he been sure that he would even make it, swallowing mouthful after mouthful of water when he'd tried to suck in a breath of air. Yet, he somehow had, before promptly passing out on the side of the canal until the rising waters brought him back to consciousness. The threat of being pulled back out to sea was enough to get him up on shaky legs, struggling to find where he'd left his horse.

"There it is," he told the horse, seeing the gates leading to the estate finally taking form on top of the hill. "We're almost there."

The horse snorted as though it could understand him and wanted to respond in some way. Who was Eryx to say the beast didn't understand its human counterpart? The only thing he could manage to do in that moment was clutch tighter to the horse's reins and hope that was enough to keep him upright.

The horse did the rest of the work.

How long had they been climbing the hill now?

Too long.

He shivered, the wind ripping against his bare skin. He knew the mermaid had destroyed his shirt, but he hadn't even been able to find his cloak. Nothing protected him from the elements of the storm currently battering the land, and him.

Each breath took more effort.

It came harder.

The muddy road ahead of him, and the clop-clop of the horse's hooves seemed to turn fainter and fainter. Even as he tried to peel open his eyes, he had to fight to do it. Nothing seemed right, his vision turning sideways when the horse slipped past the opened gate leading into the estate. His neck had started throbbing back in the water when he'd kept swallowing it instead of air, but then it had only been uncomfortable.

Now it was a painful pulsing that matched the beats of his heart. The sides of his neck felt as though they were extending with every pulse, although he didn't have the first clue as to why.

Was this death?

He was pretty sure it was.

"Help," Eryx called out when they were beyond the gate.

The yard was quiet. All the business of the day gone while the people and the court at the orchard estate hunkered down for safety from the violent storms. He doubted anyone could even hear his calls.

Still, he shouted.

"Someone, help!"

The rain pounded so hard to the ground that mud splashed up along the horse's legs as the animal came to a stop.

He thought he called for help again.

Eryx couldn't be sure.

The last thing he saw before he fell from the horse was two young men rushing out from the stables at the west side of the property. Those young men leaned over him, moving in closer to hear whatever it was he tried to tell them.

"My mother—she killed my mother."

Eryx didn't even remember hitting the ground. All he thought about was how black the sky seemed. Or maybe that was just his mind.

Because unlike his father and the rest of the people in his realm, Eryx didn't believe in the Gods they revered faithfully. He believed when one died, the only thing that greeted them on the other side was absolute nothingness.

Right then, nothing was all he saw; he liked that just fine. Now, it felt appropriate.

"Stop it."

Eryx didn't even have to shout for his annoyance to be clear because the surgeon who was currently attempting to look at his neck was fast to step back. Why his father had even bothered to call these useless fools, he didn't know. All they had wanted to do with him when they'd finally arrived—after Eryx had woken up and been feeling fine—was bleed him out.

As though that would do any good.

Then, he'd mentioned his neck.

Knowing what they did about where he'd come from, the three of them who handled any ailment of the king now wanted to take their time looking over the gills the bastards had sewn shut when Eyrx had been fresh from his mother's womb.

"Don't touch me again," Eryx warned the man. "I'm fine."

"Yes, but how?" the doctor asked, raising a thick, unruly white brow at the same time. "Because according to the stable boys who pulled you into the house, and the king, who directed them to which room you were using, you were all but dead, Prince."

And now?

"Clearly not," he said, waving at himself, "as you can see."

"It's possible the water in your lungs is attempting to be expelled through the natural route, but given the procedure done when you were an infant … If you'd just remove the scarf and allow us a look at—"

"Get out of my rooms."

"Your High—"

They were *not* touching his neck.

No one but his mother did.

"*Get out!*"

He'd had enough of being their test subject, considering they'd already had their go at trying every tincture and tonic they'd brought along. His shout was punctuated by the ornate vase he slammed to the floor from where it sat on the decorative table currently full of the surgeons' things. It wasn't the first thing he'd broken in the room since waking up, and he doubted it would be the last, frankly.

He was just in that sort of mood.

The group of men didn't even grab their belongings before fleeing the room. He wished that made him feel at least slightly pleased, but it didn't.

The things they brought along hadn't helped him before, and it wouldn't help him with what he felt now.

Nothing would.

His heart ached again.

His mind went back to his mother again.

"Fuck."

Thrusting his shaking hands into his hair, Eryx put his back to the opened doorway as he stared at the reflection in the mirror across from the bed. He should have recognized the man standing there in night clothes that belonged to him. He knew that face—watched it change day by day as he aged and turned from a child into a man.

Yet, he didn't know it now. He found no familiarity in it tonight.

Disheveled. Pale. So fucking angry. In the eyes of the man staring back at him in the mirror, however, he found the thing that bothered him the most.

There was nothing in his eyes. Deadness stared back.

Eryx approached the mirror, his thoughts racing like the beats of his heart and the constant *thud-thud-thud* in his neck that still hurt each time. More so when he breathed, he noticed. He tugged the cotton scarf, trimmed with silk, away from his throat and finally got a good look at the faint scars on either side of the thick column of flesh and corded muscle.

His Adam's apple bobbed.

The scars expanded.

Were the surgeons correct? Was his body trying to expel what water was left? Had it saved him? Or might it have killed him because they'd taken away what would have allowed him safety in the water all those years ago?

Those were questions Eryx didn't have the answers to, and they were ones he wasn't sure he wanted to know, honestly. Not that it mattered because he had more important things on his mind at the moment, and other issues he had to handle.

The approaching footsteps outside the bedchambers had him quickly wrapping the scarf back around his throat. All his life, he'd been taught to hide what would remind the people that he came from a woman caught within the sea, and he wasn't quite ready to drop the pretense yet.

Especially not with that woman gone.

Eryx turned sharply in just enough time to see his father step inside the room with Mattue close behind his heels. In the hallway, a guard stayed near the entry but didn't attempt to enter when Misael nodded for his brother to close the door.

"What were you thinking?" Misael demanded with an almost maniacal gleam in his father's eye that Eryx had never witnessed before.

And he had seen Misael do terrible, awful things.

Eryx swallowed the pain that accompanied his next words. "I'm not sure what you mean."

"Being at the orchard. The storms have come. You're not that foolish, Eryx, you know better. What on this earth possessed you to take a horse down there?"

Ah.

So the stable boys either hadn't heard him when he spoke about his mother after falling from the horse, or they simply hadn't understood what he'd been talking about.

Perfect.

"Anthia."

That was all he said.

Not *my mother.*

Or even *your favored one, Father.* Because unlike everyone else, Eryx refused to reduce his mother to nothing more than a man's whore.

No, he used just her name.

Because even that hurt.

Misael tipped his chin up, stillness and coldness settling over him suddenly. "What about the slave?"

Gods.

How could he *say* that?

"She's my mother." He flinched, correcting himself out of spite of his heart because he wanted to say it right; to make this clear so he didn't have to ever say it again. "Was. She was my mother—we were walking along the orchard, and one of the mermaids dropped from the trees."

Red hair.

Violet eyes.

Hissing.

Fingernails slicing his skin.

But the red and the purple … the face now seared into his memory bobbing along the dangerous waves … well, he wasn't about to forget that, either. He couldn't.

Behind the king, Mattue cleared his throat but otherwise, stayed quiet. Misael, however, didn't look away from his son. "We've discussed this. You know your place. And your favor toward that slave has never been acceptable."

Eryx stared hard at his father. "You don't mean that. She was my mother."

"A vessel that brought you to me. It is me who made you a prince. It was her who doomed your legacy to a constant question by the people that may fear her side of you. They will forever wonder about who you are, Eryx. And never forget it."

Right.

Because what was he, his father had liked to ask every chance he could, a human like them, or someone of the sea? He had to wonder if Misael had ever questioned his brothers, born the same way he had been, although, by different slaves, the way the king second-guessed him.

He almost wanted to scoff.

That would hurt, though.

"To be fair, my lord," his advisor said, coming in a second too late to the conversation as far as Eryx was concerned, "you did allow Anthia a great deal of freedom in her place. She often came and went without question where others would have been stripped and beaten in the square for the same actions. I even heard a certain horse had been taken by her earlier. Was that not your doing? Tis not—"

"Did I ask?" Misael uttered, jaw clenching. "You seem to be another one who constantly forgets your place, Mattue. You're are not wearing a crown—you advise it."

Eryx bet that hit a nerve.

His father was quite good at that.

Mattue was quick to quiet. "My apologies."

He tipped his head down and said nothing else.

Misael turned his attention back on Eryx. "I have had just about enough of trying to justify my only living son's affections for the slaves of this realm. It seems you've forgotten your place, Eryx, or you don't appreciate what you've been given. I can't have the rest of my people seeing it. Because then, they will think it's appropriate for them to follow the same path."

His affections?

He'd only ever cared for his mother.

Goddammit.

He didn't even love his father the way he loved his mother.

Misael didn't give him the chance to respond before his father said, "It's time for you to learn exactly what I expect of you. Nothing else will be acceptable after this day, Eryx."

"What does that even mean?"

"Mattue—what we discussed, you may relay it to Eryx, as I no longer care to stand here and stare at his face. I'm sure you know why this is fitting for him, now more so than it was when we first discussed the option."

The king left the room in the same way he'd arrived. Without a word, without permission, and without a single care in the world that he was leaving behind his son, who had clearly lost something that meant more to him than even this kingdom did.

Not that Misael cared.

He never had.

"Plans have changed," Mattue said quietly, drawing in Eryx's attention, "as your father decided while the surgeons were in here with you."

"I beg your pardon?"

"You won't return to court with the rest of us. Instead, you'll remain here, but lower in the south-west. Banished to the House of Miller until the king says otherwise. Word will travel about what happened—that you were with the slave when she was killed."

"Stop calling her that."

Mattue tipped his chin up, murmuring, "But that is what she is."

"Was."

"Eryx."

He was sure he would snap the tips of his teeth from how hard he clenched his jaw together. It hurt, but he couldn't find it in himself to give a single damn, either.

"Word will travel," the man repeated, "and when that happens, stories will get told that may not match the details of what occurred. Your father wants to ensure that no matter what, the realm sees you're being treated appropriately for your behavior and favor toward the—"

"Call her a slave one more time and I'll cut your fucking tongue from your mouth, Mattue."

Wisely, the man chose to say nothing.

"He's going to banish me."

"Yes."

"Like a shameful secret."

"Well—"

"Even though he has spent his entire reign over this realm catching mermaids to breed with them, so he could have an army of heirs and spares."

None of his statements were questions.

Just truth.

"Eryx—"

"Unless you're going to tell me something I wish to hear, you're to say nothing at all, Mattue."

The rage that coursed through him mixed heavily with his grief as he spun back around to face the mirror once again. Only this time, he recognized all too well the fractured reflection of the man staring back at him.

The boy he'd once been.

Forgotten.

Paraded like a trophy when needed.

Discarded otherwise.

Only his mother had been a constant. Only she had shown him true affection and love when everyone else in his life treated him like the spare to the throne he'd always been until it came time for him to take that seat, too. Until he was suddenly the heir, and everything had to change.

And now what did he have?

Nothing.

Again.

Just nothing.

With a shout, Eryx put his clenched, shaking fists right through the glass of the mirror, shattering most of it as he watched the shards fall to his naked feet on the floor. A shift of his left foot caused one of the pieces to slice the side of his heel, but he didn't even care.

He was crying again.

He hated that more than anything else.

"I'm sorry," Mattue said in a whisper behind him. "I know you cared for your mother a great deal, and that—"

"I want her dead."

That quieted the man.

But only for a moment.

"Who?"

Who?

Such a simple question.

He could describe the little mermaid in a single breath. How the lines of her face made up the shape of a heart. The fiery shade of her hair. Those wide, haunting violet eyes that matched the color of the skies after a storm had passed. Silken, olive skin the color of gleaming gold when wet.

Everything.

Instead, all he said was, "The mermaid. I want her dead."

"Will that make you feel better?"

Eryx laughed.

The sound was entirely bitter.

And violent, too.

Like the urges he felt inside his heart, and how dark his mind turned at the thought of having that mermaid in his hands in that moment. Oh, he'd choke the very life right out of her. Slowly, and all too happily. He couldn't even be sure she was the one who killed his mother, but she'd dared to come back. She'd stared at him in his pain for just a second too long, and he wanted her to die for it, too.

"Is that what you ask my father every time he tells you that he wants another?" Eryx asked.

Mattue didn't reply, and instead, only repeated his earlier question. "Will that make you feel better, Prince?"

"I don't know if it would make this better, but it would certainly make me happy."

Mattue made a noise under his breath. "Perhaps you're just too angry right now. I don't think you truly understand what you're saying, Eryx. All for a ... well, I won't call your mother a slave, but nonetheless, why kill for her? Why do something that would very well threaten your place alongside your father—your spot on the throne? You're irrational."

Not at all.

"I'd give anything to have that mermaid."

To kill her.

"I don't think you would," his advisor replied.

Eryx met the man's gaze in what remained of the shattered mirror. "Name your price."

Because he knew …

If there was ever anyone in this realm who could see something like this done—capturing that mermaid—it would be Mattue. His reach went farther than the king could possibly know, but Eryx did. And he didn't mind making a deal for his soul with Mattue to get what he wanted, either. Many before him had done the same.

"You know what it would cost you," the man replied quietly. "Your father expects you to take your banishment with dignity and come back to royal life ready to marry and behave. He's not going to accept anything else from you, Eryx, and if you cause him more issues, but especially where it might concern the people … Think about it."

Right.

He would be dead.

"My crown. That's what it would mean. There is no one else to come after me anymore."

"But I wouldn't mind taking it in your place."

Eryx didn't drop the man's stare. "You are next in the succession, seeing as how I've not produced an heir with a woman yet."

Mattue smiled.

It seemed far too pleased.

"It appears I am." Mattue shrugged. "I could find someone to catch your little mermaid … if that's the deal you want to make, Eryx."

Was it?

He didn't even need to ask the question of himself, really.

"It is."

In the mirror, he met his own stare. Mattue faded away in the background of the jagged reflection.

Let the hunt begin.

Mattue

The sight of his brother drunken and slovenly, puking over the side of his bed into a piss pot below was a poor one. Misael's next retch came with far less fluid to spill over onto the floor, thankfully, but it did nothing for the dankness of the bedchamber.

"Get out," Mattue snapped at the slave clutching the bedspread to her naked chest.

She didn't need to be told again.

Thankfully.

The king, on the other hand, was clearly thankful for *nothing*.

"Misael—"

"I'm *dying*," his brother croaked.

Mattue inhaled a breath meant to settle himself for another round of reminding Misael where his priorities needed to be. In the midterm, his gaze caught another item on the bedside table. The pipe and small iron canister where his brother kept the opiate salts from the Red Seas explained why it was nearly noon, and Misael had yet to answer the many knocks at his door.

Moving across the room, Mattue pulled open as much drapery on the windows as he could, and even opened a few to let the stink blow out. All the while, Misael groaned in a mixture of pain and disgust, finding his way to his back on the bed and rubbing fisted hands into his eye sockets.

"My head is splitting ... What ... what was last—*Anthia*."

The name came out of the king in a heavy rush.

Mattue only sighed where he remained standing near the window. It was easier to breathe the air in the room when it didn't also taste of his brother's vomit, semen, and many other things that he wished he couldn't discern. An unfortunate part of being a halfling.

He'd become good at ignoring it over the years.

Much like Misael, and his own sins.

"Yes, your favorite one died, my lord," Mattue said, needing Misael to get on with the day so that the two of them could see Eryx off into his banishment appropriately. Instead, the prince had already taken off, here the king still laid, clearly unwell, and Mattue needed his brother to get a handle on things.

One of them was a king, after all.

There *were* duties.

"Were you smoking the salts again?" Mattue asked.

"I'll cut your tongue out, brother."

"My lord, you forget *days*."

"I want to forget *everything!*" Misael roared.

Pity.

A heartbroken king.

Mattue truly wished he could pull some sympathy for Misael over his state and guilt about Anthia's passing, but alas, he did not. No matter how long this grief of his took to get past, Misael would never get over how he blamed himself for all of it. He didn't need to speak those words to Mattue for his brother to know it was true.

"The boys did drag the orchard canals this morning," Mattue murmured.

That news perked Misael up immensely.

"Did they?"

Too bad.

Mattue crushed his hope again. "And found nothing, unfortunately."

The king fell back into the bed. "*Fuck.*"

"It wouldn't matter. Even if they had found her, you would have had to bury her privately, without even a marker, Misael."

"Better than nothing. Better than—"

"You wouldn't even let her own son avenge her, but you'll drag an orchard bottom for a body to bury all by yourself, my King?"

Misael ground his teeth so loudly, it echoed.

No, he felt nothing for his brother.

Least of all sympathy.

The man couldn't even look his son in the face and tell him of his own pain, all too willing to let his brother convince him that what Eryx needed more was to be taught a lesson so that they could control the narrative and stories about the event, and he wanted Mattue's pity?

He had none left.

"The time away will help Eryx," Mattue said, then.

"As you told me yesterday," Misael mumbled into his open hand.

Right.

"However, I think something else might help you, my lord. Let your son's banishment soothe his heartache over his mother, and he can have his privacy in these troubling times."

Away, where they didn't have to handle him. Mattue liked to keep Eryx where he could see him, so to speak.

"And me?" Misael asked, a little sadly.

"Let's head north, back to court. There is no place where you are wanted and adored more. You can indulge all your heartache in any way you please in your gilded rooms, brother. Where your harem makes you happy."

Or something very close to it.

Misael made a thick, wet noise that came from the back of his throat. "One made me happy, Mattue. Just the one."

Yet, he had never loved her enough to prove it.

"To court, then?" Mattue asked the king. "You'll sulk over her less there, anyway, my lord. You've acquired a whole collection that reminds you of her. Why waste away here?"

Even as he said those things, Mattue didn't believe them. Looking at his brother, he found the truth.

Misael's jaw twitched, but he said nothing.

Every man had their ruin.

Every *king*.

Misael stared his blatantly in the face, lying in the mess of his own making, wearing bedclothes stained with his piss and vomit; his own damned love would do it.

So be it.

That was the king's choice to make.

Mattue didn't mind helping him along.

17. BLOOD IN THE WATER

Tak

300 days later …

"You must push, Princess," said the maiden outside the rim of Poe's nest.

"*I am!*" Poe snarled back, lifting her head enough to lock eyes with the merwoman only trying to help.

"Push harder."

"You can do it, Poe," Arelle murmured where she sat just beneath her sister outside the nest, their fingers lacing for connection and strength. The only woman of her family that she had requested to attend her birth, although Tak knew her mother waited not far from the grotto for word of the baby's arrival and her permission to join.

How she brought their child into the world was entirely her choice. From where to how, to *who*. Tak's fingertips grazed the matted hair of the baby crowning between his mate's legs. On all fours, leaning over the edge of the nest occasionally for her sister, Poe only needed to look down to see her progress.

Although right now, the lack of it.

"They're right there," he told Poe. "Feel them with me."

One shaky hand did reach down, and her trembling fingers found the same thing his hand.

"So much hair," Poe whispered.

Tak laughed quietly. "'Twas what kept you up all those nights unsettled, I think."

"*Oh, Gods*," Poe groaned.

Another contraction was coming.

The maiden told her, "Make this one be it, Poe. As hard as you can, he will catch the baby."

"It feels like it's going to rip me in half," she croaked.

Tak kissed Poe's lower back as he felt the tightening in her muscles there, and his hands went back to where they needed to be the most. "*Push*, heart of my seas, give them to me."

Poe's baby did come with the next push, and it did tear her open on the way. Tak told her, "Just the body now, my love. Easy."

"'Tis a lot of blood," the maiden murmured, "*move*."

He didn't need her to say it.

He could see the river of violet that fell over his baby and hands.

"Tak?" Poe asked faintly.

"Talk to her," he hissed at Arelle who had stood at the first lusty cry of the new life Poe had just brought into the world. "Keep her talking."

The young woman's eyes widened at the pool of purple staining the middle of the nest.

"I-I—"

Her stuttering, and then silence, made Poe look down.

"*What is happen ...*"

Her sentence didn't finish. More blood, too much, fell. Tak stood at the same time the maiden turned his mate over in the nest, yanking pillows and blankets to shove under Poe's lower half to keep it higher. Still connected to their child through her cord, the maiden only reached for the blade Tak produced to cut the still pulsing, although weak, tethered between mother and child.

He was supposed to do that.

Helpless to watch Poe bleed out as he held a bloodstained, crying baby girl in his arms, he let the maiden do the job instead.

It was only when the maiden ripped a sheet from the nest in half, balled it, and shoved it inside Poe that his mate finally opened her eyes again. The shout of pain even had her jolting up in the nested bed as if to get away with it.

Tak held their baby tighter.

"I'm sorry, Princess, I have to try to stop the bleeding," the maiden rushed to say. "You must stay still."

"*Arelle ...*"

"I'm here," Poe's sister managed to say through chattering teeth, leaning over the nest to wrap her sister.

"My baby—"

"'Tis here," Tak assured, finally stepping out of the nest that he would have to rebuild.

Poe's stare, not really focused or strong, did try to follow him as he came closer. She settled a little when their very pink, chubby baby girl with matted black curls curled upon her chest. The young's tail curled around Poe's arm the second she cradled her child. Arelle stepped back to give Tak more room to nuzzle and kiss his mate that tried harder and harder to keep her eyes open.

"*She's* here," he said, wanting Poe to know they had a little girl.

Her next breath came deep and slow.

Tak's chest ached.

"Has it stopped?" he asked the maiden.

The way her gaze snapped up to him said the blood had not.

He and Poe had talked about a lot of things regarding their child, the birth, and what would come after. There was a reason she chose Arelle to be the only member of her family as a witness; why she wanted the favored maiden of her mother to see her through it.

"You must say it to them now," he told Poe low in her ear. "Tell them now, Poe."

Somehow, she heard him.

"They cannot—" She swallowed hard, and a low whine followed. "They cannot brand her, Arelle. You mustn't let them brand her."

She spoke to her sister, but the maiden heard it, too.

"The king already has—"

"You cried all night, and your sisters, too," Tak reminded his mate, uncaring that the rest of the grotto could hear him now. "We all listened. When you screamed as they did it, and all night afterward, too. If the queen before you was told her possible young could choose the brand when they were old enough to understand, and then be put into the line of succession, then yours can, too. Let her choose."

It was important to them.

She asked him to remind her too often for him to forget.

"*Poe*, do you hear me?"

Her eyes fluttered wide one last time before she lost consciousness. She made sure they all heard her, though.

"They cannot brand her."

Arelle

"I think it has stopped," the maiden told the quiet grotto. "I'll need help to take out this packing and remove the afterbirth. This will be a delicate thing."

Arelle was not doing that.

9ine hells, she wasn't even supposed to be here tonight as her punishment of seclusion had yet to officially end. It was only her sister's request that she attend the birth, and Poe's private apology for making her sister suffer the worst of their father's wrath for what happened to Coral, that she agreed.

Well, that and the baby.

Poe and her child needed Arelle, didn't they?

They were kin.

Family.

"I'll take her," Arelle said of the now swaddled baby in Tak's arms. He had wrapped her in a blanket made of the same silver silk that matched the cushioning of her cradle in the corner of the room. "If you trust me, I mean."

"Of course, I trust you," the merman replied as his brow furrowed. "You are of her blood, Arelle."

She tipped her head to him, not able to meet his eyes as he handed the newborn into her aunt's arms. Doing her best to focus on the rooting baby trying to suckle on her fingertip instead of what was happening in the nest, Arelle imprinted the girl's features to her memory. She traced the slope of her nose and the purse of her little lips.

Violet eyes fluttered open.

"Hi, there," Arelle whispered.

The baby's tail escaped the confines of her swaddle to find her aunt's arm and coil tightly. She instantly settled, then, and her eyes closed.

"Her heartbeat is still strong," she heard the maiden tell Tak.

He didn't respond.

Arelle glanced toward her sister's prone form and the man holding her face and kissing a crown across her clammy, but unmoving, forehead.

"It'll be okay," he told no one in particular.

Maybe his mate.

"The Gods won't take her from me now. I waited too long."

18. BAIT

Eryx

62 days later ...

The clop-clop of the horse's hooves against the dirt road that led into the West Market's eastern entrance through the village gave Eryx a good visual of what lay in wait for him. Through the bustling streets filled with villagers selling their goods, from shoddy tables covered like tents with ragged cloths to keep out the elements should a storm arrive without warning, he looked beyond it all to see what was farther out.

Beyond the market.

And the square.

Even the village.

There, he found the masts of ships reaching toward a rather clear sky. Both of which meant good things not only for him, but these vendors attempting to sell their items to make what gold they could before the storm season arrived again. It felt like the last one had gone on for so long that they had barely any good weather at all before they'd been faced with the rapidly changing seasons all over again.

Did that mean the seasons were shifting? Longer storms, and shorter periods of rest?

Eryx couldn't be sure, but if that were the case, he figured it didn't mean anything good for their realm. As it was, the royal family and the people relied on the season after the storms to be able to properly live.

He didn't study the sky or the water. His education before becoming an adult had consisted of understanding royal protocol, reading, writing, and learning the languages of realms which Atlas did business or trades with. He hadn't needed any further education, according to his father. He simply needed to be a prince.

And look at me now. What good had all that focus on being the heir done for him? He was still the shunned one.

Not that Eryx minded those minor details. At the very least, his father's punishment, which had lasted the majority of the year, had actually come as a bit of a relief for him in a way. He hadn't needed to concern himself with life at court, the politics of it all, or the theatrics involved with sitting on a throne that, as far as he was concerned, had always been a little too close to his father's.

Not to mention, his advisor had managed to do his job over the past year. Mattue made sure Eryx wouldn't also have to focus on picking a wife, as the king demanded. To be frank, he assumed that was only because doing so would have meant bringing Eryx back to court, so his father could parade women from one end of the realm to the other for the people and his son to appreciate.

It defeated the purpose of hiding Eryx away.

"Sir! All your needs are taken care of with what you'll find on my table. Sickness, age, or—"

A strong gust of wind came, blowing back the fur-trimmed hood of Eryx's black, velvet cloak. He turned his head to see the man standing behind a particular booth set in front of a blacksmith's shop. As soon as the villager's gaze landed on Eryx atop the horse, he quickly realized who he had been attempting to sell his goods—medicine, likely made by using the blood of mermaids if he had to guess by what was on the table. Although, only a few people in the realm knew how to properly make such things and there were more fakes than there were real in the various markets.

"Prince," the man breathed, taking a step back from his table to bow at the middle.

Eryx nodded at the man, but just as quickly turned his attention to the road ahead. With his cloak's hood down around his shoulders, and a scarf tightly wrapped around his throat, his face was on more prominent display while he headed farther into the market. If anything, it helped to get him through the bustling streets filled with everything from a woman selling jewelry to another advertising the sale on her gowns by shouting out of a window.

Chickens wandering the road scattered at the noise of his horse's hooves beating against the soft ground. A mother was quick to pull her young son—who held onto a small, gray puppy—back from the road when Eryx passed them by as well.

Like most other people in the market who noticed it was the only remaining prince in Atlas coming through, she lowered into a curtsey, bringing her son along with her. And the same way most of the people wouldn't hold his stare for very long, the woman did the same while she murmured something Eryx couldn't hear into her son's ear.

Probably the same whispers he'd been hearing for a while.

The heir ...

Shunned and shamed ...

Yet, the punishment his father intended for him to suffer through had done very little to teach Eryx anything. Nor did it do very much to teach the people, considering they still bowed when he passed and continued to address him as the royal he was to the rest of the realm.

It seemed to him that he was only a leper to everyone else when they thought he couldn't hear because publicly, Eryx was still very much the prince he had always been. And since the majority of his days were spent alone where he could enjoy his own thoughts and privacy instead of worrying about behaving appropriately for court ... well, who had really won here?

Besides, all this time alone had simply allowed Eryx to focus on the more important things in his current life.

Like the mermaid.

And hunting her.

"And finally, he arrives," came a familiar call.

Arriving at the market square was always quite an event, for any number of reasons. The area with the square platform in the very center was the heart of the village and market. Its purpose was never designated to just one thing, but rather, many. Punishment, celebration, or otherwise. Today, it was where Mattue waited with a man who Eryx had only met a handful of times before.

Dismounting from his horse, but only after the waiting men had greeted him appropriately with a bow and a respectful "Prince," Eryx handed the reins off to a waiting boy who didn't linger long enough for the prince to thank him. Not that he minded. Climbing the steps to the square's platform, Eryx noted how much better he could see the ships waiting at the port just a stone's throw away from their current position.

Three ships, to be exact.

"A nice sight, isn't it?" the man next to Mattue asked. "I've always enjoy seeing them on the water, when the waves aren't knocking them damn near sideways."

Eryx chuckled, shifting in his leather boots before clasping his gloved hands at his middle. "I have to wonder if that might have anything to do with the cost to replace a ship and less to do with the fact you actually care for the vessels."

"Bit of both, your highness. A bit of both."

"Corval, is it?"

The man nodded. "That is my name, yes. We haven't been able to have a proper conversation yet, but Mattue has handled giving me all your directions. No worries on that."

Eryx nodded once, turning his attention back to the man. Young, he thought, to be a hunter, given his hair was a stark white blond against the shine of the sun in the sky, and his face held no lines that spoke of age. It seemed the man preferred simple trousers, knee-high leather boots, and linen shirts that weren't tied at the throat but rather, showed off the man's dusting of chest hair.

It all spoke of the style and preference of a young man, and not one with any age or standing who had to care about his appearance. Then again, perhaps it was just easier for the man to dress the way he did, given his job.

Who was Eryx to judge?

It wasn't just the ship captains who made the hunts of the merpeople work, but rather, actual hunters who went out with the ships. Men who planned the hunts with a specific skill set and knowledge of not only the water and land, but of the people beneath the surface of the sea.

A gust of wind blew through the square, sending dry dust spiraling from the ground. Mattue shook his head at the sight.

"The winds are starting."

Corval grunted his agreement, stepping toward the edge of the platform before glancing over his shoulder. "A sure and good sign the storms will be returning for a spread—only the Gods know how long it'll last this time around."

Then, just as fast, the man jumped down from the platform. A waiting boy with a scruffy hat pulled down over his eyes waited there with a sheathed dagger in one hand, which Corval took with a thanks and a pat on the child's head.

"Thanks for holding onto it for me." He looked over his shoulder, his stare landing firmly on Eryx before the man smiled slyly. "Seven caught in this hunt—care to see if your little mermaid is one of them, Prince?"

Eryx smirked. "Absolutely."

"Lead the way, Corval," Mattue added.

The walk to the wharf was rather short and quiet. Neither of which Eryx minded because it allowed him to sink deeper into his thoughts. A place he quite liked to be, considering there wasn't a soul around him who could possibly understand the things that constantly ran on repeat in his mind.

Mostly focused on the mermaid …

If only he could catch her.

Eryx's joy at having been told seven merpeople were caught in the last hunt was quickly ripped away at the sight of the nets hanging from the side of two of three ships at the end of the wharf. Even from a good forty steps away, he could plainly see that three nets held five figures that were far too large and muscular to be female.

It seemed the males had been left in their nets, and if Eryx had to guess, it probably had something to do with their outbursts and rather active behavior. Not to mention, aggressiveness. A couple, already dead and unmoving in the nets from arrows through their throats or embedded deep into their chests, acted as a warning for the others waiting to meet their fates.

"Well, I would have been a lot less excited, had you said five of the seven were males," Eryx grumbled.

Corval cleared his throat but didn't bother to glance back at Eryx or Mattue where they continued their trek behind the man. "Yes, well, the females—"

"I will look at the women."

"Of course."

"The females always tend to be frightened and quick to comply when needed," Mattue noted. "And the males … well, it takes a ship full of men to control even one of them."

"That depends on several factors, Mattue."

"Right."

"Like what?" Eryx questioned.

"Another day," Corval replied, "and we can discuss those details. For now …"

He came to a stop next to the one ship without nets hanging off the side with captured mermaids. Instead, Eryx had a plain view of the cages resting on the upper deck that had been moved to the side where they would be rolled down a loading plank.

It took him all of a glance at the two females inside the cages to know … she had not yet been caught. Yes, one was a redhead, although it wasn't nearly as bright of a shade as his mermaid. Both had the signature violet eyes that he saw in his dreams—and nightmares—every single time he closed his eyes.

However, they were not her.

She'd been burned into his memory. Her image ingrained in the backs of his eyelids, where he was sure it would remain until the day he died. He'd had an entire year to think about the mermaid every single minute of his waking hours, and unfortunately, she seemed to like visiting him in his dreams, too.

Eryx had a terrible habit of obsessing over the mermaid and what he would like to do to her once he finally captured her. His previous thoughts of a violent end for her life to answer for his mother's death had morphed into the kinds of visions that could only be described as darkly primal. He had the basest urge to find the merwoman and allow the rage that constantly festered loose as he broke her in every possible way.

Yes, an obsession was the right word.

Most certainly.

Today would not be the day he fulfilled those urges, it seemed.

"Neither are her," he murmured.

He was careful when he spoke not to expose his anger or any other emotion currently pinging around in his heart like a stone skipping over water that couldn't be contained. It wouldn't do him any good for people to see how much a merwoman affected him, especially when he didn't even have his hands around her fucking throat.

And that is enough of that, he told himself.

"My apologies," Corval said from his left.

Eryx shrugged. "Mattue did say it might take a while to find her. I'm learning more about my own patience—and lack of it—during this process."

"We have a handful of hunts left in this season if all goes well. The plans are already in the works. Care to have a look?"

Well, Eryx supposed if he couldn't have the mermaid now … the next best thing would be engaging in the hunter's plans to find her.

"I would care to have a look, yes."

Once again, Corval led the way.

Eryx breathed in the scent of the sea, hearing the echo of his mother in every breath, as he followed.

Apparently, the mermaid hunter did the majority of his planning in a fucking fishing shack. Eryx could easily think of a hundred other places the man could do his business that wouldn't smell as rancid as this building did, but he kept his mouth shut as a few scattered items were shoved sideways on a large slab of flat rock without care. Just as quickly, a map was unrolled across the surface and iron candle holders placed to the four corners to hold it in place.

"Here," Corval said, his finger dragging along the band of Atlas Islands on the map, "is where it's most dangerous for us to hunt because of the constantly changing water levels, and what's beneath the surface that we often can't see until it's too late. Sunken ships, structures that were once on parts of the island. A bit of coral reef, and in some areas, very shallow water."

"But?" Eryx asked.

Because of course, he could hear that unspoken word.

"This is also where we tend to find a lot of them. Hunting, occasionally living … whatever the case may be. It seems a good portion of their people use these islands further out as a safe haven for their activities. But without getting close enough, it makes a hunt difficult."

"Yet, you said you catch a lot from there."

"Exactly—from there, Prince."

If there was anything he hated, it was word games.

Who had time for that?

"The point, if you wouldn't mind," Eryx said dryly.

"Right," Corval replied, placing his hands flat to the map and meeting Eryx's gaze. "We've found our hunts are more successful when we sacrifice a catch from the previous hunt to use to draw them out and trap them in various places depending on the type we're looking for. Men need to be corralled with no option for escape. The females often focus on helping one another escape, and they're a great deal smaller. Easier to contain."

That was interesting.

"How are you using them as bait, exactly?"

In the corner of the room, Mattue seemed more interested in whatever scroll he'd unrolled to look over in his hands. Eryx didn't care for the man's distraction when they were trying to do business. At the same time, he liked it more when the man let him do the talking.

Win some, lose some.

"Different ways," Corval explained, shrugging his broad shoulders. "But typically, their calls will draw the mermaids out."

"Their calls."

It wasn't even a question.

Corval tipped his chin down in agreement. "Yes. They seem to recognize familial calls … maybe it's the magic in their blood or just a thing about their species. You've heard of the thrall, their bond, haven't you?"

Eryx cleared his throat. "When they bleed, you mean?"

"That, yes."

"Heard of it, of course. Everyone has heard the stories of when mermaids bleed. Never been close enough to one when they bleed to experience it myself, however."

Corval raised his brow at Eryx'x reply. "Everything you've ever heard—believe it and then some. When the creatures bleed, even the air feels like it changes."

Huh.

"I tend to think," the man continued, "that their blood calls to their kind, too, but I've not been able to prove it. It would certainly add a lot to the hunts, if I figured out exactly how to use it properly."

"I bet."

And Eryx didn't care at all unless it would bring in his mermaid.

"Back to the hunts I'm funding," Eryx said, pointing at the map before going back to his same, stoic posture with his hands folded at his middle. "And how this relates to that, if you wouldn't mind."

"Right, well … they're getting smarter, and trickier. Even this season's hunts have only brought in a small handful at most with each trip."

"More dangerous as well?"

Corval grunted under his breath. "That, too, yes. You leave a ship on the waters overnight or a net you can't pull up within the evening and it won't last. They fight back, too."

Of course.

It would be stupid to think the merpeople would simply allow their kind to continue to be hunted without adapting to the situation in whatever way they could. Undoubtedly, one of those ways would be to fight back.

"We'll pull a male from the latest catch for the next two hunts," Corval explained, "and use him to draw in whatever others we can. These ones had a lot of weapons on them, so I tend to think they were doing a hunt of their own, and that I'll have to order their stems be pierced to keep them from being too much trouble even if that only keeps the body good for a year."

Eryx considered the mermen hanging in the nets. "And the ones not used for bait? What will be done with them when they can't walk or talk or *think*?"

A part of him thought he already knew, but for once, Eryx wanted to know if he was right. He usually didn't care, but the prince had his own morbid curiosities about the happenings in the belly of the king's palace where rooms made of racking tables and bodies hung from chains remained off-limits to him.

"Owed to the crown—for bleeding." Corval gestured beyond a window to the unpleasant sky. "The season isn't over yet, Prince, and we still may catch your mermaid before the storms return."

That was his hope, too.

Not that he cared to admit it out loud.

Through the window of the shack where the shutters had been opened wide to overlook the sea, Eryx stared at the rather calm waters. The smell of the sea was still thick in the air, and he swore the scent alone was enough to have his neck pulsing with the beats of his heart. Ever since that night in the water, he'd become acutely aware of his closed gills and just how often they liked to make themselves known.

Sometimes, he even craved the sea.

Not that he understood why.

Before he could properly consider the snap decision that floated through his mind, he said, "I would like to join some of the final hunts this season."

That had Mattue finally forgetting the scroll in his hands so that he could join the conversation. "Prince, I don't believe that to be a wise decision. It would mean going out on the ships when we're close to the season and storms arrive without warning. Should the king find out—"

"You'll make sure he doesn't."

"Eryx."

Ah, his name this time.

He gave Mattue a look. "I'll join the hunts."

Mattue didn't reply.

That was that.

19. THE TRAP

Arelle

"Father, *please*—"

"Poe, I have discussed this far more than I wanted to. You know my opinion on the matter, and it will not change simply because it is your mate. Your mate is not any more or less important than anyone else in this colony."

Her father and sister's exchange had the rest of the merpeople in the throne room quieting instantly. The change in the air was palpable, and Arelle could sense it without even needing to look at the two. Still, she peeked up from the infant in her arms, if only to see if she might need to step in to calm the situation down.

Although could she really?

Likely not.

Poe stood in the middle of the room. Exactly where their father had demanded she stand while addressing him. Except now, her sister's body leaned forward a bit while she did little to nothing to hide the contempt and pain coloring her features.

On her father's side, King Zale sat unbothered on his throne of twisted, sharp glass. With a face made of what seemed like stone, he was unmoved by his child's plight. Perhaps Poe's place as his favorite made her sister forget that at the end of the day, their father only really ever cared about one thing. He made it seem like that thing was his people, when really it was only himself.

Arelle had learned that already.

It was a shame her sister learned this way. Poe was not different simply because she was to be the next queen.

"But—"

Zale held up a hand, silencing Poe instantly. "I have made my decision."

"He is my mate! The father of my child!"

At the rising voice, the baby in Arelle's arms perked. The tiny girl's eyes fluttered open, still so new in her life under the sea that she had a hard time focusing her sights on any one thing in particular unless it was close to her. So, when her pretty violet eyes landed on Arelle, a comforting sight to her, as she was used to her kin, the girl settled. Her tail had wrapped around Arelle's arm the same way it did for her mother whenever they swam or traveled. It was a baby's way of staying attached to its mother until it came time to learn to swim. And even then, their young never went too far.

"And his error in judgment is something he will have to suffer for," the king finally replied to her sister. "Because the rest of us will not also suffer for the results of his stupidity, Poe. I won't do what you want. That's the end of it. It's settled."

Arelle let out a sigh.

Not a happy one, though.

This couldn't be happy.

The soft clearing of a throat drew Arelle's attention to the woman perched at the floor near Zale's tail fin. It was strange to see their mother outside of her private chambers unless their father was holding court or something similar, within the palace, considering how rare it seemed to be for that to happen. Their father liked to keep her away where no one could touch her, and she had no opinions to share.

Both things that terrified him.

Funny how that worked.

Which was also why, when her mother did get to come out and spend time around the rest of her people, Zale made Rosel sit at his feet like a pet. As if she were an octopus or sea snake he'd trained to behave a certain way, sweetly entertaining while also mindful of her presence. Or rather, the lack of it when the moment demanded it from the king's wife.

She should be a queen.

Instead, this is how she lived her life.

Arelle often wondered how their people viewed her mother—a woman meant to be their queen—but she had learned that it wasn't her place. Everything went far smoother in her father's kingdom when everyone stayed in their respective positions without argument.

That didn't mean they liked it.

"She says she still hears him. Something *of* him. You could send out the guard to ch—"

"Hush," Zale hissed, his reprimand swift and sharp for the woman sitting beneath him. And just like that, Arelle watched as her mother's expression reverted back to a statue's, with no soul and no life to her eyes. A sad thing, really.

Shameful.

Just as fast, Zale's attention went back to his daughter in the middle of the room. Poe still looked ready to kill, but Arelle knew this discussion was over. It had been over before it'd ever really began.

Nothing ever changed in the Blu Seas. Determined to stay the same, she was sure they would all die for it, too.

"Do you still hear your mate?" Zale asked.

Poe swallowed hard. "I do, but—"

"Then, perhaps he will find his way back."

"He went hunting two weeks ago."

"And according to the mermen from the party who returned, he went too far past the Isle of Broken Islands. Chasing a creature, from what I understand. How many times did I tell Tak that he needed to put his enjoyments aside and take his proper place beside you—a princess? Many times, Poe."

"*Yes, hunting for your people to eat!*" she shouted.

Zale's jaw tightened at Poe's snarl. "This was his mistake, and I will not sacrifice who knows how many of my guards on the chance of returning him to you. Give it time. Speak to the maidens upon the end of the bond, should you feel it. You'll find a companion, and your child will have someone to help raise her."

"You know that's not possible for me now. I will want only him."

It was the ache in her sister's voice that had Arelle holding a little tighter to the baby in her arms. The girl had yet to be given a name, which wasn't uncommon in their sea. Typically, by around their first year if not sooner ... a name would be chosen for the little ones born during the end of the last season of storms.

So far, her sister hadn't picked one for her child.

However, as Arelle stared down at the baby girl ... well, she couldn't help but feel the pang of sadness echoing in her chest. Things had not been good with her sister ever since she had been made to suffer through confinement for Poe's lies and manipulation, but they had gotten better after the baby had been born. Her sister, like any other merwoman, depended on the help of her kin after a birth and Arelle couldn't have refused.

Because of the baby.

So, without needing to be told, she knew very well how painful this was to Poe. Not just because she was left with a child that now had a father who was missing, but also because the two were a mated pair. That was for life. Those bonds would never be broken even after death. Her sister would never properly mate again.

A companion was one thing. A mate ... quite another. If the man was dead, then eventually, her sister would follow to meet the same fate as many did. The only thing that would hold back a mermaid from doing exactly that was their young in some cases.

"If the landwalkers caught him," their father continued, "then there is nothing I can or will do. That is my final decision on the matter, Poe. The rest of us still need to live safely and he, better than anyone, knew that before he went out with the party."

"Your guard never leaves the colony! How does that even keep us safe? It doesn't. It keeps you safe, and the rest of us are just left to figure it out on our own."

Poe's outburst had their father rising from his throne with the grace of a king, but the slowness of a predator. The same way the sharks cut through the water, going directly for the kill, their father's movements were the same.

Arelle recognized the danger quickly.

She was not so sure Poe did.

Then again, this was about the woman's mate. That couldn't be forgotten, and she thought … their father should have known that, too. Instead, he felt like making an example out of his child, the same way he'd done with Arelle the season before.

Shocking.

Except it wasn't shocking at all.

"What did you just say to me?" Zale hissed. "Or did you forget who sits on this throne?"

Poe tipped her chin up. "That throne will be mine someday. You seem to forget that, Father."

"Not for two hundred seasons or more. And what will you do until then?"

Arelle's hold tightened around the baby cradled in her arm. And for the first time, she dared to speak if only to remind Poe that she had other priorities to consider here. "Poe—"

That was all she got out.

As fast as the conversation turned bad, it just as quickly ended with her sister pivoting on her tail and leaving the room. Without permission, and with no expectation of decorum from anyone else in the room at her exit.

Arelle let out a shaky exhale.

Her father's harsh stare turned on her. "Follow her. Remind her of her place—what we all expect, Arelle."

"You could try—"

"I can and will do nothing. The maiden will take the child. It'll give your sister time to think clearly without her infant squawking every moment."

No, it wouldn't.

She knew better than to argue.

Arelle handed off the baby, who cried loudly when they unfurled her tail from around her aunt's arm. She didn't like the maidens who were charged with looking after her during Poe's time in the palace. Not because they treated her badly, but rather … she knew they weren't her family.

Moving to follow the same path her sister had taken, Arelle only hesitated when her father's voice rang out from behind her when he said, "As for you, Arelle, we've not finished our discussion about your mating. Soon, Mav will arrive with his traveling party from the Emerald Lands. It'll have been a long and tiring trip, so I, of course, expect you to be on your best behavior for his caravan. We'll resume the discussion of what will happen after his arrival when everything else calms down."

"I—"

Glancing over her shoulder, Arelle's words quickly cut off at the sight of her father's arched eyebrow.

She wanted to refuse.

How could she take a mate now?

After everything?

She only needed to witness her sister's pain at having lost her mate—even if right now, it was only the belief that her mate wouldn't return—for Arelle to know she never wanted that. Before, she'd been scared of a love that couldn't be, and now, she had an entirely new reason to fear bonding herself as Poe had done. But wasn't that half the problem?

If one took a mate ... one could lose a mate.

Arelle didn't know Mav. Only the stories she had heard about him from others, but that made no difference to her. If she never mated, then the pain she watched her sister suffer through day and night wouldn't someday become her own.

"Well?" her father demanded when he resumed his position on his throne.

She shivered.

Just say what he wants to hear, Arelle.

"Yes, Father."

"Poe! Poe, wait!"

It seemed like the louder Arelle called for her sister, the faster Poe swam through the colony. Not that she blamed her or anything. She simply picked up the pace, determined to catch up and let her sister know that things would—somehow—be okay.

Surely.

Her fast pace cutting through the water had her guards trailing far behind, but the men didn't seem to mind. They likely assumed the women would head to Poe's grotto at the islands, because that's what Arelle thought, too.

It was the direction Poe went, after all.

The problem was her sister didn't stop at the islands. At first, Arelle thought Poe was just burning off some energy. Maybe she was even taking a moment to truly be alone. Or perhaps she felt her grotto was too tied to her mate; everything inside had been his just as much as it had been hers, after all.

However, Arelle quickly realized that her sister wasn't even just swimming along the safe boundary lines of the narrow seas before she

224

headed beyond Atlas Islands. She kept going. Past the islands, out into the raging sea where a school of blue fish scattered at the oncoming mermaid, and straight toward the forbidden.

"Princess Poe!"

It was only the distant shout of the guards trailing Arelle that reminded her they were still behind the two sisters. Their decision to keep a distance had not been to their benefit because she knew the men had been ordered to forcibly bring back anyone if they went past the boundaries the king set forth for his people. If they didn't have permission to go beyond the islands, then they could expect punishment for breaking the rules.

With the men so far behind her—Arelle checked again, seeing that they had picked up their speed a bit—it gave her the chance to still follow her sister. One of their duties was to ensure the women never went beyond the boundaries, and if either Arelle or Poe did, to bring them back. She doubted they would go so far beyond it that it threatened even their own lives.

It took her a second.

She hesitated on the decision …

If only because they all knew the landwalkers were still hunting them day in and day out. Not to mention, the punishments she had witnessed others in their colony suffer through for disobeying the king were enough to make her want to be careful. Not that her confinement had been particularly easy to get through when their kind was always happier and stronger when they stuck together.

"Princess Arelle—return to the colony immediately!"

She didn't bother to even answer the call at her back. Instead, she followed after her sister, cutting through the water as fast as she could go without thinking about what would happen when they returned to the colony. The guards would only follow so far, and they were already so far behind she didn't think they would catch up before they lost them entirely.

Besides, there was nothing her sister could do alone out in the sea. At least, Arelle might be able to convince her sister to come back and then perhaps they could plan something. But even that was all left up to chance.

She didn't even think the Gods were helping them now.

Arelle continued following her sister farther beyond the islands until she could no longer hear the shouts of the guards behind her, and the seafloor became shallower than it was by the islands. Although, it was still deep enough for a ship. Another bad sign.

Poe slowed enough for Arelle to catch up.

"We have to go back," she said, coming up behind a trembling Poe.

"I can't."

"Poe—"

She reached out to touch her sister's arm, wanting to at least give her some sense of comfort. The two didn't have to be as close as they once were for Arelle to recognize Poe's pain and appreciate it for what it was.

"Don't," her sister mumbled, spinning in the water away from her reach. "Just don't ... they don't care, Arelle, because it's not their mate. But if it were ... if it were, they'd want to move the land and seas to get their mate back, too. If he meant to them what he means to *me* ..."

"I know. I do know that, Poe."

The bond was like that.

Unforgiving.

Final.

It's what scared her the most.

"It's been two weeks," Poe hissed, "and he doesn't call for me as much as he used to, Arelle."

She frowned at that. "I don't understand."

"No, because you're not mated."

But she did know.

Mates had a call.

They could hear it across the seas. In their hearts. In *dreams*.

"We have to go back where it's safe," Arelle said, glancing back over her shoulder through the darkness of the water. She still had a good range of view, though, and it was enough to tell her the guards had stayed behind. "We've come too far. What if a ship—"

"Listen."

Arelle did.

At first, she heard nothing.

"There's nothing there."

Poe shook her head, turning west. "There is ... I hear it."

It took another second before Arelle heard the call, too. As faint as it was, even she couldn't deny that it was absolutely a call from one of their kind. Distinct in the tone, the high notes pierced through the water to travel to their spot.

"It's a bit that way," Poe said, "we have to go after it. It might be—"

"Poe, it's not Tak. You'd know if it was Tak."

And she would.

Without question.

"But what if it could take me to him?"

Hysteria, she thought.

That's all this was.

Her sister's desperation was acting out in dangerous ways. This couldn't possibly lead them anywhere good, but who was she to tell her sister to stop when Arelle knew this was all instinct for Poe at this point?

She couldn't.

Still, she had to try ...

"You can't chase every sound in these seas, Poe!"

"But I can chase this one."

Poe darted toward the surface of the water before Arelle could say another thing. Every smart piece of her knew this was a bad idea, and yet she couldn't stop the protective nature that seemed ingrained in her very being. The part of her that wanted nothing more than to protect her own kind. Because they were hers.

She only took solace in the fact that the day had been rather dreary, with the promise of an oncoming storm. The humans weren't particularly foolish and didn't tend to take the ships out to hunt if they believed a storm would arrive when they were out at sea.

But that wasn't a promise. It wasn't a guarantee they were safe.

"Poe, it could be a trap!"

Hadn't their father's scouts warned of that? The landwalkers were using catches to draw out more merpeople.

Her sister didn't act as though she'd heard her. Arelle continued to follow until both broke the surface of the sea.

And then ...

Well, that's when Arelle learned she was right. It had absolutely been a trap.

20. A LIFE FOR HERS

Eryx

It happened fast.

One moment, Eryx was watching the black clouds roll in overhead and in the next, the lookout in the crow's nest of the ship gave his call.

"*Aye*—on the west!"

What happened next came just as quickly as the lookout's confirmation on sight of a mermaid. No one questioned his call; they simply moved onto the next part of the plan. Eryx supposed that was because they only had one shot at this working, and the lookout needed to be absolutely sure that his call was correct.

The cannons on the right side of the ship were fired, all four of them at once, sending the vessel rocking back and forth in the choppy waters. Across the waves, he watched the other three ships that had come out on this hunt begin to move. Pulling farther apart than what they had just been, he knew their anchors had only been grazing the seafloor. Just enough to keep them in place.

Eryx found himself fascinated by how swift and organized the ships seemed to be even while separated. They planned and planned and planned more … and when push came to shove, those same plans left no room for questions or deviations.

"Pulling the nets up," Corval said, coming to stand next to Eryx on the middle deck. "Down on the seafloor, dyed a dark blue, they're barely even noticeable to the merpeople. Or that's what we've found."

Eryx heard everything the man said, of course, but his heart raced so fast in his chest that the blood rushed in his ears. He couldn't seem to take his gaze off the lifting and lowering waters of the sea, his stare cutting through the waves to just see …

To find *her*, maybe.

Was it even her?

The anticipation curled tightly around Eryx's throat, keeping him quiet even as the wind blew hard enough to rock the ship. With the sails pulled, the wind could blow as hard as it wanted because they weren't moving.

Yet.

"Two," the man from up in the crow's nest called down.

Corval nodded back. "And?"

"Both female."

Eryx let out a slow breath.

A good sign.

"Anything else?"

High above, the man's beady black eyes met Eryx's. A brazen display, really, considering many wouldn't even meet a royal's gaze.

"Both redheads," the man said just loud enough for them to hear.

"How can he see that?" Eryx demanded. "The water is already turning as black as the sky. If they're under the waves—"

Corval smirked. "Been scouting for twenty years, Prince. He knows what he sees when he sees it. Care to question his calls?"

He thought about that.

For all of a second.

"Not particularly," he said.

"Right. Then, stand back and let us work."

"Storm is here, Cap!"

Thirty feet behind Eryx and Corval's position mid-deck, the captain cursed at the warning from the man who was designated to watch the skies. The team of men on these ships had been doing this more than long enough to know what was happening in the sky and waters.

Even if it changed in a blink of an eye.

"Corval!"

Beside him, the mermaid hunter stiffened. "What?"

Like Eryx, he never took his gaze from the water.

"We knew this was a risk given the time of year, Corval. The storms—they come in bursts. We won't have time to get back to the wharf safely if we continue with the hunt."

Every word the captain spoke had Eryx's heart beating impossibly louder.

Both redheads.

"Don't call off the hunt," Eryx warned Corval, "or you'll see nothing for this effort."

Corval's jaw tensed, but a nod answered Eryx before the man called to the captain of the ship, "They're lifting the nets. We're too far into this to turn back now. Ride the storm out, Captain."

"This is *my* ship!"

"And we'll replace it if need be. Josef says it's two women—imagine the price they'll fetch."

"Corval—"

"There she is!" came the call from the crow's nest. "One in the net!"

Corval waved a hand high. "Close in, Captain."

"Corval, the storm will send us into the fuckin' water!"

"Close in," the hunter repeated. "We've got two ships."

Eryx met the man's stare, and Corval lifted one shoulder as if he were silently asking, you're sure this is what you want?

He understood the dangers.

"West, he said?"

"Yes, he saw them west, Prince."

Eryx reached for the spyglass dangling from the hunter's grasp. "Let me have a look, then."

The sails dropped. All it took was a simple shift of the ship's direction, and they were sailing across churning waters as the first drops of rain spattered against Eryx's cheeks. Not that he noticed. He was a bit busy scanning the surface of the sea with the hunter's spyglass. All the way to the side of the ship where a blue net was being dragged handful by handful from the waters by a line of men.

They struggled. From the water or the possibility of something being inside the net, well … he couldn't be sure.

Eryx followed the line of the net through the water and there it was.

It was nothing more than a brief flash maybe a few inches beneath the surface of the sea, but he saw it. The flip of a fin—black and green and blue scales that shimmered even when there wasn't any light to help it reflect. But it wasn't so much the color of the fin as it was the distinct markings.

Markings that, like her face, Eryx couldn't forget. He dropped the spyglass to his side.

"It's her."

Corval's gaze cut to him as the rain and wind came harder. All around them, it smelled like the sea. Salt and water. Cold and crisp. A high wave crashed into the side of the ship, sending a spray of water up over the rails and across the deck.

"She can't go far," Corval said, "because we've got the area covered."

"Make sure of it."

A cannon fired. This time, it wasn't from their ship.

Up in the crow's nest, another call came down to make Eryx smile. "They're in the nets!"

However, his smile didn't last for long. The problem with the beginning of the season for storms was that the bursts of violent weather were more dangerous than even the spreads of never-ending storms.

At least that, they prepared for. Bursts … well, they couldn't. And it all changed in a blink of an eye. They really should get off the water.

The ship rocked dangerously when a wave came in to take them thirty feet higher than they had been, before dropping them just as fast. Except when they came back down, the only thing Eryx saw was water.

Black water.

Arelle

Arelle's biggest mistake had been diving deeper into the water when she realized her sister hadn't returned back to the surface with her. If only she had stayed near the top of the raging sea, then maybe she could have skimmed over the net that seemed to rise up out of nowhere.

She blamed herself for this because she surely couldn't put the fault on Poe, given her sister's state. Had Arelle just paid more attention to their surroundings then maybe she might have noticed how all the sea creatures had seemed to vanish out of nowhere. A good sign that something was in the area which they didn't want to be around.

Like a ship.

The net came up fast and caught Arelle off guard. She spun against the scratchy, woven lines but the more she fought, the worse she twisted into it. Until finally, the netting had her completely covered and all she could do was feel herself being lifted through the water.

"Poe! *Poe!*"

The net jerked hard to the left, giving Arelle ample view of her sister and the reason why Poe wasn't answering her back. A good twenty strokes away under the blackened sea, her sister's body had become so twisted into the netting that there wasn't even an inch for her to move. The ropes cut into her sister's tail and fin and with each pull from somewhere out of the water, the net turned again, tying her sister up more.

Arelle's heart pumped hard.

Right in her throat.

"Poe … Poe, cut the net!"

Poe had her knife.

They all carried one.

Even as Arelle shouted for her sister to try and save herself, she knew it would be pointless. The sea raged too violently, only aiding in the spiraling knots that had become the net around Poe's trembling form.

"Help me," Poe cried, her fingers fisting into the netting around her face. Teeth bared and eyes wide, Arelle didn't think she had ever seen her sister look so terrified. "Arelle, help me!"

Everyone had a sense of self-preservation. There was no denying that. It didn't matter if one came from the sea or the land … when a dire situation arose, one only really thought about saving themselves.

There was no shame in it.

It was a natural reaction.

But for her, the instinct to help, if she was capable, always overtook the need to save herself. She had to do what she always did—the pull impossible to ignore, even though Arelle knew trying to help her sister might very well end with her sacrificing her own life. It was entirely possible that Poe wasn't owed that, she still had to do what she could.

"Arelle, *please!*"

"I'm coming, Poe."

She was.

Or she would certainly die trying.

The underbelly of the ship had finally come into focus a good fifty strokes behind Poe. With every pull and twist of the net, they came a little closer.

Arelle managed to free the knife she kept secured on her hip with a bit of fabric that she used to tie around her waist.

"Arelle!"

She couldn't answer her sister—not when she had to focus on getting free of the netting first herself before she could make her way to Poe. She was all too aware that with every passing second, they were both being pulled closer to the ship.

Her sister had precious moments left.

"Arelle!"

"I'm trying, Poe!"

Arelle pulled the blade of her knife along the netting and watched the ropes fray with the first slice. It wasn't nearly enough, so she yanked the blade across it again. And then again. Finally, the first rope split, making a small hole, although it wasn't nearly big enough for her to fit through.

She kept cutting.

Kept slashing.

Even when she sliced both her palms in her efforts. The purple hue of her life source leaked into the water, and trailed down her skin, sticking to her flesh and reminding her that inside … she was warm until she began to bleed.

Still, Arelle worked.

She barely even felt the pain.

When she had finally created a large enough hole to fit through, the netting spun around her as she tried to slip out through it. Her tail became twisted in the crisscrossed ropes, leaving Arelle mostly out of the net but still trapped.

"No, no, no," she mumbled, looking back over her shoulder at her sister.

She was so close to the ship.

The netting around Poe seemed to lift up even more.

Poe stared back, horrified.

Now, though, her sister didn't shout for help. She didn't say anything at all. Arelle couldn't speak either.

She cut at the netting around her tail, but she knew without needing to be told that it took entirely too long to get the job done. Not to mention, the tightening of the net around her fin left small cuts that bled into the water as she finally pushed away from the netting.

"Arelle!"

It would be the last time she'd hear her sister's voice.

Arelle spun around in the dark water in just enough time to watch Poe, twisted and bound by the netting, be pulled up to the surface of the water.

Gods.

A cry stuck in her throat.

Hopelessness raged.

"I'm sorry," she tried to say, even as she rushed to cut through the water. It didn't matter that it would be too late because she still wanted to try. "Poe, I'm sorry."

Even to her own mind, it didn't sound right.

Nothing was right.

The only thing that stopped Arelle from breaking the surface of the water was the heavy wave that pushed her backward. She spun into the water, twisting and spiraling around and around. It was dizzying, and when she finally came to a rolling stop, she had no sense of her direction.

From which way had she come?

Where were the nets?

The ships?

But then she felt it ...

When something sank in water—especially if it was something big—it created pressure that dragged everything else around it down, too. Flipping over to her back, a scream burst from her lips when the entire side of a ship came into view only a short distance away from her face.

She had a second to react. A moment to get out of the way.

Arelle still felt the ship graze the back of her tail fin when she came to her senses and decided to move. Although the sinking ship was just one problem because there had been more, she knew. It wasn't the ship that had pulled her sister out of the water in the net. They very rarely hunted with only one vessel.

She still couldn't break the surface to see where she was. How did she get away from here without—

Arelle's mind blanked as a figure took shape in the churning waters. Like the other bits of debris and bodies now sinking in the water, one stood out amongst the rest. Undoubtedly from the ship that had probably capsized from the storm.

For a moment, she simply stared. His eyes were closed. Jaw slack. With his arms extended over his head, the pressure from the sinking ship was quickly dragging him deeper and deeper into the water. In dark water, her vision wasn't the absolute best, but there was no denying that face.

That man. Though she didn't know his name, she remembered his voice. So distinct with its thick pain as he called for his mother.

His mother. Who had been a mermaid.

Arelle turned away from the sight of the drowning man—his death would be silent, even if the sea was screaming; that was simply the way of the water—but hesitated in swimming away entirely. Looking back over her shoulder, she felt a tug in her chest.

A pull.

It wasn't because he could see her and would know she didn't try to help or even for the fact someone was drowning in waters they couldn't possibly swim in ... no, it was what she knew about him that made her hesitate.

His threat to her from a season before echoed in her mind.

I'll kill you.

Arelle couldn't forget the sight of him begging for his mother, either. Or how he'd been willing to risk himself to wade into dangerous waters if it meant he might be able to save the woman.

He wasn't like her.

But he was one of them.

She heard whispers of the halflings. Of young birthed to merwomen who had been taken as slaves for the landwalkers. Anything was possible with the right circumstances, and though he'd threatened her, she couldn't ignore the urge to help him.

Didn't she owe him that? She hadn't been able to help his mother. She'd watched the woman die. It would be easier to let the man die in this sea ...

But that wasn't who Arelle was.

She turned back for him.

For a man whose name she didn't know. She turned back to save a life that only wanted to end hers.

21. THE BOND

Arelle

Arelle sucked in a lungful of damp sea air as she heaved the man's body over the sharp rocks leading into a heavily forested part of a smaller island. She hadn't realized how close they were to Atlas Islands until she dragged the man up to the surface of the sea to get him in the air.

Not that it seemed to matter that they were now on land.

He still didn't open his eyes.

Didn't breathe.

She suspected his lungs were full of seawater, considering how long he had been underwater before she'd gotten him up for air. Another landwalker would have been dead from that alone, but this one wasn't. His throat pumped under her palm when she stopped on the rocks to pull in another breath, letting the magic in her blood do its work to change her tail to legs. Tired legs. The blood from the cuts on her palms smeared across the three faint lines on his throat where gills should be.

Scars.

Still, his body tried to save him.

Arelle panted heavily, her body tired. The crisscross pattern of cuts on her legs, from where the netting had caught her too tightly and the rocks scraped against her tail, left smears of violet on the rocks as she continued dragging the man farther from the water.

Rain pelted down.

It stung her skin.

He still didn't open his eyes.

"Come on," Arelle breathed, dragging him by pulling under his arms through muck and rocks and seagrass until she found some coverage under a patch of trees. It wasn't nearly enough, and it truly didn't help that much. The long branches and fanned leaves whipped back and forth under the heavy winds. But at least she had gotten him out of the water. *"Breathe."*

A good portion of his clothing had been ripped away. Some from his own hand, she suspected, when he'd fallen into the water. Others, by her, as she'd attempted to get him out of the water. Another time, and she might have stopped to admire the man's lean form, and the way his muscular chest led down to a narrow waist with torn breeches resting low on his hips. Breeches that had split right down the middle of the crotch. His flaccid cock rested half against his thigh, and partly on the fabric.

Instead, the only thing she concerned herself with was climbing on top of the man so that she had better support to do what she needed next. Pushing both hands against his chest while her legs straddled his waist, she put all her weight down against him.

And then again.

And *again.*

All her efforts were for nothing. Only a small bit of water came out of the man's lax lips. For someone of her kind, this would have been more than enough to clear their lungs, if that's what was needed. Except for a second she had forgotten …

This man wasn't entirely like them.

He was only half.

She struck her fists against his chest, feeling the hard pulse of his heart beating against the hit. "What do you need? What is it?"

Of course, he didn't answer her.

Could he even hear her?

Behind her, the waves lapped at the rocks, spitting water and sea foam at her naked back while her mind raced to figure out whatever it was she had missed here. If he was like the landwalkers, too, then wouldn't he need air?

Yes, that's it.

Triumph filled Arelle, even if she couldn't be sure that's what the man needed. Still, she wouldn't know if she didn't try. Before she could think better of it, she opened the man's mouth wide, leaned down, and pressed her lips against his. The first thing she thought as she breathed air from her lungs into his?

He tastes like the sea.

Arelle dug her fingernails into his chest, still feeling the beats of his heart steady under her touch. Dragging in another breath, she gave that air to him, too.

"Open your eyes."

She waited.

Nothing happened.

Arelle let out a noise thick with her frustration, and then wiped away the red strands of hair that stuck to her face and lips. She could taste the blood left behind from the swipe of her hand, but she ignored it.

A lot like the way she pretended not to see the trickle of blood from her cut palms left trails across the light dusting of hair on the man's chest. With the wind blowing like it was, she couldn't smell it at first—she'd been too focused on trying to save this man's life instead of the dangerous situation she suddenly found herself in when all at once, the wind quieted.

At the same time that she dragged in a heady lungful of wet air that tasted of her own blood, she realized there was a hint of something else, too.

His blood.

Arelle looked back, quickly finding the spot on his body that bled. A cut along the side of his calf, but that wasn't really the problem. He wasn't entirely like her, landwalkers couldn't mate with her kind, but he wasn't entirely human, either. Not if his mother had come from the sea. This was how the matings started. The scent all around, blood from the struggle, and then when it mixed …

She closed her eyes, letting out a slow exhale.

With the scents of their blood mingling in the air, her stomach clenched.

In a good way.

A *promising* way.

Still, she ignored it.

She had to.

Because if she allowed her mind to become lost in the scent of their mingling blood, what came next would be … well, she wouldn't be able to come back from that. Instinct would take over—it already was; she could barely breathe from the sudden need that surged through her bloodstream to make her hot and hazy—and she would be fucked.

You already are.

Thrumming deep in her veins, she could already sense that change.

Arelle fought it.

So fucking hard.

Like the storms in the sky and the unpredictable sea, everything changed in the blink of an eye. Or rather, the opening of a pair of brilliant blue-gray eyes.

His.

He stared up at her, unblinking and wide, his mouth opening to say something … but no words came out. Only a choking sound before his hands that had previously been limp at his sides flew up to his throat. He struggled under her, his body lifting as he choked out another sound that she couldn't understand.

Arelle's shock kept her pinned on top of him as he grabbed at the side of his neck, his fingers digging into the three little scars there.

And finally …

Finally, she understood as she watched his throat pulse every time his chest heaved upward like he was trying to take in a breath.

His gills.

She bet his body looked different on the outside. But inside, it still worked just like hers and every other person of the sea.

Arelle didn't even think about it.

Not what it would mean.

Not what might happen …

None of it.

She simply slipped her hands in with his, her fingernails digging deep into the scars there. Filed into sharp points that she could use to eat, hunt or protect herself if needed, her fingernails tore through the soft tissue at his throat, ripping open the scars and slipping deep into the canals of his gills. For the first time, he made a sound. Or rather, grunted out in the pain she caused him, but she couldn't stop. Not yet. Not until … there it was. She felt the water and blood pour through her fingers, and she breathed deeply.

Because she could smell him.

And *her*.

Purple mixed with thick red.

He exhaled.

Water and blood poured down from his opened gills.

They could sew them shut on the outside, but that didn't change the inside. It didn't change who, and what, he was.

Every part of Arelle knew it, now.

Every single part of her could feel it.

Their blood mingled.

Purple and red turned a shimmering maroon.

She shuddered on top of him when he stared up at her—her throat flexed with every swallow, her heart racing as though the organ were about to come right out of her chest. Each shift of her hips on top of him reminded her that she was entirely naked, and nothing separated the softness of her sex from the rigidness of his cock.

He couldn't possibly know it.

Couldn't understand that change in the air.

The bond had begun.

They could shed their blood. Separately. Together. It could mix all it wanted, but when the mating came into play, it began something that was almost impossible to stop. There was no going back now.

She'd not meant for this.

Arelle was still powerless to stop it—not that she was sure she would even want to.

Eryx

Pain.

From the moment Eryx came back to consciousness and opened his eyes, the only thing he had felt was just *pain*. From the bottoms of his feet, to the very top of his fucking head. At first, he thought the pain was just that widespread. He quickly realized it was localized to his legs, chest, and throat.

The second thing he realized?

He was staring at her.

The mermaid.

The mermaid.

And she'd saved his life.

As the air sucked into his lungs with every fast pull, tasting of dampness and earth, water poured from the aching gills in the side of his throat. It was a strange feeling—the sensation of them opening for him like that, as natural as breathing.

Because shit ...

That's what he was doing.

Breathing.

He should have been amazed by that. Fascinated how the parts of him that he'd taken from his mother helped to keep him from drowning just long enough for this mermaid to save him, but he couldn't focus on that.

Not when he stared at her.

Not when that smell in the air had him sucking in another lungful. It tasted like nothing that had ever touched his tongue before, and he was sure he wouldn't ever find anything like it again. His gaze darted from the shimmering spattering of blue-green scales at her temples to the backdrop of the black sky behind her.

The whipping branches of trees.

Falling rain.

Swirling clouds.

Eryx swore the air around her shifted when her thighs tightened around his waist. She moved again, and he fucking choked on the words that burst from his lips without any warning, "Stop moving like that."

He needed to think.

To *breathe.*

But wasn't he?

Her wide violet eyes stared down at him, and for a second, he was stuck staring again. At all her nakedness, the softness of her curves and the way her wet, red hair fell over her bare breasts. Her nipples that had already hardened into little peaks.

Was that because of the cold air? Or because she could feel his hard cock pressed against the soft cleft between her thighs?

She looked ... wild.

Not because she was naked, or even because those crazy curls of hers had started to frizz at the ends to make them curl even more. But rather, the look in her eyes. The way her pupils had blown so huge and dark. It was in the parting of those red lips, and the way her tongue peeked out to wet the seam that had him grunting out another sound.

His words didn't seem to want to come.

Just noises.

Sounds.

He felt like an animal. Like the scent of her, and the sight of her streaked with bright purple and red—their blood, he knew—was enough to make him want to put her on her back, spread her wide, and split her open with his cock until the only thing he could hear was the sounds of her pleasure while she cut lines down his back with those same nails she'd used to allow him to breathe.

And *Gods* ...

He knew that was wrong.

Everything about that was so entirely *wrong.*

He hated this creature.

This *woman.*

He'd spend months obsessing and dreaming about the things he wanted to do to her once he had caught her. And here she was atop him, waiting, like he might tell her to get on her knees and she would do exactly that.

Why did his mind feel so light?

So high?

She shifted again, her next inhale of air catching in her throat when his hands landed hard on her hips. His fingers flexed, digging into soft flesh that felt entirely like the curves of a woman. Oh, she didn't say a thing.

She also didn't have to.

He swore he could still hear her.

Somehow.

It's the thrall—the blood.

The smear of red blood on her upper lip disappeared when her tongue licked it away. The guttural sound that followed from Eryx had her shuddering on top of him. He grabbed tighter to her hips, worried she might move.

And if she did ...

Don't let her go.

His thoughts screamed loud enough to scare him.

"Careful," he breathed.

Her chin quivered.

Speak, he wanted to demand of her. *Tell me something—tell me why.*

Instead, her hand laid flat to his stomach and she moved again. A little rock of her hips. Back, and forth, and then back again. Although this time, he thought her intent in doing so was quite clear, considering the way she shivered and the low moan that fell from her trembling lips. There was no hiding how she rubbed herself against him, those needy but raw sounds following each time she rocked her hips. She made him harder with how unashamed she was while she willingly showed him her lust.

Women were trained to think they should all seem demure and innocent. Eryx hated that and quite enjoyed breaking women of the notion that only pureness was attractive.

He liked a woman wild.

A woman like the one on top of him.

He would have leaned up.

Would have went to her.

She came down to him, instead, her hands still splayed to his chest.Each breath came slow and measured.

Her nose grazed his; her closeness had him stilling even as she started a slow, circular motion that had her hips grinding against him. A heat shot up his spine when the slickness of her slit drove into his cock over and over again. Then, she switched that rhythm from circles to lines. Faster and faster until a groan pushed out of his lips that should have warned her what was about to come fast

Him, that was.

All the while, the water pelted down faster and harder than ever. Drenching her hair into ringlets that plastered to golden skin. Dribbling in trails down the planes of features that had haunted his dreams for what felt like as long as he could remember.

There had been a him before the day in the water orchard.

And a him after that moment in time.

Everything that came before seemed irrelevant for more reasons than he cared to name. He'd stopped caring about the life he had before, to fulfill the need for vengeance. Even if it meant his own eventual end.

So, yes, he stared up at a face he felt he couldn't ever forget when it was permanently burned into the back of his mind. Except in those moments, he didn't stare at it with only hatred, but in awe and lust.

The trails of rain on her face caught the smears of her blood, slipping over smudges and taking the purple to his redder life source streaked on her chin from her own hand. It fell from her face to his, their taste hitting his tongue with a hint of the rain it mixed with.

Finally, he found that taste he'd thought he wouldn't ever be able to find again. It was them. Their blood mixed, and it tasted of the Paradise where every God his father promised was real—if only he'd believe—lived.

He couldn't get enough.

Of her in his mouth.

Of her body taking from his.

All those sounds fell from her lips as she started pushing her cunt harder into him. With every flex of her hips, she had him ready to blow. He was not an innocent man; he'd had more bed companions than he cared to admit; it had *never* felt like this and he wasn't even inside her. Eryx's head fell back as the heat in his cock curled into his stomach, sending his back arching up from the ground as her hands found his throat. She squeezed, riding him while he came from nothing more than her pussy rubbing against his dick. His seed spilled hot and thick to his wet stomach.

"*Yes, fuck.*"

His words came out strained and clipped, thick with his pleasure but short all the same. Still close enough to him that all he could see was her face, he closed the distance between them. While the sparks of pleasure still had spurts of hot cum spilling from his cock, he really got a taste of her when their mouths slammed together.

All that water and blood between them made him higher than ever. The need to take from her the way she'd just done to him became impossible to ignore as her hands drifted down from his throat. Even as he yanked her down, flipping them around so roughly her back had to have stung from the uneven, harsh ground, her fingertips glided down his chest.

Featherlight, and oh, so soft.

Gentle.

But just as quickly, she leaned in to bite him. Her touches were kind and sweet, but the rest of her was still just as raw and wanton as she had been moments before. The breathless noise that left her throat when he spread her thighs wide had his chest constricting. Almost a whine, but more like a mewl, it still felt primal.

It was in that moment he realized she'd yet to utter a word to him.

Eryx fitted between her thighs, hovering above her with one hand resting flat to the underside of her jaw to force her head back against the ground. There wasn't anything about his roughness that frightened her.

If anything, she seemed to like it.

Her body trembled and her hips lifted to find any bit of him. Her fingers circled his wrist, and she even dared to try to pull him closer. A silent urging if he ever felt one.

"What?" he demanded. "You want me to fuck you here like an animal? On this muddy, rocky ground outside, where anyone could see me ruining you? Is that what you want?"

Her voice.

He was dying to hear it.

Something inside needed to hear the sound she would make when she spoke. He had no doubt the woman knew his language. They'd found a lot of her kind could speak the language of the lands and of the sea without any teaching.

She could speak.

Had to.

And yet, all she did was swallow against his hold and nod.

Just like that, Eryx forgot the woman beneath him was the source of the hatred that had been poisoning him. He lost the sensation of pain still coursing through his body. Their current situation, stranded where he didn't know in the middle of a storm, didn't seem all that important.

She'd nodded.

A silent yes.

All he wanted to do was give her exactly what she wanted. What he promised.

The hand he'd had on her hip to keep her pinned beneath him slipped between their bodies. She was already lifting her hips to meet him when he fit his cock to the slick heat of her cunt. There was nothing soft or easy or slow about the way he took her. One hard pump of his hips had her split around his aching cock.

He couldn't breathe again.

Now, it didn't matter.

All those sounds of hers rushed back—they weren't words, but he didn't need those when her noises were just as tempting. How she gasped and moaned and whispered with every flex of his body against her own.

Her nails cut into his wrist when he fucked her harder. She dared to bite his fingers—making him lean down to return the favor against her bottom lip—when he stuck two of his digits between her parted lips just to watch her suck on them.

Her cries, though.

Those was the real music.

The song he couldn't get enough of.

Eryx certainly didn't need her to tell him when she was about to break apart beneath him. Not when he could feel it vibrating through every piece of her straight into his own bloodstream. An echo of pleasure that turned his mind into a total mess. And when she did finally release under him, the world tilted.

Or it sure felt like it.

He fucked her like he hated her.

Because he did.

But he also fucked her like a dying man receiving his last moments of pleasure.

Because maybe he was.

22. THE DIFFERENCE BETWEEN

Arelle

"PRINCE ERYX … Prince!"

"*Eryx!*"

"Is anyone out there?"

Arelle blinked awake to a canopy of trees and bright spots of purple behind the large green fan leaves hanging from the branches. It gave her just enough cover from the morning sun that she was sure sunlight hadn't been the thing to wake her up.

That purple …

She breathed in, and then out again. Over and over until the haziness cleared from her vision, the sleepiness in her mind drifted away, and she had a better understanding of her current situation.

It wasn't often she woke up anywhere but the palace. Never mind the fact that she hadn't ever awoken under trees, with a purple sky overhead—the only sign that a storm had passed and for the moment, all was good and safe in the sky and sea—and the earth under her back acting as her bed.

Arelle flexed her toes, not her tail fin as she would usually do every morning to loosen up, feeling dirt and rocks scrape against her sensitive skin. The sting had her hissing, but it wasn't the only thing on her body that hurt at the moment.

The warm firmness at her back relaxed her, but she had to wonder if she dared to move. The hard lines that surely felt like a man tucked into her back made her feel safe, and even in her heart, the sentiment echoed over and over again. But the very fact she could feel someone else behind her had Arelle tensing.

Which did nothing good for the rest of her.

She didn't need to test her body to know just how stiff it was. Even the slightest of movements had every muscle in her body protesting. It took her far too long to realize and remember why she was where she was, and just who was sleeping beside her on the still-damp ground.

The *man*.

All at once, memories of the night before slammed into her mind. Her sister, the ships … She'd been right because it *was* a trap. The man in the water, and then everything that had come after the moment she'd decided to save him.

She'd done far more than just save him. The very second Arelle dragged the halfling man onto land, she'd made her first mistake. The second their blood had started to mingle, there had been absolutely no coming back from what she had started between the two of them.

Had he even known what they'd done?

What it meant?

How now, because of the night before, the two of them would be tied together forever. Irrevocably. The bond was started—made. It hadn't been finished properly, or so she thought, and not even witnessed like most matings would be, but Arelle already knew that wouldn't make a difference.

How did she know?

Because now … already, Arelle could feel her mate within her. His magic was hers; hers became his. The magic, their thrall that had been unique to each of them was now shared, becoming their bond. He was right behind her, touching her, but even if he hadn't been, it would be okay. Because she would still feel him. Or hear him, if that's what he wanted. He was an echo in her mind. An imprint on her soul. Within the very beats of her heart.

That was the bond.

They would share the same air.

Linked minds.

Unable to stand separation.

And all because of what?

To save his life.

That was all she'd meant to do! Just save his fucking life. To correct her wrongs—or to assuage the guilt that never left because she couldn't get the image of his mother's haunted face out of her mind. Instead, this happened.

But did the man know these things?

Arelle seriously doubted it. He wouldn't know; he wasn't like her.

"Oh, my Gods," she breathed.

Behind her, she felt the man shift in his sleep; his arm slung over her naked hip, and his fingers pressed into her skin. He was still sleeping. She could tell by the way his breaths came out steady and even.

The calm after a storm.

But even that touch …

It was possessive.

In his sleep, he reached for her.

Like she had been doing for him, she'd bet. That was why, even after sleeping alone for most of her life, she still found herself awake and tucked into her mate's side. Because this was how it should be from now on. The bond would demand it, or it would torture her until she gave it what it needed.

"Eryx!"

"Prince!"

"Prince Eryx—call out if you can!"

That's what had woken Arelle up. Again, she felt him start to shift behind her, a groan echoing against the back of her neck. It had her shivering, a rush of memories filling her mind all over again. All those sounds he made when he pinned her down and fucked her until she couldn't think or breathe or see.

She'd wanted it.

Needed it.

It had still been a mistake.

Her worst *ever*.

Arelle would be a damn liar if hearing that groan didn't make her wet and hot and ready all over again, but she blamed the bond for that. It had to be the bond, didn't it? The man with his arm hooked around her to keep her in place while he woke up certainly wasn't the only man she'd laid down with. Her education had included a male companion, who she had been told upfront that she could not mate or fall in love with, shortly after she'd turned seventeen. One who'd taught her everything from the act of sex to self-pleasure, and more when it came to mating; Zale's only allowance to Arelle after essentially selling her off to another sea kingdom like he had done to her oldest sister. That way, with a companion, she would know and wouldn't be afraid of it when her time came.

She hadn't been.

It'd come too easily, maybe.

But her companion—he'd told her something important once. *The bond only ties you together; you decide everything else after.* The bond between mates could make her want a lot of things, but she still had a choice.

"Eryx!"

Arelle lifted just enough from the ground that she could peer through the brush that led out to the shore of the island. It wasn't the calm sea that she noticed first, or even the way the light breeze brought with it the scent of sunshine and salt, two of her favorite things.

No, it was the ship.

Quite far off, edging close to the shoreline of a neighboring island, the vessel had men all across the deck shouting a name she didn't know.

"Eryx!"

They would find them soon. There'd been more than one ship the night before, and there was a very good chance someone had seen her swimming with Eryx toward the islands.

She couldn't be here …

They were hunters. A lot like the man behind her. One she'd tied herself to. Bonded with.

All over again, Arelle was reminded of her situation. That she had mated herself to a man from the land. That she had an intended mate on his way to her colony. Once more, it seemed as though she had found every single rule she shouldn't break and yet, still managed to do exactly that.

It felt taunting almost. How dare she forget? How could she be so stupid?

Though it killed her to do so, and she had absolutely no idea what would happen when she left her mate behind on the island, she slipped out from under his arm and stood up on shaky legs. She did her best not to look back, to keep walking toward where the sea lapped at sharp rocks.

Their blood had finally washed away. The storm ... gone. Not that it mattered. The storm was inside her, now.

By the time Arelle reached the water's edge, the sore, healing scrapes on her toes and legs touching saltwater, she finally looked back.

Her heart stopped. Just for a second.

She was sure it did. He stared back at her. Burning blue eyes. Hatred and confusion warred.

"Wait," he said.

Faintly.

It didn't sound like an order, but it didn't have to. Not when it was her mate saying the word—request, plead or demand ... it didn't matter. That was the bond.

Everything inside demanded she do what he said. Wait. The calls from the sea came louder; the ship sailed closer.

"Prince!"

The man turned his head toward the sound.

"Prince Eryx, are you here?"

Was that his name?

"Eryx."

The name came out of her lips lower than a whisper.

He hadn't even heard it, or so she thought.

Then, his gaze snapped back to hers. His hand slid along the ground, and though she could tell he was still weak, he seemed determined to stand. She wanted to tell him to rest—it's what he would need for a while. Mating took a lot of energy. The bond often drained their kind of everything, and recovery was sometimes the best part.

Except he would be alone.

And so would she.

Arelle gave a slight shake of her head, a whimper falling from her lips.

She couldn't speak.

Not to him.

It would finish the bond.

Their voice and songs ...

He'd always be able to find her if he heard it.

It was bad enough that he'd spoken because now, she would always hear him.

"*Wait.*"

Her next step hesitated.

His voice was so much rougher.

Like rocks against her skin.

And still, she liked it.

"Prince Eryx!"

"*Fuck*," he snarled behind her.

She looked back again, but he had looked off at the approaching ship.

Arelle took her chance to run, darting over sharp rocks and an uneven ground beneath the water until it was deep enough for her to dive. Under the water, she breathed, feeling the change that took her from legs to tail again.

She couldn't hear him call for her.

Not under the sea.

But in her mind?

Her heart?

She heard him loud and clear.

I'll find you, little mermaid.

Eryx

Despite how his legs threatened to fall out from beneath him, Eryx managed to get up from the ground. Even through the pain and the wounds that reopened to seep blood—his throat, and the cut on his leg— he still rushed to the edge of the water. The sharp rocks that scraped the soles of his feet barely registered to him at all.

"Wait!"

She didn't.

The last thing he saw from the red-headed mermaid was the tips of her tail fin that peeked out from the water before disappearing beneath the surface again. Those bluish-green scales with the black markings seemed to wink at him—taunt him—before she was gone.

Rage filled him.

Disbelief, too.

The confusion was the worst, though. His mind raced from one memory to the next. He tried to put all the pieces together, but it felt like none of it made sense. Oh, he knew what had happened. Remembered it perfectly well.

But *why*?

His gaze scanned the water, entirely ignoring the ship that was now skimming along the edge of the shoreline of the island where he currently stood. He looked for any sign of the mermaid—bubbles in the water, shimmering scales … anything at all.

Eryx found nothing.

Why did that ache in his chest? Why did it hurt that she hadn't stayed?

He still wanted to kill her. The memory of his hand wrapped around her throat the night before had him inhaling so sharply that it hurt like nothing else in his lungs, if only because every time he'd tried to squeeze hard enough to take away her air entirely … he hadn't been able to.

But he wanted to.

Now, more than ever, he wanted to catch that mermaid. Kill that mermaid.

"I'll find you, little mermaid," he told the sea.

Whether or not she would hear him … Well, that didn't really matter.

He just wished that ache in his chest would go away. A part of him had to wonder if the ache was because of her … had she stayed when he told her to, would he still be feeling whatever this was?

"Prince!"

Eryx finally looked toward the ship. One of the men on deck seemed to have caught sight of him, if the way he waved erratically in his general direction before shouting at someone behind him was any indication.

He didn't even bother to wave back. Didn't have the energy.

Instead, Eryx's knees hit the wet rocks, the stab of pain from the stone cutting into skin echoing through his entire body. He wished he cared.

Nothing felt right. Everything was wrong.

Eryx wasn't sure how long it took for the ship to make its way to where he still knelt on the ground. Long enough, he supposed, for the sun to move quite a bit. He heard the oars of a boat slapping against water, and it was only then that he raised his head to see who was coming onto shore. Quite a ways back, they'd dropped the anchor for the ship before putting a smaller boat into the water.

"Prince," the man at the front of the boat called, "is that you?"

"Does it look like me?"

He didn't get a reply.

Eryx figured he didn't need one. Neither did they.

It was only once the men had climbed out of the boat and brought Eryx a blanket, which they quickly used to cover his shoulders and mostly naked form, that the one who'd been at the front of the boat spoke again.

"Lucky a man saw the bitch bringing you this way, Prince," he muttered, slapping Eryx on the back.

"I can't remember," Eryx lied.

He remembered perfectly fine, and if the men were smart enough to think … they would notice that the flattened spot of ground where Eryx had slept happily beside the mermaid was big enough for two people and not just himself.

"Caught one of two," the guy added, watching as two other men helped Eryx to his feet. "A fighter, she is."

"She's not the one I want."

"Have to discuss that with Corval, then, Prince."

Oh?

"Corval made it?"

"One of three on that ship who did," the man muttered. "You included."

Well, then …

"Take me home."

The man didn't even question Eryx, he was simply directed to the waiting rowboat before he found a seat to sit in alone while he surveyed the calm waters of the sea, and the sky that was just now starting to lose the purple tones that had colored it earlier. Eryx said nothing as they docked alongside the ship, ropes were dropped down, and then they were lifted up to the deck.

In fact, he said nothing at all until he stood beside Corval on the deck.

"I suppose the captain was right," Eryx said.

"And we'd have been out a mermaid, yes?"

"She's not the right one, though."

"But the other one was?"

Eryx didn't miss how the hunter was careful about not asking if it was true the mermaid saved his life. There were more than enough whispers on the ship for him to deduce his own conclusions on that.

"The other one was," Eryx echoed.

"Both redheads—I'll need a better look at the one we have, but …"

"What?"

"Could be family—kin."

Eryx glanced his way, looking the man over. He seemed in far better condition. Dressed, a cloak over his shoulders, and not any worse for wear. Not as though he'd almost died in the water.

"I'm surprised the other men on the ships didn't look for the captain of ours. He runs the fleet, no?"

Corval chuckled, dry as it was. "Always save a hunter over the captain."

"Mmm. Down with the ship, and all."

The man shook his head, smirking. "No one wants to die, and so a captain going down with his ship only works until the water begins to fill his lungs. There's an unignorable difference between the two. You save a hunter over a captain because one will only bitch about what was lost. The other only wants to get back out on the water."

Eryx stared out over the sea and didn't even bother to thank the man who brought over a second fur blanket for him to use. More than anything, he wanted to be back in those waters, but he didn't think it was for the same reasons Corval did.

After all, the man wanted to be on a boat.

Eryx craved the water in his lungs.

Still, he murmured, "Well, Corval, you're not wrong."

"I rarely ever am."

Right.

"So, the hunt ..." the man said, trailing off with a glance in Eryx's direction.

"Is still on."

23. INTENDED

Arelle

Where could Arelle go but home?

Though she knew what would be waiting for her there, she also didn't have a choice. She certainly couldn't run, although the fear of punishment terrified her to death. That was also part of the problem; death might very well be her punishment for this. Not just for her sister and what happened to Poe with the landwalkers. If her father ever found out that she had mated herself to a man of Atlas, well, that would certainly be a reason for him to end her life.

That didn't change the fact she still had nowhere else to go. Arelle certainly couldn't run, not when it would mean running for the rest of her life because her father would send guards to find her. The only way she would ever feel safe—an impossibility in itself—would be to constantly keep moving and running.

Not that it would make a difference. They would find her. She couldn't take to land. Not here, anyway.

She had nothing. No one. No protection, no safe haven, and no one to ask for help. A true testament to how sheltered and controlled her entire life had been under the thumb of her father when the sad fact was, she had only a handful of friends … two of which had been her sisters, and none of the others were capable of helping her.

So, all that left her with, was going home. Even if that place didn't feel like home.

Arelle fought with herself the entire way; a few strokes forward and a couple more back. A never-ending struggle until she finally reached the colony. Like the season before, she expected people to be waiting. She thought for sure she would hear the whispers, see their averted gazes, and know that the entire colony already knew exactly what had happened.

This time was different. No one waited. The grottos seemed empty and the streets were quiet. Arelle had never felt more alone.

Part of her struggle to keep moving forward had more to do with what was happening inside her very soul. The pull—like an invisible rope had been wrapped around her middle and was yanking her back toward the land of the forbidden. Back to where a man was waiting. One who she'd tied herself to, even though she'd known better.

She didn't need to be told—didn't need to ask—to know that the struggle would be lifelong. Bonds between mates lessened over the years in circumstances where they were forced apart, but it never went away. Not forever.

Eryx, she thought.

They called him Eryx.

But even as she thought that—even as her mind corrected her to use her mate's name—Arelle didn't want to. She wanted to pretend like it hadn't happened at all, so it didn't exist, because that would be easier. Because she had to ... no one could ever know what she had done.

Arelle soon learned the reason why the people of the colony were not waiting on the streets. They waited at the palace, spilling out from the gates because there were so many. All of the colony, the few hundred that remained, somehow managed to squeeze themselves into the palace, the court, and a little beyond the walls.

The guards stood out front waiting for her. The same guards who'd stopped following her the day before, when she'd chased after Poe.

They said nothing, simply stepped aside to let her pass through. Although, this time around the people of her colony did look at her. They met her stare. Oh, they said nothing, but she wondered if that was because this time, they had nothing to say.

The throne room was still just as quiet and foreboding as it had always been. Zale, sitting on his throne, managed to loom over her from all the way across the room with his severe expression and impressive size remaining entirely still. Maybe she expected to see more anger on his face. The rage he had showed her when she arrived at the palace the season before much the same way, but without Coral.

This time, he simply looked resigned.

Mad, definitely.

But it was as though he had said all he wanted to say, thought all he needed to think, and spilled his anger before she had even ever come home.

Or perhaps, it was that he thought she wouldn't come home.

She almost hadn't.

Arelle gave her father a moment. A few brief seconds to look her over, and to see exactly what she knew she looked like in those moments.

Streaked with blood.

Scrapes over her tail and fin.

Bruises on her arms.

But it was the things that he couldn't see—the war inside her mind—that she did her very best to hide. She didn't care if he could bear witness to her physical injuries, or to the truth that told the story of yet another loss of a princess for their kingdom.

It was everything else he couldn't know.

And she would do her best to make sure he didn't.

"Speak," her father demanded.

Arelle dragged in a lungful of water and then slowly exhaled. It allowed her a moment of calm. She wanted to ask where her mother was—ask if they'd told her yet. After all, he wouldn't be sitting there looking at her the way he did, with all their people filling the palace and spilling out into the courtyard while others watched from the streets, if they didn't already know.

Instead of voicing her thoughts, Arelle said, "I went after Poe. I couldn't save her. But I tried. I *tried*."

Zale tipped his head back, the clenching of his jaw acting as the only sign of his frustration and anger with her. Arelle expected an entirely different show. Rage and yelling. Her misdeeds and wrongs thrown at her feet. A punishment already prepared.

Oh, she suspected some of those things were still waiting for her. Right now, he simply stared at her.

"You went beyond the boundary line," her father said, "and you broke my rules. Again."

Arelle shook her head. "Poe did. I only followed—to bring her back."

Poe wasn't there but oh, she didn't have a doubt that if her sister was there … Poe would not have had a problem with putting the blame on Arelle for all of this. After all, Poe had done exactly that the season before.

There was just one difference between the two …

Arelle would admit her own faults.

She accepted her wrongs.

"I followed Poe," Arelle admitted, "and I knew that the guards would stop because they wouldn't disobey their king, but I had to try. I had to try to bring her back, Father."

Still, Zale stared hard.

Arelle waited her father's silence out.

At this point, what else could she do?

She was all too aware of the many, many eyes watching her. Yet, none of their people said a word. Perhaps they had been forewarned before she made her way to the palace, or even threatened to remain quiet.

It didn't matter.

She felt their stares, and their judgment; she didn't mind taking it for what it was.

When her father continued to say nothing, Arelle wrung her sore fingers together. She twisted them, needing that distraction. She had only one thought to ask in that moment, one little soul to worry about. Everything else was a background thought.

"Where's the baby? Poe's daughter?"

Zale let out a heavy sigh. "With your mother."

"Poe would want—"

"Well, it doesn't matter what Poe would want, does it?"

Arelle flinched. "Yes. It does matter. She's not dead; she's simply—"

"Caught," her father interjected sharply. "Caught, Arelle. A slave. Another of my daughters, gone. Do you know why we are all gathered here today?"

She hesitated.

Did he really want her to answer that?

Sometimes with her father, it was hard to tell. He asked a question like he intended to get an answer, but really it was just a trap. She played these games with him more than enough over the years of her life and she knew when to not engage. The only way not to lose a game was not to play the game.

Or to win.

And with Zale, a person could rarely win.

"I don't," she said.

If only because she knew she had no other choice.

Not only her father, but everyone else watching her, too, wanted an answer.

This was their life now.

The landwalkers.

The hunts.

Their missing.

All the *pain*.

"I gathered them," her father said, rising from his throne with his crown dangling from his fingertips.

He took a moment, just long enough to set that crown atop his head, and to make a show out of glancing around the room. She didn't bother to look at the other faces, of the people she would recognize, and others who came and went—people of their colony. People they were supposed to protect, people who were terrified all the time. Wondering if it would be them or theirs next.

Now, she supposed, this was the absolute worst situation for her father because he'd lost two daughters to the landwalkers. And how was he ever supposed to protect his people and the ones they loved when he couldn't even protect his own?

Oh, Arelle didn't wonder what her father was doing.

She already knew.

"I gathered them," he repeated when his gaze finally came back to settle on her, "because up until the moment you were spotted returning, we had to assume you were both gone. I need to address that, but here you are. Again. Seems you're my lucky one, are you not? Twice now, you've escaped the landwalkers. Twice you've managed to return alive but left behind someone dead."

"Poe is not—"

His gaze darkened and he lifted a hand to silence her.

"We assume she is because as a slave, she will be. And that is the only thing they will do with her once they bleed her nearly dry for their trades."

If only his gaze made her unsettled. She found, staring back at her father, that she wasn't really that afraid of him or what he might do. He had already done it all, and right now, death might even be a gift.

She wouldn't beg for it.

Certainly, wouldn't tell him to do it.

But there was no denying that death would be an easy way out. For him, and for herself.

Maybe even for Eryx.

What had she done?

"You disobeyed me."

Arelle swallowed hard, tilting her chin up, defiant. She had to be because she would not lie, not about what made all this happen. She was also not wrong in her truth.

"She is my sister," Arelle whispered, "and even if she wronged me before, I would not leave her behind."

"And yet … you had to do just that."

That blow struck lower than her father could ever possibly know. Or maybe he did know it and that was exactly why he said it. It hurt, the ache, it ricocheted throughout her entire body and lingered long after his voice stopped echoing in the silent room. As if she didn't feel enough pain between injuries on her body and the growing agony within her soul.

Neither of which she would lament to her father. It wasn't as though Zale would care. A king only cared for himself. Or this king certainly did.

"If you're going to punish me—"

"Oh," a new voice said, speaking up to draw attention, "well, he certainly can't do that, now can he?"

Arelle turned fast on the spot, surprised at the unknown person who dared to speak when the king was addressing someone. It didn't matter that she was a princess, no one ever thought to speak over her father.

The man who parted the crowd near the entrance to the throne room with a staff firmly in his grip looked her way with a rueful smile. A large green gem rested atop the golden rod where he rested his hand lazily.

She might have smiled back on another day. The second she looked at him, and met his violet eyes, she knew who he was. He had not been who she was expecting, in a lot of ways, but it was too late for that now.

She might have even liked his smile, if not for the night before.

If not for the bond.

A few people trailed behind the man, staying close enough for others to note they were with him but still back far enough that they also understood they were not like him. His olive-toned complexion complimented the bright green of his scales down his tail, and the shimmering black of his fin. The same scales that spattered across his chest and temples.

Those that followed him said nothing but did not lower their heads the same way her father's people did. Instead, they kept their gazes locked on the back of his head as he neared Arelle.

Muscular, handsome, and clearly confident if not a little arrogant given his introduction, he was everything that everyone had ever told her about him. She knew without needing to be told exactly who he was, although this was the first time she'd ever laid eyes on his face.

Mav of Emerald. Prince of the Emerald Lands. Heir to a realm that promised life in the sea and on the land. Her *intended* mate.

"He can't punish you," Mav said, his gaze slicing to where the king stood but had not yet moved again, "because if I understand correctly ... well, with your sister now gone, who does that leave as the heir to the Blu Seas?"

Arelle trembled.

That was not a question she wanted to answer. It was not a title or position that had ever been hers, nor had she wanted it.

Mav's gaze darted back to hers, and he smiled again. "Well, that would be you."

Arelle looked back to her father, waiting.

The rage her father had been so careful to hide ... the truth stared her in the face now. Blatant, and stinging.

"As you can see," Zale said with a wave of his hand toward Mav, "the Prince of the Emerald Lands has arrived with his companions. We have a lot to discuss. And I'm sure you won't mind taking to your rooms until we do that."

Oh, Arelle had many things she wanted to ask.

Many things to say.

Her intended mate looked her way and nodded. A clear sign she should do as she was told, but the softness in his gaze as he looked her over slowly—checking her injuries in a way her father had not done, but also appraising—made her heart ache.

For Mav, because what he thought he would find here was no longer waiting for him.

For herself, because another man giving her attention, either with concern or lust, made her stomach twist with sickness like never before.

But it also made her heartache for the man she'd left behind on an island that morning. Because he couldn't possibly know what she had done to them both.

Yet, she could still hear him.

Deep in her mind, echoing with the beats of her heart ... she could hear him.

Eryx.

Where are you, little mermaid?

What have you done?

257

24. SOMETHING DIFFERENT

Poe

10 days after capture …

"In here, my lord."

"We can drop the pretense, Corval."

"As you wish, Mattue."

The new voice forced Poe from her fitful slumber. The hunter who came and went from the shack where he had left her shackled to large timbers by her wrists and ankles barely spoke to her at all. If he looked at her, it was a good day.

Not that Poe minded, really.

No attention was better than the way some of the men on the ship had treated her, although the captain, and later, the hunter, kept the landwalkers under control.

Mostly.

The heavy click of the lock on the shack door echoed before the wood creaked open.

"I thought, given the circumstances, she might be a good pick for the king," Corval told the man he called Mattue as they darkened the dusty beam of light that spilled over a quiet Poe. She didn't pretend to be asleep, but she refused to stand up, naked like she was, and give the two landwalkers something to truly gawk at. As it was, she could feel the way the new man's—Mattue—eyes appraised her as if she were a cut of meat to price.

"Bit loud, that hair," the man muttered, his gaze landing unhappily on Poe's mop of long, red curls.

If it weren't for her circumstances, and the fact that she had rubbed her wrists and ankles raw and bloody trying to escape the confines of her shackles, she might have been able to focus on the painful hole in her chest where her heart beat. Empty of the call of the only person in the world who could, or rather, *would*, help her, right now, she had to figure out how to help herself.

If only she learned what might come next.

That could help.

"Wouldn't say he likes the redheads anymore after … that one incident."

"Take a better look at her, Mattue," Corval said as if encouraging a friend to smile. "I've heard there are certain things he looks for, no? Might she have one of those?"

"What do you—"

"On her hand, look."

Poe was quick to hide her hand, dirty from the floor of the shack that smelled like rotting fish and damp earth, behind her back. Not fast enough, apparently.

"Is that what I think it is?" Mattue asked her, meeting Poe's violet eyes.

Even if the hunter had tried to talk to Poe during her captivity, she would not have spoken back. And just like when this strange new man asked her a question as if she would willingly speak, Poe simply turned her head away.

Then, the man repeated his question.

In her mother tongue.

Poe's head didn't move, but her gaze cut to the one named Mattue. He cocked an eyebrow at her only acknowledgement of him and his trick.

Neat.

But it didn't matter.

They could beat her senseless and she still wouldn't speak. These men meant her nothing but harm, had from before they even pulled her from the seas, and Poe was sure of it. Indulging even their conversation seemed like another nail in the proverbial coffin, didn't it?

She wouldn't make this easy.

Not for them.

"Tis a brand," Corval confirmed.

"Blu Seas?"

"Yes."

"Could you darken her hair?"

"They're not like human women. It isn't worth the bother. I wouldn't."

Mattue scowled and gave Poe another once over.

Like a *pet*.

She shuddered.

"She's a stubborn one. That much I can tell just from her eyes and the set of her jaw alone, and he does enjoy breaking that," Mattue noted, talking more to himself than the room. "And she's quiet which *I* like in his whores, let me say."

Poe smirked.

I'm quiet for now.

She could get a lot louder.

"He's still quite heartsick over his last loss, I heard," Corval noted.

"It would do you well not to hear anything about the king at all," Mattue replied curtly.

"Fair enough, but I only said it to say she could be a nice treat for him. A gift to help get him through."

"We're getting a little close to the season when he doesn't like taking in slaves, honestly. The surgeons don't want to travel. It takes longer for their collars."

"I'll deliver her with a collar properly fitted, on, and branded, my lord."

The other man sighed.

"Mattue," Corval corrected, then. "Nonetheless, I have a friend who owes me a favor. I can even have her delivered on a date of your choosing."

"You make it hard to say no."

"Is that a yes, then?" the hunter asked. "Do we have a deal?"

"Could you hold her for a bit?"

Poe openly glared at the two.

Neither paid her any mind.

"I'm a bit preoccupied with Eryx at the moment," Mattue murmured, tilting his head to the side as he regarded Poe one more time before turning around entirely.

Corval followed. "Not a problem. And what about the prince?"

"He's different, isn't he?" Mattue asked as the hunter closed the door behind them. "After that hunt, he's different."

"Would you like the date for the next one? Let you keep an eye on him, anyway."

Poe heard the man named Mattue chuckle loudly.

"You really know how to make a sale, Corval."

"So, that's a yes, too."

"Tis a yes, hunter."

25. THE LURE

Eryx

Nearly a fortnight after the hunt ...

"Your highness—"

"That will be all," Eryx said to the servant still lingering in the doorway of the House of Miller's library. "If I need you, or anyone else, I will call on you."

He didn't even bother to glance up from behind the desk where he had stayed most of the day. Even going as far as taking his meals in the library, yet never cracking a book because he had far more interesting things to pour over. What with the newest map the hunter had delivered to him since their last discussion a good week ago. The place touted a full list of servants to handle whatever needs Eryx might have. They'd proven useful since he'd arrived a few days earlier, but he still wanted to be left alone.

For the most part.

It seemed no one here understood what that meant, considering they were constantly asking what the prince would like them to do next. Then again, he supposed on the rare occasions his father used the estate that had once belonged to a rich grain farmer ... well, the king was quite demanding. Perhaps they assumed Eryx would be the same.

Fortunately for them, no.

Unless they continued to work his nerves.

Knowing the woman was still standing in the doorway, Eryx sighed and glanced up from the map. Sure enough, she was standing exactly where he'd assumed she would be. No doubt because she was confused about why, with the sun still peeking over the sea through the glass doors and wall of windows on the other side of the library, the prince said he would no longer need anyone for the remainder of the day and evening.

"I did say that was all, yes?"

The woman, in her plain gray gown that all the servants here seemed to prefer to wear, nodded quickly. "Yes, Prince Eryx. I will let the rest of the house know that you're not to be bothered as well. However, if you do want something, please don't—"

"I will shout until all of your ears bleed so that someone will immediately help me. Even though I am perfectly capable of doing it all myself, thank you."

Her jaw fell slack.

Eryx simply smiled.

All it took after that was a wave of his hand, and the woman made herself scarce. Thankfully, she did manage to close the door behind her, allowing Eryx privacy to continue pouring all his attention into the map spread across the surface of the desk.

Frankly, the map was only one reason Eryx wanted to be left to his own devices. A few moments after the door had closed, he waited for the sounds of the house to quiet. The quiet meant that with the prince no longer needing their attendance, the servants headed to the smaller house on the east side of the property where they spent their evenings.

Far away from him. And his secrets.

One of which made this particular house very useful for him. The estate, named for the fields of grain one had to travel across to reach the main house's spot close to the sea and the grain mills not far away, wasn't Eryx's favorite. It served his purposes. Especially when all he had to do was glance up from the very desk he sat behind to find the thing that seemed to have taken over his thoughts lately.

He had a perfect view of the stained sea glass doors beyond the row of marble pillars, which were separated about ten feet apart and dominated the center of the room. Iron candelabras jutted up from shined stone floors on either side of the thirty or so steps it would take him to cross to those doors. Far enough away that the rows upon rows of books on wall-to-wall shelves wouldn't be in danger of the flickering flames when the candles were lit at night.

But none of that really interested him about the house. Every estate he took residence over the years had beautiful rooms and plenty of things to keep his mind busy. It was those doors he liked, and what waited behind them. Leading out onto marble steps where he enjoyed taking breakfast, he could walk right down into the sea. The water lapped at the steps, and even now, he could hear the gentle waves touching the house.

Inviting.

Teasing.

Promising.

But what it promised, he couldn't quite say. Still, it did it. Singing in his veins with every beat of his heart and screaming through his mind day in and day out. How he ever managed to behave normally, when inside he seemed to be constantly waging a war, well, he didn't know.

For more nights than he cared to admit—seven passing of the two moons—he'd walked down those very steps, too. Slipped off his clothes, dropped the cloak or scarf that was now always tightened around his neck to hide the torn, jagged gills that were open and flexing with breaths, and slipped into the water.

Because it called for him.

And he called for her.

It wasn't that Eryx wanted to, but when the skies became dark and the smell of the sea hit him … well, he didn't seem to have much of a choice.

An invisible force dragged him toward those doors, made him open them wide, breathe in the sea, and wish for her.

He hated it.

Craved it.

He didn't know what the red-headed mermaid had done to him that night on the island, but it was something. Long after the cuts had healed, and his gills remained open; when the bruises faded, and the scrapes didn't sting as much, he swore he could still feel that woman.

Inside.

All through him.

Infecting him.

This obsession was getting worse.

Eryx needed the mermaid to die.

Or on all the Gods above and below … she would kill him.

The next morning, Eryx took his breakfast on the marble steps just because he could. And there was something to be said about the salt in the air mixing with the flavors of the food on his plate. Standing just a few feet away from his small table, the same servant from the night before waited for him to acknowledge her.

He figured, might as well put her out of her misery.

He certainly wasn't good company on his better days, but lately, he was even worse. Not that anyone dared to tell him that. He might still be shamed and shunned from his father's court, but he was also the only heir to the land.

Still a prince.

He waved the fork over the dish made up of cooked fish and fresh vegetables from the garden drowned in a sauce he couldn't place but had his taste buds singing. Eryx said to the servant, "Give the cook my regards. This was well worth the wait this morning."

"Yes, Sire."

Glancing up, he found the woman was still standing there. "I'm not done."

"Of course, there's just … you have a guest waiting for you in the front rooms. I didn't want to interrupt you again, but he—"

"Insists," Eryx muttered, already annoyed.

He didn't even need the woman to announce his guest properly, or tell him who it was, because he already knew. Unfortunately, that meant his decent morning after a night where he'd gotten very little sleep because all he could hear was the goddamn sea was about to get worse, and fast.

"Make him wait until I've finished my breakfast," Eryx said with a wave of his hand. "At least allow me to eat before he makes me lose my appetite."

"I could have Mister Malsem send him away, Prince."

"That won't work, believe me."

"Um … if you say so."

"I do. Thank you. Show him in after I've rung the bell to clear my dishes."

The woman nodded, not saying another thing. For that Eryx was grateful. Nobody said he was a particularly great conversationalist. He wasn't about to start changing that first thing in the morning when a meeting awaited him. Especially not when that meeting was with a man he didn't care to even think about lately.

Eryx opted to savor his meal a bit more after the exchange. He even waited until the bright sun was a bit higher over the sea. The whispers of wind had taken the crumbs from his plate away before he rang the bell for the servants to clear the table and allow his guest in.

Mattue came to stand in the doorway leading out to the marble steps with his hands folded at his middle. The black, fur-trimmed cloak he wore billowed with the breeze that came along with the water lapping at the stairs.

Of course, Eryx should always greet someone first. He was royalty, after all. Mattue never cared for such semantics when it came to his nephew. Unlike the king, Eryx didn't have a penchant for hurting people who didn't immediately treat him like his ass sat in the clouds simply because of his legacy.

"Was breakfast so boring that I couldn't even watch you take it?" the advisor asked.

His uncle looked Eryx over as if he were already annoyed.

Good.

Eryx fought the urge to roll his eyes. "Or perhaps it's a new thing I'm trying out. Eating alone, and that sort of thing."

"*Mmhmm.* I hate being left to wait, Prince."

He didn't particularly care how Mattue felt. Not when he knew there could only be one possible reason why the man was there in the first place. It certainly wouldn't be for anything Eryx cared to hear or deal with, but that was the gift of Mattue that kept on giving. Even when nobody wanted it. He could somehow always find a way to worm himself into anything and stick there until he wanted to be removed.

The *bastard.*

"What do you want?" Eryx said in a sigh, not bothering to hide his own irritation at all. "Just get it over with, and then we can both get to the things we would rather be doing, yes?"

Mattue glanced his way, and then at the only other chair at the small round table. A silent request passed from the man, and although Eryx wanted to say no, he assumed that would only cause him more grief. So, he nodded, and the advisor took a seat.

"Seems the storm season has come a little earlier than they predicted," the man said.

Eryx gestured at the sky above, replying, "And yet, today is a beautiful day. Not a single storm in sight."

Right now, the good weather served his purpose.

"Yes, a rare treat," Mattue said quietly. "But we both know how that tends to work, don't we?"

"Or it could just be like everyone says, and the freak storms are simply warning us that the season will soon be upon us. You'd think after all these years, someone would have a handle on this. Oh, watch the weather, keep a note of changes … I don't know."

"Your attitude is strong this morning."

"Have yet to have a proper drink. Let's blame it on that."

Mattue's gaze met his. "But is that what it is?"

Eryx didn't like the way the man seemed to be searching for something without just telling him what it was. Mattue only did those types of things when he was planning … and that never ended well for anyone.

"What do you want?" Eryx repeated.

"It's too dangerous for you to be on a ship again. I know of your plans to return to the sea in the coming days with Corval's ships, but you should allow them to handle it. You're not needed—simply an extra body to protect or save. Or didn't you learn that the last time?"

This time, Eryx did roll his eyes.

Didn't even bother to hide it.

Even scoffed.

"I'll be fine," he assured.

Now more than ever.

He just knew it.

Mattue sighed. "You're playing with fire, but I'm going to safely assume I can't convince you to do otherwise at the moment, can I?"

"Wouldn't even waste my time, if I were you."

"And when will we begin working on the other part of our deal, Prince?"

Eryx hesitated.

The advisor didn't miss it.

"Oh, you mean you haven't really given it much thought? Because I, on the other hand, haven't stopped thinking about it."

Yes.

Well …

A mermaid for the crown.

Eryx couldn't exactly forget.

He simply … "Haven't caught the mermaid yet, have I?"

"*Hmm.*"

That was all Mattue replied before he stood from the table. Eryx kept his gaze on the man, even when he leaned across the table to brush his hand along the shoulder of the waistcoat he'd chosen to wear that morning. Then, just as quickly, the advisor's fingertips found the edge of Eryx's scarf and pulled hard.

Too fast for Eryx to react.

The scarf fell to his lap.

Eryx didn't move a muscle.

Mattue raised a brow, his gaze pointed on the opened gills at the side of Eryx's throat. There was no way to hide the way they flared open with each of his angered exhales. He didn't even bother to stare at the sealed gills on his uncle's throat that made the two more alike than either wanted to admit. Scars of Mattue's that had long since faded and were barely even perceptible. The man had barely aged beyond his best years, physically, anyway. He had, however, become far more conniving and manipulative as Eryx aged. "I'd heard something was different about you … seems my sources are to be trusted."

"You may leave, Mattue."

"Those will have to be closed again."

"You may leave. *Now.*"

Mattue chuckled. "Of course. Good luck with your next hunt, Prince."

Eryx watched the man go.

And willed his death the entire time.

"Ah, so you dared to come on another hunt, I see. Not even the threat of drowning scares you away, hmm? Perhaps royalty was the wrong path for you, Prince."

Eryx offered Corval a smile as the deckhands who'd escorted him onto the ship—one of three this time around—separated to finish their tasks. What a shame it would be if a prince had to walk himself up to the ship alone.

"Seems so, Corval."

The hunter smirked. "This will be the last run this year. The storms—"

"Quite aware."

"You don't seem concerned. We don't even have a sacrifice for this hunt, Prince. The likelihood of us catching anything is slim to none at this point. We're going in blind."

"You're going in with a plan, actually."

"The bay was a good idea," the man agreed, "but it means nothing if we can't lure them in."

Right.

Eryx was aware.

He nodded, and sidestepped Corval as he replied, "We'll lure them—or just the one. Let the captain know I'll remain at the bow for the hunt. I'll be better served there."

"For what?"

"Well, we'll see, won't we?"

If Corval was bothered by Eryx's cryptic conversation, the man didn't say. Then again, he simply might be too polite to do so. Or the man just knew his place against the young prince.

At the front of the large ship, Eryx turned to watch as the sails on two masts were dropped. Soon, they'd be on the water. He'd be a damned liar if he said the idea of being out on the sea didn't appeal to him.

He wasn't afraid of the storms.

Something inside wanted the water. Needed it like the air he sucked into his lungs constantly.

For the moment, Eryx ignored it.

With the rest of the ship busy, and Corval attending to a twist in one of the nets with a handful of other men, Eryx turned back to stare out over the wharf. He took a moment—as brief as it was—to appreciate the sight of the sea that stretched on for as far as he could see.

A bright blue sky with the sun so high. Not a cloud in sight.

From beneath his cloak, Eryx pulled the small knife he liked to keep tucked away in a sheath at his waist. He'd had an idea since the last time he'd been in these waters. A memory that'd kept poking the back of his mind and wouldn't let go.

Of their blood. And how it mixed.

As he healed, he still bled. Usually from his own stupidity of doing too much when he should rest, but that wasn't the point.

It wasn't how he bled, but rather that it was no longer a deep red. In water, he found his life source shimmered with a touch of purple. The same violet hue of hers.

Had that come from *her*?

The sea called to him. He called to her. Could she call back? Would she come if the call tasted of his blood?

Eryx planned on finding out. Dragging the tip of the knife over his palm, the blood bloomed across the surface. A little dribble at first that seeped into the lines of his hand and then dripped down the bow of the ship when he extended his arm over the railing.

Drip, drip, drip …

Right down into the water.

Time to come back to me, my little mermaid.

26. THE TASTE IN THE WATER

Arelle

"He's not ... uncivilized. I had the fortune of meeting him when I was invited to the gathering your father had. He—Mav—seemed very pleased with you. Smitten, really."

Of course, he was.

Arelle was everything Mav of Emerald should need, want, and look for in a proper mate. Her status complimented his; she was well behaved; not only should they be able to bond—if not for the fact she'd already done so with someone else—but they would also be able to produce children. There was nothing about the match that would bring cause for concern to his own realm when he returned with her.

Except he wouldn't return with her at all.

That was the thing ...

"That isn't the issue, Mother," Arelle replied. "He's a fine man."

Perceptively so, really.

Arelle simply couldn't go through with a mating ceremony with Mav when she had already done so with someone else. It wouldn't break the bond she'd already made, and another one couldn't take hold.

If she didn't figure a way out of this mating, and soon, then all her secrets would soon be on display for any and everyone who wanted to see them.

Her mother, content to rest in her nest where she spent most of her days locked away in her palace chambers, made a soft noise from the other side of the room. "Then, what is it? The last time we talked, I thought you were happy for the chosen mate from the Emerald Lands."

Once upon a time, perhaps.

But fairy tales were not real.

This would not end well.

Certainly not happily.

Instead of answering her mother, Arelle glanced up from the cradle made of shark bones where Poe's daughter slept with her tail tightly wrapped around her own tiny hand. Across the large space that her mother had filled with bright colors and pretty things, she found Rosel was still watching her.

And maybe that unsettled her.

It never escaped her notice how Rosel seemed far more like an unmated mermaid—living on her own, essentially, and inserting her own style and little pleasures into the spaces where she was forced to stay most of her days.

"Do you like your life, Mother?"

Rosel blinked, the shimmering blue scales at her temples winking. "What sort of question is that?"

"Did you choose him, or did he choose you?"

"A bit of both in the end, but what does it matter?"

"I just ... wonder."

"Is that what it is? You worry you won't love the Emerald prince?"

If only ...

"Unfortunately, that isn't my worry," Arelle said, drifting away from the baby's cradle to near her mother's nest, made up of seagrass and the softest of moss. "My worry is that the time will never be right, I suppose."

Rosel made a soft noise, smiling a bit. "The next storm, no? Or, that's what I was told."

Yes, that's what she had been told, too. At the next storm, they would take to the land. Arelle would then have her ceremony with Mav and would leave soon after. She had been allowed her companion before he ever arrived, to do with as she wished, and with the current circumstances in their realm, the prince demanded the king allow them to mate and leave as soon as possible. It was the only option afforded to Zale. Although, now, with the promise of returning when the Blu throne became hers.

All things that would never happen.

She didn't tell her mother that, though.

"To your other questions," her mother said softer, her gaze drifting to where the crib rocked with the water. "Well, those aren't as easy to answer."

"I never thought they were."

"I love what my life has given me, Arelle."

"What about what it's taken?"

"Those keep me from sleeping."

"I'm sorry," she whispered.

Rosel shook her head, the red of her hair twisting wildly.

"Are you lonely without Coral and Poe? Sarha left so long ago, I never think to ask if you miss her, too."

"I still have you," her mother replied. "And the baby."

"But—"

"I chose all my children, Arelle. It's the only choice I was allowed to have as your father's mate, and queen. I wish things were different more often than I don't, but this is what the Gods gave me. I am determined to make the best of it for the rest of my days."

Arelle stared back at the baby, and the string of shiny baubles her mother had tied down over the small cradle to give the infant something to stare at or play with when she was awake. Little golden mermaids that danced in the water and twinkled when the glowing fish became brighter as the night fell.

"When the queen was captured, before your father took the throne, everything changed for me. I was picked—the chosen one, he said. I thought that made me special, but all it did was give me this."

"And if I don't want that?"

"Your duty is the same," Rosel replied, "and like me, you will do your best and make the choices you can, Arelle. Speak when it counts."

"What if I can't?"

"We all can mate."

Except her.

Because she already had one.

"Have you thought of any more names for her?" her mother asked. "We should pick one and announce it soon. The colony is waiting."

"I thought … Poe would like Lilee. I heard that was Tak's mother's name."

"One," her mother said softly.

Too quietly for her to hear well.

"What?"

"A perfect name for a princess." Rosel turned her smile on Arelle, then, giving a wink that had her daughter smiling back if only because her mother didn't do so nearly enough now. "As for you …"

"What about me?"

"Your hesitance about your mating … I believe it's nothing more than, well, nerves. Once it starts, everything will be so easy. Natural, even."

Her mother wasn't lying.

Arelle now knew exactly how easy mating could be. She also understood why the land could be incredibly dangerous for mermaids who were bleeding. No wonder her father had always been a king who refused to take war to the land.

Then, Rosel gave a conspiratorial grin. "Really, you'll see. Take a swim, hmm? Clear your head."

That had Arelle laughing.

Bitterly.

"To where? I'm not allowed to leave the palace. And when I do get to travel within the colony, I have guards from Father and from Mav. I'm not nearly as fast as Poe so I can't—"

"As fast as Poe used to be," Rosel corrected gently, although she could plainly see how it killed her mother to do it.

Ah, yes.

They were supposed to assume Poe was dead.

Spoken from the mouth of the king.

"I can't escape them like she always could," Arelle settled on saying.

"And if I could help you with that?" her mother asked.

Arelle stilled. "Do you know how to get away?"

Rosel arched her eyebrow. "Well, I wouldn't have been able to survive in this palace all these years without a will and a way, Arelle. You know, you were a lot better at sneaking down halls when you were little."

"Yeah, tell me about it," she muttered. "I miss those days."

The last thing Arelle needed was fun when everything else in her life had become so very serious in a short amount of time, but as she twisted in a spiral through a school of fish that circled around her while darting toward the light at the surface of the sea … well, she couldn't help but laugh. Their soft fins tickled her arms; their scales sparkled in the shimmery blue depths.

She hadn't gone very far from the palace or colony. Just enough that she wouldn't be caught or seen by someone who would report back to her father or Mav. Her mother had been right. All she needed was just a few free moments to simply be.

Not that this time had done anything to solve her current problems, but at least she hadn't been thinking about it all while she enjoyed herself.

Wasn't that what counted?

Arelle could go back to dying inside later.

Surely.

The school of brightly colored fish had started to circle back around to her. Turning a loop just before she would break the surface of the sea, Arelle darted for the fish once more, but the slipstream that she passed through to do it had her stopping instantly.

As though she'd turned to ice.

Water rushed into her lungs as she gulped deep, and then moved straight out of her gills. The school twisted all around her, making it impossible to see through to the rest of the clear sea. Not that it mattered. She didn't need to see when she could taste what had stopped her right in her tracks with each and every breath.

She tried to ignore it.

Desperately wanted to stop breathing in the water.

She couldn't.

That was the thing about the bond between mates. Once made, there was no possible way to ignore how it changed everything. When the blood was shared, they became one. When the voices were heard, they would hear each other until one could no longer speak.

It's why she hadn't talked. She believed he wouldn't hear her if he hadn't heard her voice.

He still had her blood, though.

That's what she could taste with every pull of water that washed through her lungs and then slipped out of her gills on the exhale. His blood tainted the water, coloring it with the distinct call of him and just a hint of her.

As faint as it was, it still had every piece of Arelle's body, heart, and mind spiraling into the baser urges of her instincts. The parts of her that tasted blood in the water—the blood of her mate—and thought something was wrong. She still heard the men on the ships calling his name. It sounded like an echo in her very soul.

Eryx.

And at night, when she was alone and he was … wherever he was, well, she heard him, then, too. Calling for her. Wanting the sea. Being alone.

She couldn't pretend that she didn't hear him, but the war of not following those calls when that's exactly what they were meant to do—to bring her home—was maddening. It only became worse with every passing day.

How long had it been now? She didn't even really have to think about it. Twenty days since that night. Because she'd counted each one. They reverberated in her soul.

And now …

Now.

Now this.

He was bleeding.

But from where?

Why?

The pull was impossible to ignore. His thrall was inside her.

He might not be calling for her, but spilling his blood was as good of a demand to find him as any. She twisted through the fish, uncaring that they scattered because they were frightened by her sudden movement and changed demeanor.

She couldn't help it.

Couldn't fight this.

Arelle was a lot of things … a princess of the sea, a daughter, and a woman.

She was also his mate.

That trumped all.

Eryx

The sting of his cut palm barely registered to Eryx as he leaned over the railing of the bow to stare over the bay. He felt like he needed a closer look. If only he could get in the water. Or that's what his crazy thoughts kept making him think.

It wasn't possible.

Pulling in a lungful of sea air, Eryx glanced over his shoulder, the hood of his cloak distorting part of his view, although he could still see enough. The man in the crow's nest, the men running back and forth across the deck, and Corval in the middle of the ship watching it all unfold in his usual calm state.

Eryx imagined that he, too, appeared calm.

Inside, he was a raging storm.

At least that was just him.

His attention went back to the sky, taking in the cloudless blue and bright sun. Even the wind had died down to a bearable state for the ships to get into position inside and out of the bay. With only one entry to the bay where their ship was located on one side, and another on the other ... well, there was no getting out.

Nets pulled along the seafloor promised that.

And a ship outside the mouth of the bay would do its job, too.

For now, he waited.

Watched the calm skies to search for a storm. Waiting for that split-second change that always seemed to ruin every single one of his plans, even when he couldn't afford for that to happen. Inhaled the sea air and willed the racing beats of his heart to settle so he could feel anything but this anticipation that promised nothing.

Yet, it was still there.

Hopeful.

Or was it something else?

He wasn't quite sure when it changed—this feeling inside that he couldn't describe. This hopeful mess that things were right now. Because from the moment the mermaid had darted off the island, everything had seemed entirely wrong.

Did that mean she was coming?

How could he possibly just know that?

Eryx's grip around the railing of the bow tightened when the ship rocked with the waves. He heard the footsteps approaching behind him, but he didn't bother to turn away from his current position when he didn't care at all if he seemed approachable.

He was a *fucking* prince.

He didn't have to be approachable.

Eryx released his grip on the railing. Corval's chuckles reached his spot with the man's final footsteps before they, too, came to a stop. "The wait is always the worst," Corval said.

"I'm enjoying the weather, actually."

"Yes, another rare event. You're bleeding."

Eryx glanced down at his hand, which he'd simply left hanging over the railing. The last few droplets of blood from his cut palm fell to the water below. Almost instantly, the red-purple stain disappeared with the waves that lapped against the ship's bow. He'd even run his bleeding hand along the railings, wanting that scent to carry as far as it could on the wind.

Because if he could smell it …

She could, too.

It smelled like them.

Him *and* her.

"Caught my hand on a splinter earlier," Eryx murmured. "Nothing to be concerned—"

Boom.

Boom.

Eryx's head lifted high at the sounds of the cannons.

Not one.

Two.

Which meant the ship from outside the bay caught sight of activity that could possibly be a mermaid. The second cannon firing, however, meant the mermaid was close enough to the surface of the sea that they could see her swimming.

Eryx didn't need to be told.

Didn't need to see her to know …

He could feel it in his chest; in the way his heart slowed, and his breathing came a bit easier. How his mind finally started to settle, and everything came into sharp focus.

She was here. *Here.*

It worked.

"*Aye*! Get the fucking ropes—on the nets, you assholes! I want them pulled as soon as she's passed them! *High, high!*" Corval's shouts echoed over the suddenly silent ship. From across the mouth of the opening to the bay, Eryx could hear the man's partner yelling the same sentiments to his men. The hunter turned to Eryx with a calmer demeanor, then. "And you, Prince … do us all a favor, and stay put for the next little bit, yes?"

Eryx didn't reply.

He was too busy watching the water … waiting.

The wait wasn't for long.

The red hair and olive-toned skin kissed by the sun could have been any mermaid swimming a foot beneath the surface of the water, but it was her fin that he looked for. Those black markings on her fin that was so distinct, they could only be her.

Her tail and fin moved like waves—steady, fast and sure.

Straight into the bay.

"Pull the nets!"

Eryx no longer cared to watch the ships or the men work. They knew what they had to do. She continued swimming farther into the bay, never once coming up for a breath of air or even to lift her head and look around. Foolish, maybe … or it could be something else.

Something she was chasing.

Like him.

The scent of *him*.

Despite being told to stay put, not to mention the many men running from one side of the ship to the other, and the line of them pulling back the nets to close the bay in time with the ship on the other side, Eryx followed the railing. The wind picked up. Just a bit, but not enough to be concerning.

Enough to make his cloak billow out behind him as his steps quickened along the deck of the ship while he followed alongside where she swam in the water. Until he was damn near at the end of the ship where the captain steered the vessel.

Finally, she came up for air.

Except she didn't even breathe.

She just stared at him.

Instantly.

Eyes on him.

Eryx stared back.

She had to know it was a trap; there would be no way out of this, but he looked forward to the final moments of this hunt when they were able to pull her from the water and dump her at his feet.

This mermaid …

This woman he believed to have killed his mother.

This soul who haunted his dreams. Because that was the thing … they'd stopped being nightmares. He wasn't sure if he liked that or not.

Two men of Corval's came up on either side of Eryx, bows drawn and ready to fire should they need to injure her in order to get her out of the water. They could paralyze her with one shot; kill her with another; or simply a wound to warn her just in case she tried to run. 'Twas his order to make. His choice, and now was that time.

Eryx dragged in a shuddering breath.

He wanted them to do anything.

Everything to get her in a net.

Even if that meant hurting her.

He told the men, "Hold fire."

27. A PRINCE OF LAND AND SEAS

Mav, Prince of the Emerald Lands

"Have you considered, Prince, that your intended won't want to leave the Blu Seas, due to her new status and how that … impacts your plans?"

Mav only half listened to the advisor his father seemed to think he must keep at his son's side at all possible times. As if he couldn't possibly think, plan, or make any decisions for himself. Instead, his father had to be constantly in his ear, even when the man couldn't physically be there to speak directly.

His advisor made sure of that.

Mav, however, had become so accustomed to tuning out the advisor, even when it was most important, that a lot of the time he just nodded and made appropriate noises during a conversation to make the merman think he was responding.

"Mmm," Mav said.

"Including her staying here, and you returning?"

"Pardon?"

He had managed to hear just enough of that to turn his attention away from the women dancing in the courtyard to the advisor who always stayed a good fin-length away from Mav. Even when they walked and conversed, as was the advisor's favorite way to chat, the man never forgot to give the Emerald prince his proper respect.

Including space.

He wasn't sure how it worked here—a lot about the customs of the Blu Seas royals seemed different than theirs upon first glance—but back home, never would someone who didn't share royal blood stand directly beside or walk ahead of someone in line to the throne. Never mind someone who sat upon it.

Mav had adjusted his own expectations while being here. Not that he particularly wanted to. Soon enough, he would be back in his own lands where everything was exactly as it should be.

Mav had certainly been given prominence and recognition of his status while in the colony, and he appreciated that. But he was just about finished with his time here and looked forward to the next storm so that he could complete his mating with the princess. Then, he could take Arelle home.

With him.

Where she *belonged*.

Of course, he'd not considered a lot of factors about the abrupt changes happening within the ranks of royals within the kingdom of the Blu Seas. His advisor's decision to remind him of the fact that now Arelle was the only remaining daughter in the Sea that could take her father's place had

Mav's attention.

Unfortunately.

"Why would she not return with me?" he demanded. "Such a thing hasn't been suggested. I was pretty clear that *would not* be an option with the king, didn't I?"

The advisor—Vane—sighed and tipped his head to the side in that way of his that always managed to annoy Mav to no end. He only did that when he was readying himself to speak like the prince was still a child with little to no mind of his own. That time in his life had long passed, and he didn't intend to return to it.

His twenty-five years may not have been any match for the other man's over seventy, but he was neither foolish nor stupid. And he hated to be spoken to like he was, but especially by someone who wasn't even fit to dress him, frankly.

"The last sister that left the colony with a chosen one—Sarha, I believe her name is—never returned. Not even for a visit. Not even when demanded. From what I understand, the woman has a handful of children now, quite likes her new place, and has told anyone who would listen that she would rather eat her tail than come home to her father."

Harsh, he thought.

But unimportant.

"What does that have to do with my mate? She has no one to challenge her claim, or would, and these seas are not safe."

"She isn't your mate yet," Vane pointed out, although carefully.

They were all careful with Mav.

Sometimes too careful.

If he were honest, though, he'd say he preferred them careful than careless. One required less work and violence from him. Not that he minded getting his hands a bit bloody for his personal cause.

"Explain your point," Mav demanded, his gaze cutting back to the dancing merwomen who were now spiraling higher in the courtyard with colorful strips of cloth twisting through the water with them. "And then I can get back to my day, yes?"

"My point is—the people of the colony, they're not going to want to see their last princess leave. Certainly not when the other one won't even return. Seems their father is even more ... difficult than yours is on his good days."

"As I have been told, kings earn their right to behave however they please."

"And you will have your day soon, Prince."

Right.

He tended not to forget that, either.

"From whispers I have heard, it seems the king of this sea is going to demand that his daughter remain here with the colony. Although, he's suggested differently to us."

Mav scowled. "That was not the original agreement. Is he not at all scared of my threats?"

Not that Mav had been in total agreement with the original terms. His father hadn't been pleased at his choice of picking a mate from a decimated kingdom where their kind were hunted regularly by people on the land. He, like is father, if he were being honest, assumed she would be weak, perhaps even worthless, given her place as the third princess in her sea. Oh, but the tales of the golden sisters' beauty traveled across many, *many* realms. What would-be king wouldn't want a worthy beauty? He'd decided he rather liked her, after laying eyes on her when he'd first arrived.

At least, she was beautiful. Quite, in fact. The stories didn't lie.

A royal, nonetheless.

What good did any of that do him, however, if she would remain here while he was across the world in his own kingdom? It would have been far different for Arelle to see how she should live while controlling the land and the sea in tandem. Not hiding away beneath calm waters and only getting the land when storms came along.

"Things have clearly changed," Vane replied. "Circumstances are—"

"It is not my problem the king here cannot protect his people from those on land. If he were smart, he'd have done what we did many moons ago and taken back the land. Instead, they hide in the water as though land is a death sentence. Utter non—"

"Pardon me," the advisor said calmly, "but people are going to hear you, and we don't want it getting back, do we?"

Gods.

"And how long would she remain here after I go back, if we're attempting to avoid some bloodshed here and I get the mate I want?"

"The king is still relatively young and healthy. You're well aware of how long he could live. Your own father is nearing his ninetieth passing on the throne and will have many more before you take his place."

"*Hmm.*"

"Zale has plenty of time to produce more young with his mate if she agrees—once, or if, he does, I suspect the conversation about Arelle leaving the kingdom will be reintroduced."

Nonsense.

That's what this was.

Mav hated all of it.

"It'll be impossible to get word to your father and get a decision on negating the agreement by the time the next storm comes along," Vane explained.

Mav hummed under his breath. "At which time, the king here expects us to have mated."

"Yes."

"So, you think he's planned that."

"I think nothing, Prince. I simply give you a conversation for you to come up with your own thoughts and intentions."

Mav believed that only partially. He'd come to an understanding about his advisor years ago in which the man did expect the prince to come to his own conclusions on certain things, but at the same time, he liked to direct Mav to said conclusions as well.

"Well," Mav drawled, putting all of his attention back on the dancing women and their songs filling the courtyard, "seems we don't have a choice but to let the mating happen. We'll have to wait and see what happens after to decide where we go from there."

"How so?"

"She'll chase the bond, won't she? He'll have no say in that."

"Mav—"

"I'm not wrong."

"You're not," the advisor admitted.

Not that he sounded like he particularly wanted to.

"They're expecting storms tonight."

"I heard that," Vane replied. "Have you seen the princess at all today?"

"For a few moments this morning. Then she went to visit with her mother and the baby."

"Have they named the young, yet?"

Mav frowned. "Not that I am aware."

Which was why the child had not yet been formally placed in line to the throne or even branded with her family's royal status. He had to wonder if that was by the hand of the king as well. He didn't trust that merman. How could one trust someone who didn't even protect his own people?

"Well—"

The advisor didn't get the chance to finish his statement. The rush of royal guards filling the courtyard had the dancing women coming to a stop, their colorful fabrics falling to the seafloor in spiraling rainbows while the music silenced all at once. The guards avoided Mav and his man well enough, but the harsh whispers and severe expressions of the mermen with their chest plates and sharpened spears had the prince drawing in a quick breath.

Caught. She's caught.

The princess was caught in a hunt.

They were quiet, of course.

Clearly heading for the king so that he could learn the news first.

It didn't matter.

Their voices traveled.

Mav heard it all.

"If that's true …" Vane started to say.

The prince shook his head. "It can't be."

"If it is, it gets you out of the agreement."

"I never said I wanted out."

And he didn't.

He simply didn't want his princess to stay in this sea.

She was a much better fit for his.

Mav would make sure she saw it, too. Even if that meant staying here until Arelle was returned. For now, though …

"Let's find the king," he told his advisor.

28. DO YOU KNOW WHY?

Eryx

Mattue kept his expression a blank mask when Eryx was the first man off the ship after it docked at the wharf. He wished he was surprised to see the advisor waiting, but he really couldn't be, considering how often Mattue liked to randomly make appearances lately.

"Well?" Mattue asked.

Eryx pulled the hood of his cloak down, taking his time to peer back over his shoulder at the ship still rocking against the waves while the men worked up on the deck. Overhead, the sun had dipped lower in the sky. Streaks of purple and burnt orange colored the sky, promising nightfall would come soon enough.

It was the wind that carried through the air, sending ropes spilling from the hands of the shipmates and causing Eryx's cloak to billow wide around his legs that told the truth. A storm was on the way. They would need to work fast to empty the ship of its very precious cargo, get it moved, and make sure the vessel was well-tied down. Otherwise, they would find themselves caught up in the next bad storm when the skies quickly turned black.

But … he didn't think much about that. Or the work still left to do. His purpose here was done. Eryx finally had what he wanted.

"Prince," the advisor prodded when he stayed quiet.

Eryx came back to Mattue with a sigh he hoped voiced his displeasure with the man without him actually needing to say it. "I would ask why you're here on the wharf waiting for me, but I'm sure the answer will only annoy me."

"Someone needs to keep eyes on you."

"Do they have to be your eyes?"

"Would you rather the king send someone else?"

He'd rather his father left him be altogether. If he was still shunned from court and his royal duties, then what did it matter?

"How did the hunt go?" Mattue asked.

The shouts of men from the ship drew both men to the side of the wharf where Eryx and Mattue stood next to one another. A net that dangled dangerously close to the churning waves was hoisted higher along the ship's rear. Eryx didn't need to explicitly say it for his advisor to know, considering the man could plainly see what awaited them inside the net, but he spoke, nonetheless.

"It went well," Eryx said.

"Is that her?"

"*Aye*, to the left, boys!"

Eryx had no intention of shouting to Mattue over the calls of the men working to move the still net from the side of the ship to its position over the wharf. Corval had decided, only after the mermaid hadn't fought once she was in the net, that he wouldn't move her to the large cage on deck. Instead, he left her in the net, hanging over the sea as they sailed back. There, Eryx watched her the entire time.

Not that he thought she would get away. He just ... couldn't stop staring. Now was not the time for an exception.

"Is it?" Mattue asked him again, louder that time.

Eryx only smiled.

It took all of a few moments for the men who were not needed to hoist the net to its proper position and remove themselves from the ship. They circled around the spot where the dark blue rope of the net dangled over the wharf, spilling in piles while the teardrop shape dangling in the air spun a slow circle over and over again until it finally came to a stop.

A foot from the wharf, the net and its contents remained motionless. It only dropped to the wet wood when one of the men lifted his hand with a nod. With weapons at the ready, Corval gave the signal up above to let the net go.

She hit the wood with a thud.

All the blue netting spilled over her.

Eryx could plainly see the shape of her legs twisted beneath her as her hands flew out to catch her fall. Not that it made much of a difference in the end. The netting was pulled away from her by the hands of the men with quick tugs until she was laid bare to the prince's inspection, and that of every other man on the wharf.

It was not lost on him ...

Not her beauty. The way those violet eyes of hers seemed so wide. How she stared at him. Not even how quiet it'd become.

And she was beautiful.

The spattering of scales at her temples shimmered under the colorful sky when she tilted her head up higher toward him. Her shapely figure. Her golden skin winked when her legs shifted to fold beneath her so that she was sitting on her knees. With all her nakedness on display, from the smooth bare skin leading to the paradise between her thighs to the pert breasts with red hair plastered to her chest ... a truly magnificent sight.

He doubted a single man surrounding them hadn't noticed.

And she was all his now.

Despite the hatred and confusion and all the other emotions that welled inside Eryx at the sight of the mermaid he'd been hunting laid at his feet ... he was not so prideful that he couldn't admit she was—by far—the most beautiful creature he'd ever seen in his life. His memories had not done her justice.

Neither had his dreams.

But even as he felt a sense of vicious satisfaction at having caught her, he had to ignore the strange pull at his chest that demanded he move closer to her. A part of him screamed *she should be looking up at you from where she rests at your boots and begs or bleeds or both.* Another murmured *she would look so good there breathing your name, too.*

Did she even know his name when he didn't know hers?

Fuck.

He might enjoy teaching her it, though.

Eryx swallowed back the conflicting violence and lust warring in every beat of his heart at his throat under the tight scarf and the hood of his cloak.

"It is her," he said.

Finally confirmed it.

"The hunter will be happy to finally get his payment, then," Mattue noted.

Eryx pretended as though he didn't notice how the advisor's gaze raked over the merwoman in her human form. A violent swell of anger washed through him, but he pushed the irrational emotions down considering his uncle had never even shown interest in merwomen or halflings before. He wouldn't start with this one.

"I certainly will," Corval called from the deck of the ship. "They all will. This has been quite the season for these men."

Eryx cleared his throat, finally tearing his stare from the red-headed mermaid who still hadn't looked away from him. Overhead, Corval leaned over the railing of the vessel with a smirk that said he was quite pleased with himself.

He should be.

The prince was happy.

A large payment was on the way.

Everything had gone exactly as it should, and if Eryx got his way, it would continue to remain that way. All these men, the captains of the ships … and anyone else involved in these hunts, well, they would be paid very well for their business with the prince. But especially, to keep their mouths shut about what had happened between them all.

"The king would appreciate a look at her," one of the men on the wharf muttered.

Eryx scowled at the man. "Pardon you?"

"I'm just saying, Prince, she'd be particularly interesting to him … given his tastes, and all. She'd be a worthy piece in his harem."

His jaw clicked when he clenched it harder.

"And how do you know that?"

"All you gotta do is look at her. *Look at her.*"

Eryx had.

He did again.

She simply looked like his.

"And I'm sure," Eryx said, meeting the silent mermaid's violet eyes again, "that we'll all let the king know the final hunt was unsuccessful, won't we?"

Boots shifted against wood.

Throats cleared.

Water lapped at the ship and wharf.

Overhead, Corval finally replied, "That was the agreement, Prince."

Good.

Then, that was all he needed to know. Everything else was just … details. No one cared at all for those.

Eryx's gaze went back to the merwoman surrounded by discarded netting, and how her stare had drifted away from his own so she could survey the bigger threat around her. That was unacceptable—he needed her looking at him.

Especially now.

The question pulled from his lips before he could stop it, and the second he made a noise, her eyes snapped right back to his. "Do you know why I've hunted you?"

Arelle

"Do you know why I've hunted you?"

Every single inch of Arelle felt that question. It echoed in her bones and sang in her blood. He—her mate—looked almost godly standing among the others on the wharf in his rich clothing and aristocratic aura. The other men shifted from foot to foot, their gazes never lingering on her for long, but also coming right back to her as though they were scared she might run. He, on the other hand, only watched her.

She felt that, too.

He seemed so different from the rest with his hands folded neatly at his front, and his expression emotionless while he watched her. The intricately-designed waistcoat that peeked through his fur-trimmed cloak was a stark contrast to the plain clothes of everyone else around them. No one came too close. Not to her, or to him. A respectable distance was given, but not enough to allow her any sense of freedom.

A hunter with its prey.

Pleased.

But not showing it.

He didn't need to show it.

She felt it.

"Will you speak?"

Yes, she wanted to answer to his first question. And no to his second. Yet, Arelle said nothing. At that moment, she didn't need to, and he'd not demanded anything of her. Asking a question and slinging an order were two entirely different things.

One gave a choice.

One did not.

He took one step closer to her. Arelle tilted her head higher to keep their stares locked. She remembered his name just fine. It still whispered in her mind during quiet moments when nothing else was distracting her.

Eryx.

A part of her wanted to say it—to finish what she'd started here with him so that he would hear her singing in his mind for the rest of his life like she now heard him, but somehow ... by the grace of the Gods, she kept quiet.

Which was clearly not what he wanted.

"Do you not speak?" Eryx demanded.

There was a crack in his facade.

A single slip of emotion, even if it was one that had the other men on the wharf clearing their throats and glancing away. His rage came off so clear—painful, really.

Still, Arelle remained silent.

A pretty stone sitting on her knees, with wet wood pressed against her tingling skin. She was too close to the water here. Three steps to her left and she could dive right into the sea. If only he would look away, then she could do exactly that, too.

Or at the very least, try.

But like this, while he watched her and he was near, she had no choice. The bond kept her eyes on him. The thrall of her mate being close kept her watching him. Even as the man who stood closest to Eryx called his name, he didn't look back or respond. Not when he was too busy moving closer to her.

He couldn't know it ... didn't know, but the bond worked the same way for him. They were no better or worse, him and her. More the same than different, now.

It's what scared her the most.

Not even being caught terrified her like this.

"*Eryx.*"

The sharp call of his name had her mate finally tearing his eyes away from her. The man behind him, whose clothes were of slightly better quality than those who'd come off the ship, gave Eryx a pointed look that for whatever reason, had his shoulders tensing.

He didn't look back at her.

It was just a second …

Maybe two.

But in those quick moments, the thrall was gone. Arelle could breathe a little easier, and search for an opening in the large circle of men all around her. She quickly realized there wasn't a way for her to escape her current situation, but damn her if she wasn't going to at least try.

Not considering the consequences, she lithely moved to her feet before darting for what she thought might be the weakest men in the group. Shorter than the others, and a bit rounder in their middles, if she was going to make a run for the sea, then those two were probably the easiest to get through.

With everyone else's attention on Eryx and the man speaking to him, the two Arelle picked to use as her escape didn't see her coming until it was too late. She darted away from the pile of blue netting that had kept her trapped until they dumped her on the wharf; her bare feet hit the wood with fast smacks. Her fingernails ripped into the side of the one man's throat while her other hand raked lines down his companion's face. Her hiss of warning was the only sound she made as the two separated to give her more access to the sea behind them.

Except she didn't make it that far.

As fast as her attempt at an escape had begun, it was over when the others realized what was happening. She should have known better. There were too many landwalkers in close proximity. Some with weapons, and others with nothing more than brute strength.

Arelle didn't even know how it happened, but she found herself on her back on the wharf, staring up at a quickly darkening sky as the air rushed out of her lungs. A boot rested on her chest, keeping her pinned to the ground. In the background, the men she'd injured cursed her and promised violence.

All she could do was laugh.

The boot on her chest pressed harder.

An attempt to quiet her.

"Quite enough, there," the blonde man said above her, giving her a grin.

She recognized him.

He'd directed them in catching her.

Watched her when they'd got her in the net.

Moments ago, he'd been on the deck of the ship.

Had he jumped down?

"Easy, Corval."

Eryx's murmured words had all the fight leaving Arelle at once. She tipped her head to the side, finding him watching her behind a row of men who now seemed both wary and on edge. She wouldn't get a second attempt at escape.

Arelle already knew.

"You have to watch them, boys. Especially ones like this."

The man—Corval?—glanced down at her, his stare going right to the burned brand on the back of her hand.

"Very worthy piece, however," he added. "She should be on display."

What did that even mean?

Arelle went back to staring up at the sky, and then a second later, a heavy item dropped on top of her. It took her all of a single breath to realize it was a fur-trimmed cloak. It covered her nakedness—not that she minded; nudity wasn't a taboo to her kind, but she wasn't with her people—and seemed to remind the rest to avert their stares.

It wasn't the cloak that surprised her, really.

More who it belonged to.

"Deliver her to the estate I chose."

Eryx's words cut through the air, and by the time Arelle looked his way again, he had already turned to leave the wharf.

But without his cloak now.

It covered her.

Eryx

"As you wish, Prince," Corval called behind Eryx.

He didn't bother to turn to respond to Corval because he knew he didn't need to. All his orders would be followed without question. The little mermaid would be delivered to the estate of his choosing within mere days, and kept where she couldn't run until he was ready to deal with her— although he still had no idea what he planned to do to her now that he had her. Everything he'd dreamed up seemed ... not quite enough.

"They won't lay a hand on her," Mattue assured as they walked the wharf to the end where a horse was already waiting for Eryx to mount. "She'll be in perfect condition, of course."

Eryx grunted under his breath. "I already know."

"Thought you may want the assurance nonetheless."

"I want a dry bed and a good meal."

After that, he could decide other things.

Things about her.

The young boy waiting by the tacked-up horse kept a tight hold on the reins and didn't offer them to the prince while Eryx stopped to pull the riding gloves from his pants pocket. Mattue took his silence and stillness to mean he still wanted to talk.

Perfect.

"She's quite … she may be dangerous. Do you think you should have someone guarding her when she's at the estate with you and the servants?"

Eryx chuckled a dry sound. "Not likely."

"Did you see what she did to those men?"

"Perfectly fine, yes. They're foolish and lazy. She probably saw it, too."

"Prince—"

A commotion started back on the wharf. Yelling from the men, and the swish-swosh of rope being moved. He didn't need to look back to know what was happening. Corval's men were likely beginning the process of moving the mermaid—he still didn't know her name and that bothered him for reasons he couldn't explain—into a cage where she would stay until they delivered her by horse and carriage to an estate not far from here.

He expected her to die there.

By his hand.

Soon.

And yet, he couldn't say she would.

That bothered him, too.

"What did he mean?" Eryx asked, lifting his gaze to meet Mattue's after fitting on his gloves. "Corval, I mean. The others wouldn't stop staring at her. One made a comment. Corval, though … he called her quite worthy."

Mattue cleared his throat. "You didn't notice?"

"She's beautiful, Mattue. Many sea women are."

"It's more than that, Prince. Her coloring, the red hair, and the brand on her hand. It's very similar to the last one they caught—safe guess, they could be sisters, but if not, they're certainly related somehow."

Eryx had not looked at her hand. He'd not noticed a brand.

"And what of the brand?" he demanded.

"Well, that's the interesting bit. The other one had it, too. Arrows, if you noticed."

He simply stared at Mattue, waiting for the man to explain. Thankfully, he didn't have to wait long.

"Royals of the Blu Seas," the advisor said, shrugging one cloak-covered shoulder. "According to the hunters, and what I know of it, a brand like that means a royal."

"Arrows, you said?"

Mattue nodded. "Specifically, one atop the other. Crossed."

Arrows.

Where had he seen that mark before? *Had* he?

And why hadn't he noticed hers?

He had another thought, too. If the mermaid was a royal of her kind, then any doubt he had that she didn't understand him, or his language was nonexistent. While the people of Atlas certainly didn't communicate kindly with the Blu Sea mermaids, he knew other lands did for many reasons. Or so they had been told.

She absolutely could speak his language.

A lot like the others they'd caught could.

It only pissed him off more.

Why hadn't she answered him today?

"The hunters—they know more about those markings?" Eryx asked. "About the mermaids?"

"Corval certainly seems to."

Eryx would remember it.

Just in case …

"Thank you, Mattue. I'll be seeing you."

Turning, he finally offered a palm to the boy waiting with the horse's reins. Once mounted on the horse, Eryx clicked his tongue and pulled on the strap of leather to turn the beast. It was only Mattue's call that had him halting the animal.

"What is it now?"

Mattue tipped his chin up, a slight smile playing at the edges of the man's lips. "Well, you have what you wanted … is it not my turn, now?"

Ah, yes.

A crown for a mermaid.

Eryx had not forgotten.

"I suppose that's for you to figure out, Mattue," he replied.

He had what he wanted.

Didn't he?

29. TRY

Arelle

Something rough and dry scratched against Arelle's back and legs when she shifted in her sleep. Turning over had done nothing good for her, if only because sunlight spilled over her face and had her clenching her eyes shut even tighter than before to shield from the sudden color that filled her dreams.

No, she wasn't sleeping anymore.

And the dreams hadn't been that good, anyway.

Though the lump of ground she'd slept on felt somewhat cushiony even with the scratchy dryness, it crunched under the weight of her body rolling again. She tried to pull her legs closer to her middle, the same way she would with her tail and fin in her sleep, but the telltale clink-clink of chains that fetched up finally had her opening her eyes.

She breathed deep.

Dirt.

Hay.

Fur.

Wood.

Dust danced in the stream of sunlight coming in through a slated window. For longer than she cared to admit, she watched those dancing specks as she relived the day and night before. The grunt of an animal had her tilting her head just enough to see the brown speckled horse that rooted its wet nose against her opened palm lying on a bed of hay.

Another shuddering exhale left her lips.

The horse's lips jiggled against her skin with his next snort. It almost felt like a hello, and despite her current situation, Arelle couldn't help but smile at the animal. She had only seen them from afar before. Running along the tops of cliffs while she'd stayed a safe distance away in the sea.

They were as big as she thought.

Just as beautiful, too.

Keeping her one hand out for the horse to kiss again, if he wanted, Arelle sat up straight in the crunchy hay. She wanted to cross her legs, but a glance to the side at the chain that led out from a link on the wall kept her shackled at both ankles.

Memories of the night before flooded her mind the longer she stared at the chain. Oh, the landwalkers hadn't touched her on the long journey. They'd not even hurt her, really. They also barely talked to her at all when they'd delivered her here in pitch-black darkness.

She wasn't sure how far from the sea she was, but did it matter when all she needed to do was close her eyes? There, she could see it. Breathe deep and taste it. It felt like they'd traveled endlessly before finally stopping, but she knew if she followed the sounds in her heart and mind, it wouldn't take long for her to find the sea.

Except she couldn't do that at all.

She had all of three feet of chain to move, and as it were, in her sleep she'd rolled herself far from the wall where they'd left her until she'd had no more room to move. Even the cloak had managed to come undone and did little to protect her from the rough ground covered in the horse's hay.

Another snort from the horse had Arelle looking his way. The beast wasted no time tipping his large head down to nudge her hand before doing the same to the top of her head. If he understood she sat there naked and confused, the horse didn't show it.

She had to laugh at that.

"A beautiful sound, that."

The voice had Arelle scrambling up from the floor in an instant, pulling the cloak with her as though she might use it as some kind of shield. A completely, utterly useless shield. She didn't even bother to check where his voice had come from first. Not that it mattered. Once he'd spoken and she knew he was there, she didn't need to search for him.

She just *knew*.

Her back hit the wall of the stall, splinters of wood biting into her skin as the cloak hung from her clenched hands. She found Eryx leaning against the wrought iron gate of the stall on the inside. Somehow, he'd managed to get inside the stall. Probably when she had still been sleeping.

How long had he watched her?

Was that why she'd felt comfortable enough to wake up?

Because he was there?

The shackles at her ankles dug into skin and bone from how taut she dared to pull the chain. Yet, Arelle didn't move.

Neither did Eryx.

Gone was the fancy waistcoat and shined boots from the day before. Replaced instead by a loose shirt with sleeves that flared a bit at the wrists and hung down to his mid-thigh. Scuffed leather boots that hadn't even been tied up along the seam at the back shifted against the dirt floor of the stall, drawing her gaze up his lean form.

His clothes hid his body.

It didn't matter.

She still remembered perfectly fine how he looked without most of them.

"The horse—they call him Till," Eryx said, his voice creating an echo with every beat of her heart. While he spoke to her, he looked at the horse. "He seems to like you. Then again, animals do tend to recognize similar creatures. Similar beasts."

She wasn't an animal, though.

Or a beast.

Arelle stayed quiet.

Shifting his weight from one foot to the other, Eryx stood straight against the gate, his other hand coming around to show the folded pile of white, flowy fabric he held. He still didn't look her way, but at least Arelle could breathe like this. Once he stared at her, that would all change, she knew.

"I know you're not mute. Why you insist on this silence is beyond me."

Finally, his gaze snapped to hers.

She hadn't wanted him to look at her.

Now, she didn't want him to look away.

Gods.

The bond would kill her.

He took one step closer to her, and even though she was pressed against the wood, Arelle found it almost impossible not to move toward him, too. Somehow, she managed to stay still, even when his gaze took a slow trek over her. From the trembling cloak she held in her shaking hands to the way his stare lingered appreciatively on the shape of her hips. There was something about the way his pupils darkened—making those icy gray-blue eyes of his warmer, even if it was only from the heat of the man—that had her breath catching.

He liked what he saw.

He also hated it.

Arelle didn't need for him to say it to know.

"Doesn't matter," he muttered.

Although as he said it, she felt it was a lie. Whatever he was about to say, it did matter. His tone gave it away, but so did the electricity in the air when he came one more step closer. Now, if he reached out, he could touch her.

He didn't, though.

Not yet.

"It doesn't matter," he repeated in a sigh, "whether I hear your voice or not because I swear, I hear it all the time anyway. At night when I'm alone. In the wind when it blows past my ears. Every time I close my eyes. Whether or not that's because I've dreamed of getting my hands around your throat every single day since that night in the water orchard … or if it's something else, well, I can't say."

Impossible, she wanted to say.

The bond wouldn't make it so.

She hadn't sung for him. Hadn't even talked for him that night. He would not be able to hear the siren's call—his mate—when she hadn't given that to him on the island when the bond began to tether them.

"I think I might know exactly what you sound like," he continued, his boot scuffing against the dirt before he shifted the pile of white fabric from one hand to the other, "but it really doesn't matter now."

Lies.

It absolutely did matter.

And if he thought that was what would make her talk, then she had a surprise in store for him. Arelle remained silent even when that heat in his gaze bled away the longer the two of them stared at one another, leaving him back with his cold rage.

He was not very good at hiding it.

Not at all.

Though it ached to do it, Arelle dropped his gaze. He was near, and she only wanted him to come closer. Until she breathed in his air and felt his heat soaking into hers. But that was the bond, and she wouldn't let herself forget it, either.

"I heard you speak that night—in your tongue from the sea, yes, but I heard it. Or did you forget about that night? Was it just one of many for you?"

Arelle blinked, her tongue peeking out to wet the seam of her lips.

Still, she said nothing.

That was what pulled the final straw for Eryx.

His next words came out sharp, harsh, and fast. They impacted the same way a slap to her skin would. A warning, certainly, but they also wrapped around her heart like it was his fist clenching so damned tight. The exhale rushed out of her lungs because for the first time …

He demanded.

Her mate made a demand.

And she rushed to obey.

"*Tell me your name!*"

"Arelle."

Silence surrounded the stables, but this time, it wasn't from just her. No, he quieted, too. The animals stopped their movements, even the mice at the far end that had been squeaking all morning. She swore even the wind stopped blowing for a second.

He'd demanded.

She'd had to answer it.

Not that he knew, but he would have to do the same. That was the bond.

Arelle lifted her gaze in just enough time to watch the sight of Eryx closing the small bit of distance between them in the stall. His boots barely scuffed the floor. With a hand raised like he might strike her, she tipped her chin up.

Forever defiant.

She'd have to be.

He didn't hit her, though.

No, that hand of his found her throat. His fingers wrapped around the delicate column, pressing into where her gills flared out with every breath, but it wasn't enough to stop the air from dragging hard and heavy into her lungs. He pinned her in place.

With his stare and his touch and him.

All of him.

Having him this close was good, but just as bad, too. Because it made her want more. When he looked down between them, surveying her nakedness and the state of her captivity. He could do whatever he wanted to her shackled and vulnerable like she was.

Part of her wished he would.

Another wanted to hide.

"Arelle," he repeated thickly.

Her chin trembled.

It was done.

She'd spoken.

Like she could for him, he would hear her forever.

What good was her silence now?

"Arelle," she whispered in kind. "And you are Eryx."

His hand tightened on her throat, and she swallowed hard.

"Prince—"

"Eryx," Arelle said. "To me, you are *only* Eryx."

He stiffened.

She looked past him at the horse who was now grazing from a bucket that hung on the door of his stall.

"What will you do with me now?" she asked.

"I wanted to kill you."

Arelle's stare snapped back to his in a blink. The hard planes of his face called to her in a way that nothing else ever had. Like the scar through his right eyebrow, or the way his lips curved with his satisfaction. Not in a smile, but something else entirely.

Something more wicked.

She could study his features forever.

It would never bore her.

"But why?"

He exhaled a shaky breath.

Arelle sucked it in.

"You killed my mother. Or do you even remember her at all?"

Of course, she did.

But that hadn't been her.

She didn't lay the final blow, but a part of her knew that probably didn't make a difference to him. It had been late—the sky was blacker than the seas. She and Poe looked a lot alike, but especially to someone who didn't know them well. He could have easily mistaken her sister for her. Perhaps, because she had been the one to come out of the water after it had ended and watched him from a safe distance … maybe that was why her memory had seared into his own.

What did it matter?

Here she was.

"Now," Eryx murmured, leaning closer until their noses touched and his hand at her throat flexed just a bit, "I'm not so sure what I'll do with you."

As quickly as he'd caged her, he stepped back. Not that it made any sort of difference because Arelle could still feel that man on every inch of her body in more ways than one.

She expected him to leave her there chained to the wall, but even as he turned away, his hand snagged her wrist. He held her hand high and eyed the brand on her skin of the two arrows, as though he knew exactly what he was looking at and the significance.

"Which would be worse to you and your people," he asked, "killing you or keeping you?"

He didn't expect an answer. Not when he dropped her hand, and the pile of flowy, white fabric to the stall floor.

"Get dressed. You'll take breakfast with me when a maid deems you suitable. Try not to fight—I'd hate for this to end sooner than I'd like, my little mermaid. Even if I haven't decided exactly how I'll kill you, I still will … it's just a matter of time."

Wrong again.

And once more, Arelle didn't correct him.

Eryx

"The trousers, waistcoat, and overcoat you chose for the day will be at the end of your bed, Prince, and if you need help—"

"Did she fight the maid?" Eryx interrupted.

The male servant who usually helped him ready for the day quieted at the other side of the den attached to his chambers. He didn't like the stable house and estate nearly as much as he did the House of Miller, but it served his purpose of moving her—Arelle, his mind practically screamed; now that he knew her name, he certainly couldn't forget it—farther away from the sea. He thought perhaps the closer she was to it, the more she might fight to get away.

But who was he to say?

The servant cleared his throat. "No, my lord, I was told she behaved well."

Eryx nodded, surprise fluttering through him. He didn't turn away from the window as Arelle was led from the stables by the two guards he'd hired to watch her from a safe distance. The maid who had helped dress her in the gown he'd brought came out of the stables right after to trail close behind.

Even from his position up high, safe in the chambers he would use for the duration of their stay at the stable estate, he could plainly see the gown fit her well.

Someone had thought to brush her hair into manageable curls that shone in the cloudy daylight. He realized in that moment how hard this would be for him.

Not because he wanted to kill her.

But because he'd like to fuck her.

Again.

"Would you like help dress—"

"Leave," Eryx ordered.

The man didn't ask for the prince to repeat himself.

Eryx was grateful.

At least alone, he wouldn't have to pretend like he didn't have a raging hard-on from nothing more than watching that mermaid be escorted from the stables to the house. Closer to him. Which was a problem, considering how much he seemed to enjoy that. He found great pleasure in having her this close—so close, in fact, that she was entirely under his control now.

So, why did it feel like she was somehow controlling him? Why did she make his emotions run wild, or perk his cock up from only the sight of her?

He owned her.

Not the other way around.

Eryx would have to make sure she knew it, too.

Her voice, though?

It was still singing in his mind.

Literally *singing.*

No, this wouldn't be easy at all.

Then again, nothing ever was.

It was closer to midday by the time Eryx was able to sit down for breakfast. He was sure the food had been cooked and ready to serve for a good hour or more, but not a single servant of the house spoke about it one way or another, and the spread was still hot when the platters were brought to the table.

"Duck eggs, my lord, your favorite," said the woman who kept the large kitchen running at this particular estate. "And of course, the assortment of cooked fish, bread still warm and crisped the way you like, milk fresh from this morning, and—"

"It's wonderful," Eryx interjected, giving the woman a smile. The way she looked his way with wide eyes but a hesitant smile, told him the servants had likely been talking amongst themselves about him once again. Not that anything they said was a lie. All his difficultness, the arrogance and abrasive nature ... it was all true. They didn't expect or wait for compliments from him; he should try that more often, maybe. "Amalia, is it?"

She nodded before stopping near the other end of the table to drop into a curtsey. He'd never cared much for those, but as the royals do ... "That is my name."

"We'll be here a while. I will attempt to remember it. Have them bring her in, please."

"Absolutely, Prince."

Eryx could have asked for a handful of servants to remain in the dining hall to serve the food and remove whatever they finished with as they were done with it, but he preferred to take his breakfast alone.

With Arelle.

The two women who helped to carry in the food followed Amalia when she exited the room. Eryx had already placed a linen napkin across his lap and was reaching for his favorite item on the table—the boiled duck eggs—when soft footsteps echoed just outside the dining hall. He glanced up in just enough time to see Arelle come to stand in the arched, stone doorway of the hall.

Now, he was fully able to appreciate how the soft fabric of the gown he'd chosen for her to wear today fell over her curves. A material so thin and almost translucent in the light that when she walked past the window, he could see the shadow of her body moving beneath the gown. Dropped modestly in the bust, tied in the back at the waist, and just breathable enough to move easily when she walked, it fit her well.

Perfectly, really.

If not for those scales at her temples and the gills—now flattened—at her throat, one wouldn't know she was what she was.

A single strip of the gauzy dress was tied at her throat. Like a pretty little bow for him to unwrap, maybe.

Her face had been cleaned. Those wild red curls of hers seemed slightly more tamed, but a part of him was grateful no one had attempted to tie them back.

All those things came secondary as Arelle's stare landed on him at the table, and she headed his way without a second thought. Perhaps it was because the woman was waterborne or hell, it could have just been the fact that she was … so entirely unique and dangerous for him, but there was something about the way she walked. Something in the sway of her hips and the delicate lines of her shapely legs that had him watching her every step.

There was a strength to her walk.

A confidence.

And it made his mouth water.

Eryx did his best to hide it. He didn't need to be seen panting after a merwoman like a dog in heat, but he couldn't help but notice. It was hard not to.

She had nearly reached the table when the two guards tasked with watching her made their appearance in the doorway. He had a good mind to shoo them away. What could this merwoman really do to him like this with no weapon at her disposal?

But he didn't.

The image of bloodied men was enough for him to keep them right where they stood.

For now.

"When did you learn to walk?" he asked her.

She came to a stop at the other end of the table, and her hand came up to toy with a ribbon of red curls that had fallen over her shoulder. "I can't remember the last time my hair was dry."

Huh.

"And the walking?"

Her gaze darted to his. "Sixteen—like all of my kind. Three years ago now."

"And yet, it's like you've been doing it your whole life."

He couldn't help but smirk at the way her brow furrowed. The little knot in her otherwise smooth forehead said she was confused about their conversation, and the softness in her stare told him that she didn't know what to do here. But that wasn't really his problem. Not at the moment, anyway.

Just as fast as she'd showed the vulnerability, it was gone when she looked over the spread on the table. Without asking if she could be seated, she dropped gracefully into the chair at the opposite end from him.

Eryx might have chided her for it. Then again, he never cared for royal semantics, either.

"So, is this how a prince of Atlas spends his days?" she asked, leaning over to pick likely one of the only things on the table she recognized as food for her to eat. The fish. "By being spoiled and pampered in a big house far away from the sea. Although from there, I suppose you wouldn't have to be bothered by the sight of my kind being pulled from the seas. How many of us do you own?"

Eryx made a noise under his breath.

Appreciative and surprised, really.

The nerve of her …

"Just you," he decided to reply. "I don't have a taste for slaves, really. Bit too much work to keep them as you want them."

Her lips formed a grim line.

"Or is it because of your mother?"

If his new ward felt the change in the air at the mention of Eryx's mother, he couldn't say. Of course, she would know … not only had he told her the woman she'd killed was his mother, but she'd undoubtedly heard him calling and begging for Anthia the night she'd been dragged into a dark sea.

Swallowing hard, his appetite entirely gone without warning, Eryx decided he no longer wanted to entertain while he took his breakfast. Perhaps allowing Arelle entrance to the house and giving her a dress and a brush for her hair had been just a little too much.

She'd forgotten her place here.

Took no time at all, either.

Standing from the table, he tossed the linen napkin from his lap down to the mostly untouched plate. "Enjoy the meal, Arelle. I understand your kind can eat like the rest of us do."

That was all he offered before rounding the table and heading for the guards at the doorway. It was only the question she threw at his back that had his steps halting and his shoulders tensing like they were made of the same stone as the echoing hall.

"What, you can dress me up after you rip me from the sea, but you can't hold a conversation at the same time? Were you only raised to be talked to, Eryx? Does the problem start when you need to talk back? Seems like poor treatment for a prince, doesn't it? How dare you."

How dare he?

Yes, she certainly had forgotten her place and he didn't mind giving her a reminder. Starting right now.

Spinning on his heel, Eryx lost what remained of his cool, controlled demeanor with every step he took back toward the table. Arelle stood from the chair as he neared, not looking the slightest bit scared of her current situation.

Which was wrong.

He wanted her scared.

Needed that.

That was the entire fucking point of her being here. Not for him to dress her up into something she wasn't, and play pretend at the table with breakfast spread out for them both. No. She was here for him to make her suffer for what she had done to him.

Eryx's palm connected with her throat, but even when he shoved her back to the table, spilling contents to the floor and staining her white dress with the red wine that had already been poured into gold goblets, she never once flinched. He realized, as her legs widened for him to move between her thighs, that the shoes he'd sent out with the maid hadn't been put on her feet.

She was barefoot.

Like she just came right out of the sea.

He supposed she had, in a way.

Below him, Arelle's hands circled around his wrist as he kept her pinned to the table. Those violet eyes of hers locked on his, and her lips spread in a wicked smile. As though she were pleased with herself.

Had she tried to make him react?

Did she like what she was getting?

It only served to piss him off even more because now that he was touching her, he didn't want to stop. It was like the second he got too close, or his hands found any part of her body, he became drunk from it. He only needed more and more and more. He wanted to fuck her until all that fight was gone, and she was compliant and soft and perfect.

That wasn't right.

Couldn't be.

"What is this?"

He felt her swallow under his hand, the softness of her skin a match to the silk linen of her gown and the bow at her throat.

"*Why do you make me behave like this?*" he asked.

His questions landed with no impact.

She stayed quiet.

That only pissed him off more.

He'd moved closer until his lower half molded to the apex of her thighs. The skirts of her gown had risen up, but she didn't seem the least bit ashamed about it. She had to know there were guards watching from the doorway.

Where was the dignity?

The respect?

Or did her kind just not care?

Because right now, he certainly didn't … and wasn't he a little bit like her, too?

"Well? Will you even speak?" Eryx asked.

"You don't want me to."

Her words were a whisper.

A weapon.

And a tease.

He let her go, stepping back all at once even though she didn't right herself on the table straight away. Chewing on his inner cheek, his jaw clenching as he worked over what he wanted to say, he turned away from her.

"You're free to look around," he told her, never looking back, "but you'll have guards on your person until your collar is ready."

"Collar?"

Eryx didn't bother to reply.

She'd learn soon enough.

It was only once he'd left the dining hall and traveled up to his bed chambers that he finally felt like he could breathe. As though a sense of relief waited for him there.

So did the maid who'd looked after Arelle earlier. She was just setting the cloak that belonged to Eryx—the one he'd dropped on the mermaid the day before to hide her nakedness from the men on the wharf—on the end of his bed.

"Have the head of the house cancel any appointments I have for the week," he told the woman, his gaze never leaving the fur-trimmed cloak.

"But lord, your advisor—"

"Have her cancel them all. And leave."

"Certainly."

A small curtsey, and she was gone, too.

That left Eryx.

And the cloak.

A rage swelled within him at the sight of the item all over again. He knew it was irrational and nothing more than her strange pull on him that entirely fucked with his emotions. That didn't mean it wasn't there because it was all too real.

He snatched the cloak from the bed with the intention of ripping the garment into useless pieces. Because if for some reason he couldn't work out this craving for violence on the person it was owed, then at least he could find relief in something as silly as this.

Except it didn't work.

The second he drew the garment closer to himself, Eryx found the scent of that merwoman downstairs come rushing with it. That first pull of air into his lungs was coated with her. It didn't matter that he'd been with her only seconds before. He'd been between her thighs with his hands on her damned neck, and still ... still, the smell of her on his cloak sent him spinning.

That hate in his heart became wrapped in something tighter and hotter. It didn't disappear, but rather, sharpened the lust that shot straight down to his cock. Eryx had many better things to do than rip his trousers open before shoving his fist with the cloak down the length of his erection. Hell, he hadn't jerked himself off in more years than he cared to count. Not since his first lover had been bought when he was just fifteen to satisfy any and every need he'd had but he opted to take a trip across Atlas and find his own. One of many women to keep his bed warm.

He hadn't the need to do it himself when someone else was always at the ready to do it for him.

Yet, he barely even considered it. Nothing else mattered when the textured fabric of the outer liner tightened around his cock with his fist. Every stroke came faster. The distinct flavor of her flooded his tongue with every shallow breath he took.

That threw him right over the edge.

He spilled his seed into the cloak with a groan that echoed. Surely, the servants down the hall readying a room for Arelle would have heard it.

Eryx burned the cloak in the fireplace. He never left proof of his sins.

Ever.

Arelle

She counted the days.

One passed. Then two ... Three.

On the third day's night, another passing of the sun where she walked the halls of a house that seemed so entirely strange to her with guards not far at her back, Arelle could already smell it in the air. An oncoming storm.

She'd known it was coming from the second she'd woken up that morning. Yet, it'd become painfully clear to her that the landwalkers around her had little to no idea about what the skies and seas were brewing for them.

It was later in the day, when the sun began to fall from the blackening skies, that the wind finally picked up. It was only then that the people in the house began to shut the large shutters on the windows. They hid in their rooms all throughout the estate, including Eryx. But she only knew that from what she had been told.

Certainly not because she was allowed his presence.

Arelle both hated and loved that.

Her guards shut her into the chambers she had been left to use after the maids came in to close the shutters. While the rain battered the side of the house and the winds howled, she was alone.

They were afraid.

She opened the windows and laughed.

Breathing in the wet air that tasted of a sea she couldn't even see from her windows, Arelle felt slightly closer to home. She would be a liar if she said she didn't wonder what mess she'd left back in the depths of the Blu Seas, but for now ... it really didn't matter.

Did it?

If they hadn't gone after Poe, they surely wouldn't come for her. No, she would have to get back to them. Even if what she left behind might be a more terrifying fate than what was with her here. Still, the sea was her home. She needed to go back.

As she pulled back inside the window, Arelle noticed the thick wooden lattice attached to the side of the stone of the house and the strong vines growing all through it. She glanced over her shoulder at the closed doors, knowing the guards waited behind it.

But right now?

Everything sounded like a storm.

They wouldn't even know.

Part of her screamed to stay.

She was with her mate.

Another needed to go.

One way or another, the land or the sea, she would still die.

Arelle climbed out onto the ledge and grabbed the lattice and vines. She made it to the stables and mounted the same horse who had greeted her the first morning she'd awoken on the estate. She only knew how to get up on his back because she had watched others do it over the past three days. At first, the beast didn't want to venture into the storm, but eventually, he went with her urging.

Then, she heard the bell ringing behind her.

She'd not heard that before.

A part of her knew, though ...

Tis for me.

30. BELONGING

Eryx

"*Yah*," Eryx urged the horse, his palm flat against the animal's throat letting him feel every single heavy beat of its massive heart. It never failed to amaze him how the animals weren't as frightened of the storms as people seemed to be.

Ahead on the dirt road that winded through a forested area just outside of the estate's walls, Eryx could see the current reason for his fury rounding a corner. How Arelle even knew which direction she should take on the roads leading out of the estate so that she would eventually find her way back to the sea, he didn't know. She'd chosen the right one, though.

She still had a way to go yet.

Unfortunately, she'd thankfully not picked the fastest horse in the stables. And when the guards dared to hesitate to chase after her through the storm, Eryx had quickly lost any semblance of his patience. He took the horse, and he went into the blackness of the night while the rain pelted heavily against his back.

Unafraid.

And entirely fucking angry.

She'd had to know now would be the safest time for her to attempt an escape. How long had she been planning it?

He wanted to punish the guards.

Cage her.

And yet, he was the most enraged with himself.

He'd let fickle emotions distract him from what was supposed to be his plan. She should have been dead by now. Every vision of ending her life and discarding her remains with as much disrespect as had been shown to his mother had become a background thought to the fact that she was there.

With *him*.

He had her.

She was supposed to be his. His to do with what he wished. His to ruin or keep or end; to make suffer and ache or just to watch her simply lose. Lose anything at all. Something that meant even a fraction to her what his mother had meant to him.

Instead, he found himself chasing after her in a rain that stung his skin with every drop that slapped against him, on the fastest horse he'd ever ridden. And not to get her back so that he could kill her. But rather, because she was not to leave. She *couldn't*.

The thoughts made no sense. The emotions, even less. So, he ignored them as he pushed the horse harder. To its very limits, if the heavy panting and snorts that accompanied every stride from the animal were any indication.

Eyrx caught her, though. Right around the bend of that turn, his horse slid against hers, and with a twist of his body and a snag of his arm around her waist, he'd easily yanked her from her horse to his in seconds. He was sure she didn't even know what had happened at first. Not until the sight of her horse running ahead of them while his slowed.

She tensed, and then the struggle began. Her nails caught his skin; her teeth found his wrist when she damn near fell from his grasp.

Gods.

The horse would kill her when it trampled over her. The thought would have sent him to his knees, had he not been focused on staying atop the horse while subduing Arelle in his hold. It was the only reason he stopped the horse because it was dangerous and *fuck* ...

If her life would end, it would be from his hand. Not because he dropped her under the hooves of a galloping horse. The second it was safe for him to drop to the ground, he did. Arelle went with him, kicking and fighting the whole way.

"*Let me go! Let me go!*" she screamed.

Yet, even as she said it, her body pressed into his like she didn't intend to pull away once they were on the ground. She said one thing—did another.

He couldn't let her go.

Wouldn't.

The horse trotted on while Eryx kept his stronghold on the now-sobbing woman in his arms.

"You don't understand what I've done," he heard her say into the wind. "You have no idea at all. Let me go!"

"Stop!"

"Let me—"

"Stop it," he snapped, the words flying straight from his mouth and into her face.

Never had he been so harsh with a woman. He probably deserved what came next because of it, too.

The slap landed to his cheek with a crack that sent his head flying to the side. The hit had come fast, but he swore he heard her hand pull away from him quicker as she sucked in a hard gasp. Never in his life had a woman dared to put her hands on him. Not even a man would, because they all thought royals were something handed to them by the Gods above.

A joke, really.

Yet, Arelle had done exactly that.

Even as the anger inside him swelled, so did the heat for something else.

"I shouldn't have done that," she said, her words all rushing out at once.

"I—"

"*Why?*"

Just like that, the fight had left her, and all it had taken was her hand hitting his cheek. Was that because she thought he would answer her in kind, or something else?

"What?" she asked.

She might not have been struggling against him anymore, but Eryx refused to let go of the hold he had with his one arm snug around her middle. He used that to his advantage to pull her closer, flush against the hard lines of his body while his face hovered over hers. Then, all she could see was him while he spoke and nothing else.

He wanted the next things he said to be very clear.

"Why shouldn't you have done that, Arelle?"

There was something delicious about the way her throat jumped at his demand. He could practically hear the words wanting to come right out of her mouth, but she was a stubborn one. Occasionally, he might appreciate that.

Not tonight, however.

The rain continued to pound down from the sky like paradise had opened up to welcome them home with a flood of tears. The wind had her soaked hair flying out behind her with a wildness that any human woman would have been scared of, from the sheer force alone. Arelle, on the other hand, stood steady and unafraid at the storm and the man.

"I belong to the sea," she told him softly. "I belong to my pe—"

"You belong to *me*."

The sky cracked open with more lightning.

It was his voice that still boomed.

The heat that burst in his chest at the declaration could only be matched by the reflection of him in her blown out pupils. She didn't even have time for her next breath before his mouth crashed down on hers. There was no fight in her kiss to stop—only an answer when her tongue slashed along his for a taste of her own.

Eryx had no idea where the horses had gone, and he couldn't find a single shit to give about the fact they were currently on a muddy path that typically had a lot of travel.

In good weather, that was.

Like this, no one would dare to be outside.

Except for them, it seemed.

Her fingers slipped through the low-hanging neck of his nightshirt to scrape across his chest. The sting had his cock daring to punch through the trousers he'd barely managed to pull on before leaving his chambers when he heard the bell ringing to signal her escape.

"You belong to me," he breathed against her mouth when he finally dragged himself away from the kiss. His hand came up to grab tight to her jaw when he added, "And unless told otherwise, you will behave like it, Arelle."

The same heat flashed in her eyes as before. Now, he only saw it as an invitation when she flexed her sharp fingernails against the carved muscles of his chest one more time.

"If you claw me like that again, I will bend you over, rip your dress up your back, and fuck you against the boulder behind you."

That was the only warning she would get.

"You wouldn't," she returned.

It almost sounded confident.

Eryx chuckled. "Wouldn't I? You are mine to do with what I want. And you say it like you might not enjoy yourself—we very much know you would."

The pink came back to her cheeks, too. It did wicked things for his lust and he wouldn't pretend differently. His next kiss came harsher and harder. The force of it propelled them off the path and into the wet, cold grass until her back hit the rock he'd promised would be there. He released her jaw from his hold, but only to shove that hand between the silk of her skirt. The sopping fabric molded to the sweet slit between her thighs for him to stroke when she widened her legs for him.

He wished he cared that she was brazen enough to let him have her like this, but he found he craved it. The wild rawness of it called to him, and before he knew it, Eryx had her turned around on the rock so that her round, pert ass fit tightly against his groin.

He kept another promise when the silk of her dress ripped apart from the seam where the skirt had been sewed into the bottom of the bodice. Her heavy intake of air answered the cold wind that whispered across her naked skin.

The crack of his palm to her ass accompanied his next words when he asked, "Why won't you wear undergarments? They're brought to you for a reason."

All she breathed back was, "But why bother?"

She would kill him.

Eryx believed it to be true.

He ripped her dress further. Arelle pushed up to her tiptoes to bare her ass even more. He couldn't get his trousers pulled down fast enough when she widened her legs and looked over her shoulder at him. Already harder than rock, his cock ached in his palm when he stroked the head along the wet heat of her slit.

He wasn't expecting her to reach back to grab his cock from him, though. She slid him into her pussy herself, hugging him tight and making him grunt when he settled a little deeper. And then just as fast, she pushed him out, still keeping her hand tight to his base as her thighs closed around him. Only then did she let him go. The soft skin of his cock rubbed against her wet pussy and warm thighs. It wasn't the same pleasure as fucking her, but it still made him feel like his balls were about to empty faster than he could control them. With her ass pushing into him, all those soft sounds she made and the slickness of her fluids coating him … fuck, it was just enough to make him crazy.

"Come like this."

With every flex of his hips, the head of his cock slipped over her hand, which was now working fast circles into her clit. When she started shaking and those sounds of hers came louder, he lost what semblance of control he'd maintained.

The sticky heat of his cum coated her fingertips and thighs, and his dick only stopped jerking with spurts as he pushed her stomach flat against the rocks. She widened her thighs, and he buried himself as deep as he could get into her clenching cunt.

"Yes," he groaned, "now you give it to me."

Somehow, she'd managed to hold onto that orgasm until he was inside her. He got to feel every muscle of hers work and flex around his cock as he stretched her open and filled her again and again.

"*Eryx, Eryx … Eryx.*"

That chant of hers echoed in his mind.

He kept fucking her even when he felt the spasms of her orgasm bleed away. She started chasing the high all over again by backing into his fast thrusts.

Eryx couldn't get enough.

Not of the sight of her.

The feel of her.

The flavor of the skin on the back of her neck, dampened with rain and heated with their fucking when he leaned down for a taste. All of it was like the best drink to have ever slid down his throat. Even if it would kill him, he planned to swallow every single drop.

"You're going to make me come again," he told her, his teeth grazing against the top of her ear, "and then you're going to get on your knees and lick me until I'm clean, Arelle. Do you hear me?"

She answered him back with a moan, but he felt the nod of her head that accompanied it, too.

That worked for him.

He fucked her until she screamed again.

She was all too pleased to do exactly what he demanded of her, dropping to her knees to clean his cock of their mingled cum while his hand threaded into the tangled strands of her hair. Under the wetness of the rain, it somehow shone a brighter red.

But even when she was finished, she stayed on her knees. He kept watching her. The sight of her down there, submissive after all her defiance, was not at all how he'd thought this evening would end.

Once again, she surprised him.

A million questions raced through his mind.

Only one felt appropriate.

"Why?"

Arelle replied simply, "You don't know what I've done."

She'd said that earlier, too. He didn't think she would explain what she meant, even if he asked.

"You will learn," he told her.

"Will I—or will you?"

Just like that, he decided she absolutely would learn. He'd enjoy teaching her, too.

The guards all but demanded they lock Arelle in her rooms and nail the shutters closed on her windows during the days following her attempted escape. Eryx could have agreed—probably should have, if he were being honest—but he just ... didn't feel the need.

The memory of her kneeling at his feet, soft and pleased and submissive, was far more than enough to tell him something had happened with them. Something between them made this different.

He just didn't know what.

So, no, he didn't allow the guards to stick closer. He refused to lock her in her rooms, and in fact, demanded everything return to some semblance of normal after the storm had passed. Arelle continued on with her freedom, never seeming as though she might run again but also not seeking Eryx out.

He offered her the same.

Besides, watching her was far more interesting. When she didn't know he was doing it, and more so when she did.

Like now.

"Like this?" he heard her ask.

The woman who managed the kitchen and cooked for the entire house nodded behind the large oak table. "Knead it like that, yes. Well done."

"This isn't so hard."

"Not if you have a knack for it, and you certainly seem to."

For whatever reason, Eryx found himself smiling at the sight of Arelle kneading dough for the bread that would be served later at supper. Not because he liked the thought of her cooking for him—although, he did on that side of things, too—but because she was learning something new and seemed to be enjoying it. He had little to no interest in learning the mundane things like cooking or otherwise.

He had people for that.

Always had.

Did she?

"My lord," came a familiar voice from behind him. "The hunter is here, as requested. Shall I show him to—"

"The den, please," Eryx replied to the man.

"Yes, Prince."

He'd not forgotten about the meeting he'd called with Corval. In fact, he'd sent word to speak with the man during the storm, knowing they would get a brief pause in the weather before another would come through to wreak more havoc. He hoped, however, that they would have a long enough break between one storm and the next that Corval would be able to show his face.

It seemed he had.

Thankfully.

Eryx had questions.

And every single one of them revolved around that woman smiling on the other side of the kitchen while she kneaded raisins into the dough.

While he would much rather stay hidden in the enclave leading into the kitchen so that he could continue watching Arelle from afar, he also didn't want to keep Corval waiting. Even if the man would say nothing about waiting, considering it was a prince he waited on.

Nonetheless, the faster Eryx finished with that meeting, the quicker he could get back here. Perhaps in just enough time to watch Arelle learn how to make his favorite pie.

Hmm.

Spinning on his heels with a sigh, Eryx headed for the den of the large house. The handful of servants moving from room to room nodded and waited for him to pass through before returning to their duties. Corval, to his benefit, was dressed like a man of status for once. And he was standing to greet the prince.

"Prince," Corval said, bowing a bit.

"Even threw on a waistcoat for the occasion, did you?"

Corval chuckled and took a chair next to the window when Eryx waved at it. "How often does one get called to visit the prince of Atlas during storm season?"

"Rarely."

"So, the waistcoat was appropriate."

"It is always appropriate, Corval."

"Ships would beg to differ."

Eryx gave him a look. "Ships can't talk."

"But the seas can," the man replied just as fast.

Well …

He wasn't about to argue with that. The sea certainly seemed to speak to him.

Eryx took the chair on the other side of the window and reached for the glass filled with ale that was already waiting for him. Watching the dark clouds streak through the sky, he already knew another storm would soon be on the way. They would progressively last longer and longer, until it felt like for weeks at a time all it did was rain and blow with winds strong enough to rip the trees right from their roots.

"Did you find out anything I wanted to know?" he asked the hunter.

Corval cleared his throat, but Eryx kept his attention on the sky. It was easier to hide his intentions when he didn't need to look someone in the eye. Not that they needed to know that. "If you're asking if I have confirmed that the mermaid is a royal of the Blu Seas, then yes, I have. The heir, actually, seeing as how she would have replaced her sister's place in line to the throne after her capture."

"So, the other one that was caught … she is her sister."

"Quite vocal, that one, from all accounts. Beautiful, certainly, which was why she was picked by the king amongst the rest of the catches this year. She's to be added to your father's collection soon, I think, but you know how he feels about the noisy ones. We'll see if she lasts."

"Was she how you learned—"

"Partially. I have other ways, also."

Eryx arched a brow, turning to face the man entirely. "Don't interrupt. It's rude."

Even if Eryx did it to others constantly. He could afford to.

"My apologies, but yes, it's confirmed."

"*Hmm.*"

"We assume the people of the sea believe the sister to be dead, given how long it's been since her catch, and they've not attempted to force her return."

"And her?" he asked.

"Whether or not they know she's been caught as well is all up in the air. It's not like they send a messenger to speak with us. Our relationship is … tenuous, at best."

"That does happen when you hunt them."

"We need them, Eryx. They keep Atlas rich. The export of their blood is what protects this kingdom."

"Other realms don't use them the same."

Corval sighed. "No, they don't, but other realms have also fought wars that lasted for the entire lives of men to have the standing they do. And even today, in Hades, two kings still spend their days attempting to burn each other to the ground. One from the land, and another from the sea."

"There are nine realms. That is just a portion. The same as us."

"You're not wrong," the man replied, "and that's also why the Emerald Lands have never joined in the discussion of exports with us. Merpeople who rule the land and the sea ... well, they have an army more than large enough to keep their realm well protected from anyone who doesn't appreciate the way they live."

"Fascinating, really."

Corval chuckled. "Then, why do you sound bored?"

"I'd like to know more about her."

"Her?"

"Her. Them. The sea. How they live. Anything about them at all."

Across from him, Corval's brow knotted. "*Why?*"

"Because I asked. Need there be another reason?"

"Right, no," Corval was quick to say. "My apologies."

Eryx only nodded.

"What we know has mostly come from other realms—four of the 9ine kings are mermen. Ah, apologies. Eight. One of the 9ine is a queen far north. Nonetheless, of the seas, their people often live in colonies. Families tend to be large and remain together through generations because it's how they raise their young. A village, and all. Royals tend to live closer to land, for whatever reason. If they mostly stick to the seas, the colonies can be quite spread out."

"What else?"

"It varies from sea to sea, my lord. Each kingdom, each species, is different."

"So, you really know nothing."

"I know enough," Corval replied fast, his stare pointed and sharp, "because it's what I need to know to hunt them safely and make enough to live happily."

Eryx hummed under his breath, nodding to himself. "Fair enough."

"It's why I learned as much as I could about the mated pairs. They're often the most dangerous, but especially when separated. It's why when we've caught a male, if we can tell he's one half of a mated pair, he's usually bled dry before being killed. They become violent when separated from their mates. Uncontrollable. Unrecognizable. He won't even be passed on as a slave or sold to another realm. It's not worth the risk of keeping him."

Now, that had his attention.

"The what?"

"The mates, Prince. They call it the bond. Not that I know how said bond comes to be, but mated pairs … they're different from the rest. They live with their colonies, their families, make their young and whatever else, but together, they're different."

"How so?"

Why was his heart beating so loudly?

It felt like it was in his throat.

"We know it has something to do with their blood. The magic, you know. We think they can call to each other somehow."

Eryx's next breaths came a little harder.

Thicker in his lungs.

"And?" he urged.

"Well, if they can call, my lord, then they can find one another, too. And when a man of the sea can burn down half a village square in a single night while trying to get back to his mate, imagine what several of them might do to this kingdom."

The story jerked a memory to life for Eryx. He remembered a fire, four seasons before, that had burned down half of a village square. Although, it had been blamed on lamp oil spilling onto a flickering flame. Or that was the story told. It made sense to lie about the fire's origins. People would be a lot leerier about the hunts—more so than they already were—if they knew how truly dangerous the merpeople could be.

It also didn't settle well with Eryx for more reasons than he cared to name.

Corval glanced over his way and flicked two fingers at him with a smile that almost chilled Eryx. It was like that smile said *I know exactly what you're thinking.*

The man then shrugged, saying, "As I said, not worth the risk, really."

He swallowed the lump forming in his throat.

"How do they reproduce?" Eryx asked.

"It changes," Corval replied. "Depends on their lifestyle. I've been told the women can choose a pregnancy unlike our women, but when they remain on land for a period of years, it seems their fertility changes to be similar to ours."

Which explained his and his brothers' births. Before, Eryx had never held any interest in these things, but now … he felt like he needed to know it all. Whether it was true, or correct, or not.

"Humans, however," Corval continued, "can't mate—bond—with a mermaid the way they do. As we've come to learn, reproducing with their species isn't the same as mating. If it's the magic in the blood, well, we just don't have it, Prince."

Eryx said nothing.

Why?

Because he wasn't like the rest.

He was half. Not entirely human. Not entirely like her. But maybe he was just enough …

"And you don't know how they mate," he said.

Corval shrugged. "No, it's never been witnessed, but we have our assumptions. The blood from both, perhaps. Other than that … well, you could just ask the source."

"Pardon?"

"Her. You have a mermaid here. Ask her."

Eryx's jaw clicked from clenching. "Well, that's a problem, then."

"Why is that?"

"Because the more time I spend near her, the less I understand."

"About what?" Corval asked.

He let out an aching breath. "Myself."

Arelle

The cast iron tub, filled nearly to the rim with hot water, wasn't helping Arelle's newest problem. The itch under her skin continued, even after she took the roughest cloth she could find in the bath chambers and scrubbed and scrubbed until her flesh was red.

Almost raw.

She called for more hot water, and the guard waiting outside the chambers was quick to fetch yet another boiling bucket from the kitchen downstairs. Droplets of condensation dribbled down from the tub onto the shell-shaped claw feet before spilling to the stone floor. She was sure the cracks between the stones were filled with water, now. How the candles filling every flat surface in the chambers still flickered with light and managed to shine through the amount of stream, she didn't know. The steam rolled through the room like a cloud, filling every nook and cranny as she tried her very best to stop the sensation of something crawling under her skin.

The itch she just couldn't scratch.

She had a good mind to drag her nails over her legs and arms again and again until she bled or the itching stopped altogether. Whichever came first, as long as the itching stopped. That was all that mattered to her.

Adding onto the sudden itchiness was the loneliness. She didn't think the people on the estate understood the meaning of community or friendship, considering they barely spoke to one another and most of the time, they didn't bother with her, either. That probably shouldn't have bothered her as much as it did, but she wasn't used to this.

Her people didn't live alone.

They weren't alone.

Not like this.

She could count the exact number of days she had been here—seventeen—and not a single one of them had been spent like they would have been, if she were back home in her colony. The bigger problem was the fact she couldn't seem to leave.

Not because guards watched her. Or because someone would come after her again. All those things were a given.

No, she couldn't leave him.

Eryx.

That wasn't how this worked and the longer she spent with him, even if it was in separate rooms and without his attention, the stronger the need became.

Which was exactly why Arelle found herself—once again—in a bathtub while the sky was dark outside, the storms raged all around them, trying to scrub these feelings right out of her fucking skin. That's what she blamed the itch on, although she didn't know if it was true.

Couldn't say at all it was the problem.

In her mind, however, it was.

She would get it out.

A sob slipped past her lips as she pushed the damp strands of her hair out of her face before she went right back to scrubbing her legs all over again. "Gods, why?"

Why did she feel like this?

Why wouldn't it go away?

Just ... why?

She'd probably asked the same question ten times. It wasn't as though she expected an answer, and honestly, other than the guards waiting outside the chambers for her to finish bathing, she assumed she was alone.

Arelle should have known better.

Eryx had a way of sneaking up on her.

"As I understand it," came his voice from the arched doorway leading into the bathing chambers, "the ... unpleasantness you're experiencing comes from being out of the saltwater for a while. They call it the leeching. Because it leeches from your skin over time and it can cause quite a feeling. A common complication for your kind. Apparently, it'll get easier with time until it passes completely."

Fuck him.

The shocking swell of anger at his answer—that he just knew what it was—pissed her off like nothing else.

Arelle didn't even bother to glance up from her task of scrubbing her now-red skin into a raw mess as she said, "Why are you still there?"

It wasn't like she needed him to enjoy her pain and struggle. He certainly did that more than enough at every other point in her days and evenings. He thought she didn't know when he watched her, but she did. She could feel it most times.

Foolish girl, her mind taunted, *because it was you and only you who did this to the both of you.* As though she needed the reminder. Really.

"Leave," she repeated.

His footsteps didn't follow her demand, but frankly, her tone hadn't been that strong. She wasn't even sure if she wanted him near or gone.

The confusion was the worst. Look at all he'd done to her—all the things he promised to do that would hurt her still—and yet the damned thrall of her mate had every part of her craving the man more and more. It never went away. A constant in her breathing days, it tortured her.

She hated him.

She *wanted* him.

"Or is it you who would like to leave?" he asked quietly. "Then you could return to a kingdom now meant to be yours. Isn't that what would happen if you found your way back to the Blu Seas?"

Arelle froze.

How did he know that?

Lifting her gaze from her tender knees, she found him leaning in the doorway. He'd shed the day clothes from earlier, now wearing only his evening clothes and a robe stained a rich red with a satiny sheen on the fabric. Tied loosely at the waist, the robe still showcased the broadness of his shoulders and brought out the golden sheen in his skin, even under the flickering lights of candles and thick steam. He seemed ready for bed.

So, why was he here?

"You know who I am," she said.

It wasn't a question.

She could see the truth in his eyes.

"You are the hunted," Eryx told her, shrugging one shoulder. "And so, what good would we be if we didn't make an effort to learn about our chosen prey?"

"Is that what I am—your prey?"

He didn't answer.

She really didn't need him to.

"You don't know anything about us," Arelle said softly. "Not what we do or who we love, or even why. All you care about is what we can do for you. You use us, hurt and break us. Don't pretend like you know things

317

about me or my kind for any other reason than to use it against us when it benefits you."

Eryx nodded, his lips pursing in a way that hardened his handsome features further. As though he needed to seem more attractive to her than he already was. "You're not wrong, darling."

"What is that?"

"*Hmm?*"

"That thing you called me—the *darling.*"

Eryx shook his head. "Nothing. And you deflected. Will they come for you?"

"Who?"

"Your people. Someone. Will they come for you, thinking your sister is dead, which leaves only you as the heir to your undersea kingdom? Will they?"

Arelle let out a shuddering breath. The only good thing coming out of this conversation was the fact that the itchiness had lessened. For now.

"Will they?" he asked again.

This time, though, he didn't stay in the doorway. Instead, he pushed away from the stone wall and crossed the space between them. His bare feet smacked against the damp floor, and before she could even blink, he leaned down over the tub; his face came to a stop only inches away from hers. Like this, she couldn't look away.

He was too close.

All of him.

She saw all of him.

Dragged in his scent with each breath.

Wished to touch him.

Fuck him for it, too.

"Will they come for you?" he asked.

Arelle wet the line of her lips. "He might."

"Who? The current king? Someone—"

"The man chosen for me."

Something dark flashed in Eryx's eyes. "Chosen. Your mate—isn't that what it's called?"

"The one chosen for me."

It seemed better to repeat that sentiment, seeing as how she couldn't exactly lie. Not that it mattered because the darkness was back in his face, and his jaw clenched with his next breath. All at once, she knew exactly what bothered him, when moments ago, he'd been perfectly calm.

Eryx was jealous.

"Say it," he murmured, "that he is your mate."

She still couldn't lie. Not like this. Not with him.

"No, he can't be my mate," she whispered.

Their locked gazes didn't budge. She wasn't sure how long the two of them stayed like that. Did it even matter?

"I only wanted to kill you," he said, voice thick with pain and frustration and something else entirely. "So why are you still alive with me like this?"

She didn't think he really wanted an answer. He proved her right when he stood, turned, and left without a look backward. The urge to follow him was almost too much. It nearly dragged her out of the hot water.

Arelle sank beneath it, instead.

If he wanted her, he would tell her.

Wouldn't he?

He was punishing her.

Of that, Arelle was most sure.

What other reason would Eryx have after their encounter that night in the bath chambers to do what he'd done? What he was still doing?

They'd moved—in the middle of the night, during a break between storms when the sky was still dark, and she'd had no real understanding of what was happening. From the house he'd brought her to, all the way to a new estate the guards called the House of Miller. She thought the new estate was worse, if only because they were so close to the sea here that she could smell it, taste it, hear it and even see it.

Outside the windows of the bedchambers where she was being kept, without any freedom this time around, she could watch the sea lap at the stairs leading down from the back of the house. She was so close to it that the itchiness became worse. And she was so alone in her confinement that had, so far, lasted five days that she was sure she would soon go insane.

Eryx wouldn't see her.

No one did.

Arelle stayed locked in her rooms with only the windows to keep her company, and the occasional guards that came to remove what they needed or bring her what she asked for. They didn't speak more than they had to. A servant never once graced her presence. She ate, slept, and lived alone.

At least before, she could leave her rooms. There were people around.

Now, it was just … nothing.

It had to be a punishment.

Didn't it?

Pacing the length of the chambers, Arelle did her very best to ignore the sounds of the sea. It sounded like the most haunting song—calling her closer but warning her to stay away. She had never wanted anything more than the water and her home, and yet she knew the punishment and pain that waited for her should she return.

There was no winning here.

She would only lose.

But it was how she lost that scared her the most. Would she pay with her freedom, her life, or both? As it were, Eryx had already taken one.

What was another?

The fragility of her mind wasn't lost on Arelle. Nor was the fact that she felt as though she were crawling out of her skin because of the bonds that tied her to one other person in the large house. She had no idea where he was within the estate, and yet in her mind and heart, she heard him all the time.

They were close.

Not close enough, her soul screamed. Not where you should be. Not where he's touching you or seeing you. Not where you can see and touch him. It's not enough.

She would break.

And maybe at the end of it all, that was what Eryx had wanted. Maybe it hadn't been a punishment at all, but rather, an inevitable end. Because if she were feeling like this, then he had to be experiencing the same. That was the bond, and it was only fair. The bond didn't affect only one half of the pair—it ruined them both.

Forever.

After all, if he had learned other things about her that she hadn't been the one to tell him—like her proper place in the sea—then how much else had he learned and not yet said?

Did he know what she had done?

What it meant?

Arelle spun on her bare feet, the flowy fabric of the white silk gown blowing wide around her legs. The heavy wooden door that was always latched surprisingly opened when she attempted to pull on it. The guard still waited outside in the hallway, but in that moment, he didn't seem bothered that she was leaving her rooms.

"Yes?" he asked.

She let the truth slip out. "I want Eryx."

The man nodded once. "He said you would know where to find him."

How? she wanted to ask. How, when she'd never been in this house?

And yet, she said nothing.

He wasn't wrong.

All she had to do was listen, like every mate searching for her other half, she only had to wait for him to call.

She finally found him in a room, surrounded by shelves filled with books. A long table separated them, and he stood at the far end. In front of large glass doors that led out to the steps she'd been watching for days. Where the water lapped and the waves raged. Rain slapped the glass and the wind howled.

The storms raged on.

He had to know she stood there, yet he didn't turn around. If he did, he would see her crazed and broken and willing all of this to be different.

Wishing she had done this differently.

"I have a theory," he said.

His words were quiet.

They still made an impact.

"About what?" she found herself asking.

"Well, about us."

31. A KING OF BLOOD AND PAIN

Poe

The moment the bastard pulled his cock free from her mouth, Poe spat every bit of semen and blood mixed spit as she could at the king. The ropes binding her arms and legs at the wrists and ankles didn't allow for much else except to remain open and wide, and bent over the foot of the bed. Only the very tips of her toes touched the cold floor, but she couldn't even feel those now.

She had gone numb.

Misael laughed darkly, unbothered by the spittle that stained his bed sheets but unfortunately, missed him.

Next time, she wouldn't.

That was the thing, there would be a next time.

A king of blood and pain, Misael Bloodhurst cared nothing about the torture he leveled upon her, what he took from Poe's body, or how she would never be the same. No, he simply saw a pretty gift presented to him with a brand on her hand that he couldn't stop staring at, then decided that he didn't like her smart mouth, and opted to send her to be roped in his rooms where the horror began.

"You'll learn, bitch," Misael told her, breathless as he pushed off the bed.

Poe's narrowed eyes followed his every movement—it was the *only* thing she had. He took everything else, including her ability to defend herself. Out of all the things the landwalkers had done to her since pulling her from the seas, *this* was the worst.

She hated this place.

The castle and king.

His court and harem.

The way it all smelled like her mate.

As if that were somehow possible, but she just thought that was her mind's way of messing with her because she no longer had control of anything else. She didn't know how she would get back to her daughter. Tak still didn't call for her. And now she had become the latest, favorite fuck-toy of an unforgiving king.

At least, they hadn't taken her toes.

Yet.

"You're almost a record for me, you know?" the king asked, hastily throwing on a robe that he left open. He barely gave her a second glance over his shoulder, more interested in the jug of ale and the pipe waiting for him.

The salts smelled sickly sweet.

322

But when he smoked those, he also fell asleep.

"A record," he continued after gulping down a goblet and not even bothering to wipe his face when he was done. "The longest I kept someone in my chambers was four days before I took my leave."

Someone.

Did he think she was stupid?

Other than to tell people they could address her by her name—Poe—which earned her more than a few lashes from a whip, and far worse threats, she didn't speak to anyone. Not the mermaids in the harem, unless absolutely necessary, and only in their mother tongue. Not one of the landwalkers. *Definitely* not the king.

Not even over the many hours that he enjoyed raping her.

A part of him hated it, and she knew it. He craved her words, and in that way, she thought he might be an easy man to manipulate. Except that would mean being able to pretend as if this man *could* touch her and not eventually die for it, and she just simply didn't believe that.

He would die for his sins.

Especially those against her.

In that moment, Poe finally spoke.

"You mean a *slave*," she snapped, throat aching from how tightly she had been clenching her jaw, and the strain on her throat from his latest assault.

He cared for *nothing*. Begging for mercy from him would be pointless, a waste of her time, and she wouldn't let him break her like that, anyway. So, she took the worst of it, and when she couldn't, she just made herself go somewhere else.

Some in the harem whispered about the king being a soft and kind lover. That was nonsense. Total *shit*. Even if he did for someone else, he could also do the very worst. The current state of her body was proof. The way he spent his days was proof. His entire castle.

All of it.

"Tis true," the king said, then, conceding her point, "but that one loved me. I'm surprised you're not mute, mermaid."

If only she cared.

"None of them *love* you, you fool. They just learn how to survive."

Those were the wrong words.

Poe knew it before Misael had even crossed the room, but it was far too late for her to do anything to change what came next. The first slap cracked hard enough against the side of her face to send her head flying, just not far.

He even roped their necks.

"*Shut your mouth,*" he hissed into her face.

Poe blinked against the hot breath of a man that she had felt against her body more times than she wanted to in the past three days. Not even the storms battering the windows of his private bedchambers was enough to let her mind go to a different place, anymore.

Perhaps that was why she provoked him.

She needed this to end.

"If I get the chance," Poe told him, her chest aching as she tried to laugh, "I'll kill another of your whores just like I did to the one in the orchard, King."

She had heard the whispers.

That slave had been his favorite.

Fire raged in Misael's eyes. "You little cunt!"

Poe had her regrets over that day, sure.

She'd ask for forgiveness for those, eventually.

Wasn't it his time to hurt?

His next hit wasn't a slap.

It was a punch.

The hits didn't stop coming, either.

He didn't break his record, after all.

More importantly, Poe didn't break under him.

Mattue

"Corval," Mattue greeted the hunter as he rounded the hallway just beyond the king's private chambers. "How is the court treating you?"

"Better than I thought, my lord." Corval grinned. "I was told it's most boring during the storms, but …"

Without saying another thing, the man widened his arms as if to explain what he could not, and it did. The loud music from downstairs and the laughter mingling spoke to a life in the castle that wasn't usually present this time of year.

Whatever pleased Misael.

Quite normal.

"The king is trying to make himself feel better," Mattue replied, unbothered. "And you are …?"

"Just about to take my leave, actually, if I could get a moment with the king."

"He's been locked away in his chambers since you brought the slave. I appreciate you keeping her for as long as you did. She wasn't much trouble, no?"

Corval shrugged. "Nothing I couldn't handle."

His tone suggested he had been given some trouble, but Mattue couldn't be bothered to ask what it was when, in the end, things had clearly worked out to all their favors.

Even Misael's.

"I'll let my brother know you appreciated his hospitality."

"Thank you, my lord."

Mattue nodded. "Anything else?"

"A matter of my curiosity, perhaps, but I've learned to be careful about sharing that sort of thing."

The advisor did love indulging curiosities.

Sometimes.

"And what is the matter that makes you so curious?" Mattue asked.

"Your nephew, the prince."

Mattue's eyebrows jumped slightly higher. "What about him?"

His business should be long done with the hunter now. Eryx got what he wanted, and even if he didn't behave as Mattue preferred, and kept his uncle far too busy for his own good, those things would work themselves out. Or he would help them.

Corval's next words told Mattue that might have to be the case, after all.

"A while back, he called upon me to ask questions about his slave. Has he taken up his father's interests so much so he might keep one close? He seemed quite enamored with her, from the talk in the house I heard."

"She isn't dead already?" Mattue barked, probably a little too loudly.

Good Gods, she should be. If Eryx knew what was good for him, she would be by the time his uncle saw him next.

"Well, I—"

The hunter didn't get to finish his words. In the next moment, a door creaked open from down the hall, drawing both their gazes. The guards posted at either side of the king's private chambers turned to see what had finally drawn his majesty from his pleasures for the first time in two nights, and three days.

Nearly a record.

The slave who continued to call herself Poe, despite being told not to use her given name, found the floor hard, in a heap that included ropes still tied to various limbs. Misael, the very picture of rage with his chest bare, cock out, and fists bloody, shouted at anyone close enough to listen. The redness to his face and eyes spoke of the salts he had likely been smoking again, but that couldn't be the entire reason for his rage, surely.

"Take her to the whorehouses! Let them teach her how to behave and when I'm ready, I'll have her brought back here to take her toes myself!"

The door slammed shut.

The crumpled form on the floor didn't move.
"Making himself happy, you say," the hunter murmured.
Mattue ignored him.
Between the king and Eryx, he had bigger problems now.

32. A THEORY AND THE TRUTH

Eryx

"A theory?"

Her question came out like a whisper, and yet it still traveled all the way to his spot as though she had shouted it. Eryx had wondered how long she was going to last … when he couldn't seem to drag the answers he was looking for out of her any other way, he'd defaulted to the last option he'd had. Changing everything.

Here she was.

So had he been wrong?

He would soon find out.

"What theory, Eryx?"

He smiled. His reflection in the wet windows, the clear sections of glass, mirrored the expression when the lightning streaked across the blackened sky. Looking up, he was able to see just how thick the rolling storm clouds were and just how much water was dumping down on them. The wind had already ripped several trees from their roots on the property. Word of floods in the surrounding villages had come in yesterday.

Not that there was anything they could do.

The storms would continue.

They would only get worse.

Thing was … Eryx was no longer afraid of them.

"Before we get into that," he said, finally turning away from the glass doors that were stressed under the pressure of the storms, "I have a question first."

He found she was still standing at the far end of the room and Gods … what a sight she was. Wrapped in silk, with fire-red curls that sprung out in every direction, and something haunted in her beautiful face.

A treat, really.

It took every ounce of willpower he had to stay right where he was and not cross the room to go to her. Despite how the last while had been meant to force her into coming to him, it hadn't been particularly easy or kind for him, either. Not that he'd expected it to be, but he certainly hadn't thought it would be this hard. For one, because he suspected none of this would end the way he wanted it to. And for two, because he was determined to get his answers tonight.

He couldn't do that if he were fucking her.

However, it simply confirmed things he believed.

Something was different with them.

She would tell him what it was.

"What would happen," he started, tilting his head toward the doors that led to the stairs currently kissing the sea with every wave that rushed up to touch the marble. "If I opened those doors?"

Arelle's gaze darted from his to the rain-drenched glass. "The rain and wind would get in, wouldn't it?"

"And make a mess." He chuckled. "But that isn't what I mean. What would you do?"

"I …" Her pretty bow-shaped lips turned down at the edges. "I don't understand."

"If I opened these doors, stepped back, and said *go* … what would happen?"

Her sharp inhale rattled through the room.

The following silence echoed.

At her sides, the shaking hands she balled into small fists hid the truth of her nerves. Not that it mattered because he had already seen them. He wondered if she might lie again … would she make him chase circles that answered nothing and leave him with more questions?

She surprised him.

Shocking.

She was always doing that.

More so than she should.

"I would go home because it's the only place I know."

"And?" he pressed.

Her audible swallow had him taking three steps closer to her. He still had quite a way to go to reach her spot, but this gave him room to still breathe.

"And *what*?"

The sting in her tone had him grinning. A defense of hers, he'd noticed, just happened to be that she got a little nasty. It meant he was hitting a raw nerve and she wanted him to stop. Except he couldn't—not on this.

"And what would happen after you went home?" he asked.

Arelle's jaw worked with the words she tried to hold back, but she still spit them out at him, anyway. Like they were dirt she wanted out of her mouth. A truth she wished she could hide. He saw and heard it all.

"I would be forced into a mating with a man who isn't mine, and who I cannot be mated to. And when the bond didn't take like they all know it should—"

"They'll know the truth," he interrupted, his tone saying calm.

Although how, he didn't know.

Her chin quivered. "They'll know it's already been done. I've already mated."

"When?"

"Eryx—"

"*When?*"

328

Arelle glanced away, the anguish saturating her pretty features causing an ache to spread within his chest. Yet, the harsh noise he made that had her stare snapping back to his hid the truth of what he was really feeling.

"You'll tell me when," he said. "And you will tell me how."

"'Tis a hunt, a chase, between the pair. Then, the blood. It mixes. We have to be on the land—it's always the same way. The struggle between the chosen pair; for some, it's like a fight—"

"Was it much of a struggle?" he asked.

Her cheeks heated to the prettiest color pink. "Maybe that came after. It wasn't natural, I think. We didn't go into that knowing it would happen like others do."

She had a point.

Eryx only said, "So, keep going. The struggle. And then ...?"

"We mix the blood to be one, and then the heat comes."

He remembered that.

Vividly.

The fire in his chest.

The heat in his cock.

All of it.

"The island," he murmured.

"I only wanted to help."

Oh, he certainly believed that.

"Humans can't mate."

"You're not entirely like them," she said simply.

Not that he needed her to.

He just couldn't pretend anymore.

Not like his father and the kingdom needed him to.

Nothing would be like it once was.

Not after her.

"And what does it mean, hmm? What does ..." His own trembling hands waved between them. "What does this mean now?"

"Don't you feel it? Don't you hear—"

"All the time," he snapped, the invisible pull between them dragging him halfway across the space in a blink. He only needed a few more steps, and he would reach her, but he forced himself to stop. "All the fucking time!"

"That's what it is. That's what it means."

"For how lo—"

"Forever. That's what mates are."

He hated that.

Something else inside him loved it even more.

The emotions slapped back and forth inside him like a whip cracking over every inch of his soul. She'd done this—she'd bound them. He couldn't be without this woman, and he constantly thought about killing her, too.

What had she done?

Nothing felt right or true.

And yet, nothing felt wrong or false, either.

Another thought drifted through his mind, sharp and cutting. Making his insides clench and sting and bleed as it echoed through his blood.

"You're mine," he said quietly.

Arelle tipped her head up slightly, those violet eyes of hers flashing with the storm behind him, and the truth they could no longer escape. "And you'll always be mine."

"*Mine.*"

"Yes."

"And now, you'll let me do anything to you, won't you? Hurt you, take care of you … send you away, or keep you with me. Love you, hate you. Because you're mine. To do with what I want or not. That's what this," he said, a fist hitting against the middle of his chest, "means, doesn't it?"

"If it's here, Arelle," he added, taking those few steps to her slowly and painfully until their noses touched and his fist pushed against the spot over her heart, "then you feel it there. You can't ignore it either."

"I can—I have."

"Before," he returned.

She didn't lie.

"Before you caught me."

"Why?"

He caught her quivering chin between his forefinger and thumb, tipping her head up so their lips hovered over one another's, and she couldn't look away when she said, "Because when we make the bond, we speak—it sings. And we'll hear it forever, too."

"You didn't speak that night. You spoke in the stables."

"I—"

"You did what you did, and then you tried to break it, too."

A tear slipped down her cheek. The trail it left behind glistened until it stopped at his thumb. He wiped that drop across her warm skin, never once letting her go or breaking their stare.

"Would you do it again?" he found himself asking.

He hadn't intended to.

"Would it mean saving you?"

Eryx let out a slow, steady stream of air that ached in his chest and rattled on the way out. "Wasn't that the only reason you did it?"

"Then, you have your answer, Eryx. I am who I am, and I cannot change."

"I *hunted* you. I only wanted to kill you."

The smallest of smiles painted her red lips. "But will you? *Can* you?"

It both infuriated him that she dared to ask that at all and flared his lust into a roaring fire that she seemed to enjoy challenging him. Absolutely nothing was going to quell the rage that lifted hot in his gut or satisfy the ache in his dick that was now so hard it strained against his trousers.

How did she do that?

Enrage him and turn him on all at once?

How?

Eryx's hand jumped from her jaw to her throat. He squeezed hard enough to draw her right up to her toes, a wicked smile curving her lips at the same time. There was a glint in her eye—a taunting gleam that said you won't, and he loved and hated that she was unafraid of him like this.

It only infuriated him more and made him hotter.

Damn her. He still tightened his hand on her throat. Willed everything she said to be a fucking lie—tales of crazy people with magic blood that lived in the seas. Hogwash. Bullshit. He wanted it to be nonsense, demanded his hand cut off her air more than he already had and squeeze her neck until the bones popped.

But he just kept staring at her.

She stared back.

He just … couldn't do it.

As though Arelle could read the thoughts in his mind and feel the desperation in his shaking hand at her throat, she said simply, "I know."

And since he couldn't bring himself to kill her like he wanted, Eryx went with his only other option in his current situation. If he couldn't sedate his need for violence, then he might as well sate the urge to fuck this woman until he felt like he could no longer breathe.

Why waste the entire night, after all?

Arelle didn't seem at all shocked when Eryx kissed her. She was ready for it—all too willing to part those full lips of hers to give him a taste of what he craved. It took him all but a few long paces before he had her backside hitting the edge of the long table in the center of the room. In a blink, never once breaking the war of their kiss, he had her lifted to the table while she yanked the yards of silk that made up the skirt of her dress up around her waist.

Eryx drew in a hard breath when she widened her thighs, and he finally pulled away from her mouth just long enough to glance down. "Nothing under there again—you know, I think when I do find you've put undergarments on, I might cut them right the fuck off. You've made it too easy like this."

"I think you like it."

"Yes, I think I do, too."

Her high, already-breathless laughter answered him back before she leaned forward and bit his bottom lip hard enough to draw blood. The tangy sweetness that burst across his tongue when he bled, and she sucked his lip into her mouth, had him slamming her down to the table. His hands went between her thighs to spread her wider before his fingers found her soft heat. With nothing more than twisting strokes of three fingers inside her cunt, he had her whining against the table while he pinned her wrists high above her head.

"Yes, there …"

She sounded all broken, now.

Still airless, though.

Her fingers wrapped around the wrist of the hand currently between her thighs, while the other tightened around the edge of the table. Every thin muscle in her neck strained with her hard cry when he told her, "Let it go and give it to me—let me slide into that cunt while you're soaking wet and it feels like it's begging me to fill it all up."

She was beautiful like this.

More perfect than she should be.

Entirely dangerous.

She spent herself by his hands alone—the spasms in her pussy echoing throughout the rest of her body, too. The choked shout of his name had him leaning down close to her, just so he could watch the way her pupils blew wide when she came.

Why did she need to be like this?

"I hate you," he murmured.

Arelle's bottom lip trembled when she replied, "You wish you could."

Fuck.

Fuck her, this, and every other bit of it, too.

There was nothing gentle about the way he ripped down his trousers and freed his cock to his waiting palm. The slickness on his fingers from her pussy smeared to the soft underskin of his erection with the two strokes he managed before he shoved his cock into the tight heat of her cunt.

He wasn't soft, slow, or anything of the sort. Every flex of his hips came harder. She didn't even tense when his fingers dug hard enough into her thighs when he widened them again that he left red marks behind.

All she whispered was, "More."

He gave her that, too.

Arelle strained against the table and his hold when his grip went from her thigh to her throat. Pinned to the table, she still managed to arch into his body when he leaned over her. His next kiss had his blood staining her lips and he felt a dribble slide down his chin.

He hadn't lied.

He did hate her.

He also adored her like this.

Taking every bit he gave. As wet as the sea. Brazen and wild and begging. Letting him use her to her own end and only asking for more.

This part of her was perfect. It was the rest he struggled to settle.

"Eryx, *please*—"

Her pussy clenched hard around his cock with his next thrust, and the high cry that cut off her next plea had him groaning thickly. Those pretty eyes of hers rolled back when she came, and her thighs clamped against him to keep him deep. It was just what he needed to send him into a release that had colors bursting behind his clenched lids while her name spilled from his lips in a shuddering breath.

By the time he opened his eyes again, the tremors had passed, but he wasn't quite sure he could move. Beneath him, he felt the rise and fall of her chest turn in tandem with his, the longer time passed without either of them speaking.

He waited her out; he didn't want to speak first.

She didn't make him wait long.

With her back flat against the table, as still as could be under his hand at her jaw and the one keeping her wrists high above her head, Arelle sighed. "What was your theory?"

Eryx swallowed hard, still searching for the breath that would have to come eventually. "What?"

"When I came to you tonight—you said you had a theory about us. What was it?"

"It was right," he replied. "The theory, I mean. I was right."

Arelle tipped her head to the side, those red curls of hers spilling over the edge of the table when her gaze met his. "Do you want to know what would happen if you opened those doors and let me go?"

"You told me what would happen."

"I lied."

He wanted to look away.

He didn't.

"I would come back," she said, her fingertips running over the flaring gills at the side of his throat. It was only with her that he allowed his neck to be bare. Both a vulnerability and a reminder to others, it was her that he trusted to know. "I have to."

"Do you still want the sea?"

A nod answered him back. "All the time."

She looked past him at the large doors leading out to the stairs filled to the very top with the sea. On the offseason, there were a good forty stairs to the bottom. Like this, they could see the sea reaching as high as it would be for the season of storms.

"And yet, you would still come back?" he asked.

Even if he knew the answer ...

Arelle smiled. "For as long as you can call for me."

Arelle

In the time that Arelle had been taken from the sea and put in Eryx's care, there were a few things she had not been allowed to do. One of them was to access any of his private chambers. It hadn't been permitted in the previous estate, and as he'd made the guards keep her locked in a room, it hadn't been an option in the House of Miller, either.

Until now.

Maybe that was why she found the space so fascinating. From the sitting room, situated between the bedchambers and the private bathing room to the ornately carved four-poster bed that dominated the space, it all felt comforting to her. Candles, piled high on a corner shelf, flickered, giving the space a bit of light. The shutters had been pulled on every window, but she thought that was more to keep the water out from the pounding rain hitting thin glass than the storm itself.

Large rugs made of black furs kept the stone floors warm and soft to walk across, while the drapes hanging from the closed windows matched the color of the spreads on the bed. Black. A color the prince clearly preferred considering everything from his private spaces to his daily dress put it front row and center.

A book lay open on a chair trimmed with gold in the sitting room. She had just bent over to pick it up, curious to see the language she'd learned to speak as a child in the written word. Not that she would be able to read or understand it this way, but it still created a sense of wonderment for her all the same.

"Do you read at all?"

Eryx's question came from somewhere behind Arelle—toward the bedchamber. She flicked over a page in the leather-bound book, unable to understand the writing on the cover.

"I was never taught—not an important piece of my education."

His dry chuckle followed his next question. "Ah, well, do you care to learn?"

She peeked over her shoulder to find him leaning against the wall next to a portrait painting of the sea. "And who would teach me—you?"

"Do you think I couldn't?"

"I think a prince wouldn't have much time, actually."

"I had enough time to do all of this, and if you haven't noticed, my duties to the crown and people are … nonexistent at the moment."

She hadn't really thought about it. Now that he mentioned it, however, he had a point. He rarely left whichever estate he was using, didn't often take meetings or visitors, and rarely talked of the realm or the crown.

Eryx smirked a bit. "I wasn't following the rules an heir should, you see, and so I've been sent away to consider my behavior and how it should change when I am called to return to my rightful place."

Oh.

Well …

"That explains quite a bit," she noted.

"It's been … enjoyable."

She grinned.

He returned it.

Arelle went back to the book in her hands, asking, "But would you teach me?"

"I will, but not tonight."

She placed the book back on the chair. "Not tonight, then."

Continuing her search through his private chambers, she was amused at how he stayed back and let her pry without saying a word or stepping in to stop her. He never even hinted that he might. The one time he left her alone was to answer the knock on the door to take the bedclothes from the servant who brought them from her rooms down the hall. She didn't even get a peek at the woman before the door was closed and Eryx deposited the items to the table.

Still wearing the gown Eryx had fucked her in earlier, Arelle didn't care to redress. She hated their clothing anyway. Restrictive and meant to cover all the beautiful parts of a body, she really didn't see the purpose of the clothes at all, except for the wealthy to show their riches in expensive fabrics and bright colors. Anyone with a lower status wore simple grays, whites, and black in materials that itched and barely served any function in the first place.

Besides, she didn't mind being wet.

"Am I staying in here?" she asked.

Eryx picked up the goblet from the table and eyed her where she stood in the passageway to the bedchambers. "I think you should."

"Okay."

"That's … all?"

"Shouldn't it be?" she returned.

"I'm not sure. I don't understand how any of this works."

"Easily. Of course, if you let it."

Eryx let out a heavy sigh before emptying whatever ale remained in his goblet. It clinked on the face of the table when he finished with it, and then he said, "The obsession started before the night on the island."

She gave him a look, deciding it was probably better to let him talk at the moment.

"My mother was the only person in this realm who I cared for, and that night in the orchard … after everything, you just came out of the water and stared at me," he murmured, his finger tracing the rim of the goblet while his gaze locked onto something else sitting on the table. She was more interested in staring at him than finding out what held his attention when she knew it was only so that he wouldn't have to look at her while he spoke. "It felt as though you were taunting me, then—enjoying my pain. With her gone, I had nothing. My crown and name, they'd meant little when she'd been alive and they mean less with her dead. And there you were, knowing what you had done to her, watching me while I was bleeding inside … it started then. This need I have to do to you what you did to me, I mean."

He took a moment, a breath and then another. He watched the flickering flames from the pile of melting candles create shadows on the wall. Then, quieter, he said, "It seems unfair that you did this to me now. I don't get a choice at all in how I feel or what I want because of this thing we have."

"Wrong," she murmured.

Eryx lifted his head and met her gaze. "Oh, you don't think so?"

"You consented to the bond, but that doesn't make you love me. The bond between mates is everything else—love is what we get to choose. You can hate me for the rest of our life, but it won't break the bond."

He cleared his throat. "Right … is it really all that different?"

"What?"

"Love and hate. Both are possessive. Obsessive. Dangerous. Selfish, even. One kept me moving for years—the other got me to this point."

"They are different, Eryx."

"How so?"

"One is devotion to another soul. The other is devotion to your own."

He swallowed before he nodded once. "Fair enough. I have something for you."

If he wanted to change the subject, he was free to do it. Besides, they had forever to discuss the rest, and tonight didn't need to be the night when they ripped it all open.

When he asked—and was truly ready—she would tell him anything he wanted to know.

Passing by her in the passageway, he headed into the bedchambers. She turned to watch him go but didn't move from her place. She was surprised to find him press against something on the small table next to the bed, which made a drawer pop open. She hadn't noticed that when she'd been snooping earlier.

Then, he pulled out something she didn't recognize at first. It flattened against his hand, the ends curving a bit. Two inches wide, the leather was a buttery brown with an engraved design flaked with gold. The metal clasp at one end and the holes in the other told her exactly what the item was.

A collar.

It wasn't so much what it was that bothered her but rather, the metal spikes on both ends that glinted under the flickering candles when he came to stand in front of her.

"The spikes," he explained, "will fit into your gills and fill them in such a way that they will not be able to open. You will change when the sea water enters your lungs, but you will not be able to breathe. It should discourage you from heading into the water—a prevention method, if you will."

Horror filled her the longer she stared at the item. A memory flashed through her mind—one of his mother and the metal collar that had been around her throat. She hadn't been able to breathe before Poe had killed her. It was a terrifying thought that they could be in their natural form, and yet, unable to breathe as they should.

"On Atlas, it is the law that your kind wear a collar," Eryx said, his hands grabbing both ends as he held the leather wide like he was offering it to her. "You'll need to wear it until a permanent one is made. This took longer to arrive because of the season, and because I needed it made quietly."

"Permanent?"

"Those cannot be removed once placed."

"Like your mother's."

A harsh sound escaped him.

Arelle let out a shaky breath. "Do you expect a fight?"

"Maybe. I have a feeling you don't need the collar to begin with, and I'm not particularly fond of them myself, but I'd rather not draw attention to myself or you at the moment."

She smirked, her gaze lifting to meet his. "Put it on me, then. Tis the law."

"Not even a little fight?"

His dark smile had her shivering.

"No."

"Why?" he asked, fitting the collar around her throat at the same time. The spikes were uncomfortable at first as they fit into her gills; their flared bases did exactly as he said they would. "You fight everything else."

"The purpose of this is to kill me if I run away, yes?"

"If you go in the water."

Arelle nodded. "But see, you can't kill me now. No matter how much you hate me for what you think I did—and you do still hate me. No matter what you want to do to me … you'll never be able to kill *me*."

His fingers stilled at the back of her neck as he fit the one end through the metal clasp of the other.

"Not unless you want to die, too," she added with a little shrug, "because that's the bond, and you needn't love me for it to be, remember? I may want to please you because of it, but you still need me to do so, Eryx."

Forever a give and take.

He didn't have to like it for it to be.

It already was.

The collar didn't scare her.

Neither did the man.

Eryx's hand found the center of her throat, then, and something wicked flashed in his eyes as he gave her a rueful smile that promised fun would soon be coming for her. His fingers flexed at the spikes in her gills, making her drag in a hard breath at the sensation it caused. He dragged her from the passageway to the large bed with a yank of his arm.

She didn't mind following.

Her back hit the bed, and he hovered above her with that hand still tight to her throat.

"Then, please me," he said huskily.

She could do that.

That was the easy part.

"Your breakfast is waiting to be served, my lord."

Arelle blinked awake at the new voice. Sitting up in the bed, she found the curtains had been pulled around the bed to give her some sense of privacy. Not that she ever cared about that. The way these landwalkers lived, with their constant sense of shame about their most natural functions like nudity never failed to annoy her.

Through the sheer piece of fabric toward Eryx's side of the bed where he must have exited but not pulled the second curtain quite far enough, she watched the female servant hold out a waistcoat. Eryx slipped his arms through the item before she walked around him to button up the front. She was careful not to touch him directly, but only his clothing. Never did she lift her eyes to meet his gaze. The black velvet of the waistcoat buttoned up the front with large silver clasps from the navel straight up the column of his throat. She'd noticed that—how he always kept his throat hidden.

He glanced Arelle's way.

And found her awake.

"And the weather?" he asked.

"Still as horrible as yesterday, Prince."

He grunted under his breath. "I'm learning to like it, actually."

"Can't understand why."

"I didn't ask if you liked it, did I?"

"Sorry. Anything else?"

"Send Mara up for her to dress Arelle. And promise Arelle won't fight today about needing to wear a gown and whatever else she puts on her."

"Yes, my lord."

"You may leave."

While the servant found her way out of the private chambers, Arelle sat up in the bed and pulled the sheets higher with her to pool them around her waist. Eryx continued his trek through the space, picking up things here and there that he'd set down the night before. He didn't, however, speak to her.

Arelle wasn't sure if that was intentional, or not.

"I don't fight Mara, but if the woman might speak to me, then she would understand—"

"They're taught not to speak to slaves unless told otherwise, Arelle."

Swallowing that was difficult.

"Is it true your mother was allowed different freedoms than other slaves because of your love for her? She was privileged, even?"

Eryx opened his mouth to speak.

Arelle beat him to the punch, saying, "I hear talk. Some walls are very thin."

He glowered at the wall; a scowl settled deep.

"Do you only ignore the wrong of your people when it suits you, Prince?"

Eryx pulled in a sharp breath. "I have—I do. Often."

His admittance of ignorance surprised her. The privileged rarely admitted their fault—only their victimhood.

She had a mind to ask if he ever planned to change. Arelle decided against it—he would be who he was meant to be; change like that came from within.

He passed her a look from the side, adding quickly, "They will get better now with you, however."

"Because I'm in your bed?"

"Call it what it is, darling."

She continued watching him ready for the day. He flipped through a stack of papers the servant must have dropped off for him earlier, because they hadn't been on the table the night before. He then pulled back all the curtains on the bed, but they didn't speak.

Arelle hated the silence.

She blurted out one more truth she figured he needed to know. "She asked to die."

Those gray eyes of his shifted to a stormy blue when they nailed into her. At the foot of the bed, he stilled, with his hands curving around the carved footboard that showcased two swans in an embrace. "*Who?*"

"Your mother. She asked to die in the water—to be taken to the sea. One of my sisters tried to help her, the other attacked. That was how she died."

Eryx tilted his head up, staring down at her until all her fidgeting stopped, and she was helpless but to wait until he spoke again. "Would you have done it?"

"Done what?"

"Killed her. She asked to die, you said. Would you have done it?"

"She may have walked on land for all your life—that's how you knew her, but she was my kind. *Your* kind. And ours have suffered enough. I won't make even one suffer more."

A tremor worked its way through his jaw.

His hands flexed on the bed.

Then, without another word to her, Eryx turned and left the bedchamber. The silence echoed when she heard the door to the room creak open before it slammed shut.

He'd thought he'd known the truth. She bet it was hard for a man like him to learn he actually knew nothing at all.

33. THE ADVISOR

Eryx

Seven.

Seven nights the little mermaid had spent in his bed with that collar on her throat and naked for him—waiting for him. She let him fuck her until his mind stopped running; woke him up in the middle of the night with her lips around his cock; she hid beneath the sheets in the bed every morning with the sweetest smiles.

The only good thing about landwalkers are the blankets you have, she'd told him once. It bothered him more that he wondered if she might actually be right.

The bigger problem he now faced was the fact that he'd allowed that woman a space in his bed for seven entire nights. Oh, and he was no closer to figuring out what, exactly, he wanted to do with her than he had been before. He certainly wanted to hurt her. To take the breath right from her lungs and watch her eyes as her heart stopped beating because of him.

And yet, he couldn't.

Wanting and doing were two different things.

It hadn't helped his situation that when she'd said it wasn't her who killed his mother that he'd had no choice but to believe her. He'd learned she was incapable of lying to him because he couldn't fucking lie to her, either.

A strange thing, this *mating.*

It messed up everything.

And now, Eryx had no idea what he was to do next. Not with himself, her, or anything else about his life. Everything was different. Nothing could be the same.

That irked him.

A lot.

The laughing that accompanied clapping drew Eryx's attention back to the center of the room from where he sat near the entry to the corridor. There, he found a handful of the estate's staff still standing in the semi-circle that encased a dancing Arelle. The man who headed the servants had been playing an instrument that'd drawn Arelle's attention.

And just like that, she'd made a friend.

Then, another.

And another.

Nearly all of the servants in the house greeted her now. They took time to make sure she had what she wanted or needed, no matter the time or night. Part of it, he knew, was because of him. The rest, however, was all on her.

She made friends.

Too easily, maybe.

She could walk amongst them, behave like them when she wanted, and it was just enough to trick them all into thinking she could be just like them, too. He'd been right when he'd said things would change for her with the servants in the house, but he'd been wrong to assume he would be the catalyst to it happening.

Eryx wasn't sure what he hated more. Her, for being who she was and for doing what she did. Or himself because he liked her, when he wished he could still feel that same loathing he used to every time he looked at her beautiful face.

He'd not planned for this. What would happen now? Did he even have a choice in what he did with her? That was the real question.

Eryx was dragged from his thoughts when the singing started. His attention flew back to the woman in the middle of the room, her cream-colored gown spinning wildly like the curls flowing down her back as a song he didn't know—but he swore his heart did—spilled from her painted red lips. She'd taken to letting Mara paint some of her features when she felt like it. The red on her lips was the one he enjoyed the most.

Especially when it left stains on his cock.

Those memories flashed through his mind as the invisible rope came to wrap around his middle. He didn't even think about it, simply crossed the room to join her. She had already turned to reach for him, as though she'd known he was coming, when she hadn't even been looking his way.

The man kept the tune.

Arelle continued to sing.

It was haunting, really. The melody soaked into every corner of the house, he was sure. And yet, she pulled him closer, molding his hard lines against her soft curves so that every movement she made dragged against his body. The swish of her gown when she swayed her hips had his own moving to the beat with hers. One of her legs stepped in between his as she moved forward to him, and then back out again for him to come to her.

One of his hands tangled into the hair at the nape of her neck. His other wrapped tightly with hers before he pressed it over the racing beat of his heart. His teeth found her bottom lip and tugged just enough to make her voice hitch in the song.

The closeness, their movements …

All of it was not appropriate for dancing.

More erotic than he knew it should be.

He was certain no servant in this house had ever seen a royal behave the way he currently was, and yet Eryx didn't care at all.

Of course, someone always had to ruin his fun.

Why would this be any different?

"My lord, you have a visitor."

Eryx slowed the dance just enough to answer to whoever was talking—
he didn't care to look. He didn't take his eyes off a grinning Arelle, though.
"I'm not taking guests."

"Prince, he's already here. It's your advisor. Your uncle. Mattue. Sent by
the king, he says. Your appearance is required and not a request, my lord."

Perfect.

"Mattue."

The advisor glanced up from the map he was surveying in the library
with the large doors that faced the sea. He smiled at the prince as though
there wasn't a thing wrong with his presence at the estate, and then had the
nerve to say, "Oh, don't look so sour, Eryx."

"We haven't been separated long enough to excuse your ignorance."

"I beg your pardon?"

"You know how to address me, Mattue."

The advisor gave a little shrug under his cloak before sweeping his hand
over the edge of the map. Instantly, the paper curled and then violently
rolled itself up into the middle of the table. He would have corrected the
man for that, too, because those maps were precious.

He didn't think the fucker would care, though.

So, he stayed quiet.

"I always loved this room when I stayed here," Mattue noted, peering
around like he hadn't already seen it a million times before. "Barring the
doors leading out to the sea, of course. I wanted to rebuild that piece and
get rid of the steps. No need for them myself, but someone denied the
request."

Eryx was not here for a conversation.

He wouldn't indulge one, either.

"What do you want?" he demanded.

Mattue rolled his eyes back in Eryx's direction, clearly annoyed. "Where
is your couth?"

"Where is yours? You don't announce your oncoming arrival?"

"I have made attempts to get a word through to you, but you either
ignore them or have the guards turn them away. Apparently, you're so very
busy—with whatever you're doing here, of course—that you can't even
write back a proper letter with a seal, Eryx."

His jaw worked to relieve some of the tension starting to form there when he replied, "It's storm season, Mattue. No one wants to be out in those winds on a fucking horse delivering letters."

"But they'll do it for a prince. What are they supposed to tell you—no? I have it on pretty good authority you'll send for someone in the storms, Eryx, so let's not try it."

Why did the man have to be right?

"What do you want?"

Mattue leaned down to pick something up from one of the chairs pushed into the long table. Standing straight, the man brought up with him the piece of white silk that he'd used the day before from Arelle's dress to gag her when he fucked her while she was bent over the table exactly where Mattue currently stood.

"Is it the storm season keeping you locked away and busy, Prince, or something else? Say … someone, perhaps?"

Eryx simply stared at the man. "Do you have something to say to me? And next time, don't use my father as a reason for you to interrupt my day. He won't send word to me until at least after the season passes, and we both know it."

A chuckle echoed from the other man. "Fair enough. And yes, I do have something to say. You're well aware, I have eyes and ears everywhere. Do you think they wouldn't get word to me that you're becoming a little too enamored with your new slave?"

"*Arelle*," he corrected instantly.

Mattue's brow raised. "Oh, you use her name?"

"Mattue—"

"Her name is nothing. She is nothing—a creature, Eryx. Owned. That is what she is, and you would do well to remember it before you take her out somewhere and think someone else will forget her place, too. I was under the understanding you planned to kill her before you saw a new moon, and now look at you."

"I don't like your tone. Don't forget your place, Mattue."

The advisor grinned and shook his head. "See, that right there. It's concerning. We had a deal, or did you forget it? You have gotten what you wanted, and now I want what you promised me."

"Take the fucking crown," Eryx snarled. "If you want it, then take it. Who do you have to go through, when in one way or another, you've killed the ones standing in the way before now?"

Mattue's head snapped back, and his gaze zoned in on Eryx with a warning flashing brightly.

"Oh, you think I forgot about that, too?" Eryx asked. "*He fell from the horse, Eryx, that is what you must say. He fell from the horse.* I might have only been four, but you still sound the same now as you did then. If you want the crown, I'm certainly not stepping in your way."

It took him a minute, but Mattue made his way around the side of the table and all the way to where Eryx stood on the other side. That piece of white silk was still tight in his hand, and he dumped it to the prince's feet without warning or care.

Then, Mattue said, "You don't seem to understand, Eryx. While you remain alive, the crown will always be yours when it is not your father's."

"I will abdicate."

The advisor stared at the piece of white silk like it meant something more than either of them would say. "I'm not sure you will, actually. Not if the crown means you get to keep something ... your father did that once, too. Thought he loved a slave. Thing was, she never loved him back. She only ever loved you. Did you ever see your mother without her collar?"

"What does that have to do with anything?"

"It has to do with everything that you are. Your father, well, he would have allowed her anything, even removing the collar later had she only asked. Did you ever consider why she didn't? And then you were born, and everything had to change because you were a *boy* and you came from her. She didn't need the collar with her fin clipped and you on her hip, but I think she still wore it to hide what you and the rest of them could never know. Not if she wanted you to live. And Anthia ... your mother only ever wanted for you to live."

"What are you—"

"The crown is yours while you're alive. More than you know, Eryx."

What?

Eryx would figure it out.

Another time.

"Leave," he demanded.

Mattue did.

Still, Eryx heard his advisor's parting words before the door closed. They would haunt him for days, he was sure.

"You'll regret this, Prince."

34. THE FAILING KING

Zale, King of the Blu Seas

"Are you listening to—"

"I hear him perfectly fine," Zale replied shortly, his tail fin snapping hard to the floor of the private palace chambers before he continued his pacing. "I'm hearing too much, in fact."

The silence that answered his outburst satisfied Zale, but he knew it wouldn't last long. It couldn't. That had been his biggest problem since the last of his daughters had been captured by the landwalkers.

Nothing was as he wanted it to be.

Not as it should be.

"You have to understand how dangerous this could be for you, your highness," one of his advisors said, daring to be the first to speak in the group of four. "The Emerald prince has been seen gathering guards—we know he's sent back a messenger for his father, but we were unable to intervene before the man was out of our colonies. He's been spotted nearing Atlas, probably scouting. There are talks, Zale. Talks between the people of an uprising. They feel even more unsafe than before. They don't believe you can protect them. And if someone is willing to say they will be the one who will do it, what do they have to lose after everything? Don't you understand—"

"I'm not stupid or foolish. I understand what it could mean."

"There's more," another one of the men said.

Oh, really?

What more could there be?

Zale had agreed to the mating between Arelle and the prince, Mav, from the Emerald Lands when she'd been only fourteen, nearing her fifteenth year. He'd assumed it would be a good match, and even better for his rule. Yet another one of his princesses married to a strong royal bloodline of merpeople from another realm.

It meant power and a hand he could extend.

Things his people needed.

Unfortunately, that merman had been nothing more than a prickly thorn in his side from the moment he swam into Zale's seas.

"What else?" Zale asked.

His pacing finally came to a stop, and he dared to shoot a look over his shoulder at the enclave entrance that would lead to his wife's private chambers. She had made it very clear he was no longer invited in there unless she said otherwise.

He didn't even get to see his grandchild.

Not that those things really bothered him. It was the fact that she'd refused his presence because he'd asked for another child—an heir to replace the ones he'd lost these past two seasons. It only seemed fair, to be honest, even if Rosel was a little along in her years to be having children.

He couldn't force a child on his mate—one of the only choices they had in mating was the woman's decision to have the child. Spill the first seed outside of the womb, and she was safe from impending pregnancy. And even if she didn't waste the first, it seemed like chance whether she even would conceive otherwise. The man was helpless to his partner's control. As the stories went, it prevented children from arriving to a merwoman in a mated pair that was not a happy or good one. But they didn't have to be happy or good at the moment. They needed an *heir*.

"Well?" Zale demanded when his men stayed silent.

His gaze skipped over his gathered advisors, waiting for yet another grievance about Mav that would put him one step closer to either banishing the man from his kingdom or killing him altogether. That option, however, would probably mean a war for him.

The favored son.

An heir to a far larger realm than his own …

Killing Mav would not end well for Zale, but that didn't mean he wasn't considering it or thinking about it more often than he should.

"Seems he's been asking about the last queen," the man in the middle of the others said quietly. "And what anyone might know about her … unfortunate end."

Zale stiffened into ice. "What?"

"We told you—we told you the stories of her capture would be spread. You could only twist the narrative so much when there were witnesses. The kingdom knew the prince on land had an obsession with hunting her after the talks of peace she'd attempted with the king. And if the truth comes out that she wasn't killed like you said she was, then it's not that far of a step before they learn you planned for her capture, too."

Disbelief and rage swelled through Zale like never before. He darted closer to the advisor, his hand already reaching for the dagger he kept sheathed at his back as a last defense. Glaring at the man, his hand wrapped around the butt of the knife, but he didn't pull it out just yet.

"You will watch your tongue, or I will cut it out and place it in your hand for you to stare at for the rest of your days," he warned.

The man to the right of the one he'd just threatened let out a sigh before saying, "The sacrifice of the last queen didn't do what you promised it would do, Zale. They continued hunting us. And look at us now—decades later, and even your own daughters have been captured. What now?"

The sea king had a good mind to cut the throat out of the man instead of his tongue. At least then, not only would he be unable to talk and anger his king, but he'd also be dead. A good thing for Zale, at the moment.

347

Unfortunately, he couldn't do it.

He had so few people left who he could trust, and these advisors were some of those. He couldn't afford to lose anyone.

"Bring him to me," Zale ordered, finally letting go of the end of the knife and dropping his hands to his sides. "Mav, bring him to me now."

He didn't need to say it a second time. The advisors were quick to scatter from his presence, but then again, that seemed to be happening to him a lot. Even his subjects couldn't stomach to be in his view for too long before they, too, found a reason to leave.

He'd wanted to be king, once upon a time.

Wanted the world for his mate the day he chose her.

Complacency would always be a death sentence for men like him.

While he waited for the Emerald prince to be brought to his chambers, Zale went back to pacing. The entire time, the brand on the back of his hand of the two arrows—the only thing other than the crown he wore and the throne he sat on that deemed him a royal of the Blu Seas—burned and itched.

He swore when it did that, it was telling him *you don't belong—you're the false king.*

Even his own heart knew the truth.

"If he'll usurp you," came a soft voice from behind, making Zale spin around to find his mate had come to stand in the shadows of the enclave leading to hallways that led to their private rooms, "then at least allow me the freedom of escape before he does it, Zale. If you know you'll die for what you've done to these people, let me take the baby and run. You can't kill him, and if you do, it'll be a season before his father's army lands in our kingdom and burns it to the ground. Either way, you lose. Allow me to save the baby."

He opened his mouth to respond, but she was quick to ask, "What happens, Zale, if they find Anthia alive somewhere on Atlas with the brand of her reign still on her throat? If you think what the Emerald prince or his father would do to you will be even a fraction of what these people will do to you … in the end, you will still lose."

"Don't say her name again, Rosel."

She tipped her chin up, ever defiant. "You were wrong, Zale."

"About what?"

"You are both stupid *and* foolish."

She didn't give him the chance to respond before spinning on her tail fin and heading back into the shadows of her rooms where she couldn't be seen. Not that it mattered; he couldn't focus on her for long, when the noise outside in the corridor signaled the Emerald prince had been found and would soon be delivered.

But what good would it do?

They were all right.
His advisors.
His wife, too.
No matter what Zale chose, he would eventually lose.

35. THE DAY THE KING CAME

Arelle

When the rising sea threatened the House of Miller a short few days later, reaching so high that it began seeping into the house, Arelle found herself put in the back of a carriage without Eryx and returned to the stable estate where she was first delivered after being captured. A small break between storms allowed them the reprieve to travel, but with every gallop of the horses' hooves against wet ground, her heart hurt a little more.

Eryx joined her soon after, with the rest of the small army of servants that seemed to follow him wherever he went.

She liked this house far less.

It was farther from the sea.

Her heart felt every single mile traveled away from it, and it was only made worse by the fact she had to travel alone, but for Mara, who sat across from her in the carriage. Not that she would consider herself friends with the servant Eryx preferred to look after her, but the woman never treated her as though she was just a slave for the prince to do with what he deemed fit.

That couldn't be forgotten.

Despite her feelings about the stable estate, there was one single room in the house that she enjoyed. Well, it wasn't so much a room that was a part of the house, as it was attached to the east wing. A small corridor led out from the house to the glass doors that allowed entrance into what a servant had explained to her that they called a solarium.

Filled with plants, trees and more from all the many realms, it smelled like the earth. Inside, the air was always hot and damp, no matter if it rained or the wind blew so hard the trees toppled over. From the walls to the ceiling, glass that was kept clean allowed them a beautiful view of the miles and miles of fields.

The few birds and butterflies that called the solarium home weren't bothersome and tended to stay away when anyone was inside. Water continued to dribble from a stone fountain in the middle, which was fed from the water wheel outside that took from a creek that ran along the side of the house. It overflowed just enough to fill the cracks in the stone floor of the solarium that then led to the many beds of flowers and plants to feed the soil.

Currently, the entire space was filled with purple light from the sky above. A promise of peace.

Even the white, flowy gown made of soft satin with yards of chiffon blowing out the skirts was stained with the purple hue from the sky. Standing in front of the farthest wall in the solarium, she stared up and watched the clouds roll by faster than she knew was normal. It meant another storm would soon be coming in, and in a blink, the wash of purple would be gone. Replaced instead by the blackness of the rain and wind.

Arelle sighed, ignoring the noise from the house behind her. She'd left the doors to the solarium open just because she wanted Eryx to find her easier when he was finished throwing around his orders to the servants. Moving an entire house—or rather, what items he wanted saved from the House of Miller—had been quite an event in a short amount of time.

Tiring, really.

Now, the estate bustled with activity to move and place whatever needed to come inside from the caravan of carriages before the rain and wind started from the next storm. She could have helped, or even watched from afar, but she was missing the sea.

Again.

Now more so than before.

Maybe it was because she could taste it in the air.

Or simply because it was so far away.

What did it matter?

Whatever the reasons, the heaviness in her chest wouldn't leave. And that was difficult enough for her.

The click of a door had her tense posture softening slightly. She didn't need to turn around to know who it was—she could feel him.

"You look as though you're bathed in purple."

She smiled at the reflection of herself in the glass. "Do I?"

"You do," Eryx murmured.

His footsteps against the stone tiles approached her spot, but Arelle still didn't turn away from the glass.

"Shame," he said, his voice close enough that the small hairs on the back of her neck raised at his proximity, "that you look as you do, but all you feel is sadness standing here. Why is that?"

The unspoken parts of the bond left nothing to question between them, even when one of them wished for it to be different. From the emotions to sometimes, even the thoughts in their own minds.

Nothing was secret.

It all depended on what was needed.

"Did you know," she said when he slipped in behind her with one of his arms wrapping around her shoulder and chest, "that my kind believe we're cursed?"

"Oh?"

He pulled her closer; her back molded to the hardness of his chest, and for a second, she could breathe easier. She shouldn't. Not with this man who promised to take her life, and as it was, had already taken everything else from her and changed the very world as she knew it. Even the way he fucked her was raw and brutal with little softness or care involved ... although, she found that was exactly how she liked it anyway. Still, she shouldn't find a sense of peace in the arms of a man who had only seemed to want to hurt her. Yet, she did.

"Why that idea?" Eryx asked.

His lips grazed the back of her neck, making her shiver while his one hand cupped her breasts through her dress, and his other slipped down to fist into the skirt of her dress.

"We're designed to need the land to carry on the legacy, but to be desperate for the sea because that is where we are most natural. It wouldn't be such a bad thing, but when one is taken away, we crave it more than ever."

"*Mmm*, like the land now."

Arelle let out a shaky breath when he finally managed to get her skirts high enough that his hand could slip in beneath the heavy fabric. His fingers stilled when they slipped over the thin, delicate lace between her thighs.

"What is this?"

A breathless laugh escaped her. "We're having a conversation. Ignore what's under my gown."

"No. I closed the door so I could come to fuck you without interruption, actually. I find that there's anything under here at all but your skin to be very interesting. Besides, you've been quiet the last few days."

"So have you. Since your visitor, I suppose."

He made a harsh noise under his breath but didn't reply. Instead, his fingers stroked her overtop the lacy undergarments covering her pussy that matched the thigh-high stockings she'd also decided to try that morning.

It was as she thought it would be, also.

Restrictive and pointless.

Eryx would get his way, however. He would fuck her insane in the solarium until someone dared to knock on the doors and call him away from her.

She would enjoy it.

No point in denying it.

So, she made sure to say what she wanted before that could happen. If only because she felt like she needed to say it. "I used to crave the land. Now, I only miss the sea."

His hands tightened on her body to an almost painful point. "Is that your way of asking for something without really asking for it?"

"No, it's me talking. Sometimes, I enjoy doing that. You could talk back."

"Well—"

"I feel like I'm being pulled in different directions. What I'm being pulled to changes depending on the day, or … you."

"What does that even mean?" he asked.

"There's no certainty," she tried to explain. "Not with you, or the sea. Not what would happen if I left, or even if I stayed. My kind, or all of this … I say it like there's a choice, but there really isn't when everything else will seem unimportant without my mate."

"Arelle—"

"But what is my life with you? A slave at your bidding. I warm your bed and entertain you in the times between. That seems … well, it seems like nothing, doesn't it?" Then, she lifted her hand that had been sitting overtop his on her breast to touch the collar at her throat. "And even if I could leave, you seem determined to make sure that I can't, one way or another."

The pain that burst in the center of her chest felt hollow and foreign. That was the only way she understood it wasn't her own, but a reflection of his. He didn't acknowledge that he'd felt it; not physically or otherwise, but she still sensed it all the same.

"Do you want to leave—to go? Will they take you back? Would you still come to me when I called?"

"I want certainty."

"That doesn't answer my questions, Arelle."

His statement wasn't quite a shout, but the level of sharpness in his tone still had her closing her eyes.

"If I left, would you want me to come back?" she asked.

"I …"

"It should be an easy answer, Eryx."

"It is."

Arelle tipped her head to the side even as his fingers tightened into her hair. "Then why not say it?"

"Because I already did." His hand between her thighs grabbed tight to her pussy overtop the lace while his lips found the line of her jaw. "I gave you certainty—you're *mine*."

In that way, he certainly had.

"Now," he murmured against her cheek, "hush and let me fuck you here, as I first intended to before you had to go and make this an entire discussion. How opposed are you to letting me hold your ruined gown together when we leave here? I wouldn't want to … scar the rest of the house with too much wickedness."

Her lips split in a grin as his hand drifted away from her throat. "You landwalkers and your ever-ignorant shame."

"I think more the opposite, really. I would take pleasure fucking you in here, walking you naked through the house and then letting them all listen to the rest of our evening. And I appreciate even more that you would let me do it and enjoy it. But I'm not quite sure they could … settle it. So, are you opposed to me helping with your ruined gown instead? Because I am not leaving this room without fucking you. And since I promised to cut off anything you wore under a gown, I feel it's only proper I keep it."

"Do you even carry something to cut this apart? Do they train spoiled, arrogant princes to even use a blade, or—"

The next words caught in her throat when the cool, sharp edge of a blade found the curve in the back of her shoulder. The hand between her thighs stroked her over top the delicate lace covering her sex and his teeth grazed over her jaw.

"In fact," he said, letting the knife draw down to the corset of the gown, "we are trained in that, yes. And sword fighting. Now, do hush."

She couldn't promise anything.

He had that effect on her.

Eryx's blade found the bottom ribbon on the corset at the same time his fingertips began to press harder against the seam of her sex. Every cut of the knife through the criss-crossed silk at her back had his fingers moving a little faster between her thighs.

Though she felt the cool metal kiss her skin, his hand and objective were steady. Never once did he bite or even nick her with the knife. All the while, he managed to get her panting against the smirk of his lips while his hand at her pussy moved faster until she was begging him not to stop.

"Please, please … oh, please."

The low, broken whines faded into the noise of the solarium and the ripping of her dress when he pulled the delicate bodice down to her waist.

The bliss came on in a wave—a crest taking her under and then dragging her oh, so high. Her palms found the glass while she trembled her way through the orgasm. The loss of his hand between her thighs echoed in her bones, but her body still sang on.

The chiffon and silk of the skirt met the floor under his handling. She stepped on expensive, delicate fabric embroidered with sparkling beads that she was sure had taken its maker days to create. She ruined it in seconds with the soles of her feet when Eryx spun her around right where she stood on the gown.

The knife was still in his hand, and he spun the tip against her collarbone. "Ready me, sweet Arelle."

She liked the tease of the sharp blade entirely too much as she lowered down for him. The tie of his trousers came off easily under her handling. The thin undergarments beneath his pants were the only thing keeping his erection from her. His cock strained against the gray fabric that she found was rather rough under the softness of her palm when she rubbed against him.

"In my mouth?" she asked, peering up at him.

"Suck me until I come, and then take very single drop."

Arelle flashed a smile, the flash of heat between her thighs making her sigh. "As you wish."

Untying the one small bit of leather keeping his undergarments tight to the cut-V of his groin, Arelle freed his cock to her waiting palm. She stroked him tight and fast, but only twice. He wanted her mouth, and she just wanted a taste.

He was silken, hot, and salty against her tongue. The second her lips wrapped around his length, his hips jutted forward to get her swallowing his entire length. The blade traced the delicate line of her throat while his other hand fisted her hair at the top of her head.

She found paradise in his irises the color of a churning sea.

"Just as you do," he told her, still pumping his hips to a speed he wanted. "Keep looking at me and start singing for me, my little mermaid."

Yes, because he loved the music she made. She would swear, though, that there was nothing more fascinating than the sounds he made. Those deep, heady grunts as he worked himself higher with her mouth around his cock. It made her wetter, and the softness of the delicates between her thighs were sticky from her arousal.

His heart raced.

She could feel it in the pulses of his dick.

"Fuck … *fuck*," he muttered.

Her eyes blurred with water, but she loved that too. His rough handling only made her empty pussy clench with need.

He gave her no warning before he came. Just a harsh moan that followed the hot spurt of his semen hitting the back of her tongue. She took every single drop.

Just the way he wanted.

Those fingers of his tightened into her hair until she gasped from the sting, but he held her firm to his cock until all at once, he pulled her away. In a breath, Arelle faced the windows again. The blade was back at what remained of her clothing when he'd spread her legs wide enough that he was satisfied.

"Perfect."

Eryx sliced through the delicates with ease.

The blade hit the floor.

His palm found her ass.

She turned back to kiss him while he rested the head of his cock against her slick slit. His tongue slashed to hers when his hips jutted forward.

Just like that, he was filling her.

Fucking her.

Making her forget.

He was always so brutal. Unforgiving when he handled her. Fast and deep and raw. It made her ache, but in the best way. Pleasure was far better when twisted with a tinge of pain. She didn't shy away from it, either … simply urged him on for more.

Eryx delivered.

She hoped he always would.

Especially like this.

"Gods, what are you doing to me?" His voice in her ear was a harsh, guttural whisper. "Why are you like this?"

She could ask him the same.

He fucked her just like that, yanking on her hair and then shoving two fingers into her mouth to silence her, until she came again. Her arousal soaked his length, and she could hear it in the slick smack of his balls against her backside.

"Don't you move after I come."

That was the only thing she heard before a thick groan fell from his lips. He held her tight to his cock, deep enough to hurt, when he released inside her. She was still trying to catch her own breath. The gulp of air came faster when he pulled out of her and kneeled down. His hands spread her ass wide, and his teeth found the still burning cheek from the earlier slap as she felt his semen slip out of her sex and fall to the gown at her feet.

"Yes," he murmured, "love watching that, my darling."

Arelle sighed when his rough touches came softer after her orgasm had turned into nothing but a shiver working its way through her body. His fingertips stroked the strands of her hair when he stood up behind her again and leaned his jaw against hers to nuzzle. She didn't think he knew, but that was how her kind—their kind—greeted people they loved dearly.

Like a mate, or their young.

It was moments like those that reminded Arelle that no matter what she thought of this man, their mating, or the things he was capable of, he was also one of them. She'd kept marking Eryx as different—a landwalker, because that had been his entire life.

But he was more.

A prince.

Insufferable.

A man who could walk the land and sea.

Flawed.

Her mate.

Hers.

"You seemed sad," he said, "and I didn't like that at all."

Arelle laughed lightly. "Was that why you did this? Not everything else you said? You can't fix everything by fucking me, Eryx."

"But I can at the moment. And I consider it to my benefit also when I get to see you like this."

"*Hmm?*"

"For a brief second, I get to see you still trembling, as sweet as a newborn kitten for a graze of my fingers in your hair. For a moment ... I don't want to kill you."

A grin fettered over her lips. "Do you want me to complain about the last bit? Can't say that's a bad thing when it means my heart still beats."

His dark chuckle skipped across her jaw before he muttered, "And just like that, you make me go back to wanting to strangle you."

"You do know that threat has never scared me, don't you?" she asked.

"I do—I enjoy that in a very distorted way, too. And so, as I was trying to explain, if fucking you fixes everything for even a few moments, where we get to be just this and not the rest, it is worth it."

Arelle's heart thundered loud and those silken touches of his continued. Eryx was not the type of man who enjoyed his charming sweetness to be pointed out to him. He much preferred the arrogant, spoiled prince persona that he'd carefully crafted for the rest of the world to see.

But he softened when he knew she needed him to. Like now.

As a mate should do for the soul's other half.

So, instead of saying thank you for what he'd done, or even acknowledging his tenderness, she gave Eryx the thing he seemed to need to keep his vulnerabilities hidden: the sharp-tongued, challenging little mermaid he wanted to kill as much as he wanted to fuck.

Arelle cleared her throat, her tongue peeking out to wet the seam of her lips. "Well, you better figure out how you want to hold this ruined gown for me before you get me to the bedchambers and show me all that distorted way you mentioned."

"Are you still sad?" he asked.

The heaviness in her shoulders had left for the time being. All that sadness roaring in her heart for the sea she so dearly missed was a dull echo.

He had fixed it. For a moment.

She knew, however, the calm between every storm only lasted for so long.

Still, she answered him honestly. "No, I'm not still sad."

Eryx

"Have you settled on a book yet?"

Arelle glanced over her shoulder at him. A teasing glint lit up her violet eyes before she went right back to surveying the rows of bookshelves in the room where they were kept at the stable estate. He'd made a promise to teach her how to read though he didn't quite know how to teach anyone anything.

Thing was, she learned quickly.

And he found he liked her smile.

"This one, I think," she finally said.

Eryx couldn't discern which book she pulled from the shelves with her body blocking his view, but that was just fine, too, when it gave him a glorious view of her trimmed waist and the way the silk skirts of her dress fell over the curve of her ass. "Is it a good one? It'll need to be a good one to keep my attention long enough that you can read a bit before I get you into bed again."

She turned her head just enough for him to see the sensual curve of her lips that said she liked that idea of his just fine. "You have to let me read a bit first."

"A bit, then. Fine."

"And it's an old one. I don't know if it's any good."

"What is the title?"

"It doesn't have one."

Eryx laughed. "They all have titles."

"Not this one."

"Let me see it, then."

Arelle flashed him with a brilliant smile when she turned away from the bookshelves with the book in her already outstretched hand. When she was close enough, he took the leather-bound book, ready to find the title that he was sure had to be there. Perhaps it had faded where it was once embossed on the cover, or even the title page had been ripped out.

Eryx soon figured out Arelle wasn't wrong.

There was no title page.

That was a lie.

There was a title page.

Anthia, Queen of the Blu Seas.

Eryx lost his ability to breathe for a second, his gaze darting up to see Arelle had turned around to let her fingers dance over the flame of a flickering candle nearby. She wasn't looking at him when he flipped the first page, and he took the risk of looking back down again, though he knew it would be a stab in the heart.

Queen, he read again.

The word kept jumping from the page.

He knew her writing.

Those soft curves when she twisted the letters with ink on a quill.

Yes, he knew his mother's handwriting. That pain in his chest came.

Why had she never told him her true title?

Mattue's words in the House of Miller about the things his mother wanted to hide roared into his mind with a vengeance. He knew the implications; he understood perfectly well what that meant for him and yet, he couldn't linger on that for long when on the next page he found his mother's words in the form of a journal entry.

He swore he could hear her voice.

Eryx read the first page. The way she'd quickly scribbled a few paragraphs to fill up the page and all at once, explained the journal's placement in the estate's library and its purpose.

A few times a summer, they bring him here. I'm leaving this journal here because despite how Mattue claims to be worldly, he does not seem to spend much time learning the words of the world, regardless of what he leads others to believe.

It's the only shame about spending any days here because the rest of it is almost perfect. Eryx spends a spread of time with Mattue at his father's demand ... Misael intends for the man to be his advisor. He's only a spare, the man says, but he should be an educated spare, nonetheless.

I hate him—Misael.

My son, I love more than the moons and stars and seas that call for me. But who else will?

Back to the problem, however. Mattue, that is. Misael adores him—brothers are brothers, he says. The court believes he's loyal.

Eryx ... well, sometimes it's hard to tell what he thinks at all about any of them.

Then again, between the father who would only spoil and ruin him; the court who sees the halfling princes as a twisted, amusing show; the advisor who manipulates him; and the mother who always asks him if he can smell the sea? I imagine it's a lot for a boy of only four.

I suppose we're all giving Eryx one thing—an ability to think for himself. May that save him when I cannot.

A couple of scribbles marked up the bottom of the page, as though the quill stayed to the paper, but she glanced up. Right below it, the last few lines of the page were clear as day when she'd come back to her writing:

I have to stop writing—here, I get more time with him than at court, but here, he can't smell the sea. As long as I ensure he always knows it's there, he'll never forget how to find it.

Dt. Orchard Season, Journal of Anthia, Stable Estate, yr 762

"Well?" Arelle asked.

"Did you open it up?" he asked, snapping it shut. He wasn't ready to flip the next page; had she written in it again that year, or waited until the next? Did she ever hope someone may find it and that was why she left it there, or did she know his love for the estate might bring them back here someday where she could resume her place? He could distinctly remember Anthia requesting to learn to read and write alongside him, which the king agreed to, but his mother had always seemed far more advanced at the skills than she let the rest believe. He had too many questions to ask, and now the only thing available to answer them was this book in his hands. If he had time, might he find more? Had his mother written in others? "Because it seems to be a journal, of sorts."

"Oh."

He cleared his throat. "My mother's."

Lifting his gaze, Eryx found Arelle had swung around and was staring at him.

"*What?*"

"Ah, yes, it seems like—"

"My lord. I have just gotten word your father, the king, is nearly here."

He spun on his heels to find one of the servants had come to stand in the doorway. The man waited for the prince to reply.

The king was coming.

Unannounced.

They needed orders.

Eryx's hand squeezed tighter to the book in his hand until his knuckles turned white from the pressure. "How long do we have?"

"The scout said he noticed the royal caravan at Rock's Turn."

Not long, then.

"He traveled in the storms?" Eryx demanded.

"Apparently, my lord."

"Eryx?" Arelle asked softly.

There were many reasons his father could be coming. None of them good. He suspected there was only one reason, however.

The woman behind him.

To the servant, Eryx switched into royal mode because he had to. "Ready the house and everyone in it for a proper welcome."

The man bowed. "Yes, my lord."

He didn't wait for more direction; he also didn't need more.

Then, Eryx turned to Arelle. Her hand reached out, an unspoken request for the item he still held.

"I will put it under your pillow while you man the house—I swear I won't open it."

He gripped the book tighter; his mother was a topic he didn't want to touch with Arelle. Not when it still felt raw, and avoiding it altogether was easier when he looked at her and knew Anthia's last moments had been in this woman's presence. He was well aware that no, she had not killed his mother, but the twisted thoughts in his mind made everything far more difficult and complex.

"I—"

"Eryx, I know we haven't spoken again about your mother, but I am sorry. You were right about one thing—I did see your pain that night. I have apologized for what happened though it wasn't me who landed the final blow and your mother asked for it nonetheless … but this is not the same. I am sorry you lost your mother. I am sorry you hurt."

That made him pause.

His grip loosened after a second. "Sometimes, you make it hard for me to keep hating you."

"Is that such a bad thing?" she asked.

Eryx swallowed hard. "Take the journal; put it where you promised."

"Of course. Is the king—will it not end well when he arrives? For us?"

How did she just know?

He wanted to lie.

To reassure her.

Those words stuck to his throat like tar, refusing to leave his lips. Instead, he was left with only the truth and he knew it wouldn't help.

"I don't know," he murmured.

"They whisper, you know? The servants. They say your father has a penchant for pretty slaves, and he can take any single one that he wants whenever he wants."

His next breath ached. "It is the law, yes."

"Including me?"

"You're not his, Arelle."

"But—"

"*You're not his.*"

But would that make a difference?

That was the real question.

Eryx's gaze swept the entrance hall of the stable estate's main house. Every single servant had come to stand on either side of the corridor to wait for the impending arrival of the king. They kept their gazes straight ahead, never once looking Eryx's way as his boots hit the floor with soft smacks while he did his final check.

They had very little time to be perfect.

It didn't matter.

Everything would have to be perfect.

The king expected nothing less.

The clanging of the bell outside had Eryx stiffening as his gaze went to the guards standing ready at the doors. He gave one last glance over his shoulder, his stare zoning in on the woman who stood at the very far end of the line of servants. He'd wanted Arelle to attempt to blend in. He'd even had her change her dress to something less … attractive.

It didn't make a difference.

She still stood out.

Beautifully.

Perfectly.

Fuck.

The bell tolled once more.

Eryx had no more time to waste.

The galloping of hooves from the royal caravan accompanied the third and final toll of the bell. Eryx headed for the doors and didn't even need to say a word to the guards before they opened them for him. He came to stand under the large enclave that led into the stable estate's main house. There, he was able to watch the caravan come to a stop.

It was quite a show.

All four large carriages. He knew exactly what they carried without even needing to be told. Whatever his father might want and need, whether the king's stay was for a minute, or weeks.

The heavy rain fell in sheets, creating a distorted curtain Eryx was forced to watch through while the men jumped from the caravans to ready for his father's exit. They readied the makeshift cover they had created using one of his father's seals embroidered on a flag that was tied at all four ends to golden poles. Standing on either side of the carriage with the gold trim, the men waited for the door to open.

Misael exited his carriage under the safety of the cover, hidden from the heavy rain. He even wore his crown—the large bulbous tips nearly tall enough to touch the cover with their ruby jewels.

Behind his father came a man Eryx should have known would accompany him.

Mattue.

Because of course.

It was right then and there that Eryx knew exactly why his father was here. He'd suspected, sure, but Mattue's presence only confirmed it further.

It didn't take long for Misael to make his way to the safety of the enclave. Eryx, though his stomach clenched when he did it, gave his father a small bow.

"Your highness," he murmured, "quite the weather to travel in, isn't it?"

Misael eyed his son, a cold gleam telling Eryx all he needed to know. "I was told you were doing very interesting things here that I might find … curious. How much truth is there to that, my boy? And if there is something interesting here, I would certainly like to see it."

Eryx's gaze darted to the man waiting behind his father.

Mattue only smiled back.

He would kill him for this.

That was a promise.

"I'm not sure—"

"Is the house ready for my arrival?" Misael asked.

Eryx didn't know how many passings of the two moons it had been since he'd last seen his father, but it was almost funny how things hadn't changed a bit in all that time. Misael was still the same, rancid asshole he had always been. The only problem was, Eryx no longer had the motivation to care about keeping the king pleased.

"It is," he said simply, "if you consider the lack of time you gave us to prepare."

Misael smirked ever so slightly. "Perhaps, Eryx, that was the point. I would like to go inside."

He had no other choice but to move aside when his father took a step forward. Misael entered through the opened doors, and because everyone else had to walk behind the king, that left Eryx with Mattue beside him.

"I warned you," the advisor said quietly. "You gave me your word."

His jaw clenched from holding words back. He had more important things to deal with at the moment than Mattue's feelings.

Like the fact his father had already spotted Arelle. He didn't even greet the guards at the doors like he usually would. Instead, he headed straight down the corridor past the servants. If he even seen their bows and curtsies, Eryx couldn't say.

"Your highness."

"King."

"My lord."

The greetings rang out from every person Misael passed. He returned none of them.

At the very end, Arelle stood in front of the entry table piled high with melting candles. Eryx's steps caught up to his father's only a second or two after the king came to a stop in front of the red-headed mermaid who held her head high.

"Were you not informed on how to greet a king?" his father asked.

Arelle's gaze darted to Eryx over Misael's shoulder. Eryx nodded once to her—a command as much as it was a silent plea.

She curtseyed for the king.

"My lord," she murmured.

Eryx couldn't miss the way his father's lips pulled into a pleased smile. Before any of them even knew what had happened, Misael reached out and caught one of Arelle's loose curls between two of his fingers. He wrapped the strands tight to his fingers, and his gaze drank her up and down as though he'd found something he very much wanted.

Misael then glanced over his shoulder at Eryx. "Seems you and I have more in common than I thought—hunted this one in particular, did you?"

Eryx pulled in a stinging breath but said nothing.

Besides, his father had already turned his attention back on Arelle. "Mattue was right—there are very interesting things happening here. Dinner will be soon, yes?"

"Within the hour, Father," Eryx replied thickly.

"I would like for this slave to sit beside me."

Of course, he would.

And Eryx decided right then that he hated hearing his father call Arelle a slave. Except that's what she was now, wasn't it?

After all, he'd hunted her. He'd done this.

36. PROPERTY OF THE KING

Arelle

Dinner ran much later than it usually did. King Misael positioned himself at the head of the table where he could see everyone, and the first thing everyone else saw was him. And unfortunately, Arelle, too. Sitting directly beside him, she had the perfect view of everyone else sitting at the table—most who had come with the royal caravan—and of Eryx at the far end.

He sat at the head of his tables.

Not tonight.

Arelle didn't think that was the reason for rage swimming in Eryx's gaze whenever his stare came his father's way, however. Oh, he was quite good at hiding it. So good, in fact, that his expression stayed neutral and blank throughout the dinner. If one didn't know what his icy irises looked like when he was angry, then they wouldn't be aware of his current state.

She did know.

And she could feel it.

That bothered her more. Mostly because for the moment, she couldn't do anything to help calm his rage. And also because a part of her just knew … this evening wouldn't end well.

"Hmm, no," the king said, leaning over to swat away the hand of a servant who was currently offering the second pick of what was apparently Misael's favorite sweet to the slave across the table from Arelle. The man tipped his crown-topped head in Arelle's direction, saying, "Her first, and then the other."

The servant never missed a beat. "Yes, your highness."

A shuddering sigh echoed from the other end of the table, but with the amount of noise between the people eating and the quiet discussions reaching across the room, no one really heard it.

Or they didn't care.

Arelle did.

"Would you like one?" the servant asked, having come around to Arelle's side of the table. It drew her gaze away from Eryx at the other end whose gaze still burned with the fire of a thousand suns. Not at her, she knew, but right then she was the only thing he was staring at. "They are—"

"I know what they are," Arelle interrupted. "Water fruit dipped in white cream."

"My favorite," Misael said with a grin.

One couldn't tell the man enjoyed sugary treats. Though she knew Misael had to be at least in his fiftieth year, or beyond, if not nearing them, he had not a touch of gray in his hair, no age showing in lines on his face,

365

and he seemed fit and muscular as both the men of her kind and those who walked solely on land preferred. Shame that she'd bet his good looks and healthy appearance came from the enchanted medicines made from the mermaid blood and not a single thing else.

A click of a tongue and a chirp came from across the table, making Arelle lift her head subtly to answer the call of the mermaid on the opposite side of her seat. With a large metal collar around her throat, and her hair pulled back to showcase it with the royal stamp engraved at the front, the woman's piercing violet eyes made her still in place.

But what she'd said—in their mother tongue—wasn't lost on Arelle, even if the merwoman had said it quietly and quickly so that the exchange was missed by the others at the table who were still busy between food and conversation. Even the king.

Do not refuse him—the punishment is always far worse than giving him what he wants. Always.

She swallowed hard, and nodded to the slave, grateful for the help she hadn't had to give, when the king was clearly treating Arelle like a favored whore over her for everyone to see.

"Yes," Arelle told the servant, "I'll have one, thank you."

"Of course."

The servant didn't move the silver-plated tray until Arelle had taken her pick of sweet from the bunch. All the while, the table's movement continued on, the king grinned her way as though he was quite pleased, and Eryx's jaw became tenser when she brought the sweet to her lips for a bite but passed a look his way at the same time.

It was bad for her to do that.

He was screaming for her on the inside. She heard it as clear as a bright day in her heart and soul.

"Is that true, little thing?"

Arelle's head swung around to find the king was looking at her expectantly. She hadn't a single clue what he was asking but thought it better to behave as though she did than to ask him to repeat himself. "Likely."

The man flashed his teeth in a pleased smile before saying, "Then, you should dance." His hands clapped together loudly, silencing the table all at once while every pair of eyes turned on him. "Find the music, I want to watch the slave dance—find the music!"

Servants rushed to obey.

The king told Arelle, "Well, get up. You won't be sitting there to do it."

Gods.

She should have just asked him to repeat himself.

Slowly, though it was the last thing she wanted to do, Arelle stood from the table. Turning away from her seat, every muscle in her body froze when a crack echoed throughout the room and an accompanying sting radiated over her backside.

He'd hit her.

Slapped her ass, in fact.

Disgust rolled heavily through Arelle as laughter filtered down the table. Her stare found Eryx, who was now grinding his teeth and not even making an effort to hide it. In the sea, that act alone would have gotten another man killed by her mate.

Here …

All the rules changed.

The man who had been sitting beside Arelle stood, saying, "Perhaps the den would be a better place for a show like that. We're a bit tight in here, Misael. Care to let me walk her there while you finish your treats?"

The king nodded. "Sound plan, Mattue."

Mattue offered Arelle his arm, smiling all the way. She took it reluctantly, if only because she didn't trust this man, and his encounters with Eryx before this evening had never seemed to sit right with her. They followed a few others who readied to leave the table out of the room. It was only once the king—and Eryx—were behind them that the man spoke to her.

"She was right, you know," Mattue said.

Arelle glanced his way, wary. "Pardon?"

"The other slave. She makes a valid point about King Misael. Give him what he wants, and it will always hurt less."

He could speak their tongue—or at the very least, understand them?

What other secrets did the man hold?

Usually when the storm reached its raging peak, the house hunkered down. The servants went to their quarters, while Arelle spent the evening with Eryx watching the rain pour down and the lightning streak across the black skies.

Tonight wasn't the same.

With every spin of her body as she danced, Arelle took in the room around her and the people within it. Their hands clapped in time with the tune being played on the three-string instrument by a servant, but she knew it was forced. Their gazes kept darting to the windows where the rain slapped at the glass—the king didn't want the shutters closed—and the wind howled louder.

Every so often, the next crack of thunder boomed. Then, the lightning followed. Besides the flickering candles in the room, the lightning was the only thing brightening the space and people.

But not the person she wanted.

Not Eryx.

Where had he gone?

Her feet ached from dancing nonstop—how many hours had it been now? Long enough that a man had added more logs to the fire.

At least now the king had drunk enough ale and wine that he was seeming sleepy and less interested in the conversation. Unless it was Mattue who wanted to talk. Then, Misael gladly chatted with the man.

Like now.

"She'll make a wonderful addition, don't you think?" she heard him ask the advisor.

Mattue smiled her way. "Far better than the other one—the sister? The hunter thought so, anyhow."

The king made a noise under his breath. "Mouthy, that one. Couldn't even beat it out of her."

"She's being handled until you're ready again, remember."

What did that mean?

Was Poe—

"Right, right. Well, for here … Have it done tonight," Misael said, "while I take my rest."

"Even in the storm, my lord?"

"Yes, even with the storm. Careful passage, of course."

With that said, the king stood from his chair and nodded at a servant and the slave that wasn't too far away from his seat. They'd barely left his side all night, and when he moved, so did they. Although, always behind him.

Without even a goodbye or an order that Arelle could stop dancing for the room, the king disappeared through the far entry.

Her twirling came to an immediate stop, the relief flooding through her veins as everyone turned to watch the king leave. For a single moment, no eyes were on her, and Arelle did the only thing that felt rational—even if it absolutely wasn't—to her.

She turned and left the den through a back corridor that led to the rear of the house. Her skirts blew out behind her as she ran as fast as she could down the darkened hallway with only one thing—one person—on her mind.

Had she been a smarter woman, or even cared of what the people she'd left behind must have thought of her departure, then Arelle would have considered more before acting on impulse. She would have been mindful about her exit so what she was running to or from wasn't as obvious to anyone watching.

Yet, she didn't.

Couldn't.

"Well?" Arelle asked, all of her air gone.

Eryx's hand flexed on her bare ass; hard enough to hurt, too. "Not a single mark."

She swallowed hard, knowing that didn't make a difference to him or the way he was feeling. She'd known it from the moment she'd stepped inside his chambers and the first word out of his mouth had been *strip*.

Arelle dared to ask why.

The look he returned her was more than enough for her to know he didn't want her questions. He didn't want her words or her stares or anything but for her gown to be a forgotten pile on the floor. The second she'd stood in nothing but her skin, he'd crossed the room and began what could only be described as inspecting her.

"It's almost fucking insanity the way I can smell you from across the room. And when you lick your lips, I taste you on my fucking tongue. I can nearly imagine the feeling of you milking me."

He'd told her those tantalizing things after he had moved to his knees to rove his palms over her backside.

She knew exactly what this was when he'd said, "He touched you."

He wanted to see if the king—his father—had left a mark from when he'd put his hands on her backside at the table. How long had Eryx been stewing on that jealousy?

Jealous mates could be a dangerous thing.

So, she grinned when he murmured that pleased, "Not a single mark."

"Even so," she found herself replying, "I'm sorry."

His grip on her flexed again. "Don't be."

"I think ... I think they're planning something."

Eryx leaned close enough for his hot mouth to drag over the back of her thigh. He kissed the curve of her ass, and then inched over a bit more to bite the plump skin. Her air caught in her chest when a delicious heat shot through her body.

It certainly wasn't the right time.

She should tell him what she heard—the wild things running through her mind that made her think they weren't safe. That was hard to do, however, when Eryx's hand was already between her thighs massaging her clit and slit before his mouth was in the same spot to tease her as well. He always looked his best after he'd buried his face between her thighs and ate her until she was a sobbing mess in his bed. There was something about the way he looked with her arousal still damp on his lips and hungry for more.

Shivers raced through her.

Like nothing at all, she was sky-high.

Somehow, she managed to tell him again, "I think … I think they're planning something."

"Undoubtedly."

"Shouldn't we—"

"They'll be doing nothing tonight."

She decided to trust him.

What other choice did she have?

Besides, they always seemed to talk far better when the two of them were tangled in his bed. They could talk after … or plan.

Arelle panted and moaned her way through the first wave of pleasure. The roughness in Eryx's touch when he bent her over the closest flat surface said he'd choke the second one out of her.

That was just as good, too.

Later, when a man from the stables came to knock on the bedchamber door to say there was trouble with the horses that they needed the prince for, Eryx had told her simply to, "Stay."

She would wish after that he had done the same.

Stay.

Eryx

The man who handled the stables had been right—unfortunately. There was definitely something wrong in the stables. Eryx knew it the very second he pushed open the doors, struggling against the wind that only seemed to blow harder now that he'd come outside.

It was too quiet.

Something that was incredibly unusual, considering the fifteen to twenty horses that typically boarded in the stables on any given day or night. Not to mention, they had added another twelve horses that belonged to the royal caravan that evening.

And it was storming.

That always had the animals acting up.

Not tonight, it seemed.

A dark silence greeted him when he finally managed to pull the door open. The smell of hay and hide smacked him fair square in the face. The musky heat of the stables caused him to shove back the cloak's hood from his head. That way, he breathed a bit easier.

Shooting a look back at the main house, he let go of the heavy door. At the rear, south-west side of the estate, he couldn't see very much. Certainly not the front of the house, the barns for the carriages, or anything else. Only a few oil lamps and candles remained flickering in windows, but it was hard to distinguish with the rain.

Something felt wrong.

The longer he stood there staring at the house, the worse the feeling became. He didn't quite know what, but the dread wouldn't leave, no matter how hard he tried. Instead of feeding into it, he simply let the stable doors close behind him, knowing that soon, he would be back in his bed with Arelle.

And everything would be fine.

At least, until the morning.

"I wish I could find it in me to apologize, but you know me, and I cannot, my lord."

The familiar voice had Eryx's head swinging back around to face the long corridor of the stables that was lined on either side with stalls for the horses. At the very far end, he found the source of the voice.

Mattue.

He waited there in a cloak trimmed with black fur—his favorite. Silver rings with black onyx stones rested on each of the man's clasped fingers. Sitting on a stool under the only current source of light in the stables—a high hanging metal rack with fifteen thick candles sitting in a circle— Mattue smiled grimly.

Eryx took a step toward the man, and then another. All the while, his gaze darted back and forth in the stables when he passed stalls. He kept thinking … the horses are too quiet; even when they rest in their hay in the storms, they're never this quiet.

It was hard to see the beasts in their stalls with the high doors keeping them blocked from his line of sight. Through the slate where the doors didn't quite reach the floor, he could see the tips of hooves, and even a snout when he reached the middle of the stables.

"What is wrong with my horses?" Eryx demanded.

Mattue chuckled, tipping his head to the side. "Do you remember, Prince, when it was me who lived at this estate? You used to love visiting me when the weather was better … you spent more time on these horses than you did talking to me."

Though it felt out of place in his current situation, Eryx's mind drifted to the journal and how his mother must have watched him with Mattue, knowing what the man was like but helpless to stop it when it would mean her death. And which would have been better for him—an altogether dead mother, or one that reminded him without ever endangering her presence in his life that he was not entirely the same as the men around him?

A lump formed in Eryx's throat as he realized the only thing he could hear in the stables was the sound of his own heartbeat, and his breathing alongside Mattue's. The horses made no sound—not even a breath.

"Mattue—"

"And then when you came of age, your father had to just … give you anything. His favored son all because you came from a certain *cunt*. A gift for a prince. What was it you said you wanted, hmm?"

Eryx grinded his teeth as he came to a stop at one of the final stalls in the long corridor. This one belonged to two of the smallest horses—colts, actually. The door wasn't as high, as he could plainly see inside the stall.

The two colts lay dead.

It was apparent by the lack of breath, and the tongues lolled out of their mouth. Their eyes were open, staring dead at the wall where they had died in a bed of hay.

"Are all of them dead?" he asked.

Mattue chuckled coolly. "Every single one. Seems they still enjoy their little bits of fruit. Don't even question it, even if the first taste is a little bitter. We'll blame that on the poison powder I sprinkled on them. Don't worry, it was quick, my lord. I know you fancied the beasts."

Eryx spun a fast circle, eyeing the stalls and realizing something else. They were missing horses—at least a dozen.

His father's horses.

"Where—"

"You didn't answer my question," Mattue interjected. "What was it you told your father you wanted?"

His chest ached.

"This estate," Eryx murmured. "I wanted this estate, and the House of Miller, too."

"Things that were mine. Much like the crown your father wears upon his head."

"Those properties were appointed to you by the crown, but they didn't belong to you."

"*Mmm*, same difference, no?"

"Where are the royal horses?"

Mattue sighed, shifting on the stool a bit and crossing one ankle over his knee. "Gone from the estate right about now, I imagine. See, we came here with intention and a plan. We will leave here with the same, Prince."

"What have you done?"

The man stood, letting his cloak fall around him and fixing the ring on his middle finger as he smiled at Eryx. "I did warn you."

"You bastard." Eryx lurched forward, the threat already falling from his lips. "I will kill—"

Before he could reach Mattue, the man swooped down, grabbed the stool, and then swung it high. The wood crashed against the metal holding the flickering candles. They spilled to the floor, catching dry hay and sending flames licking across the floor to Eryx's boots.

He took three quick steps back.

On the other side of the fire, Mattue continued smiling. "I never did like the way they kept these stalls—always too much hay and dryness everywhere, with all these candles. Let it burn, Eryx, it'll be an easy way to dispose of the horses."

The heat climbed higher.

"Oh, and the king wanted a message passed along," the advisor added.

Eryx didn't reply.

Mattue didn't seem to care when he said, "All slaves are the possession of the king, and as such, he can remove whichever one he pleases to keep in his personal collection. Your slave has been confiscated to the crown of Bloodhurst. She will not be returned."

A shuddering exhale left his lips, and when he sucked in a breath, all he could taste was death and fire. "You've made a grievous error, Mattue. One I will make you pay for dearly."

"She's only a slave—you'll find another. Your father always did."

Except he was not his father.

Arelle was not his mother.

The flames licked higher, making shadows dance on the walls and ceiling. He didn't have long before the embers sparked a bigger fire in one of the stalls.

Eryx shook his head. "She is far more to me."

Mattue hesitated as he turned to leave, ready to exit out a back door. Over his shoulder, he said to Eryx, "Everything you've taken from me, I've now returned for it. All you had to do was give me the crown, Prince."

"I would have!"

"Not fast enough."

The flames jumped higher and Eryx pulled his arm up to cover his face from the embers dancing off the heat. By the time he dropped his arm, Mattue had already exited from the rear of the stables. The beat of hooves against wet ground was the last thing he heard before he turned and ran for the other exit.

An echo started in his heart.

The mantra for his soul …

Arelle, Arelle, Arelle.

Eryx ran through the rain, uncaring how the wind bit at his skin and the droplets fell hard enough to leave welts on his skin. He burst through the rear door he'd used to leave the house to check the stables, only to find it as dark and quiet as he'd left it.

That only had his heart racing faster. The blood in his body seemed to thicken, and everything slowed as his long strides carried him through the house. The closer he came to the bedchambers where he'd left Arelle still naked in his bed, the darker his mind became.

Twisted with hate.

Scarred with worry.

Aching with all the what ifs.

Surely, nothing could feel worse than this. If they'd taken her from him, he would burn this kingdom down. House by house. Name by name. He would ruin them.

Eryx's walk and his violent thoughts came to a halt when he found a servant standing in front of the open door that belonged to his bedchambers. The woman—Mara; the only one who Arelle really seemed to have taken a liking to—passed him a tearful glance.

"I'm sorry, my lord," she whispered. "I tried. I *did.*"

He'd been wrong.

That was the moment everything blackened.

His thoughts.

The heart in his chest.

Every breath leaving his lungs.

They would regret this.

All of them.

And when he tore apart the room in his rage, that rage only calmed enough to make him hesitate when he found the journal resting under his pillow. Exactly where Arelle promised she would leave it. Just like that, everything changed. He turned to stone. But it was long enough for him to know he didn't have time to waste.

So, he opened the journal; he read the next year's entry from his mother. And began to plan.

Arelle

The carriage rocked as the man sitting at the front with water dripping from the rim of his hat snapped the reins hard against the two horses. The animals slowed their trot at his order. "Easy, boys, the road is washing out."

As the curtains had been pulled, Arelle couldn't see where they were, but they had been traveling for what felt like hours. Surely, the night had already passed and it was morning. The problem was, with a storm raging down on them, one couldn't tell the difference with a black sky.

And even if she did know, what difference would it make?

The shackles at her wrists and ankles clanged with every bump the carriage hit. A horrible reminder of her current predicament, as though she might forget the last few hours of her life.

Being dragged from Eryx's bed.

Forced to dress and then be chained, too.

Thrown into a carriage.

Looking to her left, Arelle found the only other person she believed was probably awake in their caravan of carriages. The merwoman—currently resting her head against the side of the carriage where the drapes had been pulled to save them from the rain and wind as much as possible—stayed quiet.

"What is your name?" she asked her.

"Nothing. I am not called by my name."

That hurt her heart.

"What was your name?"

"Kisa. My mother was a maiden to yours ... the princesses were never allowed to play, though."

"What will happen now?"

Kisa lifted her head, and her gaze turned on her companion with a resounding sadness. "The same thing that has been happening for decades. They hunt us; they keep us; and then they kill us."

The woman's words were an echo in Arelle's heart. A warning, if she ever heard one. Something else—someone else—whispered with wind, too, but she knew Kisa couldn't hear it.

It was a voice made only for Arelle.

A song that belonged to her.

I'm coming—I'm sorry.

You're still mine.

Arelle closed her eyes and fell into the rocking of the carriage as Eryx's voice filled every howl of the wind. For now, it was all she could do.

37. GIVE THEM ONE

Mav, Prince of the Emerald Lands

"And you're absolutely certain?" Mav asked, cutting quicker through the choppy waters as he neared the Blu Seas palace and court.

The handful of his men following him kept a respectable distance. All but one, that was, and he allowed the man his moment if only because he had information for Mav. Information that was incredibly valuable and would prove priceless for his current cause.

"The spies confirm it. The princess is alive. As of yesterday, she was on route to the Atlas court with the king and his caravan."

Mav came to a stop and swung on the man. "The landwalkers—they're traveling in the storms?"

"Appears so, Prince."

Were they getting … confident?

Or stupid?

Mav couldn't say there was a true difference between the two when it came to the people of the land. They often made foolish choices for their own selfish needs and wants. Rarely did they think about the consequences of their actions, but especially when it involved someone other than themselves.

So was their way.

He really wasn't surprised.

Moving beyond the thoughts of the landwalkers, he went back to the current topic at hand. Arelle, that was. The fact that they had spies on Atlas who had managed to get eyes on her and confirm that yes, she was alive. At the moment, she was being moved to the king's court.

Before that, Mav hadn't been able to find her at all. It was as though she'd disappeared on Atlas, because none of the sources they had to feed them information had been able to find anything.

Like she hadn't existed at all.

Except she had.

And she belonged to Mav. He intended on getting her back for many reasons. Starting with the fact she was his intended mate, and ending on the note that with her by his side and the impending doom the king of the Blu Seas faced currently … well, not only would Mav rule the Land of Emerald, but he might also be able to take the land and sea here, too.

He couldn't find a reason not to.

Perhaps it wasn't only the landwalkers who were selfish, but this would be better for others and not just himself. The people of this kingdom needed safety. Freedom, too. The ability to live and procreate and be happy without the threat from the land.

They had barely any young.

Rarely left their deep colonies or grottos.

Even their hunting was reduced to small schools of fish that were easy to catch but offered very little for sustenance. When was the last time they'd cooked something instead of eating it raw? Not that it mattered—their diet allowed either, but one was far better than the other, he had to admit.

The people even refused to mate. Despite finding companions and lovers they wanted to bond with, they wouldn't, for fear their mates would be taken away.

They didn't have a life here. Certainly not one worth living, anyway. Every single one of them wanted something different. Mav knew this because he'd taken the time to talk to as many of the merpeople as he could. They wanted to believe things could be better, and he gave them someone to believe in. On the cusp of a rebellion, all it would take was the right push. He wouldn't need to wait for his father's army to arrive here, in a season or more, once word traveled back to the Emerald Lands.

He would have an army right here ready.

So, if he could give them what they so desperately needed and get what he wanted, too, where was the problem?

Mav did not see one.

"Prince, we need to know what comes after this," his advisor said.

Lifting his head, Mav stared at the court leading into the palace carved from the coral. "They are certain it is her?"

"Undoubtedly. The brand was clear."

"Bring whispers of the rebellion to the people of the Blu Seas. Let them spread it ... allow them to talk. I want it to reach Zale all on its own, while he sits alone on his throne."

"And then?"

Mav smiled, flashing teeth that had been sharpened into points. A distinct feature for the people of his land that came from the sea. "Well, then they will need a leader. And I will give them one."

They already had a reason to fight. They simply needed the push to begin, and once they started ... Atlas would burn.

38. MORE LIKE THEM

Arelle

"We're here."

Arelle's head popped up from the palm of her still-shackled hand to peer around. She nearly fell asleep over the four-day travel in the royal caravan. The swaying of the carriage was almost enough to remind her of the way the waves in the sea rocked them back and forth.

Except this wasn't the sea.

And she couldn't forget it.

She couldn't see much through the heavy drapes that had been drawn on the carriage, but she could tell the rain was coming down far easier than it had been. At least now it didn't sound like a thousand drums beating down on the roof of the carriage.

"Where?" Arelle asked.

Kisa, her one companion throughout the long travel, gave her a shrug from the side. "At the Atlas court."

Oh.

How long had she been lost in her mind, listening for a man who had stopped calling for her throughout the very long trip?

"Open the gates!"

The shouted order accompanied the jerking of their carriage as the creak of iron echoed. Arelle pulled back the draping on the window in just enough time to see them pass a large gate with a cursive B prominent in the middle.

Bloodhurst.

The sky was still black with circling clouds and the occasional streak of lightning. The clouds moved too fast for her to think the storm would be ending soon, but the wind had died down, and the rain came lighter than the days before.

It was apparently enough, however, for the landwalkers to feel safe, as the court square leading to the looming castle moved through the yard freely and unconcerned. She could easily distinguish the wealthy from the poor because those with any status had someone to hold a covering over them to protect from the rain, and the others did not.

The square appeared to be a market of sorts, too, with vendors selling everything from fruit to jewelry. And yet, the chaotic court square seemed to come to a complete stop as a call rang out from the carriage drivers in their caravan.

"Royal caravan. Move out of the way! It's the royal caravan!"

Arelle was almost fascinated by the way the people stopped everything they were doing to turn and watch the caravan of carriages move through the square. Women pulled children out of the way, and held tight to them as though they were scared they might dart forward. A few dared to check the windows of the passing carriages, but she wasn't sure if any of them even noticed her staring back.

The sight of the little ones with their mothers or siblings had Arelle smiling—the one bright spot in everything else about this situation that was horrid. Yes, she had three sisters of her own growing up, but they were the exception to the rule in their colony. Her father only had as many children as he did because he was king. Most refused to mate—though many took close companions—and have children because of exactly what happened to Poe, but her father even controlled their ability to do that.

"I have never seen so many children," Arelle said softly.

Mostly to herself.

Kisa still heard her.

"You know, I hear there are places in this world that mermaids can mate and produce freely without fear of capture," Kisa said thoughtfully. "What a dream that would be for us all."

Except nothing was free here.

Especially not them.

The remainder of the ride through the court square was quiet. People followed the caravan all the way to the entrance of the castle where they pulled the horses and carriages beneath the safety of a stone enclave.

It was only once their carriage had stopped and a guard appeared at the door the driver pulled open that Kisa and Arelle stood. She followed Kisa's lead, figuring the merwoman knew much more about what to expect or do than she did. Surprisingly, the guard held keys to remove the shackles at her wrist and ankles. He discarded the metal before allowing her to exit the carriage.

No one helped her down.

She was fine with that.

Arelle was careful to watch her step, still rubbing the ache in her wrists from the bite of metal, and by the time she raised her head to survey what was around her, she realized everyone was staring at her. Everyone.

It was a strange feeling.

To be surveyed.

Appraised, even.

Some appeared unsure by her presence. Others looked quite pleased that she stood there, for whatever reason.

The galloping of hooves pulled their attention away from her for just long enough that Arelle felt like she might be able to breathe. The man on the horse passed the rear carriages and even theirs, before halting a few steps away from where the king currently stood with Mattue. The advisor she hadn't trusted from the moment she laid eyes on the man.

"Well?" the king asked.

The man tipped his head down before saying, "Your highness; I hope your travel was well."

"Could have been better. What's the word?"

"We've received word the prince left the estate some time ago after procuring a horse."

Mattue's gaze drifted to Arelle.

She stared right back.

Misael, on the other hand, smiled as a king should. "See if you can find him and if you do, well, you know where to find me."

"Yes, Sire."

Mattue was still looking Arelle's way when the king turned to leave. It was only then that the man turned to follow, breaking their stare.

She still watched him go. One should never turn their back on a man like that. They were always far better to see coming.

Two guards followed Kisa and Arelle as they walked through halls that felt like they were closing in on her with every step she took. It seemed as though from the moment she'd stepped into the castle, Kisa's demeanor changed from one of a friend, to a woman who was just doing what she was told.

Including taking Arelle to what she called the harem. The gilded rooms.

Arelle didn't fault the woman for the change or even the sudden spike of loneliness driving into her heart because she suspected that here … well, within the walls of this prison they called home, it was all about survival.

They did what they had to.

"Nearly there," Kisa murmured.

The heavy slap of boots against white marble had Arelle glancing over her shoulder at the guards following close behind with heavy swords hanging from the sheaths at their sides. They walked in tandem and kept their gazes straight ahead.

Unsettling, really.

Then, a scent hit her.

They rounded a corner at the same time, coming to gates that were smaller versions of the ones leading into the court's square with the same cursive B in the middle. The smell in the air was stronger now, mixed with heat and promising something she needed. She could even hear the quiet conversation in a language she missed, whispering from whatever was behind those locked gates.

"Is that—"

"Salt, yes," Kisa said. "I think, over the years, the king has found keeping some of us happy in little ways keeps him happier as well."

But what did that even mean?

"Move aside," one of the guards ordered.

He opened the gates, the heavy gold shuddering and moaning when he pulled it open. Kisa nodded to the man and then looked Arelle's way, waiting.

"Welcome home," she told her.

"This isn't our home," Arelle replied.

Kisa sighed. "It is now."

Behind the gates that the guard locked once they were safely inside, Arelle found the same white marble that dominated the castle. The salty dampness clinging to the air had her dragging in lungful after lungful of a taste she missed so badly.

"This way," Kisa said, tipping her head to the side and taking a corridor that led away from the noise Arelle wanted to follow. "The king expects you to be dressed as the rest of us do inside the harem."

"What does that mean?"

The woman took in her gown. "Well, you'll wear a lot less."

That wouldn't have bothered Arelle any other time. She hated the restrictive clothing, anyway, but she suspected the reason for the lack of clothing here was more for ease of access and less about style or personal choice.

Sheer robes waited on a chaise inside a room Kisa walked to as though it belonged to her. With a large bed dominating the middle of the space, and the personal touches including a set of paints setting near an easel, Arelle knew …

"This is your room?" she asked.

"One of the largest. You're favored, you receive more. You cause issues, you are removed entirely, and your next home won't be as kind or rich."

She thought about someone else, then.

About Poe.

"Is there … my sister, Poe. She was captured and—"

Kisa's gaze snapped to hers. "Let's hope you fare better than she did."

Did that mean her sister was no longer alive?

Or something else?

Kisa picked up one of the two robes and held it out for Arelle to take. She hesitated, and the other woman didn't miss it. "It's past hunting season—it'll take a while for them to get the man here who will fit you for your permanent collar, and the one who will come to clip your toes. Your sister was lucky that way, too."

For the first time, Arelle glanced down. Sure enough, Kisa's pinky toes were gone in her sandal-like shoes.

"Once you are considered safe by him," Kisa continued, not at all bothered by Arelle's staring, "the king may call on you to please him. But not before they've ensured you'll neither hurt him nor run. Well, it depends on his preference for you, too. If they retrieve you, fighting is pointless."

Arelle swallowed hard. "I—"

"The pool is where most of us gather. It's warm and the salt in the water keeps us comfortable and sane. Steam rolls through it constantly. You'll find sea lilies throughout the gilded rooms to abort pregnancies you wish to not keep, but these are of things I suggest you do not speak if you wish for us to keep the privilege, as I am sure you know. I would also suggest you use them regularly, if you are clever. If you birth a child, at worst, you never re-enter the rooms and no one knows what happens to you. Nothing good, probably. At best, he lets you hold the child for a day or two. Don't cause a problem, and there won't be a problem, Princess. That is how we survive here."

She met the merwoman's gaze.

"You don't have to call me that," she said quietly.

Kisa nodded. "Perhaps not, but understand, it would be wise for you to make the rest of them think they should. For your own good, I assure you."

Well, then …

Arelle would keep it in mind.

All the while, her heart continued to break.

Where are you, Eryx?

Eryx

"What brings you to my doorstep in this weather, my lord?"

The fact that Corval was a snake.

Nothing more, nothing less.

Eryx smirked at the man sitting across the table from him before tipping the goblet in his hand up for a good swig of the ale waiting inside. He had to give the guy credit—he said nothing about the fact that the prince was dripping wet, and undoubtedly ruining the very expensive rug beneath the table.

But frankly, if Eryx were being honest, he knew exactly why the man across from him wasn't quite sure what to say or make of the prince's presence. This had not been in any of the agreements the two of them made.

Corval had never expected to see him again.

That was the deal.

The hunter had more to lose than either of them would admit when it came to capturing the mermaid for Eryx. Given how much of Atlas's riches were made from the hunts, to the crown, a hunter working on the sly for someone else would be treason.

The deal had been simple.

Capture the mermaid.

Get paid.

Never speak of it again.

Eryx shouldn't be here.

He doubted Corval would tell him to leave.

"The house is quiet," Eryx noted.

Corval cleared his throat and smiled. "It always is."

"No kids—a wife?"

"I always assumed it better not to tie a woman into this life with me. All those months on the sea—as dangerous as it is ... would it be fair?"

"Fair enough if she wanted it."

Corval nodded. "True enough. Perhaps I haven't found her yet, then."

"Or you're not looking at all."

The hunter would fetch an easy wife if he truly wanted one. Eryx didn't need to be told to know that was the truth. He had wealth—a good lot of it. Respect. A place at the royal court because of his success on the sea.

A line of women would jump at the man.

Corval clearly had enough of the line of questioning when he raised a brow at the prince, done with pretenses, and asked, "Are you going to tell me what you want?"

"What makes you think I want something?"

"The fact that you showed up at my door, looking anything but a prince, with fire in your eyes. I saw you look like this once—right after we pulled you from that island. Remember that?"

Eryx did.

Better than the man understood.

Dragging in a heavy breath, Eryx murmured, "Seems someone has decided to take my little mermaid away from me—I would like to get her back, but considering the circumstances, I may need help."

That quieted the hunter.

But for a mere moment.

"By whom?"

That was the more difficult part of this equation.

"The king," Eryx replied.

What had seemed like interest in Corval's eyes—Eryx thought the man enjoyed a good challenge, which was why he first took the prince up on his original offer—disappeared in a blink. He shook his head and sat a little straighter in his chair when he folded his arms over his chest.

"She's a slave, Eryx," the man said, "and that means she belongs to the crown if they so want her. I suggest you find another. Hell, I even know a man who trains them, if you need one soon. I will pass his name along."

His stomach rolled at the idea. The rage swelled again. It was the harder of the two to handle if he were being honest.

"You were willing to defy the crown once for me—"

"Plausible ignorance," Corval interjected with a sardonic glint to his eye. "I could easily have said I assumed the hunts with you were for the crown, given who you are, and that you tricked me so I didn't know otherwise. Might have saved me from getting my head cut off. A banishment, I could deal with. The other bit, not so much."

"And you think they would have taken the word of a hunter over that of a prince?"

"A shunned prince, you mean."

Corval certainly knew where to hit so that it would hurt. Eryx might have appreciated that on another day, but on this evening … it only served to anger him more.

Standing from his chair and waving at the doorway to the dining room where they sat to converse, Corval said, "If the king has claimed a slave, then there isn't anything one can do. I can't—and won't—help you. I cannot be more involved in this mess than I already am, my lord. I think—possibly—there is more here than you're telling me, and I can't risk doing business with a man who holds secrets. You're a prince. A royal with the only claim after your father to the Bloodhurst throne. And what, you'll risk it all for a creature with a beautiful face? Find another. I hope you understand why I have to ask you to leave."

"She is not just—"

"Do you know what will happen to her, should she not obey? Or if you cause issues for the royal house because of a slave?"

Eryx swallowed hard but stayed quiet.

Corval didn't seem to mind because he continued on without missing a beat, saying, "The same thing that they did to the one we believed to be her sister—she'll be taken to a whorehouse in the west village and taught her fucking place, under whichever men pay for her time until all she knows is how to *please*, Eryx."

His heart ached.

Because he knew it was true.

Still, Eryx didn't show it.

"And if she's my mate?" he asked the hunter. "What am I to do then?"

He didn't need to explain more to Corval. After all, it had been the hunter who explained to Eryx the dangers of a male being separated from his other half. How they would sooner kill him than risk giving him any opportunity to get his mate returned to his side.

Well, now it was Eryx.

He was the mate without.

And Corval was looking him right in the face.

Corval tipped his chin up, eyeing Eryx with a bit more wariness than before. "That's not possible. You're a—"

"Oh, but it is," Eryx returned as he pulled the scarf from his throat so the gills flaring at his neck with each heavy breath would be easily seen. He stood from the table, his gaze locked with the widening stare of the hunter as he came closer with purposeful, rage-fueled steps. "See, I am far more like her than I am any of you."

"Prince—"

"You did give me something I might possibly be able to use, and for that, I'll make this quick. Easy, even."

The sister, that was.

He could find her now.

What he would do with her was another matter, and one he would deal with once he retrieved the mermaid.

As for Corval …

Eryx used the knife on the table that Corval had been using to carve a little mermaid from a stick of wood. He drove it straight through the other man's throat. Corval bled out on his table.

He made sure the man kept his eyes on the half-merman while he gurgled and choked on his blood. Eryx wanted the hunter to know why this had happened as it had—he wanted no question as to why he'd taken the man's life. Perhaps, he should have felt some remorse or guilt for the murder, seeing as how Corval had been the one who'd brought Arelle to him. But no. The hunts had become an inevitable part of their lives and ways on Atlas.

That didn't make them right. Neither was the man dying in front of him.

All he thought about was his mate and where she needed to be. Where she wasn't. With *him*.

"Did you think it would be the seas that killed you?" Eryx asked.

Corval didn't answer.

He couldn't.

Eryx nodded and smiled thinly. "Seems the tables have turned, Corval."

The hunter became the prey.

"As they should," Eryx added, "and as my mate might say, our kind is owed this."

The prince left when Corval stopped gurgling.

Arelle

The first thing Arelle learned about the royal court of Bloodhurst?

She was on display.

At all times. Even if she thought no one was looking. Someone always was.

At times, she might be treated like delicate art. Expected to be perfectly still and quiet, as though she were an unmovable statue, in the corner of the room while the king ate sweets and drank wine with his favorite people.

Other times, she would be expected to dance. In the court square. While it rained. And everyone looked on through the safety of a windowsill.

They even came to watch the merwomen of the harem through a wall made of bars that overlooked the pool where they all preferred to spend their time.

Always naked. Or practically.

Collars at their throats.

She was a thing.

A prized possession.

An object to move at someone else's will.

Kisa had been wrong when she'd said Arelle would only be called upon when she was considered safe. Well, partially. Arelle was never left alone with the king—a guard was always nearby to make sure she stayed in line. He did, however, call on her quite often to do whatever he pleased.

Except for fucking her, it seemed.

That wasn't safe yet. By the whispers of how the king had treated her sister, Arelle simply did not believe that to be true. If he wanted to have his way with her, then he would. The way he constantly returned to request for her time, to eat, to talk, or even to watch her sit in silence, told Arelle the man didn't *want* to take it from her.

And, he wanted information.

Probably about her and his son.

"Were you more interesting to look at or talk to when you were with my son?" the king asked. "Or are you just that good of a lay that your lack of conversation makes up for it?"

Arelle turned her head slowly to meet the man's gaze, her brow raising at his blatant question and the implication behind it. "Are you asking me if he fucked me, or if I liked it?"

The few people that were close enough to the king and his new favorite slave, who he had yet to get a night with, quieted instantly. A guard took one step forward, closer to the circle of pillows where Misael apparently liked to spend his evenings watching the court attempt to entertain him with many different things in the grand room made of marble carvings and high archways.

The king raised a single hand, stopping the guard from coming any closer. Never once did he move his gaze from Arelle.

"Both," he settled on saying.

"Then yes," she returned before smirking when she added, "and yes for the other, too."

"Bold, mermaid."

"I get the impression you like that, my lord. My boldness, and that your son has had me."

The king didn't reply.

Arelle lifted one dainty, naked shoulder as if to shrug him off. She'd not even bothered with the sheer robe they'd demanded she wear—she was bare for them to see, anyway. What even was the point? If they wanted to watch her walk around naked like a show to scandalize their minds, well, she could absolutely play along with that.

The king reached forward to snag one of her red curls between his fingers, and out of instinct alone, Arelle moved away. He gave her a look. She merely stared right back.

"You will learn to behave," he told her. "You do well, but you can do better."

"He thought the same. Until he learned to love me."

Eryx had never said it.

She didn't need Eryx's own words to know that was true.

Misael's eyes darkened with merely a spark of rage. A bit of disbelief colored his expression, too. She welcomed his challenge because he likely thought she would be the same as every other mermaid here.

Afraid.

Compliant.

His.

She was none of those things.

Arelle turned back to the rest of the room but only because a man approached the king from his left, and that allowed her a reprieve from his attention … or punishment. She wasn't sure which one it would be.

Here, one trusted nothing.

The second thing she learned.

"What?" Misael snapped at the man who stopped next to the king's seat on the pillows.

"Word has come from the west, Sire. Seems there's been a fire … and then an attack."

"Why on earth would that concern me?"

"The fire happened in the row of the west village, my King. The attack was on a whorehouse in that row. A slave was taken."

That quieted the king.

But only for a moment.

"Which slave?" he asked carefully.

"The one who called herself Poe." The man cleared his throat, his gaze darting to Arelle and then back to the king before he said quieter, "There's more, my King. It seems there's those who say they saw the man who started the fire and attack—they spotted the prince, my lord."

Arelle felt the eyes turn on her, but she continued watching the room with a smile. In her heart, she could hear him again.

Eryx, that was.

I'm coming.

How, she didn't know.

When, it didn't matter.

He was coming for her.

39. THE ONE NAMED POE

Eryx

Over the flames licking toward the roof of the makeshift shelter, Eryx watched the mermaid stare into the black nothingness of the forest around them. It didn't matter what he did, whether it was actively attempting to engage her in a conversation or even just adding more driftwood he'd found to the fire, she wasn't speaking.

In fact, she refused to even look at him.

At first, Eryx hadn't minded. He wasn't quite sure what he was going to do with the mermaid he'd stolen from the whorehouse where Corval had said she would be, but one part of his plan at a time. It was all about patience, he was sure.

Now, though, as she was safe in the camp he'd created away from the storms and anyone who might see them, he wanted to fill the silence with anything but the thoughts in his mind that threatened to send him running crazy if he fed into it, and the dread that had his heart racing with thundering beats.

"I won't fuck you."

Her first sentence since the moment he'd taken her from the whorehouse days earlier. It'd taken him a while to get a horse that would travel in the storms after they'd killed all of his at the stable estate. And then, by the time he'd arrived at the west village to begin the process of removing the mermaid from her current prison, well … it had all taken too much time.

Or, that's how it felt.

Eryx cleared his throat. "I don't plan to fuck you. Apologies if that was your first assumption for why I took you."

He saw the roll of her eyes, and the pull of her lips turning them down into a frown. "You would be the first. Seems their favorite thing is to break a mermaid at the whorehouse by having a constant line of men waiting. And when you don't shut up, they invite a second one in to make sure your mouth is—"

"What is your name?" he asked because as of now, he couldn't do anything to help her pain in that regard except not be another name on her list of who had raped her. "Poe, yes?"

He knew she'd heard him, if only because a small knot formed between her brows, although she still didn't turn her stare away from the dense forest.

"Arelle told me—my mother, she killed the one. Coral, I think. And then you killed—"

Poe turned burning violet eyes on Eryx and quieted him from the intensity he found there. "She begged to die. *Imagine* … I dare you to even consider what it would have been like for that mermaid to go back to a colony with her fin destroyed by your people, having been a whore to landwalkers for only the Gods know how long. And that is before we consider the collar on her throat so she couldn't breathe. Disgusting. I did her a *favor*. You should thank me."

He was struck at the bright contrast between the way Arelle had treated the murder of his mother, and how this woman did. Like night and day. One had almost soothed him in that she hadn't suffered. This one, however, had him struggling to stay on the other side of the fire so that he didn't rip her into pieces.

He couldn't kill her.

Right now, he needed her.

She may help his cause.

"You thought that was a favor?" he asked in a murmur. "To take her from me? Even if I told you she was all I had? All that was real to me?"

"I have a child," Poe returned, "and I love her. I love her enough that if my death brought her clarity or success, I would be the first to feed my blood to the seas. I'm not sure what your mother's death has done for you, but I am sure she would have done the same had she needed to. But having a child does not negate the need you have in your own heart because you are an individual. I did not say it was a favor to *you*. If she asked for the death, was it not right for her? Was it not her choice to make?"

Eryx's jaw ached from clenching so hard. He wanted to argue, but he knew it was better to let it go. Or, as much as he could.

"You know," Poe said, sighing as she turned to stare into the forest again instead of Eyrx, "we believe that's why we can hear the calls of our mates. All that magic—when we die, we go to the sea. We can't take what changes us with us when we go, and so we give it back. It's also why in water, the blood changes. Stickier. Not potent, except when we're dead. We give the magic life. Because the sea is us, and we are it."

"Is that why the matings always happen on land?"

Her gaze cut to him again. "And what would you know about—"

"I'm mated. Someone took her from me. I would like to get her back."

Poe stared hard at him, waiting for him to fill in the blank, clearly. Eryx figured it was better for her to do it on her own. The longer he stared at her, however, the more easily he could find the similarities between her and Arelle in her features. From the shape of her lips, the color of their eyes— though all full-blooded mermaids from the Blu Sea had those violet eyes— to the shade of her hair, and even the way she regarded him in her annoyance.

It bothered him.

She looked just enough like his mate to make him pause. It was not enough to quell the rage or rawness in his heart.

"My sister?" Poe asked quietly.

Eryx shrugged. "Seems I'm stuck with her, considering how this works, and so I best get her back, no?"

That urged a smirk from the woman across the fire. Oddly, despite the hatred he felt in his heart for Poe because of what she had done to his mother, he still thought that hint of a smile was a battle won for him here.

Then, it quickly faded away.

"When?" she asked him.

"The night you were caught."

Poe's brow lifted impossibly higher. "That night, I heard whispers myself."

Eryx swallowed audibly. "Did you?"

"Who the hunt was for—*why*. Look at you now, Prince, of the land, on your *knees* because he's done the same thing to you that he did to all of them."

He let her have the words.

Perhaps she was due them.

"I don't hear him anymore," she eventually muttered, her words nothing more than a whisper after her gaze turned back on the darkness. "My mate, I mean."

Eryx's brow furrowed. "Is he—"

"If he were dead, I would be, too. I promised myself."

"What of your child?" Eryx asked.

The bright burning in her stare faded; what replaced it could only be described as agony. He regretted asking her that question—she undoubtedly asked it a lot of herself. That was where Eryx found his understanding with the mermaid. He found familiarity in her pain because he shared the same between her current grief and the unknowing.

"You don't hear your mate, you said?" he asked, wanting to give them both an out.

"I don't hear him, but I feel him. Sometimes, I swore I could smell him. Tis the only reason, after every chance I've had to run, why I didn't. He is here. I need him. My child needs him. So, where is he? Why doesn't he call for me?"

Eryx flinched. "Perhaps ... he can't."

Poe scoffed hard. "That's impossible. It's not how the bond works. He can always call—the same way I do for him. He never answers back. If he's not dead, then he might as well be."

"Except he isn't, if you're still alive."

Then, Eryx had another thought.

Because as he assumed, the longer time he spent with this woman and the more their conversation went on, the better he knew exactly how to use her to his own gain.

Here she was, the rightful heir to the Blu Seas. Hadn't they said with her assumed dead, it was the only reason why Arelle would take the throne after the current king? Eryx refused to even consider his own claim to it through his mother—if her journal entries and the way she signed them with Queen every time were to be trusted—because that wouldn't help him at the moment. He didn't have time to learn the sea, prove his place, and take it back.

How would he even go about doing that?

No, he had to get to Arelle first.

Make them safe.

And only then might he come back for the seas.

But Poe?

What would her people do for her—their supposed lost heir?

What would she do—tear a kingdom down, possibly, looking for her mate?

Eryx thought he had a very good idea of what she wouldn't do if she had any idea that she was staring at the man able to take it all away from her. So, he opted to be very careful here.

Above the rickety roof he'd made of fallen logs for their shelter, Eryx could hear the winds howling high over the trees and how they snapped and cracked with the pressure. If the landwalkers hid in the storms, and the mermaids came alive … what better time than the season of storms to invite the people of the sea to take back what belonged to them?

A war they could finally win.

"What would you do for me," Eryx said, "if I could remove that collar from your throat?"

Poe's hand flew up to the metal around her neck. "I was told it's permanent."

"It is … unless it's removed by someone who knows how."

The dancing flames colored her features.

Eryx waited.

"Can you?" she finally asked.

"A blacksmith who makes them showed me once when he needed to change my mother's because a spike had come loose in one of her gills. I was … maybe six."

And he didn't have a good memory of that day at all. Simply something he had asked his mother.

Did that hurt, Mother?

He did not think he meant her collar.

Rather, whatever it hid. Probably, a brand that looked very similar to the one on Poe's hand, and the one he had touched on Arelle's.

"There's a pin in the back that is impossible for the person wearing it to reach properly and just as difficult for anyone else to remove. But it can be done, if you can manage the pain for the duration of the process."

Poe smiled.

Cold as it still was.

"Pain doesn't scare me."

"No?"

She shrugged. "My mate taught me to enjoy it."

Well, then ...

"Let me grab my knife, and we'll talk as I work," Eryx murmured.

"I still won't fuck you."

He chuckled. "I still don't want you to."

40. TO POKE BEASTS

Zale, King of the Blu Seas

When the mood of the court was dismal, so was the colony. Thing was, this time it wasn't Zale's court reflecting a bad atmosphere to the rest of the colony, but rather the rest of his people making their mood about him and his choices very clear.

Another time, he would have handled this better.

Surely.

Perhaps, he would have controlled his subjects with the same fear he'd once used to keep them away from the land and people of Atlas for all this time. The greatest threat to his place on the Blu throne had always been his misdeeds—should they learn the truth—and how it had radically changed their world more than it already was.

He'd handed over a queen for a throne.

She had wanted peace.

He'd known it would never come to be.

What did it matter now?

"We should move the colony to a safer place. Far from Atlas, and the hunters. Somewhere we can live freely. There are smaller colonies without ruling realms that will—"

"'Tis our home!"

The shouts of the people in his throne room had Zale glancing up from the crown that rested in his lap. It felt more like a burden than it did a statement of his place now.

"We needn't shout," came a lazy drawl from the back of the room.

That voice.

It instantly made the king want to rage because, if not for the owner of the voice, this wouldn't be happening in the first place. The people of his kingdom who had dared to storm his home with the demand that they be heard would not be separated at opposite ends of the room shouting at one another.

Mav.

The foolish prince.

"Are you happy now?" Zale dared to asked him.

He didn't bother to address anyone else. The room was full of merpeople who had—at first—threatened to rip him from his throne. A good portion of his guards had stopped protecting the palace when the rebellion started to worsen in the Blu Seas. The people of the colony, however, were no longer important to Zale when he couldn't bend them to his will.

What use were they?

If they wanted to die for their home, then who was he to tell them no? If they were willing to do anything—even remove him from his seat as the king—then how could he possibly stop them? There was only one of him, and he could already tell that he was not worth very much to the rest of them now.

"Have you gotten what you wanted now?" he shouted at Mav.

The Emerald prince smiled—just a ghost of a smirk that enraged Zale further. Had he been closer to the man, he might have ripped it right from his fucking face.

Had he no understanding of what he did? How he would lead these people to slaughter?

Yes, Zale had done awful things … but at one time, his intentions for doing them had been for the greater good. He'd hoped that with the trade of a queen, given to an obsessed prince on land, they would find a safer home and life.

Instead, it'd only gotten worse.

He had paid for that sin many times over. He still paid for it today.

"No," Mav finally replied. "I have not. I was promised a mate, Zale, and I intend to have her returned to me. Your court, they have demands, too. For some, it's peace. For others, it's a place where they can be free to live how they wish. And they deserve to be given what they want, too. So, no, I have not gotten what I wanted. Not yet."

Liar.

Oh, his words sounded so good to the ears of those around him. Because yes, Zale had heard all of the whispers. Every little thing that Mav told those around him. How he promised a better life for the royal guard. How he assured the colony they would have both the sea and the land to live their life. How he made it sound perfect when he described the droves of children they would safely be able to have once they'd just done what they needed to do.

Overthrow Zale.

Take back the land.

Burn Atlas to the ground.

But him?

Zale wasn't as easily manipulated as the rest of the people around him. Pretty words and promises meant very little to him when he knew a war with the people on land was not something that would be over just because they started it.

Other realms had done this very thing. One way or another, they suffered for it, too.

"What you want," Zale said, standing from his throne, uncaring that the crown fell from his lap and rolled across the floor, "is to take this kingdom from me and keep it as your own. Deny it."

"I have a kingdom waiting for me."

That response sent Zale cutting across the floor in a flash. Too fast for the people to understand what had happened, but Mav only tipped his chin up as the king stopped when the two of them were face to face.

"But what would be better than two kingdoms?" Zale returned, sneering. "How long has your father been chasing the throne of Hades? 'Tis so close to the Tar Lands I hear you can smell the dragon shit. How proud would he be if you handed over mine to him—how much closer would it get him to the realm he really wants?"

The tensing of the other man's jaw told Zale he'd hit a nerve there. The right one.

"This is their home," Mav murmured. "Let them take it back."

"And what of you?"

"I want the mate I was—"

Zale didn't give the man the chance to finish his statement before he was reaching for the blade at his back. He'd barely thought of the consequences that would come from him drawing a weapon on the man who his people were now following as though they were blind with no thought of their own.

He only wanted the Emerald prince dead.

Mav had apparently planned for that because Zale didn't even get the chance to pull his weapon from behind his back before the prince reacted.

The staff with the green emerald that never left the prince's hands came apart in two pieces. On either end were sharp blades that glinted when they caught Zale's eyes. Mav smirked as he twisted those blades in his hands, unafraid and clearly comfortable with the weapons.

As though he'd been trained.

"Fifteen seconds," Mav told him. "That is how long it will take you to bleed out when I finish the last slice. I have done it to better men than you, so just give me a reason to do it now."

Zale snarled under his breath. "You—"

"I will let you run if that's exactly what you do. I'll do it for your mate and the grandchild she protects—I'll let you both run, but you never look back. Give me your word."

The king said nothing.

And then one blade met his throat.

"Give me your word," Mav uttered, too low for the rest of the room to hear, "and the truth of what you've done to this kingdom and the queen who sat on the throne before you will never reach their ears. It's my last option, and I will use it if you give me no other choice."

"Her reign is long over—undoubtedly dead. What good would that even do?"

Zale would not ask how the man learned those secrets. It no longer mattered, truly.

"You know what it would do. And what if her legacy lives on—I was born where the sea meets the land. Children are born to mermaids and landwalkers all the time. It's rumored that every son born to the Atlas king was a halfling, and they tried to hide it. And that king—wasn't he the prince that hunted their queen? They say he keeps merwomen to breed. If she carried on her blood, and that blood lives even after her death, your entire rule was built on a lie of your own making."

Ah, that was why Mav really said nothing about what Zale had done. Not for the king, but for himself. Because if there were offspring from the previous queen, that child would have claim over Zale, his children, and anyone else who thought to take the Blu throne.

"I will use it," Mav said again, "though it will hurt to do it."

Of course.

"Where would we even go?" Zale demanded.

"You'll figure it out. As long as it isn't here."

"Zale."

He didn't dare turn at the call of his mate. He hadn't even realized Rosel had left her rooms when the court was stormed by the people, but he wasn't surprised.

"Please, Zale," he heard her whisper.

She didn't know it, but a lot of this and many of the things he'd done that hurt her ... well, he did those things for her. Some, because he was scared that she would be taken from him. The very idea scared him to death. Others, because he loved her and it made him oh, so selfish.

He understood that over the years, she'd grown resentful. Of his ways, his treatment, and his demands that felt like a constant hand around her delicate throat.

But she'd been his proper mate.

A good queen.

The perfect mother.

As though Mav could see the change in Zale's mind through the stare he leveled on the man, the prince nodded. "You take nothing but the child."

"How long do we run?"

"Until you're dead."

Zale chuckled. "I hope the realm you're willing to slaughter them for is worth the sacrifice you'll pay to have it."

Mav nodded. "Me, too."

"*Listen!*"

The order cut through the room, blanketing it and everyone inside in total silence. No one had to ask what they were listening for; the call traveling through the sea, filling the water with its faint familiarity.

A call.

A song of a royal.
She was calling for them.
But which one was it?
Mav's gaze stayed firm on Zale. "Do not be here when we return."
It killed him.
All he'd worked for.
Still, the king replied, "Agreed."

41. CALLED HOME

Eryx

"This is the worst storm so far this season."

Eryx might as well have not bothered to say the words at all. Between the winds that screamed all around them on the high cliffs, the waves that crashed to the rocky ledge a hundred feet down below, and the haunting melody coming from his companion at his left, the words were lost.

If Poe heard him, she didn't say.

Not that it mattered.

The storms no longer scared him.

The wind hit at their backs and then switched just as fast, coming in from the front. Then to the side, and around and around it went. He was sure if he could distinguish the clouds from the sky or the sea—it was a canvas of black—then he would see them rolling and circling to create the most dangerous part of the storms.

The tunnels that came down. Wicked, ravaging wind tunnels that sucked up everything it touched and destroyed anything on the land in mere seconds.

It was the only part of the storms that caused pause for Eryx, but at the moment, he didn't have much of a choice but to be where he was ... waiting.

"Are you cold?" he asked Poe.

She wore nothing but the thin gown the whorehouse had provided—or perhaps it was what she'd been given when they sent her away from the court. Either way, Poe didn't respond to his concern or even acknowledge that he'd spoken at all.

In fact, she just kept singing.

That call ...

It didn't feel familiar in a way that he'd heard it before, but it still seemed as though the song she sang into the wind almost pulled him forward. And if her call made him want to answer it, somehow, then he could only imagine what it did for the people of the sea who would hear her song and know it.

At the moment, his own cloak was doing very little to battle the wind and rain. Soaked to the bone, and mildly cold already, he imagined she was no better.

She was, however, focused.

A grunt and the beat of hooves against wet rock had Eryx glancing over his shoulder. The horse who had done well in the storms the last few days was finally showing his edginess at the top of the cliffs overlooking the seas. Restless and jittery, the animal moved back and forth, already seeming like he wanted to leave.

Eryx needed him, though.

So, he'd tied the reins down to a small tree.

Turning back to the sea and the wind, Eryx breathed in. Slow and deep. Filling his lungs and then releasing the air with a low hum that started in the back of his throat. Instinct, he thought, because he'd never made a sound like that before.

"They're coming," Poe said, never looking away from the sea. "Look."

He did.

It took him a second.

Then, two.

But against the sea of blackness, the color started to show. Flashes of silver, and slivers of green and blue. Fins cut through the surface of the water before they disappeared once more.

Poe let out a sigh.

It sounded like relief.

But also, of mourning.

He understood perfectly well because he felt the same. This was good for them. The sight of the mermaids coming to the land meant the plans he put in motion were working. At the same time, all he felt inside was pain from his mate being in limbo away from him.

"Why doesn't he call?" she asked. "Why doesn't he answer me?"

"This may give you the chance to find out exactly why."

Finally, she looked his way.

Poe nodded.

Eryx nodded back.

"Good luck, mermaid," he told her.

That earned him a cunning smile from Poe when she replied, "Luck has nothing to do with winning a war."

He didn't have the chance to tell her she might be right because in the next breath, Poe ran forward and jumped from the high cliffs.

At least, he thought, *I managed to get her collar off.*

Arelle

There was nothing more uncomfortable than the feeling of the spikes in the leather collar around her throat being pulled from her gills. It was entirely unnatural, and her gills flared with the first exhales it'd had in far too long.

"Beautifully made, this," the man said, admiring the collar in his hands. "But not acceptable if you're going to be staying here, young one."

Arelle side-eyed the man she'd been told was a blacksmith there to fit her new, and permanent, collar. He talked as though they were friends, and even dared to ask her permission before putting his hands on her to remove Eryx's collar.

Thing was, she didn't care to talk back.

And they were not friends.

She wouldn't pretend differently.

"Now, tip your head up, I like to get the measurement a bit loose, despite what everyone else thinks. It may be the law to wear it, but you should at least be comfortable in it, I suppose. Lift up for me, thank you."

Arelle's jaw clicked in her annoyance, but she did as he demanded. The man—whose name she didn't care to learn, though he had been respectful enough to ask hers—pulled what appeared to be a strip of material from the pocket of his waistcoat. He wrapped it around her throat, and for the first time, she tensed.

He clicked his tongue; his gaze darted to hers. "I know you must think badly of me, but I am only doing my job. I try to do it kindly, little mermaid, because they give me no choice. I am either here to do what they demand, or they kill me and mine. Do not worry, it is not my hands who will hurt you."

For the first time since she'd met the man, Arelle acknowledged him with a nod and a soft, "Thank you."

"Let me measure."

"Sure."

He took the measurement of her throat in a tense position, and then proceeded to mark the soft material with a piece of black charcoal.

"There we are," he said, packing the items away. "And that is it for today. I'll put this one back on you for the sake of doing it, although what good it does, I don't know. You could have removed it yourself."

Arelle smiled. "I couldn't."

"Ah, I know. The law again."

"Not at all."

Her mate placed it.

She wouldn't remove it.

And she hadn't.

When she didn't explain further, even at his raised brow, the man chuckled with a shake of his head and raised her leather collar with the embossed detailing to place it back at her throat. Before he could, however, a ruckus in the hallway drew Arelle's attention to the doorway of the room in the harem where she'd been told to go to meet with the blacksmith for her fitting.

"What is that?" he asked.

"I don't kn—"

She didn't get to finish her statement before a servant of the court and two guards filed into the room while what looked like many more passed by the opened doorway. Each of their fast steps seemed to have a purpose. Their orders outside of the room rang out at the same time the ones inside the room told Arelle and the blacksmith, "There's a revolt in the seas—they're coming in from the water. We have limited time to move the king and court farther inland where he'll be safer. The entire harem needs to be moved now."

"Pack up! Only your robes and gowns. All else is not needed. Head for the entrance. Keep in line. Carriages will be waiting!"

Outside the room, the orders echoed.

What did they mean?

A revolt in the seas?

"Well, give me a moment to—"

"Now," one of the guards barked.

The blacksmith made a dismissive grunt under his breath, then gave Arelle a smile as he pocketed her leather collar. "Seems you won't be needing this, and I'll be taking my leave until we meet up again."

That was the last thing the blacksmith said to Arelle before she was pulled from the room by the guards.

Without her collar.

Mattue

"Are you even listening to me?" Mattue snarled at his brother from the other side of the rocking carriage.

"Oh, what does it fucking matter?" Misael returned with much less heat or care than his counterpart. "We're ahead of him, Mattue. We'll head into the heart of Atlas, and the army will march to the shore."

If they could stay standing in the winds, maybe.

And his brother was still wrong.

"It matters! It matters, Misael, because—"

"This will be settled in no time. Eryx *will* learn his place."

So no, the king hadn't listened.

Not to a single damned word.

"You truly believe that man has done what he did to spite you again, Misael? Are you serious?"

"Quiet, I'm trying to think."

About nothing, as usual.

Surely.

He would kill them.

All of them.

Simply because he would not *listen*.

Mattue's gaze narrowed on his brother as the men outside the carriage attempted, poorly, to get it unstuck on the road. An unfortunate, but common, problem whenever they tried to travel in the storms. Only fools tried, but Misael had no choice. He had to move the harem.

The king needed safety.

"He hasn't run off, taken the kin of his slave—"

"*My* slave," Misael snapped at his brother.

Mattue slammed back into the hard seat, and then decided that he would try reason with Misael one more time. "'Tis the problem with you, brother. You're assuming she is yours, but there are ways in which she may not be, but you don't want to hear me say it. One I don't think you've stopped to consider with your son, but alas, here I am to fill you in. It has come to my attention in recent days that we may have gone too far with Eryx here. Taking the mermaid—"

"*You* told me of her, Mattue. And she is mine to do with as I wish."

Yes, before he saw the mermaid away from Eryx, and that made all the difference. Perhaps it was his own halfling side that allowed Mattue the privilege of nuance when in the room with those who shared the unknown part of him, but things tended to stand out.

"You didn't notice the things she did at all, did you?" Mattue asked the king.

Misael shot him a look with furrowed brows. "What are you talking about?"

"The *whore*—the slave. Eryx's!"

"*Mine!*" Misael shouted right back, nearly coming out of his seat.

The rocking and struggle outside the carriage continued.

Mattue had more important things on his mind. "At the palace, my lord. She could be sitting in a room full of people but staring off as if her mind was somewhere else entirely. I've seen them do that—it means they're *listening!*"

That was the moment, actually. The very second Mattue thought they might have gone too far and, more concerningly, that they may not be able to come back from it.

"Yes, yes. You said—"

"Who would she be listening *for*, Misael? I think—" Mattue's words cut off momentarily, and with the next rock of the carriage and howl of wind, he heard something even he could hear, then. Words in the wind. A call for help and a cry of war.

Tides were changing.

Misael would not have heard that.

No, he couldn't.

He only heard his brother quiet.

"I did listen, you fucking fool," Misael hissed at his brother, turning his attention back to the rain and mud-spattered window of the carriage. "But he hasn't mated with the little mermaid; he's only *half*."

"If she is … if they *have*, you'll kill us," Mattue warned. "You are a fool."

Misael, crown on, turned his glare back on Mattue. "*I am the king.*"

Mattue's hand clenched tightly around the iron butt of the dagger he kept at his side, knowing how easily it could crack a skull. "But still quite human, brother."

Arelle

The carriage rocked hard to the left again, followed by severe cursing outside at the front before the crack of a whip sent the horses crying out.

Arelle dragged in a shaky breath, sad for the poor beasts being beaten for the errors of men. They should have known better. With roads made of dirt in the season of storms where rain poured until the ground was nothing but soft muck, travel became a dangerous event. It wasn't the animal's fault the two right wheels became buried into a pit of mud.

"Ay, you're a fucking fool," a man shouted, his air catching in the racing winds. "Stop rocking it; you're making it go deeper!"

A hiss sliced through the carriage, followed by the click of a tongue. The surprising use of their own language had even Arelle turning her head away from the windows overlooking the guards struggling outside to free the buggy.

Listen to the wind.

She wasn't sure which mermaid said it; it also didn't matter when every mermaid in that carriage suddenly lifted their heads in tandem as wind swayed the carriage with its next blow. Not a single one of them spoke.

They didn't need to when they could all hear it.

Not one call.

Or two.

Or even ten.

Their kind had many calls. For family. Their young. A mate. Royals. It was only one call that would cross any amount of land or sea—that of a mate. Because it was in their hearts. But so was the sea, and the wind that moved it. The other calls would travel, too, just in a different way.

Right then, it sounded like hundreds of calls were reaching them in the wind.

We're coming!

Hold the land!

Burn everything!

We fight.

Find me. Find me. Find me.

So many, in fact, that it had some of the mermaids in the carriage chaotic until they found their way out onto the ground. The guards shouted, their demands lost to the sudden calls from at least four of the women in her carriage answering back.

"Get in the carriage! What are you doing?"

Arelle heard the hiss of the whip outside at the same time all those calls echoed around her that one stood out.

Find me, my little mermaid.

Eryx.

A scream echoed from the woman who had taken the first crack of a whip. Hisses answered it before grunts followed. Arelle watched out the window for a brief second as the women attacked the guards.

She listened for Eryx again.

He was still there.

Her attention drifted to the front of the carriage where the guards had left the small door open between the inside and the tented bench where they sat to steer the horses. Horses that were now standing just a few feet away tucked close together, untied, to brace for the weather.

"You heard them," one of the mermaids said, "hold the land."

They could make their own choices.

She would make hers.

Arelle headed for the door as the last mermaid followed behind her but exited from the side to help her sisters finish the men outside. She slipped on the wet wood of the bench when she climbed out the door and stumbled from the carriage into the mud below.

The shouting and struggle behind her had her heart aching. She wanted to help, but this might be her only chance.

And faced with the decision of staying to help her kind or going to follow the call of her mate … well, there was only one right choice.

She mounted the closest horse. Her thin, loose white gown was already soaked through and plastered to her skin.

Arelle grabbed tight to the reins of the horse, struggling to stay atop it when her heels dug in hard. How she stayed on when the horse took off, she would never know.

Luck, maybe.

Or just a bit of magic.

It took a bit before she felt comfortable on the horse, but it was easier hearing Eryx when all she really had to do was just pull one way or the other on the reins to make the horse follow.

Her heart pounded as the beast rounded a corner, and the sight of an overturned carriage a little way down the road had her slowing. She recognized the gold detailing on it and the high, curved top because she'd watched it carrying the king away from the court earlier when they had been shuffling the mermaids into the ones waiting for them.

But it wasn't the carriage that stunned her the most. In the travel of the royal caravan over the last day, many fell behind or moved farther ahead. Sometimes they caught up and other times, they went hours without seeing anyone. It wasn't a shock there had been one close to where they lost theirs in the mud.

It was the man straddled over another man on the outside of the carriage that had her swallowing hard. They rested a few feet away from where horses lay with broken legs, and the four guards remained motionless with bloody, beaten heads and dead eyes watching the sky on the rocky, muddy road.

The only man moving was the one using the man on the ground as a chair. For a second, the cloak over his head kept him hidden, but a hard gust of wind sent it flying back as he looked up at the sound of an approaching horse.

"The king is dead!" she heard him call out. Another gallop forward, and he shouted again, relief clear in his voice, "The king is dead!"

Arelle thought time slowed for a moment as the living man's eyes widened when he finally realized who was coming closer.

Mattue turned to watch Arelle pass. She cared not for the lives lost, or the odd scene of men with beaten in heads, and Mattue sitting on a dead king with his hands clenched into bruised fists. A day would come for him—the advisor—but it wouldn't be on this one.

Not when her mate called her home.

42. A CROWN OF GLASS

Mav, Prince of the Emerald Lands

"Prince, I beg of you to wait just a mom—"

"*Burn it! Burn it all!*" shouted a princess with hair the color of fire to the gathered crowd of merpeople in the narrow seas.

She spun one way, and then the other. Too fast for Mav to discern her face as he weaved in and out of the people that shouted back for her. Too fast for him to notice anything but the bloody mess streaking down her vibrating spine. The tenor of her voice, the way it shook in its power, was unlike anything he had heard, and Mav was not the only one. The rest of the people her song had drew closer to the lands responded to her call for war and vengeance in kind.

"*Burn everything! Every night, every storm, we take to the land, and we burn what we can't overtake until there is nothing left and nowhere for them to hide!*"

"*Yes!*" came the roar of the crowd.

"Prince," his advisor hissed at his back again.

Mav just didn't have time.

Or a care.

A few mere swim strokes away from the woman he was sure to be his intended mate, he had no interest in anything his advisor had to say when, so far, the man had yet to do him any damned good. The princess freeing herself and finding her way to the seas was simply a bonus in a situation he had already pushed over the edge under the water, but one he couldn't deny would practically guarantee the success of her people.

And his plan, of course.

"And only when the people of Atlas truly understand what the Blu throne will do for its seas will we grant them some shred of mercy," she hissed as Mav finally broke through the center ring. "Even that will *hurt*."

"Princess," he murmured, holding something for her.

She would need it.

By the morning, as storms continued to rage, he planned to have them mated, her crowned, and their attack on the land in the full throes of chaos and violence. Which would be nothing less than she, and her kingdom, deserved.

Mav would make it all happen.

Heads turned his way, and finally, the mermaid in the middle of it all spun around to properly face him. Instantly, Mav recognized his mistake and likely what the advisor had been futilely attempting to explain to him.

The woman who glared at him, soon focusing on the crown of twisted glass in his hands, was not the mate he had hoped, and foolishly thought, escaped the landwalkers. No, instead he looked at her sister.

The heir before her.

"Not the sister you were looking for, Prince?" Poe of the Blu Seas asked, the question letting him know that he had not hid his shock, or disappointment, very well at all.

"Would you forgive my honesty?"

She cocked a brow at the query. "I find myself feeling far less forgiving lately for the misdeeds of men, truth be."

He could see that in her.

In her face.

Her very aura.

It radiated.

It haunted her eyes and gave her a coldness that settled as intensely as her stare. He didn't have the first clue what had been done to this merwoman during her captivity on the lands, but whatever she left behind, it had not escaped her. Perhaps she was not quite done with it yet, either, and so ... a cleansing had to begin.

What better way than fire?

"Is she free, too?" he asked when Poe remained quiet. "Your sister?"

Poe's gaze darted from the crown in his hands to his face. "Have you or my father sent word to the Emerald Lands to ask for help here?"

"I did—very recently, in fact. I could see where this would soon head with your father ignoring his people. If my father's army travel underseas, and they will, knowing they'll face storms, it'll be nearer to the end of season before significant help arrives for us. Ships will come as soon as they are able. We'll have to do what we can and hold the land."

She nodded. "But we *can*."

"I believe so," Mav replied. "'Tis a good time for it."

He couldn't find a reason why not. If they didn't do it now, would this realm *ever*? These people needed to take back their lands and seas, or they were forever doomed to be the prey of a far less worthy species.

Sickening.

"My sister ..."

His fingers flexed harder around the crown in his hands, but she didn't notice. "What of her?"

"I did not see her. I know they have her. *Someone* does."

Then, his duty here wasn't done.

He eyed Poe once more, and she did the same to him.

"And somewhere on those lands, my mate lives," Poe said, confirming the stories he had heard to be true. "I need to find him."

"A fair trade, a mate for a mate."

Poe's chin tipped up. "If you say so, Prince. Now, where is my mother and father—my *daughter*?"

The crowd of waiting merpeople seemed to close in around their

SONGS OF THE HUNTED

princess and the prince at the question. As if they knew his answer would enrage her, but it wouldn't be only his fine line to walk.

"Forgive me," Mav murmured as he fell to the bend in his tail and held her crown high. A crown she did not immediately take. "If I had not let them run with her, I do not trust your people would have let them escape the palace alive, my Queen."

He did not have to bow to her.

Well, he would when she put on that crown.

When she snatched it from his hands, her stare burned even within the depths of the dark, churning, cold seas. Atlas was but one thing she wanted to burn in that moment, and the way her hands clenched around the crown until the sharp tips cut into her skin and made her bleed said as much without her needing to say anything.

Mav, grateful that he had made himself useful to the woman with fire and hate in her eyes just a short while earlier, raised his head a bit. Enough to meet her eyes.

"I will do my very best to immediately correct that mistake," he vowed to her.

"I would very much like to know *how*."

Yes, so would he.

43. TO CHOOSE LOVE

Eryx

Five days later ...

The irony not lost on Eryx that he found himself back at the same bay where he'd caught Arelle. It seemed like the best place, given the abandoned structures, some of which still stood well and tall, that many people on Atlas assumed were no longer safe to use. They believed the storms had weakened the stone watchtower near the entrance of the bay or compromised the integrity of the scattered houses on the upper rim.

Some were, sure.

But given its easy location to the sea, and the lack of activity from anyone on land, it was the one place he thought would be safest to wait.

After he arrived, unsure of the time or the day because it felt like he'd been traveling for longer than he could comprehend, Eryx let the horse go, knowing he'd no longer need the animal. He removed the reins and the small satchel along with the saddle and gave the horse a slap to its rear thigh to send it running into the forest surrounding the bay.

The animal would be okay.

Nature of the beasts, he knew.

Under the mostly safe covering from the trees, Eryx pulled the few items he'd managed to keep with him over the last few days. A knife. The bit of fresh water in a small ceramic jug with a corked top, and bread that had somehow gotten wet hidden inside the leather satchel. His mother's journal also.

That, too, was wet.

He let out a sigh and carefully peeled back the front cover to find exactly what he thought he would. He'd not even had the chance to fully read through the journal and now he never would because the ink had bled through the pages and smudged beyond recognition from the rain.

Uncaring when he tore a few delicate, damp pages as he flipped to the very back, he did find one single paragraph that he was able to read. It felt appropriate—a goodbye, of sorts.

I worry, Anthia had written, though he didn't know what she'd written before those words higher on the page, *because he seems so much more like them than us. But I keep hoping it's inside him like it is us. And if he ever needs it, he'll know how to use it.*

The date written below that final entry was three years before his mother died. One of her final trips to the stable house. Because it was around that point when his father decided Eryx spent just a little too much time with Anthia and made an effort to separate the two as he came of age and he had been sent to the Red Seas.

His mother hoped he was like her. He hoped she'd died knowing he was.

The wind tunneled around Eryx and the items on the ground. Pages from the journal pulled with the force of the wind, tearing at the spine from its fragility because of the wetness. He could have tried to save it, but he didn't bother.

Everything—up until the moment he'd caught Arelle in this bay—had been for the sake of his mother. From his rage to the loneliness and even the vengeance it attempted to inspire. All of it had been for her. It felt appropriate that he'd come back here to finally let her go, too.

He had no doubt that, when he could look, Eryx would find more journals like those of his mother's. More proof of whom he came from, and *why* she chose to bear a son for a land king that had only ever taken from her.

Well, a part of him did know why.

So I can do what I am doing now.

He stood and turned into the wind to listen. It was easier when he closed his eyes to do it, and this time was no exception. The low hum in the back of his throat started, and the scrapes on his palms from the cuts that he'd received both running and fighting over the last few days stung when he clenched his hands and they reopened.

He'd noticed it before, but never told anyone. Not even Arelle.

His blood no longer ran red. It made lines down his palms, snaking over his long fingers and gathering at the tips before dripping to the ground in the same hue that Arelle bled.

The purple color splattered to the green moss covering the rocks and uneven ground.

She needed something else to follow because he was so tired. After everything, his body seemed unwilling to give him anything more. He'd pushed to his breaking point, and then beyond. His body screamed enough now.

I smell you. I hear you.

Her words came with the wind.

He smiled.

"Time to come home, my little mermaid," he murmured.

He knew the moment she reached the bay. He couldn't hear the horse she rode over the thunder clapping high above or the pounding of the rain, but he felt her. Without meaning to, Eryx had found a place to rest at the base of a rather large tree that had given him decent cover from the weather. When he tipped his head down … his eyes just happened to close.

How long was he sleeping?

It didn't matter.

The shout of his name carrying over the bay had his eyes wide open in a second.

"Eryx!"

That was not her voice in the wind. It wasn't her call echoing in his heart. It was her.

She was there.

He was up from the ground in the next breath and then he moved to the line of the trees where he could easily scan the bay and the rocky ledge surrounding it like a high tower meant to protect whatever was waiting behind it.

And there she is.

He found her at the top—right in the center. Atop a horse that she jumped down from when she called his name again. In the whipping winds, and with the black backdrop of a stormy sky, the white dress she wore seemed like it haloed around her. This time, he answered her call back.

"Arelle!"

He sensed the moment she found where he stood at the bottom of the bay, directly on the other side of her. She had cliffs to climb down and an entire body of water to cross before he had her again. The relief wasn't there like he thought it would be, but he knew why.

Eryx needed to touch her.

Look in her eyes.

Be *one*.

He swore he saw her raise a hand—was she waving? He did the same.

Then, before he even understood what happened, Arelle darted forward. The skirt of the flowy dress blew out behind her and he took one step forward as his chest tightened with the realization of what she was going to do.

She jumped from the cliff.

No hesitation.

No fear.

Just … *jumped*.

His first instinct was to follow her. At least, he had mind enough to shed the cloak on his shoulders, and the rest of his sopping, ruined clothes before he headed for the shore of the bay. He couldn't see her in the water; the darkness had started to bleed together, but that didn't matter. She was close enough for him to feel.

That was all he needed.

Eryx walked naked into the water, the chill barely an annoyance to him now. It was as though he'd become so used to being cold and wet that it wasn't even a discomfort anymore. He kept walking forward, hands skimming the surface of the water, until he was up to his throat and he only had a few more steps before he'd be in over his head.

For the most part, the water was calm. Small waves, despite the storms that had seemed to calm momentarily. As much as it could in this season. Still as black as the sky, but he was no longer afraid of what waited under the water for him.

Arelle broke the surface only a few feet away from him. Her hair slicked back from the water; rivulets ran lines down her face. For a second, time stopped when their eyes met. The world remained still as he took her in, and she did the same.

"How?" she asked.

"Luck," he decided. "A lot of luck."

Her laughter echoed. His gaze fell to her throat—the collar was gone. Behind her, her fin and tail twisted in the water, making little ripples all around them. He noticed how the shimmering green-blue scales that matched the spattering at her temples covered her entire lower half as she inched closer in the water.

How had he never admired her like this?

Well, he knew.

He'd been too busy catching her.

"Come closer," he demanded.

She did.

All at once.

No questions asked.

Her lithe form cut through the water and slammed into him. The force of it was enough to send him stumbling back several steps in the mucky bottom of the bay. Her mouth found his, and those hands of hers pulled through his hair with a sting that spoke of desperation and hope.

He understood that feeling all too well, now.

Because of her.

Everything about them had been desperate.

But hopeful all the same.

He found her scales were as soft as silk when her tail wrapped around his legs. At some point in her swim from the other side of the bay to him, she'd taken off the gown. It floated around them in the water, now transparent and useless. His palms slid down the curve of her stomach and her waist before drifting lower to where smooth skin met shimmering scales. All the muscles that made up her tail flexed at his touch, tightening

413

around him even as his legs fought to free themselves from the hold.

Not because he wanted to get away, but rather, he wanted so badly to do the same to her. Coil himself around her, keep her right where she needed to be—hold her still until she understood.

Never once did their kiss break, even as the struggle between them neared closer to the shore, and he was no longer neck deep in the water. Her tongue slashed against his; her taste became the sweetest drink to him, taking him higher and making him crave more.

Now, the water only came to his chest and so did she when she dipped lower to drag in water through her mouth like she was taking in a breath of it instead of air.

She didn't want to change yet, he realized.

Eryx's hands drifted over her jaw. "You miss this."

Being in her true form.

The sea ...

All of it.

A sly, knowing grin answered him back. "I need both."

Somehow, he would give her that.

Raising from the water, but not releasing the pull of water she'd taken into her lungs, she took his hands and pulled them lower while she continued to stare up at him. He felt the way she guided him until he reached what she wanted him to find. A small cleft in her tail just below the curve of her hips. Slit in the same way the paradise he'd found between her thighs, it was the only similarity.

His fingertips graced the cleft, and he was surprised to find it warm and soft like the rest of her. Arelle released a quiet hum, and her lashes fluttered closed when she shuddered from the touch.

"Is it different like this?"

"No," she said, the word coloring her next moan. "Not to me."

Frankly, he found it wasn't all that different for him, either. Her form might have changed, but all those sounds still fell from her lips as he stroked her cleft in and out with two twisting fingers sounded exactly the same. Her silken heat drew him closer; her hands wrapped around his cock and tightened with fast pulls that had him hard in seconds. She was still beautiful—still wild in her need.

She closed what bit of distance remained between them. He lost his words when her lips grazed his, her body molded against his, and with just a shift of her lower half, she'd fitted his cock into the tightness of her cleft.

"Fuck," he grunted against her lips.

She laughed an airy sound.

And then she bit him. Hard enough to draw blood from his bottom lip, he was sure. All the while, she moved against him—riding him, in a different way. Except all around his cock, muscles shuddered and pulled though he couldn't move because her tail had enclosed his legs again.

This time, it was his turn to laugh. Even when she was sweet, she still wanted to be his animal. Wild. Uncontrolled. Entirely untameable. He certainly didn't mind fucking her like one, either.

The watchtower was both old and wet.

It smelled like it, too.

However, it was the only structure that Eryx felt was safe enough for them to use for the night. At the moment, it also smelled like his mate, him, their sex, and the crisp breeze coming in through the slated windows. That bit of wind brought with it the scent of smoke, too, but neither of them mentioned it though he knew she had to smell the fire like he did. A lot of things had started to burn on Atlas over the days and nights that chased Eryx to the bay. That burning continued even through the storms and heavy rain.

He didn't mind the mustiness of the tower or the fact that they rested on a pile of their wet clothing tangled together because at the moment, he had better things to focus on.

Like Arelle.

And that she was on top of him.

Fucking him.

The same way she'd done all night. Well, in between short bursts of sleep that never seemed to last too long before one of them woke up again and reached for the other.

Her fingernails dug into his chest, and she showed him her teeth when she leaned down just close enough that he could almost kiss her. Almost, because she was keeping that from him this time. She very much enjoyed riding him because it gave her control, like now.

How fast she went …

Whether she came, or he did.

It was all on her terms.

He let her have it.

This time.

"Tell me a secret," he heard himself say.

Even his voice didn't sound like his own. No, it sounded high with her and their fucking and everything that should be right and good. He didn't have to think about what awaited them outside of this tower, or a world that would be turned on its end.

"I would like to sit on your face instead," she returned. "And then have you taste your cum coming out of me, yes?"

Eryx laughed, but it quickly melted into a prayer—her name—when she squeezed her muscles and sat down atop him harder than before. Her rhythm stilled, but her hips grinded against his body without her own lifting from his. Hard and sure, around and around on his cock until he was sure he was going to blow.

And then she stopped again.

"You're killing me," he mumbled against his palm.

His other was wrapped in the hair that had tumbled down her back.

"Do you still want a secret?" she asked.

"Are you going to let me come?"

"I may."

Eryx grinned and she lowered just enough to finally give him a soft kiss. It wasn't nearly enough, but he felt it even after she straightened back up and tightened her thighs around his body. "Then, I still want a secret."

"I love you."

He'd expected something different.

Anything but that.

Not because he didn't want it—oh, he *did*—but rather, it seemed like the one thing she had managed to keep for herself. Everything else, she'd handed over to him. Control. Her life. The bond. Even her freedom was his at the end of the day to decide whether she could have it or he would keep it.

He was in her heart, sure.

He didn't own it, though.

Except apparently, now he did.

"Do you?" he asked.

She started grinding again, but this time, with a purpose. Above him, she nodded, the loose strands of her red hair that he'd not been able to gather in his fist falling over her shoulders and swaying the closer she brought him to orgasm.

He could feel hers, too.

The way she shivered.

How her muscles tensed.

The wildness in her eyes.

"I do," she breathed.

She came. He followed right after. His *I love you, too* came out clear, and strong, though.

As it should.

"Look," Eryx murmured.

Arelle turned her head to the left where she rested on his chest, using him as a pillow. He didn't mind, and besides, like this, he could hold her close. He'd climbed into one of the slated windows of the tower, using the stone ledge as a backrest before she'd joined him and curled into his lap. Here, they could watch the bay, the sea, and even the sky.

Arelle sighed. "The sky is purple."

It had been that way for a while.

He merely hadn't mentioned it.

"Do you smell that like I do?" she asked.

He didn't need to ask what.

"There's still a lot of smoke in the wind."

"Something is burning," she whispered.

"Atlas. Atlas is burning."

He didn't need to be told.

A kingdom was changing.

A war had begun.

Down below, sea foam gathered on the rocks of the shore surrounding the watchtower. Another good sign that the storm had stopped, and they would calm for a while. Bathed in the purple of the sky, he pressed a kiss to the top of Arelle's head.

"What do we do now?" she asked. "Where do we go?"

"I have some options. I have ... connections in places. Allies, though I'd hesitate to use them when their loyalties can be bought rather easily given the worth of whatever they make a person pay. But given the circumstances, they would be my best bet."

"Who?"

"I spent some time in the Red Seas, made friends with the king and his sons during travels meant to educate me. I had been sent at my mother's request, but my father posed it as if he had willed me to go."

"Do you think that was purposeful?"

"On her part?" Eryx returned.

Arelle gave him a look.

He sighed. "Now, yes. Going there, well, it was nothing like my father's court. *Willing* women, happy little families all about. But I had not been allowed to disclose my halfling status to them at the time. I think ... I think the truth of some things may sway their allegiance to me should we go to them for help, but once I open that proverbial jar of shit, it can never be closed again."

"My oldest sister married into that king's harem."

Eryx nodded. "So, you have someone there, too. It would help our cause more. Or we stay and—"

"Die?"

She made a good point.

Then, she made another.

"We have no ship, and you have no tail. It will not be an easy travel for you under the seas, Eryx."

But he could breathe in the water.

What else did the rest matter?

"What choice do we have?" he asked her.

Arelle remained thoughtful and quiet.

He had a feeling that allowing Poe to go back to the sea would change what happened underwater. Arelle told him what she'd seen after escaping—Mattue and Eryx's dead father—which meant the kingdom on land would be in upheaval as well.

Nothing would be safe.

After everything, he could not consider the possibility that Arelle would remain on this continent when he was so unprepared to protect her.

"I'm with child."

He hadn't asked for a second secret that morning. She gave him one, nonetheless. His joy was only dampened by their current situation, and she seemed to sense that when she smiled up at him and lifted one bare shoulder as if to say *I know.*

"How?" he asked, then.

How did she know?

How did it happen?

He had a lot of questions.

Arelle smiled softly. "'Tis taught to merwomen to spill the first seed to forsake the pregnancy. I have considered that might not be the case with those born of land and the sea. Perhaps in that way, you are more like them, however *they* are. I do not know."

What could he say to that?

Except now they had a child to think of, too.

"Does it matter," he started, wondering out loud, mostly, "if we stay or if we go? Right now, as long as we make ourselves safe first. Can't we work out the rest later?"

"Will we be together?"

"Always."

"Then, I will do whatever."

Eryx stared down over the sea again, and the foam that had become thick on the surface of calm waters. "My mother's journal—it was ruined in the rain."

"I'm sorry."

The secret could die with him.

Who he was—what he really was—could end right here.

No one would know.

"What was the name of the queen who came before your father?" he dared to ask.

"I never knew it; my sisters, either," Arelle replied, shifting on him until she settled once more with her face buried against his bare chest. "He forbade her name from even being whispered, when her death was such a source of contention for the colony. We were all told she was the lost queen. She was favored—they loved her, or so I was told, and many weren't willing to believe she had died. Rumors said she was caught, but the royal court said it wasn't true. We never understood why we weren't allowed to talk about her or what came before us—he mated after he became king, we came along to our mother later. Why?"

She tipped her head up.

Those violet eyes of hers met his, and she waited.

The secret could die with me.

Maybe it should.

Arelle reached up to drift her fingertips over his jaw. "What is it?"

"The lost queen was my mother. Her journal … If there was one, she would have left more, but that will take time we do not have to find them. Are there not those alive, from land *and* sea, who would have known who she was?"

She turned to stone in his lap. "That would mean—"

"Yes."

He didn't want to say it.

He didn't want her to say it, either.

"*Eryx*," she whispered, pleading. "You could change *everything.*"

"We are two against many. The land here is burning and that means there are already people fighting for a throne I never wanted to begin with, Arelle. It has become apparent to me that my birthright is far more than what others chose it to be."

"Right now, perhaps, but—"

"'Tis not safe to stay."

Her chin trembled when she said, "But we *will* return. When we can take it back."

It wasn't even a question.

He had never wanted to be king, not as a boy or a man, because he had only ever wanted to be happy and left alone with his mother.

With Arelle in his hands, their gazes locked and burning, he would be anything if it meant keeping his mermaid.

Eryx tucked her into his embrace again, but this time, with her back pressed against his chest and his arms tight around her middle. He nuzzled into her hair, pulling in the scent of her while the flatness of her middle was tight to his palms.

"We will take it all back," he promised, "one day."

But today, they would love one more time, pack away their clothing, and slip into the sea foam where they could disappear into the depths of the sea below although it would not be easy travel for a halfling. Then, it would be as though they hadn't existed here at all … because for a time, they no longer could.

BIO

K. Fournier is a Canadian, mother, storyteller, and the fantasy romance penname for author Bethany-Kris. She's got a lot of dogs, cats, kids, and somehow, she still manages to write. Find where to follow BK or visit her website to stay up to date with all things BK/K. Fournier.

www.bethanykris.com

www.ingramcontent.com/pod-product-compliance
Lightning Source LLC
Chambersburg PA
CBHW072019020726
47501CB00006B/1872